W9-BUE-571

HATTERAS
BLUE

Novels by D. C. Poyer

Stepfather Bank
The Shiloh Project

By David Poyer

The Med
The Dead of Winter
The Return of Philo T. McGiffin
White Continent

HATTERAS BLUE

D. C. POYER

 For information, address St. Martin's Press, 175 Fifth Avenue, New York, N.Y. 10010.

Design by Robert Bull Design.

Library of Congress Cataloging-in-Publication Data

Poyer, David.
Hatteras blue / D.C. Poyer.
p. cm.
ISBN 0-312-02926-8
1. Hatteras, Cape (N.C.)—History—Fiction. I. Title.
PS3566.0978H38 1989
813'.54—dc19 89-30125
CIP

First Edition

10 9 8 7 6 5 4 3 2 1

For all my friends on the Banks

"Gradually it was disclosed to me that the line separating good from evil passes not through states, nor between classes, nor between political parties either—but right through every human heart. . . ."

A. Solzhenitsyn,
The Gulag Archipelago

Note C: Caution
Hydrography is not charted on Diamond Shoals due to the changeable nature of the area. Navigation in the area is extremely hazardous to all types of craft.

NOAA Chart 12200, Cape May to Cape Hatteras

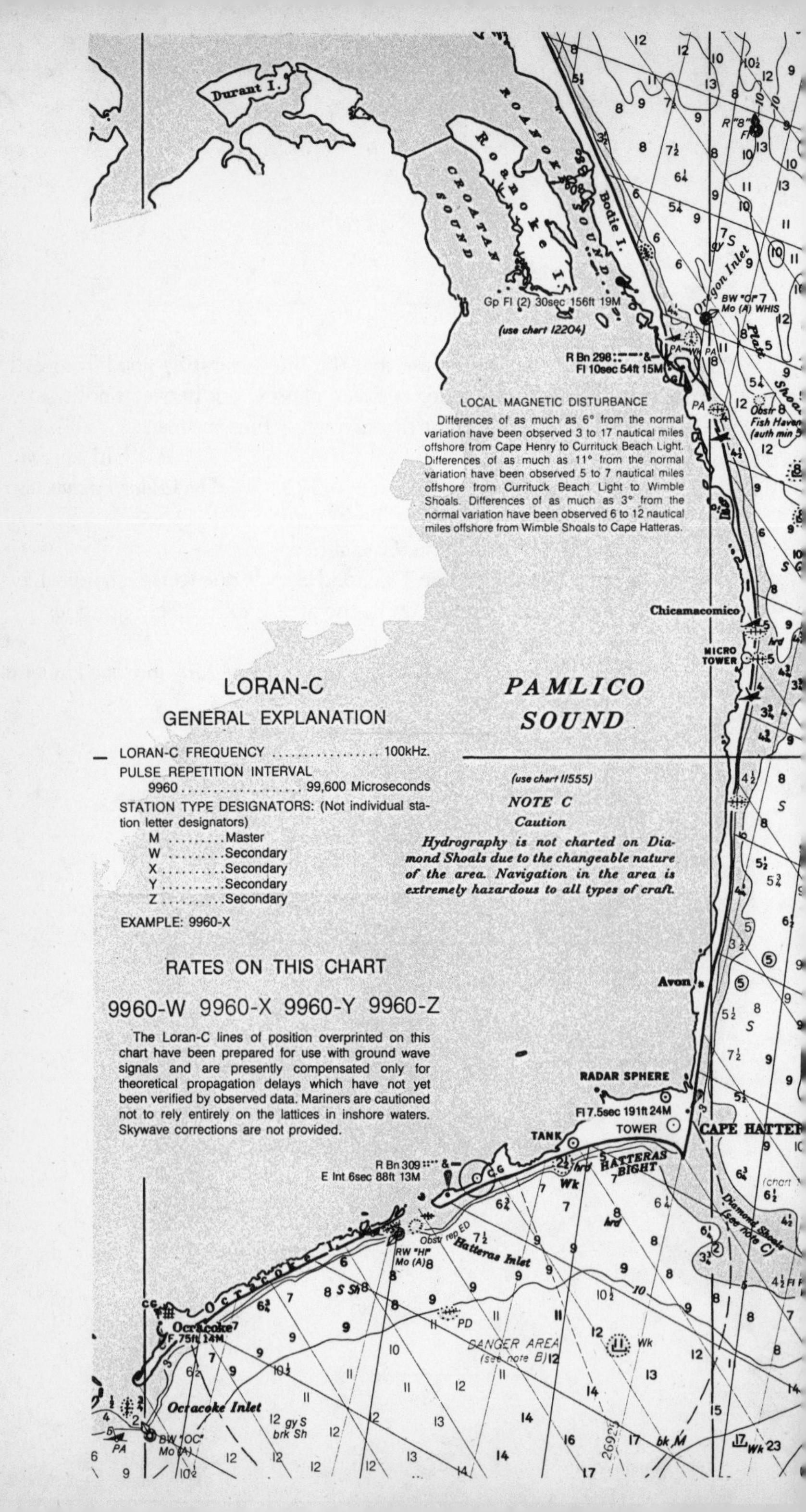
Durant I.
ROANOKE SOUND
Roanoke I.
CROATAN SOUND
Bodie I.
Oregon Inlet
Gp Fl (2) 30sec 156ft 19M
(use chart 12204)
R Bn 298
Fl 10sec 54ft 15M
LOCAL MAGNETIC DISTURBANCE
Differences of as much as 6° from the normal variation have been observed 3 to 17 nautical miles offshore from Cape Henry to Currituck Beach Light. Differences of as much as 11° from the normal variation have been observed 5 to 7 nautical miles offshore from Currituck Beach Light to Wimble Shoals. Differences of as much as 3° from the normal variation have been observed 6 to 12 nautical miles offshore from Wimble Shoals to Cape Hatteras.
Chicamacomico
MICRO TOWER
LORAN-C
GENERAL EXPLANATION
LORAN-C FREQUENCY .... 100kHz.
PULSE REPETITION INTERVAL
9960 .... 99,600 Microseconds
STATION TYPE DESIGNATORS: (Not individual station letter designators)
M ....Master
W ....Secondary
X ....Secondary
Y ....Secondary
Z ....Secondary
EXAMPLE: 9960-X
RATES ON THIS CHART
9960-W 9960-X 9960-Y 9960-Z
The Loran-C lines of position overprinted on this chart have been prepared for use with ground wave signals and are presently compensated only for theoretical propagation delays which have not yet been verified by observed data. Mariners are cautioned not to rely entirely on the lattices in inshore waters. Skywave corrections are not provided.
PAMLICO SOUND
(use chart 11555)
NOTE C
Caution
Hydrography is not charted on Diamond Shoals due to the changeable nature of the area. Navigation in the area is extremely hazardous to all types of craft.
Avon
RADAR SPHERE
Fl 7.5sec 191ft 24M
TOWER
TANK
CAPE HATTERAS
HATTERAS BIGHT
R Bn 309
E Int 6sec 88ft 13M
Hatteras Inlet
Diamond Shoals (see note C)
Ocracoke I.
Ocracoke
F 75ft 14M
Ocracoke Inlet
DANGER AREA (see note B)

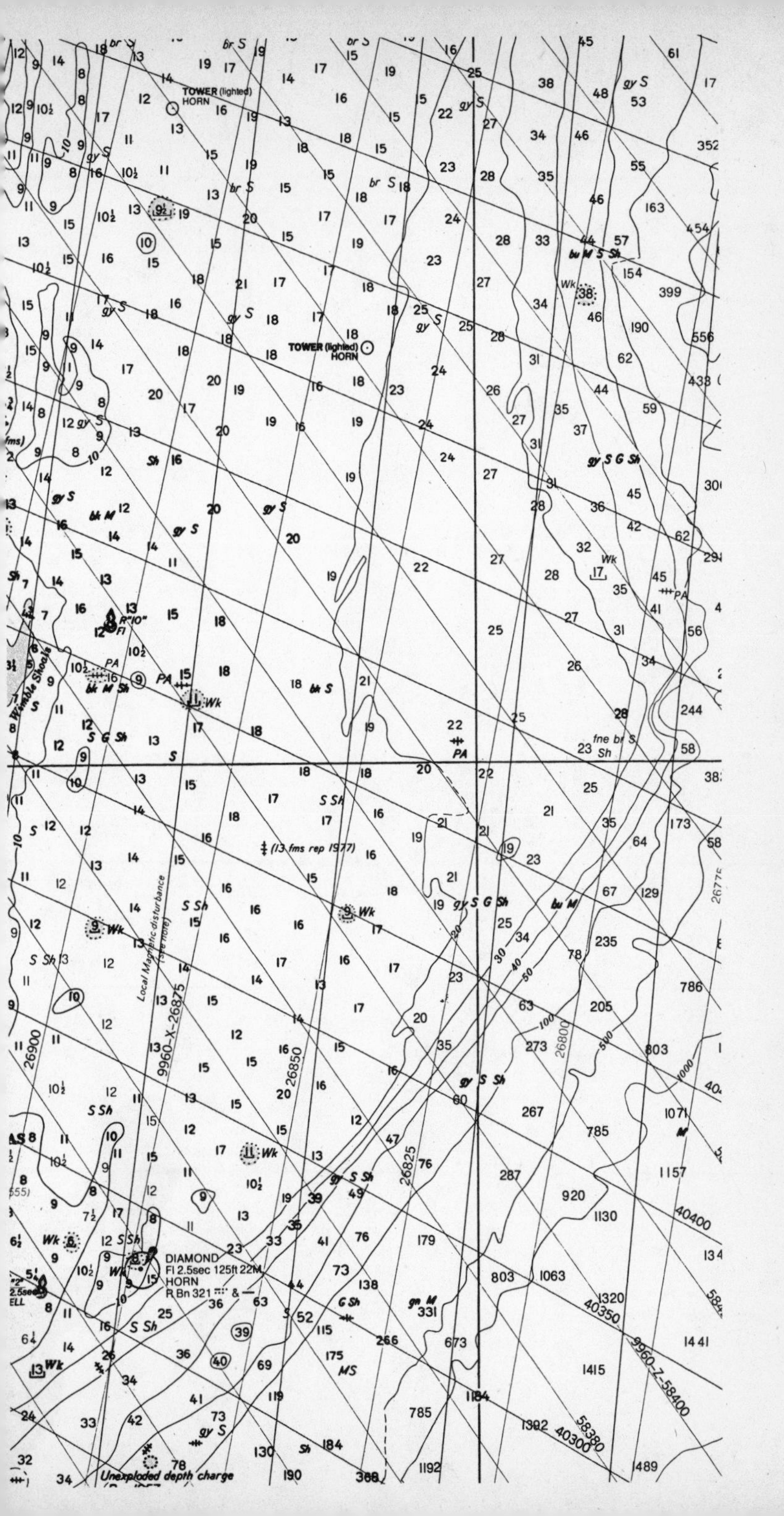
TOWER (lighted)
HORN
TOWER (lighted)
HORN
Wk
PA
Wamble Shoals
(13 fms rep 1977)
Local Magnetic disturbance
(see note)
9960-X-26875
26900
26850
26825
26800
26775
DIAMOND
Fl 2.5sec 125ft 22M
HORN
R Bn 321
Unexploded depth charge
40400
40350
40300
58380
9960-Z-58400
fne br S
Sh
gy S G Sh
bu M S Sh
S SH

Prologue

Halfway down the Atlantic coast a beak of sand juts into the sea, curved and cruel as the beaks of the falcons that soar above its dunes.

This is Cape Hatteras, North Carolina, the seawardmost point of the Outer Banks. For four centuries mariners have approached it with apprehension. Sometimes they passed safely, close-reefed, and gave thanks. Sometimes, as the timbers that still litter its beaches testify, they lost their gamble.

This is no myth, no Devil's Triangle or Sargasso Sea. Two ocean currents meet here, one warm, one cold; their eternal struggle is shrouded in fog and storm. The low, deceptive coastline has lured hundreds of ships to their deaths, the roar of surf muffling the screams of the drowning. And when war last came to America, it came first to Hatteras.

Seamen still call it the Graveyard of the Atlantic.

Fifty miles to the southeast of Cape Point, close enough that on a clear night one might see the loom of Hatteras Light, a wreck lies motionless on the bottom.

Almost undamaged, except for the slow fingers of encroaching coral, it lies on its side on hard gray sand. Its bow planes are jammed on hard dive. Its hatches gape open, wells to the dark interior. Cold silt swirls slowly amid dead gauges, twisted air lines, half-loaded torpedoes, the occasional writhe of a moray. Its cannon points upward, toward the faint glow that is all that remains of the sun at thirty fathoms. Its conning tower, flaked with corrosion, lies frozen in a roll to starboard that will last till its metal dissolves in the all-devouring sea.

Over forty years have passed since the sunlight touched it. The memories of men have eroded, eaten away by time as salt eats steel. Yet far beneath, silent except for the stir of sheltering fish, the dead ship waits.

Above it the Atlantic rolls relentlessly inshore. Below the gray light filters weakly down. Only the sleepless shark swims now beside and over the patiently waiting hull.

• • •

Beyond the rolling curve of sea is the shore. A narrow strip of wet sand where sanderlings skitter like windup toys. Then dunes, waving with sea oats and panic grass.

Beyond the dune line several men are working. In the glaring sun sweat glistens on their chests; light flashes from the sand-polished blades of their shovels. A heap of torn-up yaupon crackles as it burns. Plastic flaps listlessly atop a stack of concrete blocks. Beyond the workers a yellow machine rolls to and fro on steel tracks, spewing smoke into the clean wind, gouging away the side of a sandhill. A sign by the highway proclaims FIND YOUR PLACE IN THE SUN. SITE OF THE NEW PIRATES' REST TIME-SHARE RESORT. MARKETED BY O.R. GALLOWAY REALTY & CONSTRUCTION.

The heavy blade gouges deep into the dune. A moment later it pauses. A man shouts. Two of the laborers amble over and begin clearing sand. At first they think the black layer is trash. It is rotten and flakes as their shovels bite into it. The dune slides away reluctantly.

Both stop at the same time. Desiccated, fragile, but still recognizable, a boot sticks out from the sand. They look at it and at each other. They shovel again, less willingly.

There are bones above the boots. There are the bones of three human beings under the remains of a rubber raft. The laborers stare at them wordlessly. At last one of them shakes his head. Dropping his shovel, he trudges back to the truck and climbs in. A moment later the engine roars.

The long wait is over.

1945

one

Lieutenant Commander Lyle Galloway II, U.S. Coast Guard, dug his fingers around his eyes in indecision and fatigue. When the colored patterns stopped he straightened, and stared around the dimly illuminated bridge of his ship.

Galloway was tired. He and the *Russell* were the same age, twenty-seven, and she was tired too. After a year of near war and four of the real thing, after supporting the landings in North Africa, and North Atlantic convoy duty in winter, he was glad of this assignment: coastal patrol off Cape Hatteras, a quiet sector for two years now.

Best of all, the war with Germany had ended two days before.

Now they were running south from the mouth of the Chesapeake on the fourth day of a two-week patrol. The night was clear and starry, and at eighteen knots the knife bow of the old destroyer pared phosphorescence from the sea. No one expected contact. The European war was over, this was a milk run. Yet five minutes earlier the officer of the deck had called him from a warm bunk. The radar on the bridge showed a pip ten miles ahead.

Galloway ground a fist into his palm. "Going back to CIC," he said aloud.

"Aye, Captain," said an anonymous voice from the darkness.

Russell's makeshift combat center was dark except for the green glow of the scope. He leaned over the radarman's shoulder, watching the flickering point of light. The day before, he remembered, the sailor had been raucous with the news of peace. Tonight he was silent, intent, moving his dials slowly as if afraid to startle whatever was ahead of them.

If this was a U-boat, it had no business at sea. After six years of war Europe was quiet, a smoldering heap of bomb-stirred ash. The Soviets and the Americans had met at Torgau two weeks before, cutting Germany in half. Russian troops were mopping up in Berlin. The Führer and the rest of the high command were rumored dead in the flames of the greatest city of the Reich. It had been a close war. Twice—at Stalingrad, and in the Atlantic—it trembled in the balance. But the Russians held. And at sea, though Admiral Doenitz's *Unterseeboote* sank twenty-three million tons of shipping, the Allies had won at last. Quickly built ships, radar, air patrols, and the convoy system had cut the knot of the Nazi noose.

Now Galloway thought rapidly, hands thrust into his leather foul-weather jacket.

The day before, a U-boat had been reported by an Army B-25 on patrol out of Lakehurst, New Jersey. The bomber pilot had come in from astern, recognizing the plume of white water for what it was: a snorkeling submarine, running just below the surface. He had attacked, but misjudged the target's speed. Both depth bombs exploded astern of the sub, which promptly went deep. He reported its position and its southward course, and the Atlantic Antisubmarine Warfare Command scrambled a hunter-killer group of planes and ships east of Cape Henlopen. They had not yet found the U-boat. Had it escaped them? Was this it?

Galloway's fingers encountered a folded wad in the pocket of his jacket. Moving to one of the radio remotes, he reread the message by the faint glow of the pilot light. The comm officer had handed it to him the day before. It was from Admiral Ingram, CincLantFleet.

SECRET
THOUGH LAND WAR IN EUROPE DRAWING SWIFTLY TO CLOSE . . . MORALE AND MATERIEL OF U-BOAT ARM OF KREIGSMARINE STILL STRONG. UNITS NOW AT SEA, THOUGHT TO NUMBER APPROXIMATELY FIFTY, HAVE BEEN ORDERED BY GRAND ADMIRAL DOENITZ TO SURFACE AND SURRENDER. IT WILL TAKE SEVERAL DAYS FOR WORD TO REACH ALL SUBMERGED UNITS. THE MORE FANATICAL MAY NOT GIVE THEMSELVES UP.

ENEMY UNITS FAILING TO SURFACE, FOR WHATEVER REASON, WILL BE DEALT WITH SUMMARILY BEFORE UNNECESSARY ALLIED CASUALTIES RESULT. . . .

Galloway stuffed the paper back in his pocket. He bent over a glass-topped table on which a light traced the motion of the ship. "Datum?" he said.

"Contact bears two-three-zero, twelve," the radarman reported. "Estimated course and speed, one-seven-zero, speed—fifteen knots!"

"Here," muttered an ensign. He drew a diamond on the tracing paper, south of the destroyer.

"Fifteen?" said Galloway to the radarman's back. "You sure about that?"

"Checked it twice, Cap'n."

"Jesus, that's fast."

"Sonar reports nothing yet," said another rating.

"Tell them just to listen, not to ping. I want to take this bird by surprise, if we can."

"Shouldn't we tell the Navy, sir?"

"They're fifty miles north of us," said Galloway slowly. "But I guess I ought to."

"Recommend course one-niner-zero at twenty-one knots to intercept."

"Roger. Bridge, this is the captain speaking. Come right to one-niner-zero and kick us up to flank speed."

"Bridge, aye."

The ensign set down the radio handset. "Norfolk says to go after them. They're detaching a destroyer from the hunter-killer group to help. Coast Guard has tactical command—hey, that's us!"

"Good," said Galloway, surprised and pleased at the unaccustomed courtesy. He did a rough calculation in his head. Thirty minutes to intercept the racing submarine—if it was one.

For a U-boat did not belong here. Not now.

It hadn't been like that three years earlier. In 1942 the sea off North Carolina was the front line of the war. The U-boats had left Germany a month after Pearl Harbor. When they arrived in the U.S. shipping lanes it was sudden slaughter. They struck on the surface, at night, not even bothering to dive. Their favorite hunting ground stretched from New York to Charleston. Armed with deck guns and torpedoes, they lay in wait at night, silhouetting passing coasters against the lights of Morehead City or Virginia Beach. Ship after ship went down. Oil and debris washed up on the beaches, and beach dwellers found bodies where they had sunned in summers of peace.

Galloway had seen it. He was from Hatteras. On Good Friday of 1942 he had stood on the beach near Buxton with his bride, their moonlight walk forgotten, and watched the night sky flame as a tanker burned on the horizon. He'd cut his leave short and gone back to the ship the next day.

But since then the threat had receded, sucked back toward Europe as Germany weakened. A U-boat here, off the East Coast, at the end of the war . . . ?

He dismissed it for the present. Already he could feel the old four-piper's deckplates begin to vibrate as she came up to maximum speed.

This might be it, he thought. The ensign looked at him. He reached for the intercom again. "Bridge, Captain. Sound general quarters."

The crew, honed after years of war at sea, had felt the heel and the sudden increase in speed. They were already rolling from their bunks when the alarm began to bong. Men shoved into the already crowded compartment. One sailor, eyes not yet adapted to darkness, muttered to Galloway, "Christ, what now. I thought this friggin' war was over."

"Not yet, Sam," said the captain drily. The sailor peered, then seemed to melt away as the gold braid on Galloway's cap glinted in the dimness.

Pushing the darken-ship curtains aside, he stepped out onto the bridge again. It was even darker there and he stood still for a moment. His fingers found the strap of his binoculars. The portholes were open and a warm breeze fanned his cheek. The officer of the deck, a big reserve jaygee from Philadelphia, was taking the reports.

"Mount thirty-one manned and ready." The forward three-inch gun.

"Sonar manned and ready."

"Hedgehog manned and ready." The weapon that had turned the war at sea around. Fired by the dozens, its projectiles detonated only when they hit the steel of a U-boat's hull.

"K-guns, manned and ready." The depth-charge throwers to port and starboard.

"After mount manned and ready."

The lieutenant turned. "Captain, we're ready for action. We're making nineteen knots now, with twenty-one rung up."

"Feather still there?"

"I just checked the scope. They haven't spotted us yet."

He wondered whether he should slow. A sub could hear a destroyer at flank speed from miles away. But if he slowed it would take forever to catch up. Till long past dawn. And at sunrise the Navy would be overhead with the new air-launched torpedoes to take credit for the last kill of the war.

He smiled tightly in the darkness. That wasn't the way it was going to be. Galloways had been famous in the Coast Guard for more than sixty years, since his great-grandfather Otinus Randall Galloway had rowed into the worst northeaster in memory to rescue the passengers of the doomed schooner *Floridian.* It would be sweet indeed if here, off the coast of home, he could carry on that tradition by destroying a killer more dangerous than that legendary storm of 1878.

Minutes ticked by. Seen from the sea, the destroyer would be only a patch of darker black in a moonless night, with only the phosphorescence at her bow to betray her to a periscope.

Struck by a thought, he bent over a chart of the patrol area. The navigator's dead reckoning estimate showed them some forty miles at sea. To the west Cape Hatteras jutted seaward, its stylized wrecks and dotted lines of shoal fretting the coastline. Galloway chewed his lip. The water shoaled gradually. Still only two or three hundred feet this far offshore. If he could catch the U-boat here it would be unable to go deep.

It was so pat that he felt again that touch of suspicion, indecision, unwonted caution that had dogged him since the first radar contact. "That thing still on the scope?" he grunted.

"Minute he dives we'll let you know, sir."

Twenty-two minutes yet. He went out on the bridge wing to get a grip on himself.

The wind was warm and strong. He curled his fingers around the binoculars and leaned into it. The only light came from the stars. Immense, glowing, the Milky Way arched over the sea. He leaned over the coaming. Like reflected constellations, luminescent organisms sparked and swirled as the bow dipped and lifted, knifing through the chop with a vicious, eager hiss.

The jaygee came out of the pilothouse. "Fifteen minutes to intercept."

"Very well. What speed we making?"

"Twenty-two knots, Captain."

"Good." He grinned; the World War I four-stackers the Navy had palmed off on the Coast Guard could only make twenty-one officially. The engineers knew something was up. Well, time to scotch the rumors. He went back inside. A moment later his voice boomed through the ship, calm, enormous, metallic.

"This is Captain Galloway speaking. We've picked up what looks like a U-boat and are heading to intercept. The war with Germany is officially over, but this guy obviously didn't get the word. Or he may not feel like giving up. So we're not taking any chances. If he doesn't surface as soon as he knows we're around I'm going to attack. That's all."

Galloway hung up the mike then and stood fidgeting with the glasses. He did not look at the radar screen, though he wanted to. Its brilliance would ruin his night vision, and it might be important shortly for him to be able to see.

"Ten minutes, sir."

He ran up the ladder to the signal bridge, into open air. The starlight showed pointer and trainer below him, crouched to the sights of the forward gun mount, the loaders cradling shells. Beside him the searchlight operator was swinging his big lamp around, and from the port side metal clanged as a gunner's mate charged the fifty-caliber machine gun.

The sub was making fifteen knots and *Russell* twenty-two. Ignore the slow power of the Gulf Stream, sweeping past Hatteras like an invisible river in the sea; it was carrying them all along at an equal rate. That made closing speed seven knots. Ten minutes at seven knots was 2300 yards. Should be able to see *something.* He raised the big night glasses and steadied them very carefully just to starboard of the bow.

A faint glow wavered in the center of his vision. A plume. The U-boat was still snorkeling, oblivious of his presence. Suddenly he realized why. At fifteen knots its wake was so turbulent that *Russell* had been able to run up its tail without being heard. Luck. But also as dangerous as picking up a loaded rifle by the barrel. U-boats carried torpedo tubes in their sterns as well as in the bow.

Closer. The plume shimmered against darkness, visible now without the glasses. The faces of the gunners turned toward him. But he held, held, till he could make out the dark jut of the snorkel. Now to give the Nazi commander the chance he hoped he wouldn't take. "Illuminate!" he shouted into the wind. "Ten degrees to starboard! Sonar, start pinging."

With a sputtering hiss, the searchlights ignited. The twin eighteen-inch beams caught the plume dead center, lit it against dark ocean like a concentration camp prisoner caught on wire. At that moment, belatedly, the phone talker beside Galloway spoke up. "Sir, sonar reports a submarine contact, bearing one-two-zero, five thousand yards."

"One-two-zero? No, no, that'd put him way off to our left," said Galloway, watching the vee of foam. Odd that the sonarman would get a screwy bearing like that. Surely, he thought, this guy knows we're here by now, with the sonar pinging directly through his hull. "Hey, what's wrong with my weapons?"

"All guns forward on target," said the jaygee hastily from beside him. "Hedgehog on target. Depth charges set at sixty feet—"

The plume suddenly shrank. "She's diving," said Galloway. "Stand by to fire." He leaned forward, gauging the range to the searchlight-illuminated swirl of foam by eye.

"Sonar reports another contact, on starboard bow, range very close."

"That's our boy. Going in for attack. Count me down on range, and tell me if she starts to turn."

"They say that'll be hard, sir, a lot of bubbles in her wake."

"Right. Are the other cans on the screen yet?"

"They have one pip may be *Arnold*, eight miles astern of us, closing fast."

"Hell," muttered Galloway.

"Six hundred."

"Better get them on this first run, sir."

"Five hundred yards. Nearing hedgehog range."

"Sonar to Captain. Target slowing. Turning right."

"Hedgehogs, stand by to fire," he said.

"Right five degrees rudder," said the OOD, without being told.

"Good . . . there, steady as she goes."

"Three hundred."

"Starboard hedgehog, fire," said Galloway. Beside him the jaygee seized the firing handle.

Russell's forecastle blazed as twenty-four thirty-pound projectiles leaped off her deck a tenth of a second apart. They disappeared into the night sky. He envisioned them arching upward, hanging above the sea for a moment, then plunging downward in a circle a hundred feet across. He counted the seconds as they sank. Right on time, a dull thud came from far below.

"Have them reload right away," he shouted, already sliding down the ladder.

The combat center was packed. Five men bent over the tracing table. They looked up as he wedged in. "Looks like we connected, Cap'n."

"Let's not take anything for granted." Galloway bent too, taking in the situation. The battle would be fought on tracing paper now, a succession of chess moves played with coolness until the violent end.

"USS *Arnold* on the horn for you, sir."

Galloway grunted and took the handset. The Navy can, coming up astern, would have her weapons ready for immediate use. But her sonarmen would need time to find and plot the target. If he vectored them in they could attack immediately, keep the enemy commander reeling. "Tomcat, this is Paramount," he said rapidly. "It's your high-speed snorkeler, all right. I've made one run and got a hit. Will vector you in for immediate coordinated attack. Over."

"Tomcat here." The voice was familiar; he knew *Arnold*'s skipper, had gotten drunk with him more than once in the wide-open hell of wartime Norfolk. "Hello there, Lyle; how's my favorite Coastie? Ready for your orders. Now on two-zero-zero, slowing to twelve."

The ensign's pencil flew, plotting the enemy's position every thirty seconds. The U-boat was holding a tight turn to the right. He coached *Arnold* around to follow it. The fixes were inches apart on the paper. "It's a fast son of a bitch under water too," he muttered.

"Seventeen knots," said the ensign. "You know —"

"What?"

"This isn't your standard U-boat. They can't make more than eight knots submerged. This has to be one of the new ones."

"Could be." Galloway remembered the secret briefings.The new submarines had been Germany's last hope for victory. Twice as big as the boats that cried havoc off Hatteras, with three times the range and much higher speeds. He'd heard rumors of designs even more radical, with a breakthrough engine that required no snorkel or battery. If this were one of them it must have escaped at the last moment, running the gauntlet of Allied air and crossing an ocean totally controlled by the British and American navies.

Arnold reached the drop point and seconds later the rumble of depth charges reached them. "Our turn," snapped Galloway. "Hard right rudder. Hedgehogs to port this time." He picked up the handset and was about to speak when the deck jumped as if a giant had slammed a hammer against the keel.

"What the hell was that?"

"Captain, this is the bridge—*Arnold*'s been hit!"

The deck slammed again as he ran out on the bridge. He looked out to starboard, and stopped, unable to move for a moment.

The other destroyer was burning, an immense column of reddish flame. Secondary detonations boomed out over the water as fireballs burst from her stern, where depth charges were stowed ready to drop. She was still charging forward from her attack, but as he watched her stern began to drag. She settled backward into the water. The bow lifted, exposing the underside of the hull. Then it too disappeared; the fire winked out. That quickly, she was gone. The ocean was empty save for a deep rumbling and cracking, the sea breaking the bones of a ship.

"Torpedoed," breathed the OOD, beside him. "How could that happen? He was *above* the contact!"

"I don't know," said Galloway slowly.

"We've got to stop for them, sir."

"Stay on course," he said tonelessly. "We'll continue the attack."

Russell plunged onward, over the invisible spot where oil, wreckage, and probably men were bubbling to the surface. Galloway barked orders, and a second salvo thundered into the night. This time two thuds floated back up from the sea.

"All stop," he said. The old destroyer lost way as he brought her around in a turn. Searchlights slid over the water. The barrels of the guns moved uneasily. The men waited, fingers poised on triggers, valves, dials. U-boats were masters at playing possum and stealing away. But three hits . . . no sub made could take three hedgehogs and continue to operate. Galloway pulled a carbine from a rack and jammed a magazine into it. He went out on the wing. *Russell,* hove to, began to roll to the easterly swell.

The U-boat broached to starboard, 200 yards away. His shout was lost in a blast from the forward mount that rattled the windows and sent his cap spinning overboard. The lights pinned a dark silhouette: a submarine, deck awash, men spilling from the conning tower and running forward. *Russell*'s after three-inch fired at the same moment the machine guns began hammering. Tracers stitched the night, converging on the black shape wallowing in the seas.

A flash, a bang lost in the terrifyingly close scream of a shell ripping past! Just above him, he judged; another few feet aft and it would have gone off in the forward stack, raining fragments where he stood. Another flash! The enemy was well trained. To load and aim that rapidly and accurately under fire . . .

The U-boats carried deck guns larger than his, though their rate of fire was slower; for a moment it was anybody's battle. Another shell exploded in the dark sea, sending water pattering over the destroyer's hull. Bracketed! Blindly, knowing it was little more than a gesture, he aimed the carbine toward his enemy. Its puny clatter was lost in the roar of heavy guns.

There, a flash as one of *Russell*'s rounds hit, paler than the red bloom of gunfire. He glimpsed a belated scrap of white at the conning tower hatch before it vanished in the flash of another solid hit, this time apparently on the hull itself.

The U-boat exploded. This time the flash and roar were simultaneous, and the old ship rang like a struck bell to the shock.

The firing stopped. The last tracers hissed harmlessly into the dark. Searchlight beams, solid in the smoke, swept over an empty sea.

"She's gone," said the jaygee, breathing hard. "The murdering bastards."

Galloway stared into the darkness. "We're not sure of that yet."

"Sir?"

"Ahead full," he said through numb lips. "She may have submerged again, to shake us off. Prepare for depth charge attack."

Her screws thrashing, the old ship moved ahead once more.

"Men in the water, Captain!"

From the bridge he could see them. They waved and shouted, clinging to bits of wreckage. Men who had brought war to his homeland, who had killed his friends. He knew now their ship was gone, settling toward the bottom. By the laws of the sea, by the traditions of the service his family had served so long, he was obligated to rescue them. The old warship swept toward them, gathering speed.

He stood trembling, unable to speak. He had turned to the lieutenant, about to give the order to slow and take them aboard. Then, borne by the warm wind, what they were shouting came faintly to him.

Hail to the man who lay a cowardly suicide in Berlin.

Heil to the greatest mass murderer of all time.

He stared down at them. They were adrift, helpless, defeated. He might have disbelieved his hearing. But at that moment the searchlight swept across their faces. Now he could see them, their arms raised from the sea in defiant salute.

He could not let men like this remain in the world with his family, with the son he had held in his arms only once. With all the children, all the innocents. They had failed in their mad attempt at escape. They had refused to surrender. Now he had only to turn his face away from them.

"Fire and amen to this evil forever," he murmured.

"Sir?"

"I said *fire!*"

The charges leaped from bursts of reddish light, and splashed on either side, amid the waving, screaming men.

• • •

The sun rose, red and enormous, two hours later. It rose on oil and lifejackets and splayed-out corpses, German and American, drifting side by side in the Stream.

Saved now from time, the steel hull lay in darkness, heeled to starboard on gray sand. Its planes were jammed on hard dive. Oil and the last remnants of air bubbled slowly from ruptured tanks. Bodies bobbed impaled on knife-sharp steel. In the growing light gray forms circled slowly, drawn by the delicious reek of death.

The long wait had begun.

It would not last forever.

TODAY

two

The corroding brass ring clamped together sand and asphalt, the silvery planks of the old pier, the calm green water of Pamlico Sound. Somewhere in the gently jostling rows of trawlers and pleasure boats soft rock was playing, underscored by the burble of diesels as a charter fisherman moved by. On its deck middle-aged men tilted cans. It was a normal May morning in a normal year in a corner of the world where the years, though they passed without haste, had always left untouched more than they changed.

Behind the closed porthole a wide-shouldered man with close-cut black hair lifted an inch of liquid topaz into the sunlight. His face and bare chest were burned dark, but circles still showed under his eyes. The hair on his chest was black, that on his arms and head sun-bleached a dull copper. He wore wrinkled and oil-stained work trousers. Through the dimness of the cabin the beam passed dense and dazzling as a shaft of molten glass, teeming with dust motes, angling gradually up and down. The tumbler flashed red and blue fire as stubby fingers turned it in the silent light, the liquor heeling and quivering as the wake of the passing boat reached it.

Or, Tiller Galloway thought dimly, Is it a tremor in my hand?

He had sat there since before dawn, remembering that last time he'd sailed from the Golfo Triste.

To San Rosario in early fall the ganja came down from the mountains in two-hundred-pound bales. Even covered with ripe bananas in the backs of the trucks it sweetened the dusty air along the roads with the autumnal aroma of marijuana.

He'd waited for it that afternoon five years before on a rotting pier under four dead coconut palms. Their stiff dry fronds were clashing to a light, ominous wind, and twice in the last hour the surface of the gulf had rippled briefly with heavy drops like falling bullets. He was watching the men who grunted in the blowing dust, slinging the bales into the deep flared hull.

He had looked at the sweating mulattoes and noted the sway of the palms. He had examined the anvil-shaped thunderheads. Last of all he had glanced at the man in white linen who stood a few yards down the pier, focusing a camera on the jut of land that screened the bay from the Caribbean.

Galloway had decided then he would go for it. The big score. Everything—or nothing.

Years later, years older, the same man turned suddenly from sky and sea and sand and drained the shot glass to the bottom. Drank, then held it for a long second cocked like a grenade in a callused hand.

A moment later the porthole shattered. And into the dimness came a cry. Low and reluctant, muffled by rotting wood and the lapping waves, it lasted for only a moment. Then there was only silence.

• • •

At the sound of shattering glass Bernie Hirsch straightened from two steel tanks of compressed air. She looked toward the boat, a few berths down from her, but saw only the red-orange glare of the sun on still water.

Bernice Hirsch's mouth was too wide and her chin too strong for her to be lovely. Her brows were too dark and thick to be refined. But her face was striking; it made men look back at her, and then, some of them, look away. She seemed always a little sad. Seeing nothing amiss down the pier she looked back, toward the marina. She was looking at the lot when the blue-gray BMW pulled in. She paused, watching the man who stopped at the office, stared for a moment at the Closed for Reorganization notice taped to the door, and then approached her with long, swinging strides.

"That looks heavy. May I give you a hand?"

She didn't have to think long about that one. It was a hundred feet from her car to *Victory*. "Well . . . all right," she said, lowering the twin tanks to the hot gravel of the lot. "Thanks."

He was tall. Well tanned, with light hair threaded with silver, and striking blue eyes. She smiled again, surprised at finding a man attractive who was easily twice her age. She was suddenly glad she was wearing "visiting clothes"—a dark skirt, sensible heels, blouse and jacket—and that she'd been strict about her diet.

"I'm a little confused. Perhaps you can help me."

"I'll try."

"I was looking for Harry's Dock—"

"You found it. They took down the old sign, haven't put up the new one yet. Now it's Blackbeard's Harbour Yacht Club and Condominium Development."

"I see—"

"Were you looking for someone in particular?"

"Is the *Victory* at this pier?" He rumpled a gray suit as he levered the forty-pound cylinders to his shoulder. "Mr. Galloway's boat?"

"That's right—that is, it was his. Tiller doesn't own it anymore."

"I was mistaken, then."

"No, you're right. He's still in business. In fact, he lives aboard. He just doesn't own it anymore."

"Good." He offered his free hand. She took it; his grip was warm and strong. "I'm Richard Keyes. Obviously you know him. I wanted to see him, if he's here."

"I'm Bernice Hirsch, Mr. Keyes. I think he's here. Come on. Watch that loose board."

She led the way down the creaking pier, past several power- and sailboats in various stages of decay and disrepair. One had sunk at its moorings, and its cabin, crusted with seagull scat, showed rings of scum from the tide. A For Sale sign showed dimly in a window. The stench of rotting fish and gasoline came up from the brown water that lapped against the pilings.

"Hirsch," said the man behind her.

"Excuse me?"

"You—you don't work for Galloway?"

"Me? No. Actually, I'm his parole officer."

"I beg your pardon?"

"Don't let it bother you. If you're here on business, Tiller's an excellent diver."

"I'm sure he is."

Something had unsettled him, she saw, but she decided she'd said enough. It wouldn't do to lose Tiller a job. Any job. She stopped at the gangway. "Anybody aboard?"

There was no answer. "Come on," she said, and ran up the plank. Behind her, Keyes proceeded with more caution. As he lowered the tanks to the scarred planking Bernie looked around the deck for Tiller.

The boat was some seventy feet long. Military-surplus aluminum lockers had been bolted in along both sides of the open deck aft. The metal was battered and dinged. The gunwales were teak, but scarred as if by heavy chains. A steel diving platform had been bolted to the stern. It was rusty. The smooth sweep of her foredecks looked better—except for peeling scarlet paint—from still-graceful bow, from which a worn mooring line tended forward to the pier, back to the windscreen of a jury-built cabin that enclosed the originally open wheelhouse. Atop this was perched an awninged tuna tower. A pool of oil moved sluggishly at the transom, and here and there the wooden hull was dark with rot.

"It's not too clean," she said, "but she floats. So far. I'll get him for you." She went to a companionway amidships and kicked with a heel. "Tiller! You aboard?"

"Get off my boat," said a muffled voice from below.

She kicked again. "Open up! In the name of the state of North Carolina and the county of Dare."

A series of thuds came from below, a muffled curse, and then the companionway door jerked open. An empty bottle emerged, followed by an arm and then a man. She moved back as he climbed deliberately from below, gripping the rail. As he reached the top the bottle slipped from his hand. It hit the deck and bounced, rolled out a freeing port, and met the slimy water with a plop.

• • •

Galloway watched it drift off, bobbing in the outgoing tide. The sun glinted briefly from it before it lost itself amid the shadows of the pilings. Well, there are more, he thought. Lots more. Holding tightly to the rail, he blinked up into the sunlight, ignoring the two people waiting on deck.

"Hello," one of them said.

He lowered his eyes slowly to a big guy in an expensive suit. No, not big, exactly; tall, but slim rather than strong. Still, some men like that were panthers. His eyes were what held your attention. Deep blue, intense, protruding a little, but not far enough to knock him out as a model for *Esquire* or GQ.

"Who the hell are you?"

"My name's Keyes. I wrote a letter, care of the marina. Did you get it?"

Galloway nodded.

Keyes was frowning now. "You're . . . who? A crewman?"

He laughed briefly. "Crewman—yeah. And engineer. And dive master. I'm Galloway."

"*Lyle* Galloway? I thought you'd be older."

"Third of the name. Could be you were thinking of one of my illustrious ancestors." He slurred the last words. "Yeah. I got your letter. You still interested in watching me clear a wreck?"

"You're diving in this condition?" This was Hirsch. Distaste was clear in her voice.

"I'm going, damn right." He looked dully at her, then back at the sky. "You. Keyes. Law says I got to see a certification before I can take you down with me."

The man in the suit pulled a billfold from his jacket, flipped through it, and held it out. Galloway looked at it. His eyes focused and then opened a little wider. He glanced sideways at Hirsch. The parole officer was looking not at Keyes's hands, but at his face.

Galloway reached out casually, examined the billfold, and handed it back. "Seems all right," he said. He thrust his right hand deep into a trouser pocket as Keyes replaced the wallet. "You be needing gear?"

"Yes. Everything."

"That'll be a medium top," said Hirsch, opening one of the aluminum lockers and rummaging through a pile of rubber. "And a high-waisted bottom, because you're taller than a medium would fit." She held up a wet-suit top, black, with a pebbled sharkskin finish. "Quarter-inch thick."

"Fine," said Keyes. He crossed the deck, avoiding the pool of dirty oil, and perched on the gunwale.

After a moment Galloway sat down beside him. He looked at Hirsch, who was now rooting through a box of regulators. Her long brown hair had swung over her face, and her breasts moved under the thin blouse. "Bernie," he said, more politely than he had spoken yet that morning. "Mind doing me a favor? Check and see if the lines are ready to let go. I'll get the rest of his gear."

"Sure, Tiller."

When she was gone Keyes leaned back. "Good-looking girl."

"Uh-huh."

"Odd relationship you two have. Is it—intimate?"

"Who? That nosy bitch? Strictly official." He turned to Keyes. "All right. What's the pitch?"

"Pitch?"

"The trick with the wallet. The hundred-dollar bill."

The blond man raised his eyebrows. "You said you read my letter?"

"Yeah, I read it."

"Well, as I said there, I might have some work for you. But I wanted to see you in operation first. To do that I wanted to dive with you. As to the little—tip—it's very simple, Mr. Galloway. You asked for a dive card, and I don't happen to have one."

"But do you know how? It's damn easy to get killed down there. Especially for someone your age."

"You've seen better years."

"I do it every day. It's hard work, salvage diving. You look like an office man to me. You sure your heart'll take it?"

"I play a good deal of handball."

"Oh. Handball."

Keyes's face tightened. "Look, Galloway. You accepted my money. Officially, you shouldn't take me without a cert. I assure you I know how. But if anything happens to me, just strip the body and leave it out there. You'll be clear, and I certainly won't care. Is that good enough?"

Galloway stared at him for a moment, then shrugged. "If that's how you want it."

Hirsch came back aft. "Jack's here with the explosives," she said. "The lines are ready. Tiller, I brought a change of clothes. I'd like to come along, if I may."

"'If you may.'" Galloway heaved himself off the gunwale. "Why bother asking, Counselor? Is it to make me feel better? It doesn't. The law says you can snoop on me wherever I am, whatever I'm doing. I suppose that includes Oregon Inlet. If you've got to come you can help lash down some of this gear. Might be rough out there today."

He turned from her look, and went below.

• • •

"Cast off," Galloway called, spinning the wheel to the left and gunning the throttle astern with his other hand. The engines rumbled unevenly and oily smoke blew forward over the deck.

On the dock a boy flipped the bow line off its cleat and stood holding it, poised to spring aboard the departing boat. He stood tense and vital in the sunlight, a freckle-shouldered young man whose summer-bleached hair stuck out at angles as if he had toweled it to air-dry after a swim. He was so slim-hipped it seemed only friction held up his cutoff jeans, the only clothes he wore. He hitched them higher with his free hand as he waited.

Galloway slammed the engines into neutral, then forward. Gears chattered below, then caught. The screws spewed dirty water and the boat gathered way. As she passed the end of the pier the boy jumped, swinging himself over the gunwale into the cockpit. He dropped a worn

Kitty Hawk Kites tote bag to the deck and pushed it under a seat. "Hey, Bern, Tiller," he said, but his eyes were on Keyes.

Hirsch said, "This is Jack Caffey, the owner. Jack, this is Mr. Keyes."

"Hello—the *owner?*"

"Hi. That's right. Got anything for me to do, Tiller?"

Galloway, at the wheel, shook his head without looking around. Caffey looked at Bernie, shrugged, and squatted down, bracing himself with a hand on one of the lockers.

They were out of the basin now, moving out into the wide brackish sound that separated the barrier islands from the mainland. Galloway left the channel markers, sticks topped by black-painted cans and plastic bottles, to starboard. Each bore a brown pelican, wings folded, regarding them as solemnly as a bench of French judges. Beyond them were mud flats, dotted here and there by gray herons. A speedboat ripped past, cutting the sluggish water apart like a razor through brown velvet. They rolled heavily to her wake. Behind them the land fell away. When the channel ended at a small buoy Galloway twirled the wheel with one hand, and Pamlico Sound, twenty and more miles wide, opened before them.

Keyes had been taking in the sound and sky, balancing easily with his arms folded. Now he leaned to Caffey. "Say—Jack? Mind if I look around?"

"Sure. Come on, I'll show you." He jumped to his feet. "Boat tour," he called in Galloway's direction, but the man at the helm made no response.

Keyes meanwhile had pulled off his shoes, folded his jacket, and rolled his trousers to mid-calf. "Forward first, then," Caffey grinned at him. "Along the side, like this." He vaulted to the gunwale, tanned toes splayed, and held to a corroded aluminum rail as he worked forward. The rail wobbled.

Keyes followed, more cautiously, but with a sureness that showed this was not his first time afloat. Caffey held out a hand, but he refused it with a shake of his head. A few seconds later they stood on the foredeck.

"Hang on," they both heard Galloway shout, and the pitch of the engines increased. The deck tilted upward and began to vibrate. Caffey crouched, planting his feet for balance, and pointed at a patched area of deck. "The gun mount was here," he called over the rumble of diesels and whistle of wind. "This used to be a PT—a patrol torpedo boat. She operated out of the Coast Guard base on Ocracoke. I've seen pictures, she was quite a looker in those days. Used to have guns, torpedoes, depth-charge racks, the works. Three fifteen-hundred-horse Packards."

"How did Galloway come by her?"

"They had three of them high and dry over in Pasquotank when they closed down the old base there. They gave him fifty bucks to haul them away. He managed to put one seaworthy boat together out of the three of 'em."

"I see. Where's the anchor?"

"Bow flares too much to see it, but we got a fifty-pound danforth and a hundred fathom of line."

"Good."

They crept back to the cabin, swung around it, and regained the afterdeck. Keyes looked over the side. The water was green now. The boat slid over it smoothly, churning it to foam. Two vees of bow wave accompanied them, rolling out over the surface of the Pamlico, ruffled now by cat's-paws. The sun blazed and shimmered into their eyes. "Belowdecks?" shouted Jack. Keyes nodded, and Galloway moved aside a bit to let them down the companionway.

The noise of the engines was louder in the enclosed space below. It was dim, too, and a stink of oil, mildew, and whiskey met them. They braced themselves and looked around the cabin.

To their left a chart table was bolted to the bulkhead. Above it on a rack was an early model loran set and a marine radio of equal senescence. A tangle of wires disappeared into the overhead. A chart of the Virginia Capes area southward to Cape Lookout was thumbtacked to the table, covered by a yellowing sheet of plastic. On it quivered a set of dividers, jabbed into the chart by their points. To the right, two chairs were lashed to a fold-down bunk with what looked like clothesline. A binocular case hung from one of the legs.

"Engine room," shouted Caffey, pointing to an open hatch going aft. The explanation was unnecessary; the roar from the compartment beyond became deafening as Keyes bent to pass through the low door.

The Packards were long gone, victims of age and the cost of hundred-octane gasoline. Instead two 200-horsepower Reo truck engines had been bolted to their foundations, and connected to the props through a salvaged tugboat transmission. Keyes coughed. The single bulb swayed through a white haze.

He continued aft, turning to slide between the hammering engines. Waves of heat beat at him. Their casings were cooking-hot. He paused near the transmission and looked down at the packing boxes, where the shafts, blurred by rotation, passed through the hull into the sea. A small spring bubbled around each shaft, running down between hull timbers into the bilges, forming a black pool, scummy with oil.

He turned, to find Caffey watching him from across the compartment. He motioned him back, not smiling.

"How dependable are they?" Keyes shouted.

"They need an overhaul. But they've been getting us out and back." Caffey turned and led the way forward through a second hatch into a space that allowed them to stand upright. He clicked on another naked bulb. "The crew berthed here," he said. "Tiller tore most of the bunks out when he bought her. Now it's a dive locker. That machine in the corner's an air compressor, for charging tanks. That's a cutting-and-welding torch beside it. This rack holds ten bottles of gas and there's room for more in that old ammo locker."

"Anything forward of this?"

"Tiller's bunkroom, then a smaller space—cable locker for the anchor, a whole bunch of crap." Caffey hesitated. "I mean, gear. The boat may not look so hot, she hasn't been kept up since he—since he went away. But we can do a lot with what we have aboard. Any kind of diving, salvage you want done." His voice lowered. "Mr. Keyes, let me say something. Tiller Galloway's top of the line. He really is. Don't judge him by what you've seen so far today."

"I see." Keyes turned. "Topside, then?"

"Sure."

• • •

An hour later a gray arch grew ahead of them, rising from the sound and the low dunes. They passed only one other boat, a small trawler heading in from seaward. Galloway poked *Victory* like thread through a succession of needles between low islands covered with sea oats and scrub brush, past shallows where egrets and avocets hunted knee-deep. At intervals kittiwakes whirled up, their shadows flickering across the water, now growing a translucent greenish-blue.

"Oregon Inlet Bridge," said Hirsch. She had come up from below in shorts and a "Virginia is for Lovers" T-shirt. She smiled at Galloway and Keyes, then flushed a little, and her dark eyes dropped. Barefoot, with long brown hair twisted back, she looked younger than Caffey.

"The way to the Atlantic?"

"That's right. North of it, Nags Head, Kitty Hawk, Kill Devil Hills; south of it is all Hatteras Island, down to Ocracoke."

"It looks like it's built over land, not water."

"That's the problem," said Caffey. "That's new land. The whole Banks, all the islands are movin' south."

"Moving?" Keyes looked disturbed. "What do you mean?"

"This is all sand," said Caffey, waving his hand at the low dunes they were passing. "Just a ribbon of sand, couple thousand feet across—and the Atlantic on the other side. No one knows how it keeps resisting the sea. This inlet opened one night in a storm, a hundred years ago, and now it's closing up. Corps of Engineers been running dredges, but the sand stays ahead. It's driving the trawlers out of business."

The bridge gradually darkened the sky, the whir of tires coming distant through the concrete, and then fell behind. The channel twisted. Shoals thrust out from the shore, and along their margins tiny figures wielded poles: surf fishermen. A patch of choppy, disturbed water appeared between them and the sea. Galloway eyed it and throttled back. A moment later they saw his hands tense on the wheel as a whisper came from beneath the hull. He held course. The boat slowed, seemed to drop her head for a moment, then raised it and pushed forward again. They were over.

"There she is," said Hirsch.

The trawler lay where the channel opened to the sea. Only mast and booms showed above the chop, trailing cables in the tidal current.

"A real menace to navigation," Caffey said. "Tiller, how'd she get there? I thought she'd be up on one of the shoal patches."

"She was," said Galloway, unbending enough to turn his head. "Something grabbed her hull when the Guard towed her off. Lot of old wrecks in this sand. Got this far, then went down. Okay—let's get clear to seaward. I'll take the anchor."

He throttled back and went forward. Jack took the wheel, keeping the boat's head into three-foot swells that came in steadily from the open sea. The sun was intensely hot.

"Ready to drop," Galloway called back. Caffey gunned the engines a little, watching the wreck. "Leave her room to swing."

"Okay, Tiller." He aimed the bow a little farther to seaward. The booms poked up like dying trees a hundred yards astern, the breaking surf a white line beyond. "How's this?"

"Good. Back her."

The engines hesitated, then rumbled again; *Victory* began to drift backward. A moment later chain rattled, followed by a splash. Caffey slammed the shift several times before it went into neutral. Galloway stood waiting, watching the line come taut, then made a chopping motion.

The diesels died. "Tiller," said Bernie, in the sudden silence, "Is it my imagination, or are your engines getting louder?"

"Mufflers are shot," said Galloway, pulling himself up into the tuna tower. A moment later a red-and-white diving flag was flapping in the sea breeze.

"Bern, you coming in? Looks like good visibility today."

"I think I'll stay with the boat this time, Jack."

The three men began dressing out. Keyes stripped off a starched white shirt, revealing a pale long-muscled torso without a trace of fat. Over shorts and T-shirts they pulled heavy, buoyant rubber. The suits were hot and tight-fitting, making it hard to bend a leg or raise an arm, and in the sun a wearer soon found himself literally bathed in sweat. The blond man said suddenly, "Are these necessary? Isn't this water warm?"

"Sure, it's warm," said Galloway, working the pants over his legs. "You can go down bare-assed for all I care. But don't complain when a jellyfish makes love to you, or you tear your guts open on a piece of junk."

Keyes shook his head, but complied. They finished dressing. Over the wet suit went a buoyancy compensator, like an old Mae West life vest; lead weights strung on a web belt; a diving knife. Galloway selected a regulator, screwed it onto a tank, twisted the valve. Air *phutted* into it, tautening the rubber hose. He bit into the mouthpiece and took a deep breath.

Bernie helped Keyes and Caffey lift the tanks to their backs. Galloway put his twin eighties on the deck, bent, and with one smooth motion swung them up and over his head. The straps slid into position on his shoulders and he cinched them tight without looking. He pulled the tote bag from under the seat and unzipped it. The waxy blocks of explosive, box of fuzes, coil of primacord went into a net bag, ready to clip to his belt.

"You two ready? Okay, listen up. These old wooden trawlers don't take much demolition, but you got to place your charges right. I'm going to put three pounds, the main charge, right under the keel. Another two pounds goes back aft, to break up the engine foundations. Last pound I'll put in the deckhouse. Any questions?"

"I got one," said Caffey. His hair was already wet with seat. "What about me? What do I do?"

"Sorry, Jack, I keep forgetting you're the boss." Galloway said it without resentment, in fact without much expression at all. "Tell you what—you do the placement aft. You know where the engines are, don't you?"

"Come *on,* Tiller! I was trawlin' out of Wanchese all last summer."

"Okay. I'll give you your charge when we're down there."

Keyes had been listening. He pulled out one of the blocks, turned it over in his hand. "This stuff. Is it safe to handle down there?"

"Pentatriethylene?" said Galloway. In a smooth movement he drew a heavy knife from a sheath on his leg. The point went through the packet and chunked into wood. "Satisfied?"

"Very."

"Good. Now listen up. Watch yourselves down there. Keep away from jagged edges, loose lines and cables. Don't go inside the hull. It's been weakened already by the grounding and being pounded by surf for a week. This is just a job, a hundred an hour and expenses. No unnecessary risks. For you, Keyes, that goes double." Galloway stepped over the gunwale to the diving platform. He slipped on fins, standing on one leg as if the hundred pounds of gear was a summer suit, then gestured brusquely to the others. Caffey sat on the gunwale and rolled over the port side. When he bobbed up he beckoned to Keyes with a gloved hand. The older man hesitated, then tucked the regulator in his mouth and stepped in feet first.

Tiller Galloway lifted his face to the sun for a moment, then lowered it to look round the boat a last time. Hirsch raised her hand an inch or two, palm out. He nodded shortly, put his hand to his mask, and bent forward. The surface shattered beneath him, and he was received by the sea.

three

There was a peaceful interval as he sank, watching his bubbles stream upward to crash and shatter against the silvery undersides of the waves.

Galloway dropped slowly on his back, arms outstretched, looking up at the world he was leaving. Back there, up there, were the regret and self-hatred that tortured him every moment he was sober. It was like seasickness. Everyone felt it, if the sea was rough enough. He'd felt a touch of it himself his first time out after four years ashore. But the moment you left the pitching boat, the moment you hit the water, it disappeared like magic.

His regret and self-hatred were like that. Ashore only one thing helped. He knew he was drinking too much. But it was the only way he could go on. Though even then, no matter how drunk he was a still small self within looked on unaffected, accusing, full of ineradicable grief.

But beneath the surface, under the sea . . . life was elemental here. Past and future were alike nonexistent. Here there was only now. Submerged in it, a man became less human. He left his guilts and furies behind, hovering back in the sunlight. Surrounded by the sea, in a strange way he could become an animal again, could return to the slow instinctive unconsciousness his kind had left behind a hundred million years too soon.

Good visibility today, too. This close to shore he'd expected murk, but he could make out the bottom of the old PT. The sea was light green above, a deeper green-blue below. Diaphanous coelenterates, gauzy and shimmering as if woven of fog, drifted past as he sank. He looked around. Caffey, swimming downward, was several yards below him, and the stranger, Keyes, several yards above. He wondered briefly what the man wanted, what sort of work he had in mind; then dismissed it. He'd find out soon enough.

The bottom came into sight. Coarse white sand, rippled by current. It was nice to work in shallow water once in a while. He paused to valve air into his vest, then finned slowly west with the tide.

A shadow ahead slowly became the wreck. He eyed it critically as they neared. It had settled on its starboard side. The hull was clean of barnacles and weed, as if it had just been hauled. Too bad old McOwen had to lose his trawler, Galloway mused. But his loss is my gain. I sure as hell need the income.

He turned, to find the others close behind. He led them along the hull. A sinuous shadow drifted over him: a loose cable, part of the trawler's drift gear, moving in the inshore current. The stern was ground into the sand. The lower blades of the propeller were buried, but part of the shaft was exposed. He pointed to it; Caffey nodded.

Rounding the stern, he continued up the starboard side. The hole in the hull came into view. He could see where one of the strakes had pulled free. She must have gone down fast. The deckhouse, hatches open, loomed above them as if ready to topple. Portholes stared out, dark and blank as the eyes of dead fish. He saw Jack reach out to one as they passed. It creaked shut under his touch, then swung open again lazily. A hatch or cable banged somewhere. They swam beneath the blunt bow, reaching the port side again.

Okay, enough rubbernecking. Galloway checked the bag at his waist, then exhaled a stream of bubbles. With his lungs empty, he sank toward the bottom. He pointed upward to the wreck, and made a warning sign to the others. Canted like this, in a strong current, it could shift at any time.

He reached the bottom and began breathing again. He dug busily for a moment with one hand, shoving sand aside. Keyes and Caffey sank to the bottom nearby, watching. Sand drifted up, dispersing in the current like beige smoke. A shadow flitted over them, and all three looked up. A great barracuda, attracted by the bubbles, was patrolling between them and the sun. It hung motionless a few yards away, five feet of torpedo-shaped silver, jaws agape as one black eye studied them.

Galloway watched it for a moment. Barracuda seldom bothered divers, though the big fish, fascinated by humans, would tag along wherever they swam. It seemed to be watching Caffey, who was examining a spiral shell before tucking it into a pocket of his vest.

Dig, dig . . . sand caved in nearly as rapidly as he scooped it out. Vision contracted to the inside of his mask. He closed his eyes and mined on. In Vietnam you learned to work at night, like an octopus. Your fingers grew eyes. At last his outthrust glove touched the ridge of the keel. He paused then, his body half under the hull, pulled his right glove off, and snapped the bag open. He found the end of the primacord. Working by feel, he pressed it into a block, sandwiched it between two others, and bound all three together with the explosive line. Then he thrust the whole charge as far as he could reach under the keel.

One down. He pushed himself free, unreeling the plastic-sheathed cord. The water cleared somewhat. Caffey was above him. He waved him closer, prepared a one-pound block, and gave it to him. Caffey swam aft. Galloway looked around, but saw no sign of Keyes. He spliced Caffey's trunk line to the main with a three-hole primer.

And one last charge. He swam upward, found an open hatch just below the pilothouse level. That would do. Latching it open—he hadn't brought a light, and it would be awkward to have it close on him—he moved slowly inside the wreck, checking the overhead and corners. Morays took time to move in, but there could be other nasties. But it was clear. He estimated the centerline, wedged the explosive against a strength member, and backed out, unreeling primacord.

And that was it. On the far side he could see Jack—or was it Keyes? Couldn't tell at this distance—waving. He guessed it was Jack. The detonator was a standard fifteen-minute delay cap. He pulled it and let go. There was a dull pop and the fuze, bubbling as it burned, sank toward the bottom.

He swam aft, looking for Keyes, but found Caffey first, backing out from under the stern. So the other figure had been Keyes. Caffey saw him and gave a thumbs up. Follow me, Galloway signaled, and swam against the current, which was increasing, round the starboard side.

Keyes wasn't there. Galloway cursed silently. He was taking the order to stay clear a little too literally. He swam upward, and saw the other man on the far side of the hull. He was reaching for his knife, intending to tap on his tank to attract Keyes's attention, when something snapped.

Something big. He paused in the water, trying to locate the sound. Then he saw it. One of the booms, heavy steel posts the trawler used to lift nets, was tearing out of the wooden deck. He swam hard, instinctively clearing its path, then spun.

Caffey would be right under it.

Even as he thought it, the boom tore free. It toppled slowly, yet too fast to evade, through the increasingly murky water. The current was increasing, drawn back through the narrow inlet by the tide. Galloway straightened his body and kicked swiftly down and aft, his snorkel fluttering against his mask as he drove through the water. As he closed he caught one glimpse of a fin, kicking downward, then reached the expanding cloud of silt and plunged into it.

Vision disappeared. He drove on, trusting to his sense of direction. It was almost correct. He crashed into steel, felt something sharp bite through rubber into his arm. He gripped the edge and swam over it in a somersault, twisting to head downward. He groped. Something soft there—rubber, or flesh. He held his breath, listening for the roar of bubbles from a ruptured hose, but heard nothing. Fine brown particles seethed in front of his eyes, as if he were diving in bean soup.

He groped again, and was rewarded with a limp arm. Pulling himself down to it, he ran his hand over the body. One shoulder, no, one whole side was pinned under the boom. He located Caffey's regulator, drifting free. He thrust it roughly into an unresponsive mouth and thumbed the "clear" button, sending a surge of air into the boy's lungs. Was it too late? He couldn't feel any movement. He held it there anyway and felt around the boom with his free hand.

He was stretched out like that when a rending sound came through the water, and something massive struck him in the small of the back. Pain flared in his head. The weight slipped to the side, slid past him. He jerked his leg out of the way just in time as it thudded to the sand.

It can't be more than a minute, he thought, since I pulled the detonator on the charge. But it seemed like five. He thought of going back and pulling it off the cord. That would safe all three charges. But in this murk it could take minutes to locate it. Caffey seemed to be unconscious. He didn't respond or move. In the minutes it would take to find the detonator, the boy would drown.

He had to get him free, and worry about the explosives later.

Galloway doubled his legs under him and braced them against the bottom. He let the mouthpiece go, hoping that Caffey, even unconscious, would keep his teeth tight on it, and wrapped his hands around the boom. He pulled. The only thing that happened was that something gripped his shoulder.

His knife was half drawn before he made out a mask. Keyes's blue eyes were wide behind it. Ah, Galloway thought. He's where I want him at last. He pulled the other man's hands to the boom. Keyes nodded.

All right, Galloway thought. If we can move this son of a bitch at all it'll be on the first try. He set his knees in sand and sucked three deep breaths, as fast as his regulator would deliver them. One . . . two . . . he nodded at Keyes.

The steel mass came up suddenly, slid, and toppled away toward

Caffey's head. Galloway pulled him backward as the boom grated on sand once more. His hands moved over his partner, found a toggle. Gas thudded into Caffey's vest, and Galloway triggered his own.

Ten seconds later they broke surface. Sunlight, the smack of a wave in his face . . . he spat out his mouthpiece and breathed salt air, tried clumsily to swim. His legs were weak. He felt a hand under his arm. Keyes, vest inflated, was helping him. His eyes were worried behind the oval mask.

"The boat," Galloway sputtered. "Don't have much time . . . Bernie!"

Her head popped above the gunwale. Her eyebrows lifted, and a moment later a life ring and line sailed toward them. Galloway grabbed it, nearly done, and let her pull him in.

Keyes went up first. He and Hirsch hauled Caffey clear of the water while Galloway collapsed on the platform, pulling in great draughts of air. Blood dripped from his arm, trickling downward over rusty steel as if seeking the sea.

When he could stand he did, and looked over the transom. The two of them were working on Caffey. After a moment the boy turned his head, shuddered, and began to cough up seawater. Galloway unbuckled his tanks and climbed aboard. He went directly to the wheel and pushed in the starter. The engines whined, backfired, and finally caught. "His chest?" he said tiredly to Keyes. The older man nodded. "Bernie, watch him. Don't let him move. If he's broken any ribs, he could puncture a lung easy."

"Okay, Tiller."

"Keyes, you get forward. Cut the anchor line. Yeah, just cut it, we'll recover it later."

"Right."

When his knife lifted, Galloway slammed the throttle forward till the engines screamed. The boat leapt ahead, fleeing for the inlet.

Keyes came aft. He stood beside Galloway at the wheel, facing forward, their shoulders almost touching. "I saw what you did down there," he said. He spoke almost confidentially, though he was shouting to be heard above the engines.

Galloway glanced at him, reached back to rub his spine. "That so?" he grunted.

"I didn't help much on that boom. It was superhuman."

Galloway looked at him again and grunted again. The bridge loomed. "Hey! Bernie! Did you call ahead?"

"Your radio needs fixing. They could hardly hear me. But they'll have an ambulance at the inlet."

"No one's fault," said Keyes. "We'll back you up on that. That wreck was ready to fall apart. It confirms my choice."

"What choice was that?"

"I chose this boat, and I chose you. Not at random. But I had to sound you out, to see you personally."

"And just what did you choose me for?" said Galloway. "Assuming I let myself be chosen."

Keyes glanced aft, to where Bernice Hirsch bent over a now conscious Jack Caffey. "How's your schedule, Captain Galloway? Not too full, I hope?"

Galloway seemed to go away for a moment, as if remembering something. Then he came back. "It was. But some things have dropped out recently. What did you have in mind?"

"Historical research. You may find it interesting. It'll be worth your while." He glanced at Hirsch again. "That is—if you can spare the time."

Galloway regarded him; was opening his mouth to speak when far behind them the sea suddenly split open. A white plume raged skyward, with black bits of wreckage in it. The shock shuddered along their hull before they heard its rumble in the air. "It seemed so long," said Galloway, looking back. "I half thought it failed."

"It couldn't," said Keyes. "There are some men who succeed. Who *will* to, no matter what opposes them. Thus they force fate. And you are one of us."

Their eyes met, and held for a long moment. No one watching could have told whether it was with admiration or distrust.

four

The rescue squad had come and gone. The doctor on call decided not to evacuate Caffey north. He could recuperate from bruised ribs and mild shock as well at home as in Norfolk. Hirsch went with the ambulance. A sheriff's deputy stayed, talking first to Galloway and then briefly to Keyes. The sun was slanting toward the sound when he left and they were finally able to go below.

"Watch your head on that companionway," said Galloway.

Keyes bowed a little, keeping the stoop as he followed Galloway forward. He lingered at the door, staring around the cramped bunkroom. Plywood shelves had been hammered into the bulkhead above a neatly made single bunk. Frayed bungee cords secured the books. Navigation, history, philosophy, a Bible, a few novels. A piece of clear plastic had been roughly taped over a broken porthole.

"Drink?" grunted Galloway, pulling a full bottle of bourbon from behind his mattress.

"Don't use it much. But I guess a touch wouldn't hurt. With water."

"Unlash that chair and pull it over."

Keyes balanced it on its rear legs and lifted his glass to the shelves. "A reader, eh?"

Galloway nodded. He was pouring his second, straight, before Keyes had tasted his.

"A drinker too, I see."

"Man gets dry in four years."

"That how long you were in prison?"

"That's right."

"Where?"

"Central. Raleigh."

"You mind talking about it?"

"Yeah, I mind."

"What were you in for?"

"I was broke. A guy offered me a can't-lose deal. I'd provide the boat. He'd provide cargo and crew."

Keyes took a sip. "Marijuana?"

"Mixed. That and cocaine."

"From?"

"Colombia."

"Say, this tastes kind of . . . moldy. Does yours?"

"No, liquor's okay. Must be the water. Been sitting in the peak tank for quite a while."

The blond man looked at his glass, then set it on the deck beside him. "So. What happened?"

"About what?"

"How did you get caught?"

"Just a minute, mister. I was cross-examined on all this four years ago. There any reason to go through it again with you?"

"I told you: If I have a job for someone, Captain, I like to know who he is. What happened on the way north?"

Instead of answering Galloway got up. The only light in the closed compartment was from the dying sun. It slid through the porthole and made a swaying red ellipse on the far bulkhead. Keyes had been staring at him since the interview started. Now, in the dimming bloody light, Galloway watched the pale blue irises widen even more. The effect was hypnotic: He had to blink before he could tear his gaze away. He shrugged, turned around, found himself without pacing room with Keyes in the chair, and sat down again. "What the hell . . . we made one run without any problem. Then somebody turned. The Coast Guard was waiting when I made Virginia Beach the second time."

"That must have been hard on your family. Especially the Coast Guard involvement."

Galloway nodded, then caught himself and glanced up from under. "What do you know about my family?"

"Just that the name means something down here. All those Lifesaving Service heroes, going out in surfboats in storms to rescue the shipwrecked. Your—grandfather, was it?—helped the Wrights launch their flyer up on Kill Devil Hill. How long has your family been here?"

"Long as there's been English. Legend is the first Galloway came ashore in a whiskey barrel. They were probably shipwrecked here around 1700."

"I've always envied that," said Keyes. "Knowing your family, who your ancestors were. Don't know a thing about mine. And then there was your father—"

Galloway said nothing. He drank. A low, regular thump came from outside for a few minutes; then the wake of the passing boat died away, and the old PT settled again to a slow tilt.

"What did he think?"

"About what?"

"About your going to prison."

"He shot himself when the guilty verdict came down. I don't think he believed I did it till then."

Keyes sat silent for a moment. "That must have been rough."

Galloway shrugged.

"You married?"

"Not anymore."

"What about your mother?"

"Stepmother. She's refused to see me since my release. There aren't many people on this island I'm on speaking terms with anymore."

"No? Why did you come back, then?"

"Number of reasons. I know fishing and salvage, I thought I could make a living. There's something I have to decide, and this is the best place for me to do it. And then there's the parole."

Keyes nodded slowly. Galloway silently refilled his glass again, lifted the bottle with a raised eyebrow. The other covered his with his hand.

"How long's that for?"

"Two years mandatory."

"This Hirsch, she keeps close tabs on you."

"She's new to her job. Wants to save me."

"From?"

Galloway didn't answer. Keyes waited a moment, then sighed. "Were you in the Coast Guard?"

"Of course."

"What happened?"

"Nam."

"What did you do there?"

"I was a salvage diver in Saigon harbor. Later I got a chance to work with the Seals."

"What kind of work?"

"Combat demolition."

"Like today?"

"If this was North Vietnam, and we did it at night, and people were trying to kill us, yeah, it would be kind of like today."

"Why did you leave the Coast Guard?"

"Drugs."

"Selling?"

"Using."

"You use now?"

"Only this," said Galloway, polishing off another shot.

Neither man said anything for a long time after that. The sun dipped lower. The blond man's face was in shadow now. Galloway felt vaguely relieved. He poured himself a splash more.

"Too bad about the boy."

"He'll bounce back. Jack's always been a tough kid."

"You've known him long?"

"Since he was born. He's a double cousin."

"I see. Did I understand him right? He really owns this boat?"

"It was confiscated. After they found me guilty the Guard sold it at auction. He bought it."

"With whose money?"

Galloway flicked up his eyes, but didn't answer.

"Why don't you buy it back from him now?"

"Parole condition. I can't own a boat. Plus, I happen to be broke. He went to that knockdown with the last cash I had in his jeans."

"I see. So he owns it, but you run it."

"That's right, we're partners," said Galloway. He finished what was in his glass, looked at the bottle, then put it away. "All right. Let's have your proposition."

"I want you to do a little research for me," said Keyes. "Or with me. Dig around in some local history. If that's successful, I may want your assistance with a dive or two, and the use of your boat."

"That last part sounds like another offer I got once."

"The one that put you in prison? Maybe it sounds like it. But it isn't."

"So what is this research about?"

"It's a hobby. I'm interested in military history. Always have been. I'm ex-Army, matter of fact I was in Vietnam too. Now and then I write an article. I've published in *Military Review, Naval History, Army* magazine, and some little academic periodicals nobody reads much. That sort of thing."

"You've got a story?"

"Maybe. Got a lead. Just have to track it down."

"You said diving. Where?"

"Not sure. Somewhere off the coast."

"How far out?"

"Can't say exactly. Maybe forty, fifty miles."

Galloway glanced toward the chart table. Something gnawed at his memory. He frowned, but nothing came. "You talking treasure hunting of some kind? Pirate ship? Spanish galleon?"

"No, no, nothing like that. Purely historical interest. There might be souvenir value, if we found it first, but that's all."

"What ship was it?"

"I'm not sure yet. That's why I need to do the research."

"How deep would it be?"

"I'm not sure. Could be as much as two hundred meters."

Galloway whistled. "Six hundred feet? You're not asking for much, are you?"

"It wouldn't be an easy job. That's why I came to you."

Galloway heaved himself from the bunk and leaned over the chart table. He clicked on a light. "Show me."

Keyes picked up the dividers and rule, consulted the latitude and longitude markings, and laid off several lines with a pencil.

"There," he said. "As best I can figure, what we're looking for, if it exists, should be somewhere in there."

Galloway scratched his head. The lane, or corridor, was ten nautical miles wide. Starting roughly off Kinnekeet, it passed southward some thirty miles off the tip of the Cape before bending to run southwest. Water depth was thirty fathoms at the landward side, deepening to almost a hundred to the east. "You can't narrow it down any more? That's hundreds of square miles of ocean." He paused as a thought occurred to him. "If it's a wreck, though . . . I could check around the waterfront, up at the inlet. The charter boat captains. When you have a flat sand bottom like this, fish congregate around wrecks—"

"No!" Keyes almost shouted, then restrained himself. "I don't want that. I don't want anyone to know we're interested in this area."

"You mean search it ourselves? You're crazy. I'd love to take your money, but forget it. There's just too much ocean there."

"Oh, I agree. But now there may be a way to narrow it down." Keyes moved away from the table. When he sat down again his voice dropped. "That's where our research will come in. Listen. Do you recall, about two months ago, several bodies were discovered on the beach, a little north of here?"

Galloway had sat down too, and picked up the bottle again; but now he halted it halfway to his lips. He had the expression of a man who discovers another level beneath a conversation that up to now he had toyed with.

"The Indian grave. What about it?"

"You know about it?"

"Just what I read in the *Current*. The local paper."

"It was found by a company called O. R. Galloway. Any relation?"

After a moment Galloway said, "My brother. He's a big developer here. But I haven't seen him for years. We sort of—lost contact."

"I see. Well, one of the wire services picked the story up. That an ancient burial site had been discovered. That's how I happened to see it."

"And that made you come to Hatteras?" said Galloway.

"That's right."

"Go on."

"They weren't Indians," said Keyes.

"How do you know that?"

"I got here yesterday," said Keyes, hesitating a little then, "and called the sheriff, telling him I was interested for historical reasons, I needed more details. I didn't get much out of him. He stuck to the Indian story, but refused to show me the remains. Said there were legal problems, Antiquities Act or something. So then I went over to the site and managed to find one of the laborers, one of the guys who actually dug it up. I persuaded him to tell the truth."

"I hope it didn't cost you too much."

"It didn't. Here's what he told me: There were three bodies. They were dressed in civilian clothes and had six thousand dollars in cash on them. They also had a rubber raft. There was identification, but it was false. The ration coupons they had for gas and meat, on the other hand, were genuine. The coupons were dated 1944. They'd all been killed, it looked like to him, with shotguns."

"Christ," said Galloway, sitting up.

"Exactly. I asked him then if there'd been anything else found with the bodies. He said no—except two very rusty pistols. Well, I think there was more. Maybe not when they were found, but shortly before they died. What we'd have to find is the person, or persons, who killed them. It'd be hopeless for me, I wouldn't know the first place to go. I'm an outsider here, even my accent's wrong. That's where you'd help."

"Kind of late to try to solve a murder," said Galloway. "But I guess it'd make an interesting story, at that. So. Who were they?"

"I figure Germans."

"Obviously. And spies."

"Maybe. Or refugees. The question is, why were they killed?"

"If they came ashore in a rubber boat in wartime, on these beaches, they were spies. And the people here would treat them accordingly. This was before the road, before development. People here are used to taking care of themselves; they always have."

"Summary justice. Sure. But even then, why would the bodies be hidden in the dunes, why would nothing have ever been published about it? And why is the sheriff circulating this story that they're Indian bones a thousand years old?"

"Okay, you've convinced me there's something fishy. Go on. What exactly you lookin' for? That you think they had with them?"

"I'm not quite sure. A book?"

"What kind of book?"

"I don't know. A logbook. Or a chart, the one they were navigating on when they sank. Anything that would tell us more."

"Let's talk about that for a minute. Are you sure you want this bad enough to hire me?"

"I think I can afford your fees."

"Let's make sure. Say a hundred a day to hire me as a, I don't know, a local guide, a research assistant. If it comes to diving, that goes up to four hundred a day, for *Victory*. Hundred an hour diving time for me, hundred-fifty an hour over a hundred feet, and two hundred over two hundred feet—if I feel like going that deep; we'd have to use mixed gas, and that costs. And another thing. I don't work alone."

"I'd help, of course."

"No problem there, but I'd want Jack."

"At the same rate?"

"Oh, hell, no. Jack comes for half my fee. Once he's on his feet, I mean."

"We can use your partner, if he's not too banged up. But what about this girl? Hirsch? She won't butt in, will she?"

Galloway tapped his fingers together. "Christ, I don't know. See, she can come aboard anytime, she's my conscience. I don't get the feeling she has too many other customers at the moment. Actually she makes herself useful. She doesn't dive, but she's not afraid to work. I let her handle the boat when we're below."

"But she's in law enforcement."

"So it *is* illegal."

"No. I'd just like to do this story quietly."

"Lot of competition in the history business?"

"Something like that." Keyes grinned.

"Well, I'll try to discourage her. But that might not be easy. Especially if she gets suspicious."

"Are you sleeping with her?"

Galloway frowned. "You asked me that before. No."

Keyes looked at the overhead. A smile gradually worked its way into his eyes. "Even if she came along . . . having her might not be inconvenient. We'll see. Anything else?"

"Only one more thing. My contingent fee." Galloway paused. "You say you're after a story. Fine. Whatever you make from that's yours. But let's say we happen, some long shot, to find something valuable. No, don't say anything. But I'm putting in right now for thirty percent of whatever you make on whatever your deal is here."

"I agree to your fees, Mr. Galloway, except for that. It's not necessary. There's nothing valuable involved."

"I understand that. I'm talking, say, theoretically, if we stumble on something unexpected, you'd expect the biggest cut, wouldn't you? Since you'd be paying the expenses. Right? Or are you saying, if we find anything, it'd all be mine?"

Keyes looked reluctant even to discuss it. At last he said, "*If* we found anything like that, I'd consider five percent of it yours."

"I'll settle for twenty."

"Seven."

"Go to hell," Galloway growled. "I'd make ten percent for straight legal salvor's fee. Which something tells me this ain't."

"All right. Fifteen."

"And like I said, if we did go on to some diving, I'd need expenses, gear—a depth sounder, buoys, anchors, lots of line, food."

"We'll discuss that if it happens."

Keyes held out his hand then. Galloway took it. They both smiled tightly.

"Now. About finding out who killed them—"

"I said I'd give it a try."

"You have someone in mind?"

"Think so. She won't want to see me, but she will."

Keyes stood, stretched, and looked around the cabin. It was dark now except for the little light over the chart. "Well. A busy day. Where do I sleep?"

"There's a motel—" started Galloway, then stopped and grinned. "No motel?"

"I'd rather stay aboard." Keyes had leaned back in his chair again.

He did not elaborate. After a moment Galloway bent for the bottle again and examined it. An inch of whiskey remained.

"There's a foldin' bunk in the dive locker. You can sleep there. I'm going out for a bite."

"Seafood?"

"Mostly."

"Sounds good."

"You're a trusting son of a bitch, aren't you?"

"You're the only one who knows about this so far, Captain," said the older man. His voice hardened in the near-darkness. "Let me warn you now, I wouldn't like it if you talked about this with anyone else. It would benefit neither of us."

Galloway sat in the shadows, thinking about this. He was very drunk, but even so he perceived that there seemed to be something screwy in the way Keyes was approaching him. He said there wasn't anything valuable involved, but he'd jumped out of his skin when Galloway suggested talking to trawler captains. He didn't want to discuss a cut, even theoretically, but he didn't want him to talk to anyone. And how had he known to investigate the Indian-burial item? Tiller knew he wasn't at his best at the moment, but he could come up with only two possibilities. Either the guy was dead serious about this history thing, and wanted bad to be first in print with it, or else there was something else out there—something valuable.

In which case, it might pay to stay with the man, act like he bought his story. Keep paying out line on him, till he found out what he was after.

He waited, but Keyes said nothing. So at last he just said, "Don't threaten me, bud. It has a bad effect. Frankly, you may be wasting your time. Any ship that went down off Hatteras, at least in the last fifty years, it'd be in the records. And if it had anything worth money in it, six hundred feet isn't too much for a big firm with the right gear. There'd have been salvors out there a long time ago."

"I'm hiring you, not your opinions."

Galloway dropped it. He got up, staggering a little, and went into the head forward. Keyes looked after him, then picked up the pencil. He tapped it against his lips for a moment, then carefully and thoroughly erased all the marks on the chart.

There was the snap of a lock, the hollow lonely beat of two sets of footsteps pacing down a dock. A motor purring into life. Then silence came to stay, and the boat rocked gently in the night wind.

five

"Not much in the way of roads out here," said Keyes the next morning. He was maintaining sixty, staring out through the tinted windshield at a slim shimmering of asphalt.

"Wasn't even this two-laner till fifty-eight."

"How did they live? Or was there anybody here then?"

Galloway glanced at him. This morning the blond man wore khaki Banana Republic hiking shorts and an open sports shirt. His narrow feet were strapped into Birkenstock sandals. A Rolex and a hammered nugget ring glinted gold as he swung the convertible around a northbound pickup.

"'Course there were. Rodanthe, Waves, Salvo; Kinnekeet, Avon, Buxton, Frisco, Hatteras. Little fishing villages. They grew up around the inlets and the old Lifesaving stations. Or where the dunes were high enough so beans or corn would grow without getting salt-killed."

"But how did they get around?"

"They didn't, not much. Mostly went places by boat, or drove along the beach at low tide. I remember doin' that when I was growing up. Had to take the ferry across at the inlet—that was before they built the bridge. You still have to take a ferry to get to Ocracoke."

Now the road rose and fell as marsh spread to their left. The dunes cut off their view of the sea. But herons, stilts, and willets waded in freshwater ponds, and ducks burst into belated flight to clear the road as Keyes bore down on them.

"So tell me who we're going to see."

"Her name's Mercy Baum. She's oh, late eighties. No, she must be ninety by now. Lived on Hatteras all her life. Knows everything. Local history, that kind of thing."

"And you think she could help us."

"If she wants to. And if she's . . . still able. Anyway, it's a place to start."

When the car lifted, the bridge lofting them high over Oregon Inlet, they could see for miles. Behind them stretched the island, green of yaupon and bayberry and myrtle, tan of sand, its seaward coast gnawed by white surf. To their left the Pamlico stretched a sheet of dimpled silver to the horizon; over it, too far to see, lay the mainland. But Galloway was searching to seaward. "Looks like she broke up clear and went out with the tide," he said at last.

"Who?"

"The trawler. I can't see a thing where she used to be."

When they came down off the bridge they were in Nags Head. A few miles later the unpopulated scrub and dunes gave way suddenly to restaurants, hotels, fishing piers, and the ubiquitous cottages. Identical, boxlike, they swarmed along the shore. Above them from time to time loomed larger structures, many still being sheathed with plywood: the time-share resorts. They crawled north on the bypass, mired in moving metal. In the narrow strip between sound and ocean the summer tourists thronged the Deep Africa Mini-Golf, the Surf Slide, the Go-Kart Grand Prix, Dowdy's Amusement Park, Brew-Through, Hardee's, Tastee-Freeze, McDonald's. A few miles past an immense hill of bare sand Galloway pointed to the left. "Turn in here."

"All right." The BMW's tires hummed on new paving as it wound upward into soundside dunes. At the crests of the road they could look down on the Albemarle, immense, shining, morning-calm.

"This is it. Park here," said Galloway at last.

"You're joking."

"Afraid not."

The building was modern and low, placed not atop but amid the sandhills, as if hidden away. An ambulance stood ready at a side door. Over the entrance stainless steel letters read KITTY HAWK NURSING CENTER.

• • •

The late morning sunlight glinted off the dunes outside the window, glinted again off salt-white hair. It was cut short and pinned up with a brown barrette. Tiny hands lay softly together on a colorful afghan. Outside in the corridor came from time to time the hiss of wheelchairs on tile, the chatter of nurses.

"Mrs. Baum, you have a visitor."

Galloway smiled thanks at the attendant, then bent.

"Mercy?"

The bright blue eyes turned instantly toward him, and the old woman smiled.

"Mrs. Baum, it's Tiller. You remember me?"

The smile clouded. "Tiller—? Can't say I do. Things ain't as clear as they used to be. Still, whoever you are, I'm glad to have you to visit."

"I wondered if we could talk a little—about the old days?"

"The old days. There's right many come to ask me about them lately. Well—sure."

The attendant bent over her for a moment, wiped her cheek with a tissue, whispered loudly in her ear; she shook her head. The attendant left. Galloway drew a chair to hers; Keyes found a nearby sofa. "I appreciate it, Mrs. Baum. We'll talk a little, and then I'll ask a question or two, maybe."

The woman sat for a moment, looking out again; her eyes went distant. Then she began, not rapidly but unhesitating, as if reciting a poem memorized years before.

"I remember a lot about it. About the dirt roads and all such as that. About the last one left who does. My father and my mother have been dead for years, and my sisters and brothers too. And all my other kinfolks are dead. I've got children—four, two boys and two girls.

"You'll want to know when I was born. Well, that was in eighteen and ninety-eight. Our closest doctor was at Manns Harbor. Had to go by water to get him, wa'n't no bridges, you see. Sometimes you died 'fore he got there. But Doctor Gardner was with my mother when I was born.

"Most all my people were Service. My father and grandfather were in the Coast Guard—it was the Lifesaving Service, years ago. My father was a surfman. His father died when he was thirteen years old. He died in that storm of eighty-nine trying to save them people in the *Henry P. Simmons.* So my father couldn't go to school. He had to go out and work to take care of his mother. He had it pretty hard.

"All my people come from around here. My mother's people were Claffords. Seems I heard her say they originally come from somewhere in the mainland. Little Washington, or somewhere that way. Now my father's father, he came from Manteo. There's Stories still on Roanoke Island. And my father's mother, she was a Etheridge. There were four of them, Etheridge girls. My grandmother Casey, and Lizbeth, and Clara, and Kelly Lea. I didn't know them, that was before I was born.

"My mother died having my sister when I wasn't quite three. She's buried in Avon. All my people are in the Methodist cemetery there.

"My daddy was a hard-workin' man. And he raised a big family. I had four sisters, and I had one, two—three brothers. So there was eight of we children to raise up. And I'm telling you he had a hard time of it. But since he was in the Service we always had something to eat and a house to stay in.

"I was a little barefooted girl. We didn't have to wear shoes, no, even to school. We had a little one-room schoolhouse in Avon. The teacher she would stand in the door and ring, ring this hand bell, when we children would be playing, for us to come in. And we had to stay in at recess a lot, we'd misbehave and done something we shouldn't. Whisperin' in school, or laughing."

Keyes was eyeing Galloway. Galloway ignored him. "What kind of games did you play?"

"Oh, you'd hardly believe the silly things we did in them days. We had ball games. We had a game we called fifty-oh. And ring around the roses. And a game we called sheepie."

"I remember playing sheepie. But how do you play fifty-oh?"

"Oh, some'd go off and hide, and we try to find them. And if you found them and could make the home before they did we'd win the game. Hide and seek was what it was. Oh, and we played cat. That was like baseball sort of, but we made our own ball out of string, didn't have no factory made.

"And on Sunday afternoons we'd go to this big hill out near Kinnekeet. It wasn't as big as Jockey's Ridge, but it didn't lack much. We'd run up and down it and play until we were so tired we couldn't hardly get back. You wouldn't believe it to go down there. I hear there's all kind of cottages and such there now."

"Tell us some more about your father," said Galloway. "You said he was in the Service."

"Yes, at Kinnekeet Station, with Otinus and Lyle and them other Galloways they give the gold medals to. Most times he had to walk the night. If it was a stormy night he'd patrol twice a night. He'd walk up and down the beach—that ocean had to be watched for ships, y'know. Then when one of them got in trouble, he pulled an oar. I remember how I used to worry when there was a shipwreck on the beach. Because then the rule was you had to go, you didn't have to come back.

"I remember seein' 'em come ashore. Ships from different countries. Some men got lost, some got saved. I've seen women and little children too torn to pieces, washed ashore on the beach drowned."

Keyes glanced at Galloway again. "Sounds like a rough life," he muttered.

"Oh, you wouldn't hardly believe how people lived them days. Nobody got nowhere much—I think I did go to Norfolk once or twice when I was growin' up. That was when we saw the Wright brothers. My daddy took me through Kitty Hawk on the way up. And they flew over our cart. It looked different from planes they have now. And we were scared. Wouldn't you have been?"

"Well, I guess so," said Galloway.

"No, we had no easy time of it. But still, them were happy days. We didn't have a lot, but what we had we enjoyed. If I got a rag doll at Christmas, and a stocking full of nuts and an orange, I was happy. Now little children gets everything and in no time it's tore up. And the grown-ups are the same way. Money, money, money—they'll sell their souls to get the dollar."

"Your husband was in the Service too, wasn't he?" said Galloway. "How did you meet him?"

"Oh, I met Leford in 1914. He was from Buxton, but he lived down in Hatteras Village." A thousand wrinkles deepened on her cheeks. "I met him at the dance at Wahab's Hotel. We moved down there and lived there and then in Rodanthe for right many years. My oldest son was born in Rodanthe, and my daughter was born in Raleigh when I was visiting my sister out there.

"And, yes, he went into the Coast Guard there in the first war, and we were stationed here and there—Poyners Hill, and Kitty Hawk, and in Norfolk for two year even. But I didn't go there, the children was small. And he got transferred back to the Banks in 1937. And finally settled down in Avon, where I was born. I buried him close to twenty year ago."

"Mercy, this is interesting. Hearing about the old days. Let's talk about a little later now. About the war."

"The first one or—"

"The second war. Do you remember that?"

"Lord yes. That was when things changed so much, you know. You could go down to the base, if you had family in the service, and buy just what you wanted. Didn't have to order it, and wait and wait for the mail. I remember Leford bought me a gold watch once." Her hand twisted a plastic bracelet. "I never saw a ship actually get torpedoed; but we could hear it, boom boom boooom. Everything was blacked out. They had the shutters on the Light. I could sit out on my porch in the dark and see the blaze out to sea. I asked my husband one night, 'What'll we do if the Germans come to land on Hatteras?' And Leford said, 'We'll kill 'em, Mercy. That's what that shotgun's for.'"

Keyes was leaning forward; Galloway shot him a warning glance. He said, "That's something I wanted to ask you about, Mercy. You know the men who used to patrol the beach then, during the war?"

"You mean from the station. Yes I do. It was Leford and William Tolson, Dunbar Hooper, Jamie O'Neal and those. And that Aydlett boy."

"That's right. Mercy, one night they caught some people coming ashore. In a rubber raft. What happened to them? Did you ever hear?"

"Oh yes. They come ashore that night in the spring of forty-five. But Leford swore me never ever to—"

The nervously moving hands stopped.

"He swore you what?" said Keyes, leaning forward, despite Galloway's warning gesture. "Did he tell you? *What happened?*"

The old woman was silent for a moment more. Then she said, "You boys got to forgive me. My mind's not so clear as it was. And sometimes I take to talkin' nonsense. I'm not bodily sick, but I broke my hip a couple of year ago and something happened that it got twisted. I don't think I've got enough time for it to ever heal."

Tiller said, "Yes, Mrs. Baum, but let's go back to what you were telling us about. Did Leford tell you what happened that night? Did he ever mention anything they'd taken, anything they had with them—"

"I don't remember it well. I don't remember who you are. But let me tell you something important."

"We're listening," said Keyes.

Galloway found himself fixed by her eyes. "I don't know what you boys are wantin' to hear, or what you're after. What you're strivin' for, or what your trouble is. I've had a lot of trouble in my life, yes I have. But you got to put aside this striving and sinning and live the best way you can. I did and I'm happy now because I know the Lord's going to take care of me. Although I'm suffering, that'll be over after a while. I know I've got to die soon. But when the Lord sees fit for me to go, I got no dread."

Over her bent head Galloway met Keyes's eyes. He nodded.

They left Mercy Baum facing the window, immobile in the sunlight, watching the wind ruffle the beach grass at the top of a dune. Tiller looked back once at her, along a corridor polished like the morning Albemarle, and thought: If you were eight years old, barefoot, you could scramble to the top in a minute. And see for a long, long way.

• • •

Outside Keyes opened the car doors and flicked on the air-conditioning. He looked across the shimmering roof at Tiller. "You get anything useful out of all that ancient history?"

"Maybe a little."

"What? I got zip. She knows, all right. But she's still sharp enough to clam up on this one subject. If I could get five minutes with her without those nurses around—"

"You'd what?"

Keyes glanced at him. "Nothing."

Galloway looked at him for a long time. At last Keyes grinned faintly and got into the BMW. But Tiller didn't; only bent down, a little, to look in at him. "You'd what?" he said again.

"I'd ask her again—very politely."

"That's right," said Galloway. "You try any rough stuff with these people, you'll have me to deal with. Understood?"

"Sure."

Galloway got in. Keyes started the car and a moment later they were rolling down out of the dunes, back toward the highway. After a time Tiller said, "We got more than you seem to think."

"What's that?" said Keyes.

"She let those names drop. The men with her husband on the beach patrol that night. Tolson, Hooper, O'Neal, and Aydlett."

"Hell, that was a long time ago. They're probably all dead."

"Yeah. They are. Except for the last one. Aydlett."

"You know him?"

"Sure do," said Tiller. "I used to work for him when I was a kid."

"Great! Well, let's go see him."

"I don't think it's going to be that easy."

"Why not?"

"He hates my guts."

"Why?"

Galloway said, staring ahead at the road, "Because I killed his son."

six

"Tiller! You aboard?"

Bernie looked around the dock, shivering. She was dressed in mid-length navy shorts, a T-shirt, and a light windbreaker, and it was seven in the morning, and a light mist had not yet burned off the water of the inlet.

There was no answer. She swung her tennies over the transom and rapped at the companionway hatch, listened for a moment, then slid it open. The main cabin was empty. She paused in the galley, noting silently two torn packages of instant oatmeal, two half-finished mugs of coffee, still slightly warm to the touch.

She closed the hatch and plopped herself on one of the lockers in the stern. She dangled her legs absent-mindedly and threw her hair back. She reached for a cigarette, then stopped; she'd promised herself to cut back.

She'd planned to spend the day on the boat, perhaps checking in on Jack that afternoon at his parents' home in Waves. Now an empty Saturday yawned. She had paperwork to do, but the thought of the office appalled her.

That was one good thing about her job—you weren't tied to a desk. Mr. Moulton, the supervisor, had told her that a good parole officer spent time with clients. Sometimes it was rough. You had to deal with people society had junked. You had to understand them, what had gone wrong inside them, and try to help it go right. It wasn't easy and it didn't pay much, but you could make a difference; you could help people sometimes. And that was what she wanted to do.

Specifically, she thought she could help Tiller Galloway.

Sitting there, trying consciously not to think of a cigarette, she turned the case over in her mind once more.

Tiller Galloway was a felon. A drug smuggler, his record said; convicted under the 800 series of 21 US Code (A), Illegal Importation of Controlled Substances. She knew that the recidivism statistics on druggies were appalling, especially those in the management side. For most of them release was like returning from vacation. The lure of easy money, vast quantities of it, was too great, the deterrent of three to five years in prison too weak.

But Lyle Galloway III didn't fit the norm. He seemed to be making a genuine effort to turn away from that life. Her degree was in psychology and she tried now to think of Tiller Galloway subjectively, as if she were writing a case study.

She knew he felt guilty about his father's death. And there were other skeletons there, things he'd done when he worked for the shadowy Colombian he called only the Baptist. He'd refused to discuss them with the prosecuting attorney at his trial or with anyone since. So he hadn't turned his back completely on his former life. But he seemed genuinely to be struggling, fighting with his personal devils for some kind of redemption. Beneath the boozing and the cynicism she had an idea he was still plain and strong and at bottom even honorable as his Hatteras ancestors.

And that, unfortunately, was his problem. Because along with that, bound with it like one weak strand in a strong rope, he still had the streak of greed that had made him a cocaine runner.

Besides, she liked him. Not romantically; that would be disastrous, both for her career and her own peace of mind. But she admitted to some attraction. He was older than she was. But she liked older men. They knew what they wanted and they weren't so—childish.

Her thoughts moved from there to Keyes. Another older man. The odd feeling she got when he was around. He was attractive, but there was something else there too. She wasn't sure yet what. It might be dislike. It might even be fear. Whatever it was, it made life more interesting.

She reminded herself that she had to find out just what he wanted from Tiller.

She glanced lazily around the inlet. All was quiet in the ruddy morning light. On one of the fishing boats men were repairing a net, but for most of the locals a weekend was a time of rest. Even the pile-driving barge at the new pier-and-condo complex going in on the south side of the basin was silent this morning. Still thinking of Keyes, and how fine the decision might be between dislike and attraction, she looked ashore.

A man was watching her. An old man, short, stocky, with a nondescript face and intent hazel eyes and a tan deep even for the island. His Lacoste shirt, chinos, and tan bucks would have blended at a yacht club, or at the new golf courses in Duck Woods or Kitty Hawk. But here he stood out. When he caught her glance he came slowly down the pier, stopping opposite the boat.

"Good morning."

"Hi."

"May I come aboard?"

"I can't give you permission to. It's not my ship. Did you want something?"

His eyes slid forward, examining the boat, then came back to her. Close up, she saw he was older than she'd thought at first. He looked as if he'd been strong once, strong and ruthless. Now he was fragile. The strength had gone, leached by time like carbon from rusting steel, leaving only its form. Judging by those eyes, it had left the ruthlessness as well. His lips twitched into a not very convincing smile. "I'm looking for a friend of mine. About six-three, maybe forty-five, generally wears a gray suit. Have you seen him?"

"You mean Mr. Keyes?"

"Keyes. Yes. Is he aboard?"

"No. He went ashore with Tiller—he's the captain—I suppose for the morning. They'll likely be back this afternoon, if you want to stop again."

"Perhaps this is better after all. Would you give him a message?"

"Sure. What is it?"

"Tell him that Tarnhelm is ours."

"I don't understand."

"Just tell him those three words. He'll understand."

"T-A-R—" He spelled it out.

"And what does that mean?"

"It's a personal message."

They stared at each other for a while across the lifelines. At last she said, "You'd better write it down," and took out her case notebook. He nodded, looking at her closely, and slowly extracted an old-fashioned fountain pen from his slacks. After a moment he blew on the pad and then handed it back. "You're a very suspicious young woman."

"Sorry, but it helps, dealing with the people I deal with."

"What kind of people do you deal with?"

"Former criminals."

"How unfortunate," said the old man. "Will you give him my message?"

"I'll give it to him. That's all I can promise."

"Thank you."

He was turning away when she added, in a louder voice, "And can I tell him your name?"

He stopped, as if considering, and then half smiled. "He'll know who I am."

She wanted to ask more questions, but he was already out of ear-shot, walking stiffly away up the pier. A silver and black 280 SE pulled out from behind the office, its driver leaning to open the door for him.

She hopped off the locker, holding the pad. She craned her head above the cabin, to make sure he was out of sight, and opened it.

"Tarnhelm is ours," she whispered.

She found that she didn't like this a bit. She stared at the car for a moment more, then taking out her own pen jotted down the tag number and followed it with a terse description of the man, the driver, and the car.

• • •

Shortly after noon Keyes slid to a halt between a Jeep and a rusty Ford pickup that gave off, in the heat, a powerful odor of fish. Galloway walked behind him as they strolled down the pier toward the boat. At the south end the pile driver was banging away. Thud . . . thud . . . thud, like the bass drum of a marching band. "Hell of a racket," said Keyes, inclining his head to it. "But I guess a new pier will be worth it. This one, I wonder you don't break your neck on it at night."

"Not for me. I've got my notice."

"What do you mean?"

"There was room for *Victory* at Harry's Dock. There isn't any at Blackbeard's Harbour. They gave me two months' notice."

"Then where will you go?"

"Don't really know. The old docks and piers are going fast. It's all charter boats now, or motor yachts—Yankees with gold chains on their necks and women on both arms." Galloway shrugged. "Maybe on the mainland there'll still be something."

They found Hirsch asleep on a pile of life jackets arranged in a shady corner of the pilothouse, a diet Pepsi and the stub of a fried-Spam sandwich beside her. One of Caffey's books on coelenterates lay spine up on the deck. Galloway nudged her with a toe. "Hey. You got nothin' better to do than hang around here?"

"Oh, hi." She stuck a fist into a yawn. "Guess I fell asleep. Hi, Mr. Keyes."

He smiled down at her and she saw immediately that he was interested. There was no mistaking that look. She sat up, reddening at the thought of lying there sprawled out. She tugged her T-shirt lower, suddenly conscious of the way her nipples showed through the fabric, of her stockinged feet. This was not the way a Dare County parole officer ought to look.

"How's Jack? Any word?" Galloway asked, from down in the cabin.

"I called his house. The doctor said he'd be on his feet in a day or two."

"Good. Thanks." The last word was barely audible.

"Oh. Mr. Keyes. Here."

"What's this?" He took the paper suspiciously.

"A man came by while you were gone. Not long after eight. He left this message for you."

While Keyes examined it she watched his face. Watched it freeze, and the blue eyes tense. Then, a moment later, change to surprise. When he glanced up at her he looked puzzled. "I don't get it. Who did you say left it?"

"Late-sixtyish man, about five-eight, tanned, green polo shirt, tan slacks. Driving a Mercedes. Or rather, being driven by a young chauffeur."

"Doesn't clang any bells for me."

"Are you sure?" she said, watching him closely.

"Sorry."

"Tiller?"

She couldn't see him, but she could imagine Galloway, belowdecks, shrugging in silence. Keyes handed her back the pad.

"Look, I got his tag number along with the description. I could trace him from the office. If you want—" she left it hanging.

Neither man responded immediately. At last Galloway called up, "Dick? What about it? Want her to check it out?"

"I don't see the point."

"Thanks, Bernie. But I think we'll just wait till he comes around again. If he does."

She stared at the notebook for a moment, then closed it and padded down into the cabin. Galloway had gone forward, invisible for the moment. She found him bent over an open locker, jotting a list on the palm of his hand with a ballpoint.

"Tiller. Can we talk?"

"Sure."

"Did you know you have grease on the back of that shirt?"

"Yeah."

"This old man. You don't know him? Who he might be? You're sure?"

"Doesn't sound like anyone I know. No, I think this is Dick's business."

She glanced toward the companionway; it was empty, but she lowered her voice just the same. "He says he doesn't know who he is. But I was watching him when he read the note. I think maybe he does."

"He says he doesn't."

"What *is* his business? The two of you are getting awfully chummy."

"He says he's a historian."

"What do you mean, he says he's a historian?"

"Nothing. He's a historian."

"Well, what is he doing here?"

"He's paying me to do research."

"That's all?"

"That's all so far, Counselor."

"Don't condescend to me, Mister Galloway."

"Sorry, Miz Hirsch. But you have a habit of forcing me to do it."

They looked at each other angrily. At last he turned away and resumed his rummaging. He pulled out a wire pennant and examined it. It was very rusty and one of the swagings was cracked. He fed it out through the porthole and it splashed outside.

"What are you doing?"

He sighed. "Normal upkeep, just normal business. Checking out my gear."

"Are you going out?"

"I have no plans to, but I like to keep ready."

"Tiller—after the trawler you blew—do you have any more work lined up?"

"Not a patch of it, darlin'. This fella's the only source of income in sight at the moment. So I've got to play him close if I plan to eat next week. Do me a favor, Bernice. Don't scare him away."

"I can take a hint. Well, I'm going to drive up to Sam and Omie's for lunch. Want to come?"

"Thanks, no."

She left feeling rejected; vaguely angry, vaguely puzzled. There was something going on between the two of them. Keyes didn't look like any historian to her. But whatever he was he'd managed to rouse Tiller part way from his apathy, like a half-raised hulk. That was good.

But then what was this "Tarnhelm" business, strangers leaving laconic and mysterious warnings. . . .

She decided it would bear watching. But for the moment she dismissed it from her mind, dismissed Keyes too. She was hot and hungry and looked forward to some fresh fried clams. All the way to Nags Head she watched the road behind her. But no black and silver car showed itself.

seven

Late that evening they headed south, down the long stroke of Hatteras Island's reversed L. Near Rodanthe the roadway sagged. The sea had chewed its way through the dunes that winter and only bulldozers and sandbags had forced it back. Past Buxton it rose, winding through low forests of live oak and loblolly pine. As they purred along tiny red eyes peered back at them from the underbrush. Halfway past Frisco Keyes said, "What in hell are those things?"

"Mink," said Galloway in a monotone. "Or Russian rats, we call 'em. They say a Russian ship went aground here once—okay, slow down. Right coming up."

They moved off the road onto marl. The crushed oystershell crackled under the tires as they followed its winding course between clumps of bush. It reminded Galloway of another house, one he had not been to since his equivocal homecoming from Raleigh.

His father's house, now his stepmother's, the one he'd grown up in. . . .

Keyes interrupted his musing. "Who is this guy Aydlett? Why does he live way out here?"

"I told you, he used to be a big name in marlin fishing, back in the fifties."

"You said you worked for him."

"Yeah, used to bait-boy on the *Princess* when I was a kid. He was kind of a father figure, I guess. I liked it better than home."

"You didn't get along at home?"

"Lyle Two didn't believe in coddling his sons. Either of us. He kept a length of rope out in the boatshed I got real familiar with."

"You said you had a stepmother."

"Anna's a good woman. She'd hide me and try to stop him. But my dad had the last word. Couple times I ran away. This is where I'd come."

"He's a fisherman, you said."

"A charter skipper. He has—he had—anyway, there's three boats; the *Queen*, the *Princess*, the *Duchess*. He built them with his own hands, him and his sons. But he's been retired for years now."

"Wait a minute. He can't be that old if he was a boy in forty-five—"

"He wasn't."

"The old woman said he was."

"She didn't say he was a boy. She said, 'that Aydlett boy.' Now listen. I want you to stay in the car."

"Why?"

"Because I told you to."

"Well, good luck. Should I cut the lights?"

"Yeah."

Three small houses loomed vaguely in the darkness ahead, surrounded by live oak and red cedar. From two came the white glow of electric light. Only the last, farthest into the soundside bush, waited with windows dark. "Which one?" said Keyes.

"That one."

"The dark one? But—"

"Clifton Aydlett doesn't need the light anymore," said Tiller evenly.

When the engine stopped the night was very quiet. There was only the creak and whirr of the night insects, the distant shiver of surf, and once in a long while the whine of tires from the direction of the road. Marl crunched under Galloway's feet as he walked the last few steps to the house.

The old man was standing behind the screen, as if watching the night. He waited silently as Galloway mounted the porch.

"Cap'n Aydlett."

"Who's that?"

"Someone come to talk."

"Well come in, come in. Hold on, I'll light a lamp for you."

"It's all right, you don't need to."

But the wooden kitchen match was already sputtering along the screen. Galloway watched the thick work-warped fingers tremble over the wick, turning it up, shaking out the match. When it flared up he looked around.

It had once been, or still was, a storeroom. Against the walls were stacked bundles of hand-tied nets. In the roofbeams were racked bamboo poles, rods, old outriggers striped red and white. Shoved into corners of the plank floor were heaps of bronze propellers, fighting chairs, Pflueger reels, old cans of Athey and Pettit paint and varnish. It smelled of pipe tobacco and turpentine and hot kerosene from the lamp. The man who shuffled slowly among them was not large, but his shoulders bulged under his loose shirt as he lowered himself into his armchair.

"You'll have to trim it yourself. Sit down, sit down there at that table. You know, I believe I know your voice, but can't say I get the name right off. It was—?"

"It's Tiller Galloway, Mr. Aydlett."

"Tiller, sure, I knew right off—" He paused then, stopped sightless in the dimness to which he had retreated. In the silence Tiller could hear the crash of sea beyond the dunes. "Galloway, you say?"

"Yes sir."

"Lyle Galloway's younger boy, the strong one, that used to fish with me?"

"That's right."

The old man said in a low voice, "I'll thank you to leave now. I don't believe I want to speak with you, sir."

Galloway was thinking, has it been five years? Six? It was hard to believe this old man, gaunt and trembling, had once been able to lift a fifty-horse Johnson with one arm.

"Please listen to me, Cap'n. You're one of the people I think of as my friends."

"I know Mezey wasn't the best of boys, he went off the tracks when he was young. But you finished the job proper. Many's the night I have cursed your name, Lyle Galloway."

"I paid for it. Four years in Raleigh. It's over."

"It's not over for me. Or for your dad."

Galloway looked at the blank milky eyes. The chimney began to smoke and he turned the wick down. His own hands were trembling too, he saw. "Sir, I don't forget his—suicide. Ever."

"You were the cause of it. He loved you. When you got booted out of the service there in Vee-etnam it almost killed him."

"I know."

The old man sat and trembled. It was not from emotion, Galloway saw now. It was Parkinson's; his leg jiggled incessantly, rocking the arm-chair; his hands shook where they lay on the armrests.

"And my boy," said Aydlett at last, almost in a whisper.

Galloway closed his eyes.

He remembered fishing with the Aydletts. He remembered the aching hours of boredom as they trolled for swordfish and white marlin, dolphin, tuna, wahoo; and then the sudden disciplined panic of the hit. The day-long battle they'd fought with a huge black marlin late one July through thunderstorms and line squalls, the lightning all around them like white-hot lizards running down a vine; they'd ended it at dusk with the fading fish on deck, a massive beast that weighed out a heartbreaking ten pounds short of the IGFA all-tackle record. The brief season of the sailfish and the savage butchery of shark fishing. How Meshach Aydlett had saved his life once when he'd slipped in a patch of bloody chum and fallen overboard into a boil of makos.

Years later Galloway had killed him.

It had happened on that last run, not that far from the cape. Somewhere out there Mezey Aydlett's bones lay in the cold silt. He'd been one of the last. The Panamanian mate was dead by then, along with most of the crew. That was the Baptist's way of cutting costs.

Not that he did it himself. Juan Nuñez preferred to let the inexorable laws of economics and psychology do his work. He distributed the profits from a voyage by shares. Ostensibly that made each man a partner. What it really did was make each the enemy of all the others, since the fewer were left at the end of a voyage the more each share was worth. And of course the Baptist's cut as supplier benefited too.

The result was a hell-ship, an anarchic nightmare where each man guarded his back and even those who were satisfied—as captain and owner, Galloway would have netted over half a million dollars—had to defend themselves against men crazed with greed and uninhibited by conscience.

He stopped himself from thinking. If only he could never think again, never recall the past . . . never recall his friend's face when the bullet hit him. . . .

Now, in the honey glow of the kerosene lamp, he took a shuddering breath. "Sir, I don't ask you to forget it. It's true he done wrong, like I did, but he was as good a man as me. It was just him or me there at the end. You've got to believe that.

"But I've finished with that, the smuggling, the drugs. I've paid for it. I'm out on parole now and I'm working up to Harry's as a salvage diver."

The old man sat silent in the yellow light.

"I'm not asking you to forget Mezey. I know you can't. But I want you to forgive me."

"Forgive you? Why?"

"Because I'm sorry."

The old man looked at him with his motionless eyes for a long time. At last he said, "No."

Galloway sat numb, unable to move.

"I 'magine you're right about Meshach. He was not a bad boy. But he got with bad company up in Virginia Beach. It was that white stuff that killed him. That dope is pure evil . . . What was it really brought you here, Tiller? It wasn't to ask me that, was it?"

"Well, yes sir, that was mainly it."

"Then who's that outside?"

Galloway jerked up his head. For a moment he stared at the blank black interiors of the windows. The old man chuckled sadly then. "I could hear him," he said. "Closed the car door, then took a leak over by my motor shop. Friend of yours?"

"Sort of," said Galloway.

"He ought not be wandering around like that. Them no-see-ums will be eatin' him alive. Plus we got them cottonmouths. He scares one of them he's likely to regret it. Go ahead, get him in here."

Galloway went to the door. Keyes was standing outside by the little porch, his shirt glowing like a ghost in the starlight.

"Go ahead, tell me about it," said Aydlett when they were both settled opposite him. "I assume it's some kind of scrape. You was always in them as a kid."

Galloway took a breath. Despite what the old man had said he seemed willing still to talk. Or maybe he was just curious. Whichever it was, this was not going to be easy. "Well, I was up to Nags Head this morning," he began. "I was talking to Mercy Mae Baum."

"Is she still alive?"

"She's getting some feeble, but she's still alive."

"And what were you talking about with Mercy Mae? I remember her well. And I remember Leford. He was a good man with an oar."

"It has to do with Leford. And the other men that Mercy told us were with you on the beach patrol in April of forty-five."

The old man did not move.

"It has to do with the bodies they found up to Kinnekeet," Tiller said.

"Bodies? Oh. *Bodies.* Yeah, Abe read me about them Injuns—"

"They weren't Indians," said Keyes then. "And you know it, old man."

"Back off," said Galloway sharply. "Captain Aydlett is—was an old friend of mine. I'll do the talking here."

Keyes sat back in his chair. Tiller watched him for a moment, then turned back to Aydlett.

He told the old man the story. As it went on a shade seemed to pass over his eyes. He sat back halfway through it and passed a trembling hand over his mouth. When Tiller was done he sat like that for a time, then muttered, "She told you I was there, eh?"

"I don't think she meant to."

"Maybe it was meant to be. So the buried do come to light at last."

Leaning forward, Keyes said, "After all these years, old man, maybe you'd better tell us the truth."

Aydlett's hand moved out behind him, shaking. Simultaneously with the clang of a ship's bell his other hand came up from under the table. The knotted pale-palmed hand held a short old-fashioned double scattergun with two cocked hammers. "Just sit tight," he said softly. "You too, Galloway. Just lookin' at this you ought to could tell the only safe place in this room is directly behind it."

The door came open behind them and a moment later Galloway felt himself jerked upward, lifted bodily by the shoulders.

"Well," said a once-familiar voice beside his ear. "If it ain't old Tiller."

He had his head halfway around when the shotgun went off.

Or seemed to. White light burst against his head. He found himself on his back on the table, then felt himself being hauled up again. This time he was held from behind. The second punch, delivered like the powerful slow strike of a mako, knocked him empty of breath. He managed to recover, not enough to matter much, but he kicked the man behind him and got one arm up in time to block the next swing of a huge fist. It left an opening through which he saw for a moment a dark, broad face, one dark eye filled with recognition and rage. His own hand came back instinctively, but then he opened it, covering up, and waited for the next blow.

"Shad, don't hit him no more for now. Abe, let him go."

"Pop, this the one killed Mezey. You don't want to be tellin' me to go easy."

"You listen to your daddy or it'll be your skinny ass I'm blowing away! Sit him down. Abednego, you stand behind this other one. What's he look like?"

"Tall white man, dressed expensive. Real nice watch."

"Hm."

Galloway, still blinking back stars, found his eyes nevertheless drawn with awful fascination to the old man's hands. At the way the fingers shook, their involuntary tightening . . . "Captain Aydlett?" he said.

"Yes, Tiller?"

"I'd be glad if you'd cease pointing that shotgun at my stomach."

Aydlett laughed. He handed the gun to Shadrach and leaned back.

"What's this all about, Pop?"

"About a story," said the old man. "You boys all comfortable? Got a little story to tell you."

"We're listening," said Keyes.

The steady blind eyes were the color of old teak. And then the only sound was the soft voice, and faintly from outside the chirr of cicadas and the endless crash of the surf.

• • •

"My people come out to the Banks from Tyrrell County. Roanoke Island was in Union hands in the war, and it was a haven. So us Aydletts been here since 1864.

"My father started goin' to sea when he was fourteen years old. His name was Jason, after the sailor. He worked his way up to third mate. That was as high as a black man got in them days. He was on a four-mast schooner, I don't remember the name, till he got to be married.

"Later on he worked on a menhaden boat, and in the winter he'd guide for the rich folks up in Pea Island. He started workin' me soon as I was big enough to walk. When I was small, on Saturdays I'd go out with him fishing. In the winter the shad, I'd take and bust them and get a bucket of roe out of them and take it home.

"I worked all my life. When I was twelve I was mess-cookin' at the shark factory for sixty-five men, two dollars a week. That was a lot of money then. But the hardest work I done was pushing a clam-rake. You only got fifteen cent a hundred for 'em. And pound netting, that was hard. Those nets behind me here, my mother and us children used to tie them. You don't tie too many yards in a night. That's the way we used to work.

"Wa'n't any other Negro families out here then. We weren't welcome in the stores, had to go round to the back when we wanted soap or kerosene. And when we went up to Manteo we couldn't go in the show there.

"I recall my father had a boat called the *Sally June,* after my mother. And one time I remember we were coming across the inlet, and he revved up the motor. And I wondered why. And about that time the boat moved to the side. She had hit the current in the channel. So he caught me by the waistband and told me to look over the washboard. I looked over there and as far down as you could see the water was clear; but you could see that current cuttin' the sand from the bottom. Now little did he dream that was going to be his doom.

"My father died in November of 1930. He and another man were comin' back from Ocracoke. And the engine quit. And the tide carried them out into a storm. They said they could see them from shore for a long time.

"My family used to practically own the beach down here between Buxton and Frisco. After my father died there was some Yankees here in the thirties taking it up for taxes and my mother she sold it to them. She just let it go. We owned three mile of land out on the coast and a mile out along the sound. Now Abe reads me the Manteo paper and I see it going for a million dollars for twenty acres.

"After my father died I left school and went to be a fisherman. First I had to build me a boat. Got my juniper in the swamp, over on the mainland. Went to a white man who liked me and borrowed fifteen dollars, and bought a used Buick for the engine. Borrowed a propeller. I got me a steering wheel off a wreck. Borrowed a gas tank. That's how I started out in the *Princess*.

"Money was scarce. We got half a cent a pound for croaker, three cent for trout. I got that note paid off, though, and ain't never owed a man white or black since. And I built me two more boats, the *Queen* and the *Duchess*. And I was a fisherman for forty-eight years.

"Then my eyes started to go bad. Could have asked for a handout from the government, but I didn't. My father always told me you got to make your own way. After I couldn't see no more I turned the boats over to my boys."

The old man turned his head to the side, as if listening. Galloway glanced back; his sons were staring narrow-eyed at Keyes.

"Now you may wonder why I am tellin' you all this. But it does lead up to a point. It's this. I look back over the years and how I had to struggle. My father and I worked all our lives and our family still ain't got nothing.

"Now you two has come to see me about something that me and some other men did forty-some years back. You seem awful eager to find it out. The way I figure it, I'm past carin', but if there's anything I have or know that might be worth something, then Shad and Abe deserve to get paid for it. Now, you—Mr. Yankee—"

"I'm no Yankee."

"To me you're a Yankee. Now you speak up and tell me what my story's worth to you."

Keyes reached for his jacket pocket, but his hand halted as the shotgun came up. Then it resumed as the barrels motioned him to continue.

"What's he doing?"

"Putting money on the table, Pop."

"Folding money?"

"Two hundred—three hundred—five hundred dollars!"

"Tell him to put it back."

"Pop—"

"This here is real cash, Dad—"

The old man rounded on them and told them to shut up. They did. He sat back and shook his head slowly.

"Why not?" said Keyes tensely. He did not reach toward or look at the money.

"Seems like you want this bad as I thought you might. Let's call it a thousand."

"You're sure that's enough?"

"Don't get smart with me. Yep, I think that will about do it."

"All right," said Keyes, "But I don't have that much all in cash. I can write you a check on my Merrill Lynch account—"

"Half and half will be all right," said the old man.

When the check was written Aydlett put it and the money away in a drawer in the table. When it was out of sight the tension in the little house lessened. The old man leaned back, looking satisfied with himself. He took out a brass-ferruled pipe and began stuffing it slowly with Captain Black.

"Now," he said, "You wants to hear the story."

• • •

In early 1945 the sea off Hatteras was clear of the enemy. No longer were the beaches slimed with oil, scattered with flotsam from torpedoed ships and here and there a body, still in its waterlogged lifejacket. But no one knew whether the U-boats would return.

For one thing, all through 1943 and '44 there were the rumors. There was wartime censorship. But without news, imagination had loose rein. U-boats had been seen refueling, people whispered, in isolated inlets along the coast, had been seen in Chesapeake Bay itself. Lights had been reported along the coast at night, perhaps signals to someone lying off. And on Hatteras itself the tales took on concrete detail. German sailors, it was said, had slipped ashore by boat, were mingling with the locals and even seeing movies. Ticket stubs skimmed from the pockets of dead U-boat men proved it. And why not? Hadn't they landed in New Jersey, Canada, and Florida?

There had never been enough regular military forces to defend or even observe the immense empty bow of the Banks. And so the men of the island had taken it into their own hands. Four or five at a time would go patrolling along the empty beaches by starlight, carrying old pistols or the twelve-gauge L.C. Smith doubles they used to hunt the Canada geese that came down the flyways to Hatteras.

Clifton Aydlett had been one of them on that foggy May night. There'd been a gallon jug of clear East Lake corn, inadequately aged but potent, and doubly welcome as they passed it among the men who paced in old Coast Guard peacoats and civilian duffles along the windy beach. They'd been out for two days, sleeping in the abandoned station house, and around the driftwood fire in the dunes they agreed to go home at dawn. It was just too cold to stay out, and the fog made it hard to see a hundred yards.

They sat huddled in the dune line, smoking Leford Baum's Lucky Strike Greens, prolonging the inevitable demise of the whiskey, and looking out onto a cottony nothingness above which somewhere was the moon.

It was ten minutes to one when Jamie O'Neal suddenly kicked sand over the embers, pulled the cigarettes from the others' mouths and buried the glowing tips. Frozen by the action, they turned their heads slowly.

The sound of diesel engines was blowing in from the sea.

The five men moved apart and hid themselves in the dunes. They waited. The mutter swelled and distanced in the peculiar way of sound in fog. Minutes passed. Then, faintly, they heard splashes.

The raft came ashore to the north of them. The figures wore dark overcoats. They did not speak as they pulled the rubber boat, hissing as it deflated, up onto the beach. Metal clanked as they unloaded it. The men hidden in the dunes glanced at each other.

Young Cliff Aydlett fingered the trigger of his bolt-action .22, evaluating it mentally against a Nazi submachine gun.

• • •

The old man's voice paused then. Galloway started; he'd lost all consciousness of listening to a story. He had been back there on those lonely dunes with four half-drunken white men, all of them suddenly confronted by the enemy of their nightmares.

"Anyway," said the old man, "Dunbar and Leford called to 'em to surrender. They shot first. We killed 'em all, and buried 'em there in the dunes."

"Why didn't you report it?"

"Afraid to. When we got back we found the war had ended the night before. If you kill men in a war time you're a hero. But afterward—you see? Leford and Jamie figured the smart thing to do was not talk about it. Wouldn't you think so?"

"Maybe, at the time," said Galloway.

"So now you say they're found. Diggin' for one of them new resorts, you say? Mysterious are His ways. But why are you two ferreting around about it? Askin' Miz Baum, and tracing her words to me? Explain good now."

The old man's question hung. Galloway looked at Keyes. The tall man sat motionless, his eyes on the worn planks of the floor. At last he sighed and looked up.

"We thought there might be something else in the raft, Mr. Aydlett."

"What it is?"

"In the raft. Was there anything in it that wasn't buried with it? A book, instruments—"

"Why?" said Aydlett, and his blind eyes glimmered.

"Because that's what I paid for! Now tell me!"

"Take it easy, Dick—"

"Sit down, man!"

"Take that shotgun out of my ear, boy!"

"I don't know as I like this cracker's tone of voice," said Shadrach to Abednego.

"Stow it, you two." For a moment, in silence, the old man sat in his chair in everlasting dark. "Fact is, we're going to want a piece of it."

"You want what?"

"This time, mister, the Aydletts are not goin' to sell out for no mess of lentil pottage. This time us colored folks is in for part of the profits."

"I don't see how that can be arranged," said Keyes.

"You arrange it. Or you ain't seeing what I got."

"But a split—how would we—"

"That's pretty easy," said Aydlett, turning his sightless eyes from one end of the room to the other. "One of my boys is going with you from now on till when you collect. Now which one? Abe is smarter but Shad is meaner. Shad is stronger too. Yes sir, I think Shadrach will be accompanying you all in your venture."

Keyes looked at Galloway helplessly. At last he said, "You drive a hard bargain, Aydlett. All right. He's in. But in that case I want my thousand back."

"That was for hearin' the story. You done heard it. Now we're talking about something else. If you don't want it after you see it, that's fine. Ain't neither of us out nothing. That sound fair to you, Lyle?"

"If you got the cards to back it up, Cap'n."

The old man smiled. He rose and stretched; they could hear his joints snap like breaking twigs. He moved slowly toward the kitchen, into total darkness. They heard him shoving things aside and muttering. Galloway met Shad Aydlett's eyes steadily, conscious that here was another who would neither forgive nor forget.

When the old man returned he had a bundle of oilcloth. He laid it on the table and his hands trembled over it for a time and when he took them away a folded chart lay faded and water-marked under the slow buttery glow of the kerosene lamp.

Keyes examined it in silence. Tiller, over his shoulder, could see that it was in German. And that it had pencil lines still faintly visible across its yellowed faded surface. At last Keyes glanced up. "It's real!"

"'Course it is."

"I've only got one question."

"What's that?"

"How did you get this? You were the youngest. And you were black."

Aydlett's face closed. "What's that matter? Seems to me you got some secrets you want to keep. Goes both ways. You got what you wanted. Don't need to know nothin' more."

"There's something you're not telling me."

"If there is they's a reason I ain't going to neither."

They regarded each other, or at least faced each other, for another moment. Then Keyes stood up. He reached for the chart. The muzzle of the shotgun stopped him.

"I'll take that," said Shadrach Aydlett.

Keyes seemed about to object, then to think better of it. He straightened his chair. "Well, if that's all, I believe we'll be going back to your boat, Tiller."

"With me," said Shad.

"With Shad," said old Clifton. "Get your things, quick, boy."

Shadrach handed the gun to his brother and disappeared. Galloway stood up too. At the scrape of his chair old Aydlett muttered, his face pointing toward the sound, "Tiller, I remember how you used to come fish with us. I didn't expect never to say these words. Only part of me wants to say them now. But I ain't unhappy to see you again."

"I'm glad to see you too, Cap'n. I only wish—"

"Don't want to talk about it anymore. You go on out now. Shad'll be waitin' for you."

When they were halfway to the car Keyes turned back. "Forgot my checkbook."

"I thought you put it in your jacket."

"No, I left it on the table. I'll be right back. Put the—put Aydlett in the back, you can slide your seat forward for him."

Galloway had Aydlett's ditty bag in the trunk and the man's big frame packed into the rear seat when Keyes returned, striding rapidly forward in the glow of the parking lights. He got in and the motor roared. "Ready?"

"Ready."

"I'm ready too," said a deep voice from behind them. Tiller closed his eyes. Shadrach Aydlett, he thought.

Jesus Christ.

eight

"That's an excellent piece of equipment, sir." The clerk tore off a strip of paper and held it up for the three men to read. "Eight-color display, with a printed readout, so you can find a good fishing spot again. The bottom shows up as a black trace, like this—" he pointed—"and fish as vertical lines. Very easy to read. It's the top of the Marinetek line—"

Galloway looked away, around the interior of the store. Boots, nets, reels of cordage, foul-weather gear crammed the interior of Manteo Marine Supply. His glance met Keyes's. The historian had gone casual that morning in a light-blue jogging suit, Reeboks, and a Casio runner's watch. Behind Keyes his eye met Shad Aydlett's, distant, sarcastic, silent. They'd spent Sunday night on *Victory*. Aydlett, who had brought a ragged sleeping bag, had insisted on dossing down just outside the companionway hatch. Keyes had wakened them both at daybreak and they'd breakfasted quickly on the boat and left for Manteo for the supply run.

The assistant stopped speaking; Galloway turned his attention back to the counter, where the circuit diagrams and specs had been laid out for him. "What kind of hookup do I need in the boat?"

"Standard twelve volts. Bolt-in installation. You'll need to drill a hole for the transducer. That mounts on the outside of the hull, pointing down." Holding the sonar head poised, he looked at them expectantly. Galloway half-turned to Keyes, who was inspecting a gleaming new Hobie. "He's the moneyman today," he explained to the clerk. "Hey. Dick. This unit looks good."

Keyes glanced at the electronics on the counter. "How much?" he said. When the clerk told him he began to count out the money.

"Cash?" said the man dubiously. Keyes stopped counting. "No, no, go ahead. It's just that most people around here don't carry that much . . . would you like a receipt?"

"That won't be necessary."

"Yeah, we would," said Galloway. "Just in case it doesn't work."

"All right, fine," said the clerk, pulling out a pad of blanks. "Your name and address, please."

"Chapman, Bill, Two hundred Main Street," said Keyes. Galloway turned around and inspected the Hobie.

"Where is that, sir? Norfolk?"

"Yes."

He handed Keyes the carbon. "If anything goes wrong, Mr. Chapman, just bring the unit back. But I'm sure you'll be happy with it. We used to sell a lot of those to the trawler people."

"Now what?" said Keyes, when they were outside. It was blazing hot already. "Anything else we need? It's almost ten."

"What's the hurry?"

"I told you last night, I want to get to sea as soon as we can."

"Well." Galloway looked at the sky. "Line . . . food . . . buoys . . . fenders . . . drinks, white gas, transmission oil, new vest cartridges, torch tip, primacord. Shad, you think of anything else?"

"Sound like you bought the town clean, you and Keyes."

"Then that should do it."

"You don't want any hard stuff?"

"I think the Budweiser will be enough," said Galloway.

The trunk and half the backseat of Keyes's BMW was crammed with grocery bags, coils of line, cases of soda and beer. Keyes laid the fathometer on the console between the front seats. Galloway followed him around the car, then stopped. Aydlett had tipped the seat forward and was motioning him in.

"What's this?"

"In to the back, Tiller, buddy. We partners, right? Old Shad don't plan to sit in the backseat of this expedition."

Galloway paused for a moment, then shrugged. He stepped past the grinning waterman and wedged himself in among the supplies.

The BMW purred across the narrow bridge that separated Roanoke Island from the sandy strip of the Banks proper. It was lined with fishermen; cars from many states bumped along in slow lines; the season was in full swing. Galloway was glad to turn south, back into the empty expanse of Hatteras. As they crossed the inlet he stood up in the open convertible, holding on to the back of Aydlett's seat. There was still no sign of the trawler.

They pulled into Kinnekeet an hour later. The first sign of town was a distant sparkling over the dunes; sunlight from the windows of the first scattered cottages perched above the sand and scrub. Then the oceanfront developments, still building, and the pennant-decked sales offices where agents lurked tenacious as morays to exchange cheap cookware for an afternoonlong hard sell. Last came the soundside, old Kinnekeet. Here the houses were low, huddled close, the oldest ones patchworks of mismatched timbers from long-wrecked ships. And then the dock. They pulled past two dead gas pumps and braked in a cloud of dust. The pile driver was whanging away. "Oh, hell," said Galloway from the backseat.

"What's wrong?" said Aydlett, twisting around to look at him over the headrest.

"That Hyundai."

"What about it? Whose is it?"

"Just be patient, Shad. You'll have enough of her in about a minute and a half," said Galloway.

Hirsch was sitting on deck, under a kind of sun awning she had rigged out of a plastic tarp and bungee cords. Today she was wearing white ducks and a blue cotton tank. Canvas espadrilles sat neatly aligned by her bare feet. Her sunglasses were totally opaque. She sipped at a diet RC as the three men began carrying gear aboard.

"Hello, Bernice," said Keyes.

"Good morning."

"Who's this, Tiller?"

"Shad, meet Bernie Hirsch, my parole officer."

"Miz Hirsch." Aydlett grinned down at her from beneath three cases of beer. "You not from around here, are you?"

"Hello. No, I'm not. Going out, Tiller?"

"Yeah, thought we'd head out this afternoon."

"What for?"

"Dick thought he'd like to take a little pleasure dive, it's so hot. Maybe we'll do some fishing. Just a little stag party, you might say."

Galloway's voice was casual. Perhaps it was just that that made her pause suddenly in rearranging her hair and glance toward him. "Stag. I see. That's an awful lot of groceries . . . for how long, Tiller?"

"Day or two."

"Do you mind if I come along? Just let me call the office from the pier, and get my beach things out of my car—"

"Well, look, I don't want to get you in trouble with what's-his-face, Mr. Mutton—"

"Mr. *Moulton*. There won't be any trouble. I have some vacation days coming."

Galloway sighed. "Suit yourself."

She ran down the pier, bare feet slapping on boards. Keyes glanced after her. Galloway saw the look. "I tried. Looks like we're stuck with her."

"Well, she adds to the scenery."

"I see your point."

"I'll help her," said Aydlett, coming up from below.

"Hold it a minute."

"What, man? What's this money for?"

"The reefer's broke. Get us about five bags of ice. Block, not the cube."

Aydlett took the money and went off after Hirsch down the pier.

Galloway flipped open one of the deck lockers and brought out tools. Drill, diagonal cutters, electrical tape, a roll of light insulated wire. "We'll get this installed before we leave. Can you give me a hand?"

"Sure," said Keyes.

Below in the cabin Galloway dumped the tools in a corner and crowbarred up part of the deck planking. The inside of the hull came into view beneath. He tightened a quarter-inch bit on an extension rod and cinched that into the drill. Sitting back on his heels, he fished the sonar head out of its Styrofoam packing. "Know how these work?"

"In general."

"This converts electricity to sound and back again. Goes on the outside of the hull. Normally I'd install it with the boat hauled, but we can do it pierside. I'll go overside, under the keel. You drill. When the bit comes through pull it right back and I'll push the wire in. The edge of the head seals to the hull with monkey shit, so there shouldn't be any leakage after that. Got it?"

"Sure," said Keyes. "Rap on the bottom when you're ready."

Galloway took the transducer topside, stripped to his trousers and put on a mask. "What's going on?" said Hirsch, coming down the pier with her arms full.

"Installin' some gear."

"Be careful."

Galloway didn't answer. He took several deep breaths and swung himself over the side.

The water of the basin was warm and murky, and the mosquito whine of propellers filled his ears. The mud bottom was only three feet below *Victory*'s keel. He frog-kicked along under it to where he estimated the drill would exit, then raised the head and thumped it twice against the wood.

It didn't sound very loud. He was raising it again when a grinding sound came through the hull, followed by the glint of the bit, about a foot from where he'd expected it. When the grinding ceased and the glint disappeared he pushed the wire through. When he could feel tension on the other end he set the head firmly in place. The epoxy putty sealed and he released it and made for the surface, his arms and chest stinging from drifting jellyfish.

He popped up beside the boat and took a few breaths. That had been easy. Underwater work was like that. You could never tell in advance how hard a job was going to be. Long as I'm in the water, he thought, might as well check the stern tubes and props. They would in all likelihood be at sea for several days. Off Cape Hatteras, that had to mean at least one storm. He took a few deep breaths, then surface-dived and frog-kicked aft.

The stern tubes were all right, though he could see he'd need new zincs soon. The props were all right. But he approached the cylinder hung from one of the shafts more cautiously. He parked himself sculling in the water and looked it over from two feet away.

It was a foot-long, three-inch tube, dull gray. Attached to his starboard shaft by a loop of cheap yellow polypropylene rope. Strategically placed, right underneath the fuel tanks. It was meant to kill.

Galloway began to want air. Sculling his hands, he moved closer. The yellow rope did not foul the prop, which meant that his first thought, that it was rigged to go when the shaft began to turn, was wrong. That left two other possible means of detonation. Either it was set for time, or for tampering of other motion. There was no sound from it, no clicking of an escapement, no bubbles from a burning fuze. But he had to assume it was the former. Or was it?

The desire for air became a need. He'd been down for over two minutes. It seemed to take forever to reach the surface. When he did, coming up off the counter, there was no one in sight on deck.

"Keyes!"

"Yes?" The blond man looked over the gunwale, impatient. "You finished down there yet?"

"We've got a bomb on our hull."

"A *bomb?*"

"Gray, a foot long. Protrusion on one end, crimped off. Probably a time detonator, the acid type."

"We've got to get rid of it."

"No shit. Throw me a knife."

Seconds later he handed the tube up. Keyes set it gingerly on the deck, then turned to Hirsch, who stood looking at it, her eyes wide. "Can you run this boat?"

"Y . . . yes."

"Get it started. Quick!"

He turned to haul Galloway out as the engines sputtered and banged, then tossed off the stern lines as Tiller sprinted for the bow. Hirsch jerked the boat backward into the stream. She twisted savagely with the engines, missing the pier by no more than a foot, and then gunned out of the basin, leaving behind a roostertail of white water and a swell that set the other boats nodding and jostling at their moorings.

The throttle was full forward as *Victory*, still accelerating, skidded into the channel, hitting the waves like a skipping stone. She howled for the sound. Fishermen stared at them from small boats, and a water-skier swerved abruptly and went head over heels into the water. Galloway hesitated, then picked the thing up. "Get rid of it!" shouted Keyes.

"Too many people around," shouted Galloway. He was tearing at one of the new coils of line. He lashed one end to the tube and tossed it over the stern, paying out as quickly as he could. It bounced gaily in their wake, twenty feet, forty feet, a hundred feet astern in the roiling white water.

They were a mile out when, at the top of a porpoising leap, it went off, blowing a meter-deep crater in the Pamlico and sending spray a hundred feet into the air. The concussion boomed across the water.

When it had died astern, the mist drifting back down through brown smoke to rejoin the sea, Galloway motioned Keyes forward. But only to the front of the pilothouse. He looked up; Hirsch, at the wheel, was out of sight. They were still at full speed, the wind whipping past them and the cutwater hissing.

He turned suddenly. "All right," he said, his voice low and vibrating like a stressed rope. "Explain, and explain fast, and explain right now. Who put that bomb on my boat?"

"I don't know."

"This is serious shit, Keyes! Somebody found out we're asking questions, and they don't like it."

"I understand that, Captain." The other man's voice was cool. "I'm not stupid. But it's good news. What it means to me is that what we're after exists."

"What are we after? Who else wants it? And don't tell me you don't know! I'm not buying that line anymore!"

"All right," said Keyes icily. "I won't. I do know. But I won't tell you—yet. You're making money, aren't you? You'll make a lot more.

That's a promise. But if you want to get curious, there are lots of other skippers on Hatteras."

They stared at each other for a moment more. Then Galloway turned away. He balanced himself around the pilothouse and climbed the ladder to the tuna tower.

He took the wheel from Hirsch. As soon as she let go of it she suddenly sat down on a thwart.

"Nice work, Bernie. You really made the old bitch move."

"What's going on?" said Aydlett angrily from behind them. "Damn, Tiller, I thought you two turkeys was all I had to worry about. You mean they's somebody else after you?"

"After us," said Galloway. "Partner."

Aydlett showed his teeth in a rueful smile.

Bernie's face changed then. "Tiller—*Mister* Galloway—"

"Uh-oh."

"Below." She pointed down, into the cabin.

Galloway gave Aydlett the wheel. The big man wrapped one scarred hand around it and aimed the boat up the sound, not bothering with compass or chart. Below, Galloway pulled the hatch shut behind him. Hirsch was standing by his table. She had taken off her sunglasses and he could see how wide her pupils were.

"What is it?"

"Tiller." Her voice trembled slightly, but she looked resolute and very angry. "What the hell is going on? Was that something to do with you? With . . . the drug thing?"

"I don't think so. A silenced twenty-two in the back of the neck, without a warning, is more the Baptist's style. And he's got no reason to. I pulled the time, I did it straight; he knows I didn't talk."

"Then it's got to have something to do with Keyes. With this Tarnhelm business. I warned you about him, Tiller."

"Big deal."

"What's that supposed to mean?"

"Nothing."

"Don't play games with me, Galloway. You'd better get serious about this. I happen to be responsible for you to the Office of Corrections. I can yank your parole in a minute. And don't think I won't! My first duty is to protect the public. Only secondarily do I try to enhance the well-being of the parolee."

"Enhance my well-being," said Galloway. "Get off my back."

"I don't think so. You need my advice. You don't seem to have very good judgment about people, Tiller. Especially when they throw a little cash around. This Keyes—he's bad news. Anyone can see that. And this Shad—he's a thug if I ever saw one."

"Hold it right there! I grew up with Shad Aydlett. He's fishing folks, they talk rough, but they don't come any better. And Keyes—so he's not Mr. Law-abiding? Wise up, Hirsch. I've dealt with guys that make him look like a deacon. You have to take risks to make bucks. The bigger bucks, the bigger risks."

"That's a classic statement of the criminal mentality."

"Or the bond market."

"Not clever. I don't know what you're getting involved in. I don't think I want to, either. My advice is to turn around right now. Drop these two men, drop whatever they want with you."

"And live on what? The state of North Carolina's been paying my room and board for four years. Seems to me a little risk is worth accepting if it keeps me off the welfare rolls."

She didn't answer for a moment. Then she said, "There are other jobs. Real estate, construction, driving a tour bus. I don't know why I bother. Sometimes I think you're a real asshole, Galloway."

"Jam it. You've got your roles confused, Hirsch. You're my parole officer, not my wife. Dick says he doesn't know who tried to kill us. I believe him. He's hired me to do a job and I'm doing it. You see me doing something illegal, then turn me in. Till then, just butt out."

He turned and went back up on deck. Bernie stared after him.

"Bastard," she said, more than loud enough for him to hear.

nine

The gulls were the first to signal dawn. The eastern sky was the color of their wings, and their harsh cries fell faintly as they soared on a freshening wind.

Galloway leaned against the wheel as light came to the sea. He stared out over the swells, humming under his breath. A snore came from behind him and he glanced back. Shad Aydlett had spent all night on deck, flaked out on a locker. His massive chest rose and fell like the tide.

Galloway was thinking about Keyes.

He didn't know much. And when he put together what he had, he came to a dead end.

He knew, had suspected from the first, that Hirsch was right. Keyes was no historian. That was just a cover. He was after something. He refused to say what, and so far Galloway had no idea what it was.

That, Tiller thought now, didn't bother him. If the man had a secret he was welcome to it, long as the paycheck came. The trouble was, someone else was after it too. And that someone else—presumably the old man who'd visited when Hirsch was aboard—had no problem at all killing people.

At last, coming up to the same dead end for about the fifteenth time that night and morning, he stopped thinking about it and bent to the old chart. His eye traced the smudged pencil line that was their track, too.

As Keyes had directed, he'd made *Victory* hard to follow. He'd held an easterly heading out into the Atlantic. Then, while an observant man on Coquina Beach might still have seen them without binoculars, he had turned north. He'd held that course till dark, till the multicolored sparkle of Virginia Beach loomed to port, until that observant man—whoever he might be, whatever he might want—might have concluded that their course led to New York City, the destination he'd filed by VHF with the Coast Guard listening watch at Oregon Inlet.

Throttled back to cruising speed, the old PT could stay at sea for days. If, Galloway thought, her engines didn't give out. But lower speeds extended her cruising radius immensely. Because of that he'd slowed to twelve knots when he finally turned off the running lights, came about, and pointed the bow south.

It was a long run down the North Carolina coast. The pencil line of their course paralleled the low, shifting sands, but stayed well clear offshore. In four centuries those shoaling beaches had claimed hundreds of sailing ships. The contrary fury of the Atlantic drove them helpless on lee shores, their anchors combing the fine sand bottom. Even powerful steamships like the iron-hulled *Huron* had been torn apart in the surf of the Graveyard.

Galloway knew the same thing could happen to him.

By midnight the hectic glitter of Nags Head and the thirty-second double flash of Bodie Island Light had dropped astern. Galloway picked up the loom of Hatteras Light shortly after that, about one. When he'd timed it he'd woken Aydlett, given him the wheel, and gone below for a loran fix. He had steered south by southeast since then through gradually steeper seas. As he'd expected, the weather worsened as they neared the cape. They'd passed the flaring white eye of Diamond Shoals Tower sixteen miles to starboard, and come a trifle farther east the last hour before dawn.

He checked the chart one last time, then idled the engine and went below to roust the others out. Hove to on the open Atlantic, forty miles from the nearest land, the old boat pitched sullenly to gray-green swells. Her engines muttered, clearing their throats from time to time as salt water covered the exhaust ports. The ocean around her was empty, save for the four-foot seas that came steadily in from the east, but above her the sky was filled with the high-topped cumulus that meant a possible storm.

Victory was ready to begin the search.

When he came back up, carrying a deflated buoy, Aydlett was leaning over the chart.

"Mornin', Shad."

"H'o. Where we at?"

"Here."

The black man moved his hand slowly over the paper as if feeling the depth with his callused palm. "Right along this track here, where the old chart says."

"Yep."

Aydlett looked around at the sea and sky. His broad face took on a slow expression of doubt. He seemed about to say something, but just then Hirsch came up yawning and tousled, scratching her head. "Good morning," Galloway said to her.

"Uh."

"Is that one of my shirts?"

"Yeah. Want to make something of it?"

"No."

She paused, looking at the horizon. "Is that rain over there?"

He turned his head. Not far off to the east, a vaporous umbilical of gray united low clouds and dark water. A puff of cold wind made the buoy, flag flapping, fight to free itself from his hands. "Squall," he said. "We'll be getting wet soon. Can somebody give me a hand here?"

"Want me to take the wheel?" said Keyes, coming up from below. Galloway nodded to him. With the seas abeam *Victory* had rolled like a pig all night. The tall man had come topside twice to be sick. This morning he looked drawn, but decent enough in clean Hawaiian trunks. His blond hair looked brown combed back wet, like alfalfa honey, and even darker tufts bristled on his bare chest.

Hirsch moved after Galloway, looking glum. He'd noticed she took early mornings unenthusiastically. They made their way forward, holding tight to lifelines and handrails as the boat pitched clumsily about. Galloway knelt, then stretched out over the starboard bow, inflating the buoy. The red-striped plastic popped and crackled as air hissed into it from the tank. As the last wrinkle disappeared he twisted the valve closed and began screwing an aluminum rod and flag to its top.

She held the sphere as he sorted out line and bent on a five-pound mushroom anchor. Minutes later the first drops spatted around them as they hurried into the enclosed pilothouse. Keyes pulled the sliding door shut behind them as rain began to lash the deck outside. It was a cramped space for four people.

"I'll take it," said Galloway, squeegeeing water from his eyebrows with his hand. He put the engines back in gear and spun the wheel left. The rudder hit the stops and he held it there. The boat began a tight circle to port inside the gray tent of the squall.

Galloway glanced at Keyes across the cramped wheelhouse. He was braced against the bulkhead, eyes closed, his head nodding with each roll. Well, nothing anyone could do about that. Every man had to fight his stomach for himself. He checked his instruments, his eye lingering for a moment on the fuel gauge. The Gulf Stream had cut their effective speed on the way south. These seas would increase fuel consumption, too. Eventually they'd have to head for one of the inlets to gas up. Morehead City, he thought, might be the best, though Hatteras Village or Ocracoke were closer. But he wouldn't have to worry about that for a while.

And now they'd arrived. Out of the inchoate rain-mist ahead the buoy reappeared, lifted on a gray-green swell. It was time to start looking for Keyes's . . . whatever. Galloway rubbed his back, wincing, and stared out the rain-smeared windshield.

"It seems to be letting up a little," said Hirsch.

"It hasn't started yet," he muttered, glancing at the barometer. His frown deepened. Twenty-eight and fifty-hundredths inches. And the last weather bulletin had been a small craft warning. There was a blow coming, all right. Impossible to tell how soon, or how bad.

"What's wrong, Tiller?"

"We may be in for some heavy weather," he said to them all. "If this needle keeps dropping, I might want to run for shore. We can come out again in a couple of days."

"No," said Keyes.

"What's that?"

"We're not going back." The blond man opened the door and looked out on deck. The squall was passing and a fine gray fog hung over the heaving sea.

"Take the wheel, Bern," said Galloway. "All right. Out." The pilothouse door slammed, and with none too gentle a hand he propelled his client along the rain-slippery afterdeck.

"What is this?" snapped Keyes, whirling suddenly to face him. "Get your hands off me, Galloway. Now."

He let go, just slowly enough, and leaned toward Keyes. An outskirt of the squall spattered them suddenly with cold rain. "Listen here, mister. You won't tell me what we're looking for. Okay, we've discussed that, you've made your position clear. But let me acquaint you with some of the facts of life on this boat. I run her. Not you. I'll stay out as long as you can pay me—*as long as it's safe.* When I decide it isn't, we go in. Got that?"

Keyes's blue eyes had turned flat. He reached back with one hand, clutching the gunwale white-fingered as the boat hung on the edge of a roll.

There were no more words. But words didn't matter now. Galloway leaned against the slope of the deck, near fascination despite his own anger. It was as if two men were struggling behind those sea-fatigued eyes. One of them fought for control, for rationality. The other was murderous and not quite sane.

The hatch slid open and Shad Aydlett loomed out. At his appearance the violence in the other yielded suddenly, visibly. Keyes nodded. "All right," he said, so quietly Galloway barely caught it. "Of course. You're the captain, Tiller. But I have to ask two things. First, that you not push me, physically or—otherwise."

"Sorry."

"And second, that we keep searching for as long as possible. For weeks if necessary. Even if it means discomfort, for me or the others."

"That's what you're paying me for."

"Then we understand each other." Keyes turned toward the sea, staring into the oncoming waves as if trying to see beneath them. "Rain's stopped. Can we get started?"

"Yeah, let's do that."

Standing before the chart table, taking a sighting on the tossing speck of the buoy, Galloway considered that last exchange. Keyes looked green, but seasickness didn't explain it all. The longer he spent with him, the more he realized there was something strange about the man. Something that was not in balance. And now he was under strain of some kind. From outside, or from within?

It might be fear. Fear of whoever had tried to destroy *Victory*. Keyes knew who they were, all right. But what else was hidden behind those protuberant eyes, wide and expressionless, hard as submerged rock, blue as the shoaling Caribbean?

I don't know enough to speculate even, Galloway thought again, picking up a pencil to tick the beginning of the first run. If I knew who he was—or what he's out here after—then I could guess. But I just don't.

Maybe it wasn't important who he was, what he was after, or whether it even existed. The essential thing, as always, was the money. As of that morning Keyes owed him $900. Enough to clear up Jack's medical bills already. After that he'd be in profit. Even with the chart, it could take them weeks to find whatever Keyes was after. Galloway grinned as if through a bad sunburn. Five years before he hadn't sweated the c-notes. It had been easy green, and plenty of it. The golden ticket, the milk run north.

It might be like that again. The more he saw of Keyes, the more convinced he was that the man was serious; someone like this didn't waste time chasing rainbows. If there really was something valuable out here . . .

Forget it, boy, he warned himself then. There's no easy money. No free lunch. You paid too much for thinking that before.

He thought of his father then. He bent to the chart table, and his pencil sliced a scar across the face of the deep.

• • •

It was late in the afternoon of their third day at sea. Their time had settled into the routine of watch, meal, sleep, watch. The seas had moderated, then increased again. The barometer had bottomed, recovered, and then declined. The air warmed to the high eighties and the overcast opened to an occasional thunderhead under blazing sky. The humidity was solid as a hot ice cube.

Bernie was on the flying bridge, sprawled over a chair with an arm on the wheel and one bare leg dangling from the open window. She'd been there alone for three hours. Her breasts swung nearly free under the tiny bandeau of the new tiger-stripe bikini. Her bare shoulders were flecked with sweat. Her other clothes were getting dirty. She hadn't brought much aboard, they'd gotten underway too fast.

It's so hot, she thought. But anyway she was getting some tanning time in. She needed it. Among the college girls at the Nags Head beach she'd felt like the only bar of white chocolate in a Perugina display.

She blinked, yawned, and looked from the compass to the echo sounder. Nothing. It penned a monotonous line that dropped slowly as they wallowed eastward. Every so often a bump interrupted it, but the line always smoothed again into flat bottom. There was plenty of time to think. And she had to think. Especially about Tiller Galloway.

They'd met two months before, in the office the Dare County Board of Corrections maintained in Manteo for probation and parole counseling. He was her first client and she'd been nervous. Galloway, sitting with her in the bare room, had seen that and taken over. Put her at ease. Told her what she needed to know about him. Made it simple.

That alone put her on his side. But the more she found out about Lyle Galloway III, the more puzzled she became.

They'd gone over the facts first. Charge: smuggling. Verdict: guilty. Sentence: eight years. Served four years, paroled to two years discretionary. Current employment: salvage diver.

Second: the background. Good family. No, excellent family, known up and down the Banks for seamanship and courage for at least a hundred years. Decent work in high school, college, and ROTC. And to all appearances a good record in the Coast Guard. Until Vietnam.

Third: the man. Facing him across the parson's table in the counseling room, she had felt both the power of his personality and his profound alienation. She'd tried to reconstruct his emotional picture. His father was dead, he would feel, because of him. He was estranged from his family and friends, except for Jack Caffey. Jobs would be hard to find, money would be scarce; the words *convicted felon* did not figure well on employment applications.

In many ways, she thought, the parolee was like a forcibly dried-out alcoholic. He faced the temptation every day to slip back into crime. Of course the slippery way downward opened at every man's feet. But for the ex-convict, unlike those who'd always observed the law, crime was not unthinkable. It was a path he knew. Once lost, innocence, like virginity, could never be regained.

And prison made it worse. She personally thought the penitentiary system promoted the criminal life. Not only were prisons training grounds; they acted in a more subtle way: To those incarcerated other criminals became peers, became their standards of comparison for day-to-day conduct and even for right and wrong.

The parole officer's job was to counteract everything the parolee had picked up in prison, and to readapt him to normal life. Counsel him, build confidence, help him find work and new companions. And also to check on him: drop in on him at home, at work; interview employers and friends; find out how he spent his time. She was supposed to be half friend, half jailer. It was a narrow line to walk.

But she felt she could make a difference here. That it was worth putting in the extra time. Tiller Galloway was a man at the edge. He could decide for evil or good. She'd try as hard as she could to bring him through that decision. But it was a choice that on some not too distant day he would have to make for himself.

She brushed away a fly. Several of them had accompanied the boat on the dash out of Hatteras, and they were permanent passengers now. She checked the compass, the sea ahead and behind, the sounder. Nothing. The clouds moved steadily overhead and the seas, looking glazed, came steadily in from the green emptiness of the Atlantic.

Her thoughts moved on to the two other men aboard. Shad Aydlett. She'd changed her first impression of him as a roughneck. Tiller had been right; that was only his rough clothes, his size, and his island accent, unfamiliar to her ears. The black man was unfailingly polite to her. But he watched her. No, not just me, she thought; he is comfortable with no one; he will not even sleep belowdecks; he watches all of us, Tiller, Keyes too.

Keyes . . . she thought then, for the hundredth time since *Victory* left Hatteras, of the bomb.

She shifted on the seat. When she'd calmed down from the explosion, and from Galloway's uncooperative attitude, she'd thought about what to do. Her first impulse had been to call the Coast Guard on Tiller's radio and report it. It didn't have anything to do with Galloway. His denial, along with the note, convinced her of that. This new man, this Aydlett, had apparently invited himself along only the day before—and besides, he'd hardly want to blow *himself* up.

So the murder attempt had been aimed at Keyes.

But it was also true that informing the authorities would involve Galloway—inevitably, given his record and parole status. That had influenced her decision. She admitted that. But it wasn't the whole reason. No, she told herself, I made the right choice. I'll find out about this Keyes myself, find out what he's up to. And then I'll decide what to do.

Something called her away from her thoughts. She brushed away the fly again and glanced out and down. The sea slid slowly by, furrowed with steady swells. The horizon was empty. Yet something had interrupted her. She glanced at the sounder. That was it. The stylus had squeaked as it jumped, making a heavy line with lighter squiggles unraveling around it.

"Hold it, Bern," she muttered to herself. The bow had dropped off a few degrees while she watched the sonar. She brought it back, steadied up again on course, then looked back at the trace. The line dropped back to flat bottom as the boat churned on at three knots, corkscrewing as waves shouldered her upward.

She twisted and looked aft and down. Galloway sat nodding in the cockpit, a can in his hand. Aydlett lay on the bow, a towel over his eyes, to all appearances asleep. Keyes was not in sight. Somewhere below, she guessed, probably in his bunk. He'd had the helm through the midnight to six. She grabbed the throttle, untouched since she'd taken over, and revved it twice.

Galloway glanced up. She waved. "Tiller! Come look at the trace. I think we found something."

He swilled what remained in the can, dropped it into the life jacket locker, and came deliberately up the ladder. He leaned over her to check the trace. She caught the warmth of his breath on her bare shoulder, caught too the smell of beer.

"Yeah, I see. About three hundred yards astern by now." He laid a finger against the depth markings. "At a hundred and eighty feet? I hope not."

"Leave it go?"

"Hell no. Whip her around. Let's make another pass."

She rolled the wheel, held it, shifted it as Galloway had taught her. She steadied the bow in the center of the smoothed path *Victory* left on the sea. "Nice turn," said Galloway. She grinned, and they both concentrated on the depth sounder.

"There!"

"Another pass, a little to one side."

She ran east again twenty yards to the left of the wake. The sounder showed a steady line at 185, 190 feet. The bottom was flat and unbroken.

"No good."

"Try forty yards the other way."

"Right."

They pitched to nose-on seas. The flared bow threw thin transparent curves of smaragd-tinted spray. A stray beam of sun, sneaking through the thunderheads made distorted squares flicker in and out of existence on the deck of the flying bridge.

Galloway nodded slowly as the trace peaked again. "There's something there, all right. Sizable. And look at those lighter traces, the yellow ones."

"Fish?"

"Big 'uns."

"Is that good?"

"You bet it is. Means the charter boys haven't found this one yet."

Galloway flicked the sounder open and tore off the last foot of paper. He walked dividers across the chart and made a bold X, then fixed them like darts and wrote the latitude and longitude on the trace. "Okay," he said, staring at it. "We'd better get Dick. You mind?"

"Okay."

Excited, she swung down the ladder, legs flashing. Galloway turned the sounder on again and swung the boat in a circle. He braced himself against the window ledge as *Victory* came beam on to the seas. At the height of the flying bridge, each roll sent him in great swoops through the air.

Ten feet below him, Bernie heard the companionway hatch close behind her. She hesitated. It was darker than she'd expected. My eyes are dazzled, she thought. As they adapted she saw that Keyes wasn't in the main cabin. The dive locker, then. She worked her way forward, bracing herself against Galloway's bunk as the boat took several vicious rolls.

Reaching the forward door, she rapped lightly and went in, crossing the compartment to the two bunks. They were empty. She stopped again, puzzled, and as she hesitated she heard the door close behind her. She turned.

He was leaning against the closed door, watching her. One hand moved at his crotch; he was buttoning his trousers. The head, she thought. That's where he was. But why is he staring at me?

Then she remembered. The new swimsuit. Perhaps the brazilian-cut bottom, the tiny bandeau top, were a little . . . skimpy. She crossed her arms over her barely covered breasts. "I was sunbathing," she said. "We're at sea, no one's around but us. It's what everybody wears at the beach now. Does it bother you? If it does, I'll—"

"Bother me?" He laughed, not taking his eyes from her. He thrust his hands into the pockets of the work cottons he'd borrowed from Galloway. "Would you like that?"

"No. I wouldn't."

"Of course." He took a step toward her, swaying as around them the hull launched itself into another corkscrewing roll. His eyes gleamed in the darkness. "It's a game to you, isn't it? I've watched you around Galloway. And around me. Teasing us. Being provocative—"

"Now wait just a minute, buddy. Just hold it right there—"

He cut her off. "Why? Let's get this straight. I think you're attractive. And you obviously need a man. Why not?"

"No!" She backed away, stumbled, and sat suddenly on one of the bunks as the boat rolled again. He was moving toward her when she said quickly, "You've got it wrong, believe me. But that's not why I came. Tiller sent me down. We've found something."

The words sent a visible shock through him. His mouth opened, then he grabbed for the hatch. It banged against the bulkhead.

She heard the three men shouting at once above her. But she sat still on the bunk, staring after him, trying to swallow a sudden sob of mingled anger, shame, and fear.

ten

Above her at that moment Galloway was cursing vividly. The port engine had quit as he was setting a grapnel. When he and then Aydlett had tried to restart it, without success, he scrambled aft and below with a flashlight and the crowbar to try shorting the starter switch. When he came back Hirsch, wearing one of his sweat-stained dungaree shirts, was sitting rigidly on a locker, her face turned away from the men. He did not notice her strained expression. Instead he threw the bar across the bridge. It clanged into a corner, throwing chips of paint.

"Shot," he said, and spat over the side.

"Trouble?" said Keyes.

"Not right away. One engine's enough for cruising. But if we need power, we're up the creek." He leaned into the windscreen. "Shad, let's try another run on her."

Aydlett rolled back to the bow. He moved fast for a big man, balancing himself without wasted effort against the uncertain rhythm of boat and sea. "Ready on the hook," he called back a moment later. The three-pronged steel grapnel looked like a household utensil in his huge hand.

Galloway lifted his eyes to the recorder once again. He put the remaining engine into gear, ran fifty yards ahead into the wind, watching the trace intently, and yelled "Drop!" at the same instant he slammed the props into neutral, then astern for a quarter-minute, then into neutral again.

Aydlett had carefully made up two coils, one on his left hand, the other on his right. At Galloway's word he swung the grapnel once, twice, around his head, and then it left his hand in an easy-looking arc that sailed it lightly over the crest of a sea. The first coil rose after it, unwinding in the air. Fifty feet ahead of the bow it disappeared with hardly a splash, and flashed downward into clear blue. The line kicked up salt foam as it hummed down after the grapnel, sucking rope off the coil left in his hand. At last it stopped. Aydlett cupped his hands and shouted back, "Bottom."

"Pay out."

"Pay out, aye." The waterman paid anchor line from a flaked heap on deck hand over hand as the wind carried them backward. A marker buoy went over the starboard deck edge, red stripes gay. When Tiller held up a closed fist he made the grapnel line fast to the big samson post where the anchor was bitted off and came aft.

"See it dragging?" Galloway said to Keyes.

"It's vibrating."

"That's right. Still in the mud—there it goes."

The line tightened. It rose gradually from the sea, dripping, then straightened suddenly as *Victory*'s weight came against it.

"She's caught."

"We'll see." Galloway put the engine in gear astern. As the bow rose to a sea the line came taut again, this time weeping water along its exposed length. The propeller thrashed, but the boat stayed put, yawing with the off-center pull. "We caught something, all right."

"You think it's—"

"Can't tell from here, my friend. Got to take a look. You coming down with me?"

"Of course."

Bernie had come into the pilothouse and was looking at the chart. "How deep did you say it was here?"

"Bottom's between hundred-eighty and -ninety."

"That's deep."

"Damn deep. But that's bottom. Whatever's on it is sticking up twenty or thirty feet to make that trace. And we should have fifty or sixty feet visibility out here this time of year. So if there's anything interesting we'll be able to make it out from a safe depth." He pulled open a drawer and ran a finger down a plastic-paged pamphlet. "Say at a hundred-twenty feet. That gives us fifteen minutes stay time for a no-decompression dive."

"Say you two is going to skin dive down there now, Tiller?"

"Scuba dive. That's right, Shad."

"I reckon I'm comin' too."

"What! Like hell you are. You've never done any diving that I know of."

"Can't be that hard."

Galloway stared at the big man, mentally damning not Aydlett but himself; he should have anticipated this. "Look, Shad—it's not that it's hard. It's just complicated. There are lots of things that can kill you down there."

"I never saw nothin' come out of the sea I was afraid of."

"I don't mean animals. I mean decompression, the bends, turning the wrong valve and cutting off your air." He could see he wasn't getting through; Aydlett was looking increasingly suspicious. "I'm just not going to let you kill yourself down there, Shad."

"No?" said Aydlett slowly. "Seems like you suddenly taking real good care of us Aydlett brothers, Tiller. Like you took care of Mezey?"

Galloway saw the muscle bunch in the man's huge shoulders. He had to stop himself from looking around for a weapon. "You can think whatever the hell pleases you. But you're not going down."

"Tiller—"

"Butt out, Officer Hirsch. This hardheaded nigger and me been knocking each other around since we was old enough to bait a hook. You want to try to lay a couple on me, Shad? Feel free. Won't change my mind. May change yours."

"You're treadin' narrow line, Galloway."

"You're standin' on my deck, Aydlett. You dance to my shanty here, like everybody else aboard."

That was a principle even the big waterman had to admit. He saw the yielding in Aydlett's eyes first, even before the big fists reluctantly opened. "That's better. Now look, Shad, what I want is to have you be our safety man on the surface. I'll tell you what you need to know. But you got to break yourself in easy, you know? I'll dress you out, you can go in with us, but I want you just to watch. Don't go down farther than the keel unless you see one of us in trouble. Then come down like a burning barn."

"I reckon that will be all right," said Aydlett.

Galloway exhaled. He knew he'd only postponed the inevitable. Between his memory of his brother, his father's warnings, and his inbred wariness of whites, Shadrach Aydlett was far more dangerous aboard *Victory* than any explosive.

They slid down the ladder to the open deck aft. Galloway began opening lockers. Three aluminum single tanks bonged on the deck. He laid three metered dual-stage regulators beside them. "Dick."

"Yes, Tiller?"

"So far you haven't told me a lot about what you're after. Anything, in fact. Will you know it when you see it? Or will we have to look around for a name?"

"I'll know," said Keyes. He zipped a wet suit top, then paused. "All right if I skip the rest of the rubber this time . . . Captain?"

"Sure. We shouldn't be down that long."

They sat on lockers and dressed out. Weight belts, gauges, knives. Keyes screwed a regulator to one of the tanks and inspected the hose as air hissed into it. He set the tank on the gunwale and slipped into the harness. He took a breath and spat the mouthpiece out, satisfied.

Galloway dressed quickly. He slipped on flippers last and looked across the cockpit at Aydlett. The fisherman had imitated the others as they dressed and had most of his gear on correctly. Galloway adjusted his mask for him and guided Aydlett's hand to various points as he explained the weight belt, the pressure gauge, the operation of the buoyancy compensator and the reserve valve. "Okay, that's pretty good," he said, standing up. "Dick—"

"I'm listening."

"There may be a current. We'll swim forward and go down the anchor line. Shad, it would be best for you to go forward with us and hang on there at five or ten feet while we're below." He held up his watch and tapped it. "Remember our stay time: fifteen minutes at a hundred and twenty. I'll lead. Stick with me."

Keyes heard him out, eyes expressionless behind the oval window of the mask. He nodded shortly.

"And Bernie—say, are you all right?"

"Yes."

"You'll be in charge up here. You know the drill, you've been out with us before."

"Be careful, Tiller."

"Always am. Back soon."

Galloway cut off further conversation by biting rubber and leaning backward, kicking himself away from the rolling hull.

He slammed into cool water. Bubbles foamed above him as he sank. He let a little of the ocean into his mask and revolved slowly, drawing his first hissing breath, into a floorless world of deep blue. Deep blue . . . he felt free for the first time in days. That was what the sea meant. Here was no mourning, no regret, no vain imagining. Your needs and your fears were as direct and raw as those of its creatures, living without desire, destroying without hate.

Here he could forget.

Keyes and Aydlett appeared simultaneously in white bursts on the other side of the underwater hull. Yeah, there was a good surface current. The boat moved steadily away from him. Galloway swam forward against the current, a few feet below the surface. Wave action pulled him up and down. He reached the anchor line and grasped it, a thread of white slanting downward, its far end lost in a sapphire haze.

A tap on his shoulder. He looked back and up, biting the mouthpiece at a twinge in his back. He moved his shoulders to ease the tank and the pain disappeared. Keyes, above him, was motioning. Down?

Galloway looked around once more. Aydlett was thrashing clumsily toward the line, exhaling huge clouds of scarcely used air, swimming more with his arms than with his legs. Well, he'd learn. He nodded to Keyes then and returned his downward signal. He vented air and began swimming downward, the fingers of his right hand ringed around the line.

The sea around them was the same blue as a summer sky, as soft and as filled with light. Delicate white filaments, like smoke from a quietly burning cigar, drifted by as they descended. Galloway pinched his nose through his mask as pressure leaned on his eardrums. His ears cleared and the hiss of air and rumble of exhaled bubbles became encouragingly louder. He felt his sink rate increase as the air in his suit and vest compressed. He turned his wrist to check the gauge. Forty feet.

The two men sank together. The blue became deeper and richer. Red and yellow muted, became washed out. At fifty feet the sea went suddenly cold on their faces and hands. Galloway shivered. They sank rapidly now and from time to time he tightened his hand on the line to brake himself as he cleared his ears.

At sixty-five a flash at the corner of his mask drew his eye. Amberjack. Three, seven, a school of a dozen flashed like scimitars in the falling light. Big, three or four feet long. Curious and unafraid, they swam close to the bubbling monsters that sank slowly into their world, veering off only a dozen feet away. Their scales glittered like rhodium plating. Beyond them moved other, larger shapes, too far to see clearly.

Tiller turned his head to check his partner. Keyes was swimming strongly a few feet above, his mask turned toward the fish. They passed eighty feet and he paused to vent a little air into his vest. Not much, he still wanted to be heavy. The line stretched ahead in a shallow arc, disappearing into a void of prussian blue. He could feel the current now, about a knot, streaming past them like a slow thick wind.

Ninety feet.

At 100 he gripped the line to stop the descent. He could see nothing below but a school of yellowtail, angling away from them into the gloom. He looked upward. The boat and Aydlett's spread-eagled form were long out of sight. A murky green sky glowed between him and the surface.

Keyes motioned brusquely down. Galloway shrugged and kicked downward again.

The sea grew abruptly colder at 110.

At 120 he stopped again, and set the outer ring on his watch. The air flowed thickly past his tongue, a viscous fluid that made the regulator click and squeak. A shadow slipped by him and he glanced up.

It was Keyes, going down with powerful kicks of his fins. He had let go of the line. Galloway cursed inwardly, then let go too and followed him. The current was stronger now. The gloom deepened, even the blueness dimming toward night.

At 140 feet something took shape beneath them. At first it was merely angles, a flat surface that reflected what little light remained. At 150, where Galloway leveled off, it became a tapered stern.

He hardly looked at it. He was searching for Keyes. The other man was not in sight. He brought his arm up to his eyes and squinted at the luminous dial. It was hard to make out the hands. He blinked rapidly, then realized the trouble was not in his eyes. The beer, he thought, remembering the can he'd left on deck. That, and the pressurized nitrogen in his air, was making him drunk. It didn't frighten him. He was used to the sensation. But it made him more cautious. He bit down on the mouthpiece, conscious of it as his link to life.

Where the hell was Keyes? In a few minutes they'd have to leave. At 150 feet they were using air from the single tanks five times as fast as at the surface. He pivoted, searching the dimness below, and finally, reluctantly, angled downward.

His eyes took in what his narrowed brain could not fully understand. What he could see was light-colored with coral encrustation. As he moved along its length a taller structure took shape from the icy gloom ahead of him. Once smoothly curved, now jagged with barnacles and waving here and there with weed. Pipelike things protruded from its top. He exhaled and settled toward them, curling an arm around the tallest to anchor him as he checked his air.

Five hundred pounds left above reserve. Two minutes of bottom time at this depth, if his increasingly fuzzy calculations were correct. He looked around. A large grouper, mouth gaping, meandered across the smooth hull. It took several seconds before he realized that the stream of bubbles beyond it wasn't coming from the fish. That's stupid, he chided himself. Must be Keyes over there. Yeah. Who else? He grinned around his mouthpiece.

Even as that thought trickled through his brain, the other diver came into view around the edge of the hull. He had drawn his knife and was trailing it behind him. He saw Galloway and swam upward toward him. As he neared, Galloway tapped on his watch and held up a finger. One minute. He jabbed his thumb upward.

Keyes lunged, knife arm extended, point aimed at Galloway's stomach.

Reflex alone saved him, slow as his thought processes had become. His hand caught the outstretched arm and he pivoted, pinning it against barnacled steel. The other diver resisted, straining against him. Galloway sucked air, fear cutting suddenly through nitric gaiety. The other man was strong. They were mask to mask. In the dim nightmare light the blue eyes bulged fixedly at him. The knife quivered in their double grip, the point inches from his side.

It began slowly to move. Toward him. Galloway grunted into his regulator, conscious that he was using air too fast. But he couldn't let go, couldn't break away without running the chance of a slip. Let the other man get that hand free, even for a moment, and the knifepoint would rip through a quarter-inch of rubber into his guts.

Keyes's other hand came up and wound itself into Galloway's hair. At the same instant he changed the direction of thrust, catching him by surprise. The knife flashed between their chests, both of them fighting for control; the dull glimmer of the saw-blade just missed Galloway's face.

He breathed out hard, cleared his lungs, and let go of the hull. Locked together, they began to drop. He reached out with his freed hand then and found the toggle on Keyes's vest. Yanked it savagely. It popped and hissed and began to fill, slowly, against the terrible pressure of the sea.

Keyes fought for a moment more as his body rose, then lost his grip. He began sailing upward, silhouetted against the glow, looking like a medieval saint fighting his apotheosis. Steel gleamed briefly as it fell, then disappeared into darkness.

Galloway exhaled. He glanced around once more, then released the stanchion and inflated his own vest.

He came up as fast as he dared and broke surface 200 yards from the boat. Waves tore at his mask as he tongued out the regulator and went to snorkel. Sure rough up here, he thought tiredly. The swim back was slow. Once he saw Keyes ahead on the crest of a wave, then lost him as he disappeared into a trough. Bernie was helping him over the diving platform when Galloway, puffing and blowing water through the snorkel, reached the stern.

He rested his arms on the rusty steel, breathing hard. The violent pitching of the platform made him dizzy after the stability of the deep. Hirsch finished with Keyes and reached down to him, looking worried. He handed up the tank, then drew his own knife. He hauled himself up and rolled over the transom into the cockpit.

The tall man was sitting on deck, chest bare, holding his right hand in his left. Blood ran from narrow slices in his wrist. He looked up as Galloway stood over him, the blade ready. "My hand. What happened to—"

"What the hell was that little stunt?"

"Stunt?"

"You heard me, goddamn you! That bit with the knife!"

"I don't know what you mean," said Keyes. He looked at his sheath and his puzzled look deepened. "Where is it? I remember tapping on the hull with it . . . what happened after that?"

Galloway sat down, almost collapsing on the deck, but he kept his eyes on Keyes. Spray burst over the rail, resoaking them both. His head ached.

"Tiller, what happened?"

"He made a pass at me with his diving tool. I got it away from him, fortunately. Well, Keyes?"

"I told you! I don't remember!"

Galloway stared at him. Finally, slowly, he slid his own weapon back into its sheath. "It must have been narcosis. You were deeper than I was, and it hit me too. Have you been this deep before?"

"No."

"You've got to watch for it. Allow for it, control it. And you need more sleep . . . But why'd you go off on your own?"

"Sorry." There was real apology in his voice. "I had to find out. To see if it was the boat."

"Boat," repeated Galloway, and this time the image in his mind suddenly made sense. His eyes widened. "That wasn't a ship down there. That was a submarine. Is that what you were after?"

Hirsch, standing between them, could contain herself no longer. "I'm glad you're back, Tiller."

"No big deal. Glad to see you care, but—"

"Funny. No, it isn't that." He looked at her face, then followed her arm to the horizon, to the boiling thunderheads almost on them. Another sea came over the side and drenched them all with cold salt water. Loose gear slid and rolled across the deck.

"So our storm's finally arrived. This close to Hatteras, I wonder what took it so long."

"That's not all," she said. "I knew when you saw that you'd want to get underway. So I started the engine while you were down. But, Tiller—the other engine's quit, too. And I can't get it going again."

"Christ. What's Shad say? He's good with engines."

"Shad?"

"Wait a minute. He's back aboard, isn't he? I didn't see him on the way up."

A sudden preliminary spatter of rain danced along the gunwales. Behind her voice the wind rose to a whine. "No," Bernie said, sounding frightened. "He hasn't come back aboard. As far as I know he's still in the water."

eleven

Galloway pulled himself to his feet, ignoring the pain. His eyes came up from the sea to the onrushing storm. And then, instinctively, to the compass.

The wind was dead southeast.

It was nothing less than a death sentence for a powerless boat off Hatteras. Downwind waited disaster. Driven on a lee shore, *Victory* would be pinned on the shoals and battered to bits like a balsa toy. Their only hope, with both engines dead, was to ride it out at anchor, fixed by a thread of nylon to the mass of steel far below.

"Get this gear stowed," he snapped at Hirsch. "Tanks first. Lock the lockers. Throw everything else movable below. We're going to be taking some seas." His glance flicked to Keyes. "Get below with that hand. Wash it out with disinfectant. There's a medical kit in the head. Then get back up here. Move!"

"Wait, Tiller, wait! What about Shad?"

"What about him?"

"Where is he?"

Galloway, bent over the fuse panel, said angrily, "How should I know? He may be on the bottom. In which case we can't help him. Or he may have left the line and got pulled away by the current. In which case he's somewhere north of us. And we can't help him there, either, till I can get one of these bastards to turn over."

She stood aside from the companionway at that, her face white. Galloway slid down it after Keyes. He turned aft, ducking as he entered the engine compartment. The light was on. Tools slid across the deck. He picked them up and went to work, hearing as he did so a sudden heavy drumfire of rain above his head.

A few minutes later he looked up from the port engine as Keyes came in. He held up his hand, neatly wrapped in gauze and adhesive tape. "All fixed."

"Did you clean it out? Coral infections can be hell."

"Yes. Used the last of your bourbon. I took an internal dose, too." His smile faded. "That business with the knife—I remember it now. Vaguely. But I don't see how I could have done it."

"Narcosis is a funny thing. Sometimes fatigue—like when you're seasick for days on end, I guess—can bring it on hard. You probably thought I was some old enemy, or a shark." Galloway twisted a fuel valve closed and then open again. His fingers were ochre with rust. "Know anything about diesels?"

"Some."

"Great. Check out the fuel pump. I'll pull the filters."

"Right."

They worked silently for several minutes, bracing themselves against the engine blocks as the boat pitched. At last Galloway straightened. "It's time we got off a distress call."

"Just a moment." Keyes did not look up from the pump. "Tiller . . . I'd really rather you didn't."

Galloway stopped, one hand on the hatch. "I thought we had this straightened out."

"We do. You're the captain. But I still don't think you ought to use the radio yet." Keyes replaced the pump cover, tightened the bolts, and wiped his hands on his trousers. The bandage was smeared with red; in the dimness Galloway could not tell if it was rust or blood. "We're in no danger as long as the grapnel holds. Correct?"

"We'll get shaken up pretty thoroughly. May lose some gear. Serious damage, probably not—*if* the hook holds."

"Then why give our position to the world on channel sixteen? There'll be time to call if we start to drift, won't there?"

"What about Aydlett? We've got a man overboard here. And if that grapnel goes, we might not have time to get a Mayday out. Without power to hold us into the seas we could go right on over. What good'll it do us then?"

"This wreck may be worth money to us, Galloway. A lot of it." He looked at his hands, wiped them on his trousers again. "And not only to us. It's important we keep its location secret as long as we can."

"From whoever set the bomb?"

"Exactly."

Galloway hesitated. The deck dropped away under his feet, then quivered as it slammed down into the sea. The hull creaked as its timbers twisted. I ought to put out a Mayday right now, he was thinking. They were out of the shipping lanes, but there might be a trawler near. And even in this storm, the Coast Guard might be able to put a helicopter north of them to look for Aydlett.

But he'd have to give their position, and hundreds of people monitored the distress frequency. So far Keyes had been right. There was at least the possibility that he was right about . . . whatever it was he was after. And if he was right about that, there might be money involved after all. Real money. The kind that would solve his cash flow problems for a long time.

He saw for a moment Shad Aydlett's face, and then superimposed on it, the face of his brother. Screw him, he thought angrily. He's the one who insisted on going in the water.

"All right. No radio. Yet. I'll take the risk—considering as how you're paying for all damages incurred on this little outing."

"Thanks."

"I'm going to check the mooring. Be right back."

The wind snatched the hatch from his hands and shrieked in his ears. The sky was the color of old solder. He narrowed his eyes against mixed rain and salt spray and looked around. Topside was a shambles. Much of the gear was still on deck aft, battering itself into junk. Bernie, arms and legs blue with bruises, was fighting the wheel in the pilothouse, trying to keep the yawing bow into the seas.

"I got the tanks secured before it hit, Tiller."

"Good thinking." A full tank of compressed air, if struck right, would explode like a bomb. But the regulators and other equipment—they'd cost plenty to replace. A sea burst over the afterdeck as he watched and swept some of it through the freeing ports.

"Hook holding?"

"Yeah. Feels real solid—God, look at that!"

He turned. A line of rippled white, the crest of an enormous wave, was sweeping toward them from the rain-gray mist. "Amidships," he said. "And hold it there."

Victory dipped to the preceding trough, then rose, but not quickly enough. The wave rolled over the bow and slammed into the bridge, staggering them, pitching the little ship skyward. A series of tearing sounds came from above. "There goes the tower," she shouted above the gale.

"Part of it, anyway." And the new sounder, he was thinking; even if it remained, a soak in salt water would make it useless.

Several smaller crests came in. The old boat feinted to one side or the other and rode over them gracefully. Galloway leaned against the bulkhead, watching the sea ahead. Then he saw it. Another crest, higher than the one that had taken the flying bridge. He put a hand on

Bernie's shoulder, as much to brace himself as her, and clenched his teeth as the white line drove toward them.

It caught them on a yaw to starboard, smashing in one of the cabin windows and flinging the boat sideways until the taut line jerked them viciously to a halt.

"One more like that—"

"And there it is," said Galloway tonelessly. "Hang on." I should have put a kellet on the line, he was thinking. And I should have sent the Mayday.

Now it was too late. The antenna had been on top of the flying bridge.

Victory met it head on. Foaming green covered the windshield as she was carried up, up, and backward until it seemed she would pitchpole. Galloway grabbed for a handhold, missed, and fell backward against the hatch. Water poured in through the shattered window. At the very crest the bow jerked suddenly and the whole hull quivered. Her motion changed instantly; she turned her head from the wind and rolled far over to port. Galloway struggled upright and stared out the streaming windshield.

The nylon thread had held. The grapnel had held. But the forward cleat was gone, torn out of the hull. *Victory* drifted beam-on in the trough, waiting for the next big comber to finish her.

Well, that's it, he thought. Gambled and lost. He felt suddenly weary, and at the same time, strangely relieved. He had a sea anchor left, but he didn't have much faith in it. In a way he was just as glad. There wouldn't be much longer to struggle.

"I shouldn't have let you come out with us on this," he shouted. "It sure wasn't part of your job, Bernie. I'm sorry."

"I didn't do it because of my job."

He looked away from the sea then, at her. Shaken and bruised, in the last moments before they capsized, she was smiling up at him. "I did it to help you, Tiller."

"You wasted your time."

"That's where you're wrong," she said. "You're a good man, Galloway. Under all that bitterness and shame, you're better than you think."

And leaving a man to die? He was about to speak, about to tell her what kind of man he really was when the companionway hatch banged open and Keyes, face smeared with oil, peered up. "Try the port engine," he shouted.

Galloway glanced again at her, muttered a half curse, half prayer, and punched the starter button.

The diesel rumbled into life. He slammed the wheel hard to starboard and as the screw gave the rudder bite, the bow came round into the teeth of the storm.

"Water in the cylinders," Keyes said, climbing the rest of the way up into the cabin. He looked at the broken window. "Backed up through the exhaust line and through the valves. I drained it through the indicator cocks. Your exhaust system's in sorry shape, Tiller."

"I know," said Galloway shortly.

"I can't help you with the starboard engine. It isn't water or fuel or the lube oil supply."

"One's plenty, long as it keeps turning over. The anchor cleat pulled out just as you came up. We've lost the wreck, I'm afraid."

"You have the position?"

"Marked on the chart."

"Good."

Galloway was staring into the storm. "Okay, here we go." He spun the wheel.

"Where are you heading?"

"North," Galloway said, gritting his teeth as the bow came round into the wind and sea. Maybe it wasn't too late. A tremendous wave burst over them and green water drained like a waterfall through the shattered windscreen. "We got a man to look for."

• • •

Surprising them all—especially Galloway—they found him. *Victory* ran north for twenty minutes, following his mental calculation on the drift of a man at the surface. Then he turned into the seas, throttling back to just enough power to hold her into the wind, and sent the others out to look.

Hirsch saw it first, a tiny speck off on the glassy backside of a comber. When Galloway steered for it the speck became first a bundle, then the figure of a man, face down, kneaded and tossed by the sea. "He's got his vest inflated," he muttered.

"That's all that's holding him up," said Keyes, from the far side of the boat. "He's dead. Better just—"

At that moment Shad Aydlett lifted a lifeless-looking face. He stared up at them for a long moment through salt-swollen eyes; then took the regulator out of his mouth and lifted an arm wearily above his head.

"Bernie, take the wheel. Dick, give me a hand, let's get him aboard."

"Right."

• • •

The port engine ran through the night. Galloway headed west. Toward four the storm began to abate, and two hours later he picked up the unmistakable white and black spiral of Cape Hatteras lighthouse. The lee of the Bight reduced the force of the waves and he was able to increase speed. At six-thirty he yielded the wheel to Hirsch and folded himself into the corner of the transom. He hadn't slept all night. Out of the gray dawn the low woods of southern Hatteras came gradually into view to starboard, the weathered gray houses of the village rising beyond them.

Galloway rubbed the dull ache at his back and contemplated the ruin of his boat. He'd built the flying bridge to take weather, but not the full force of a broadside wave, and the beams supporting the overhead had snapped. Everything above the low railing had been carried away, roof, windows, antennas, sounder, everything loose. It was a shell. Looking at it, he decided that the simplest thing to do would be to saw off the jagged beam ends and use it as an open platform to steer from when the weather was good. Perhaps he could rig some kind of sunscreen . . .

Keyes emerged from the cabin with a large towel. Coming aft to where Galloway sat, he arranged it to fall over the transom. Galloway watched. "What are you doing?" he said at last.

"Covering our name. Do you have any paint aboard?"

"There's a few cans in the chain locker. Why?"

"For the same reason I didn't want to radio our position. Where do you plan to put in?"

"Well, we have several choices. Hatteras Village is over there, off to starboard. I suspect you'll want something farther away, though."

"You're right."

"Ocracoke's next island west . . . pretty harbor, but small. We'd stand out like a lighthouse on fire there. No, I think Morehead City's our best bet." Galloway nodded slowly. "There's two, three transient marinas there can handle us. Better engine shops too."

"How far is it? I want to get back to sea as fast as we can."

Galloway got up stiffly. He stared at the chart, then walked his fingers over it. "Say eighty miles . . . cut Cape Lookout close . . . we should pull in around four."

"Is there any possibility of leaving tomorrow?"

"No way. *Victory* needs work, Dick. We need rest. And we've got a lot of gear to replace." Galloway yawned. "Anyway, we can rename her, sure. How about *Tarnhelm*? That suit you?"

Keyes's head snapped up. "That wouldn't be a good name."

"Why not? What does it mean, anyway?"

After a moment the blond man said, "The Tarnhelm is . . . do you know Wagner?"

"*Wagner?*"

"The Ring Cycle. German opera, from Norse legends. The Tarnhelm was a sort of helmet of invisibility. Siegfried—the son of Odin—used it to regain the ring of power for the gods."

After a while Galloway said, "I don't get it."

"Is that so," said Keyes shortly.

Galloway squinted at him. We've got to have this out, he thought. Soon. He decided to do it while they were in port. Get Keyes alone somewhere and get some answers at last.

They both fell silent as Shadrach Aydlett appeared at the companionway. It was his first time on deck since they'd pulled him out of the water. The waterman's face was puffy and he moved slowly, but he seemed alert. The three men exchanged wary nods.

"You feeling better?" said Galloway.

"Some."

"What happened? You weren't making much sense when we gaffed you last night."

"I don't even remember that," said Aydlett. "I remember what happened, though. I let go of the anchor line to try to go a little deeper, test out that breathin' gear. The current got me and before I knew it I was a hundred feet away. Swam for a while but couldn't make any way. That stream is hell to fight." He paused for a moment to drain the beer he carried. When he came up for air he said, looking away from them, "Thanks for come lookin' for me, Tiller. Guess I owe an apology too. I'm sorry I was so suspicious of you."

"You'd have done the same. It was just luck we found you, though."

The waterman folded the aluminum can, tore it in two, and tossed it overboard. He watched it as the halves fell astern, gradually filling, and then disappeared. "Yeah. Luck. After the first half hour, I was sure you was leaving me out there."

"I can't say I wasn't tempted, Shad."

The two men stared at each other. Then Galloway said, "Anyway, you up to takin' her? I got some painting to do."

"Just bring me up another beer," said the black man, sliding himself behind the wheel.

• • •

When they nosed into the crowded harbor of Morehead City and Beaufort, twin towns facing each other across the meeting of the Newport River with Onslow Bay, Galloway's block letters were tacky-dry. Miss *Anna*, out of Wanchese. She limped slowly across the basin and fitted her nose deep into a nest of gill-netters. Their crews, off-loading crates of sea trout and red snapper into refrigerator trucks, hardly glanced at the battered old PT. Galloway cut the engine and looked at his watch. "Four-fifteen. Let's get fueled first. I got to call a guy I know over in Peltier Creek, see if we can get him started on these engines. Then I'll give Jack a buzz, see how he's doing. How about some dinner in say half an hour? They set a good table over at Austin's."

Keyes and Hirsch accepted; Aydlett said to bring him back some crab sandwiches, he'd rather stay aboard and get some more sleep. Galloway finished tying up and left the others filling the tanks with marine diesel fuel.

Caffey was at home, said he was doing fine, but that his family was driving him nuts. He insisted on coming over from Avon that night. After a few more calls Galloway hung up, grinning, and strolled back down the pier.

• • •

Austin's Sanitary Fish Market was a relaxed place. Pinballs and videos were going all out against one wall, and balls clacked in a room farther back. Men glanced at them from the bar, then went back to their beers. Hirsch, Galloway, and Keyes slid into a booth, Bernie beside Tiller. The waitress was slow-spoken but the food came fast. Before long they leaned back, replete with the clear clam chowder that was a Carolina Banks tradition, spiced shrimp steamed in beer, plenty of fried flounder stuffed with crabmeat, and mountains of string fries and doughy-centered hush puppies. When they were done with the deep-dish strawberry pie Galloway stirred sugar into his third cup of coffee and raised his eyebrows. "Been to Morehead before, Parole Counselor Hirsch?"

"No, this is my first visit, Tiller."

"Fascinating town. Hosts one of the biggest billfish tournaments on this coast. There's a museum. And there are lots of shops. Over in that direction." He pointed.

"You want me to leave so you can talk."

"Well, now you put it that way—"

"All right. All *right.*" She got up and threw the napkin down; a fork clattered to the floor. "But you can count me out of the rest of this. I'm washing my hands, Galloway. I'm renting a car back to Manteo tomorrow morning. And believe me, I'll be doing some serious thinking about revoking your parole."

She stalked out. Galloway watched her go, an equivocal expression around his eyes, then turned back to Keyes, cradling the coffee cup.

"Is she serious? About your parole?"

"She doesn't kid around." He thought briefly of the woman he'd glimpsed during the storm. "But I don't think she'd do that—yet. Okay. Let's get down to business."

"What kind of business?"

Galloway put the coffee down. He leaned forward. "It's time to get some things straight here, Mr. Keyes. I've been going along with you blind up to now. You're promising me money, but I'm beginning to wonder if the risks justify it." He paused. "Now let's have it straight. Who you are, and what you're after. If you still don't want to talk, then settle your bill and find yourself another boat."

The other didn't respond for a while. He pushed the remains of his pie around on his plate. At last he said, "I suppose you've earned it. You've taken the risk and suffered financial loss. Though of course I'll pay for your gear and repairs."

"This'd be a good time to make me sure of that," said Galloway.

Keyes looked around. The waitress had left them, and they were several tables away from the nearest fishermen. He nodded, opened his wallet, and counted out thirty more of the same new hundred-dollar bills he had given old Aydlett. Galloway stared at them in his hand. They were a little damp, but they looked like real money.

"The fact is, Tiller, what we saw down there is a German U-boat. It was sunk during the Second World War. What I'm after is inside it."

"You want to salvage it?"

"That's right."

"Why? What's in it that's so valuable?"

"Precious metal."

"Well, that's always nice to have," said Galloway, after a moment. "But what was it doing aboard a German submarine?"

"Bullion was transferred that way several times during the war. The U.S. Navy brought the Philippine treasury out during Bataan. The British did the same in Greece."

Keyes cleared his throat. "This shipment was loaded in Kiel in March of 1945. It came by special train from Berlin, guarded by the Special Branch of the SS in cooperation with the Reich's Minister of Finance branch in Prussia. The boat, one of the new Type Twenty-ones, got underway as soon as it was loaded and slipped out through the North Sea into the Atlantic, running submerged day and night to avoid Allied patrols."

Galloway studied him. "You seem to know a hell of a lot about it."

Keyes watched the ceiling fan revolve.

"Where was it bound?"

"The same destination as the other U-boats that didn't surrender. Argentina. But it never made it."

Galloway chewed that over in his mind. "But why was it off Hatteras?"

"At that stage of the war the U.S. Navy was either in European waters or on its way to the Pacific. The captain probably reasoned this area would be undefended again, that he'd stand a better chance of getting through here than in midocean. It would be risky—but logical."

"I'll ask you this one more time," said Galloway. "If I don't get an answer this time the deal's off. All of it. How do you know about this, Keyes? *Who are you?*"

"My father was aboard that U-boat when it went down."

Galloway began to smile, then stopped. The man opposite looked serious. "Your *father?*"

"Let me explain. He grew up in Kiel, on the sea. He was in U-boats from the beginning of the war. He was lucky; he not only survived, he rose to what we'd call a chief machinist, an engineer.

"The last Allied air attack on Kiel sank his old boat at the pier. He volunteered for the Volkssturm, but instead they assigned him at the last moment to another boat. It was a new kind, and was ringed with guards; once they were aboard the crew were locked in. After they sailed he heard rumors they were carrying a special cargo. Something valuable. He saw nothing, though. There were a lot of crazy stories going around in those days and that sounded like one more.

"They were attacked twice from the air heading out the North Sea. After that they ran at snorkel depth at night and completely submerged during the day. The new boat could do this better than the older types, but it was still a hardship and very dangerous.

"When they arrived off the coast here they'd been underwater for two weeks and conditions were bad. Some of the crew wanted to return to their families in Germany. They mutinied. Four men were shot. My father thought the worst was over. Then, late one night, they were attacked again." He paused there, seeming to expect something from Galloway. "This time it was an American destroyer—"

"The *Russell,*" said Galloway suddenly. His look had gone far away, years and miles beyond the restaurant where they sat. "By my father."

"That's right. By then Lieutenant Commander Lyle Galloway the Second, U.S. Coast Guard.

"My dad barely made it out of the engineroom hatch. He was hit in the arm by a machine-gun slug and fell over the side into the sea. He saw several other people in the water as well, and at one point he recalled a raft. But they drifted apart in the darkness. The Americans picked him up the next morning. Alone. As far as he knew, he was the only one who survived the sinking."

"Is that why you picked me for this job?"

"Believe me, I didn't plan this, Tiller. I was startled when the name Lyle Galloway jumped up at me from the *Marine Directory.* There seemed to be a kind of poetic justice in hiring the son of the man who sank my father's ship to find her again."

"I see. What happened after the sinking?"

"Since the war had ended, he was only detained briefly, then repatriated. But the winter of forty-six was very bad, very grim. He saw no future in Germany, though he did get married there. He went to Spain, where I was born, and then to Argentina, where he started a manufacturing firm. Things went well with him there. In the sixties I came to the States to go to college, and I liked it here; when I graduated I joined a tool and die company in the Midwest. He died in 1975. Now I'm in marketing insurance. Still, I often go back to South America on business, and to see my mother and my father's old friends."

"These old friends. Nazis?"

Keyes made a face. "That was so long ago. You don't take that seriously, do you?"

"Keyes doesn't sound very German."

"Obviously because it isn't my real name."

"I guess that was a stupid question," said Galloway. "What is your real name?"

"Does it matter? Actually it's Schlüssel. I translated it into English when I got my citizenship."

Tiller nodded. "Go on."

"One day at a gathering in Buenos Aires I overheard a discussion of cached funds. Swiss banks, smuggled gems, overseas investments. One of the old men remarked that a shipment that had been supplied by the *Reichsicherheitshauptamt* from special facilities in the East had disappeared in Kiel during the last days of the war. I pricked up my ears. It was the first time it occurred to me that the shipboard rumor my father had mentioned might be true; that such a thing had actually existed.

"I sniffed around a bit, keeping my inquiries low key. Party chatter. No pun intended. The shipment had never reached Argentina. Therefore, it might really have been aboard that U-boat when it sank.

"What did the Germans think happened? I checked with a military historian and found that the sub was listed as missing in the North Sea. It had been claimed as a kill by a British bomber pilot—one of the ones who'd attacked them there.

"I realized then, Tiller, that I'd stumbled on something of fantastic importance, and, moreover, that *I was the only one left who knew it*—my father was a silent man; he never talked about his wartime experiences to anyone but me."

"Didn't they know about my father's sinking a U-boat?"

"There's something funny there, Tiller. Apparently his after-action report was classified. The sinking took place after the war; there may have been some other reason for it as well, it's strange that it was never released. But no one else had any reason to disbelieve the English pilot's claim, and there was no way to tie your father's report, on the other side of the Atlantic, to a specific boat."

"Where does the life raft fit in? The bodies in Kinnekeet?"

"I was still without one vital item of information: where the U-boat lay. You know how hard it is to find something on the bottom without coordinates. Especially here, with so many wrecks. My father had no idea, he worked in the engine room, and the only place name he remembered was Hatteras. But when I read about the bodies I thought instantly: This was the raft he saw. There *were* other survivors. But now we know they were ambushed and shot by Aydlett and his friends that night they came ashore."

"Ambushed? He said the Germans fired first."

"Whatever. Actually I—"

His voice sank as the waitress breezed up to their table. "Moah coffee?"

"No, I think I'll have a beer. Draft, if you've got it."

"And you, sir?"

"More ice water will do me fine," said Keyes.

"Say, would you have some aspirin at the desk?" Galloway asked her.

"Why, sure. Does your head hurt?"

"My back."

"Well, now, that's too bad. Just you wait one minute." She returned in seconds with two tablets, full glasses, and a wide smile for both of them before she went back to the fishermen.

Galloway popped the pills and washed them down with a draught of Miller's. "Quite a story. But possible. Yeah. They just recovered that wreck on the West Coast, the monthly gold shipment from California, went down in 1851. Several million bucks. How much you figure's down there?"

"I heard different figures from different people. I know what the rumors my father heard on the boat were. A metric ton; twenty-two hundred pounds of gold."

Galloway coughed beer back into the glass. He dabbed at his face with a napkin and stared at Keyes. The waitress hurried over. "Are you all right, sir?"

"It's fine," said Keyes. "He gets these coughing fits from time to time. Just give him a moment to recover."

Galloway regained his voice. He leaned forward, looking after the woman, and whispered hoarsely, "When you started talking 'wreck' I thought bronze propellers, scrap metal, deck cargo—maybe even weapons from a wartime freighter. This isn't in the same league! And you're doing this alone?"

"All by myself," said Keyes. "My money, my effort, my profit. You understand now why I had to hire a small salvor, not a big firm. If we mounted a large-scale operation word would get out, people would be curious. In the end there'd be legal fights, other claimants, tax difficulties. The state, the federal government, maybe the German government—the court actions would take years before we saw a penny.

"As it is, if no one but us knows what we recover, I can broker it in small lots in New York and Europe. You can take your percentage in raw metal if you want, but it'd be smarter to let me convert it and give you and this Aydlett your cuts in U.S. currency."

"We can discuss that later," said Galloway. He sat back, eyes intent. "Let's not get starry-eyed. Neither of us has seen it yet. You'll bet your ass it's down there?"

"In a sense I have. If *Die Spinne*—the Spider, the organization of old Party members in South America—finds out this is still at large, they'll do anything to get it. They'd look at it as theirs."

Galloway nodded slowly. "And you think Mr. Mysterious could be one of them?"

"Who?"

"The old guy, the one who left the note."

Keyes looked after the waitress. "I'm not sure who he is. Short, fragile—the girl's description isn't very helpful. But yes, I'd say there's a damn good chance of it."

"Uh-oh," said Galloway.

Keyes nodded somberly. "So you see why we have to move fast and cautious."

"Yeah. . . . Okay, one more question. This Tarnhelm. You say it's some kind of mythical helmet. Obviously it means something else to these people. What?"

Keyes thought about that for a while. At last he said, "How much do you know about World War Two, Tiller?"

"More than most, I imagine . . . growing up I'd read my dad's books . . . why?"

"When they realized they'd lost the war the top Nazis started making plans for afterward. One plan was called Werewolf—for a guerrilla campaign after the war. It was a failure. A second was Operation Odessa—to smuggle out as many high-ranking Party people as they could. It was a success; years went by before the Allies even suspected its existence. I figure Tarnhelm was their name for the third—to get this gold to them in Argentina, so they could set up a new organization there."

Neither of them spoke for a long time. Galloway scratched violently at his head. Days of salt water had made it itch. "Hell," he said. "A ton of heavy metal. At a hundred and eighty feet. That's the absolute limit for air diving. We'll have to fight narcosis the whole time we work. We'll have to time ourselves to the minute, or we'll end up with more bends than a pound of pretzels. What we want is inside a steel hull built to resist depth charges and gunfire. Problem: Find it, get it out, and get it to the surface, *off Cape Hatteras.*" He exhaled noisily. "Any bright ideas?"

"You're the underwater expert."

"I was afraid you'd fixate, as my parole counselor would say, on that inconvenient fact."

"I do want to say one thing, though."

"I'm listening."

Keyes leaned forward. His finger tapped the table as his cornflower eyes sought Galloway's earnestly. "Sure there are obstacles. Don't get hung up on them! Remember what I said about will, out on that trawler?

"Very few people on this planet want anything. I mean, want it with all their power! But without that kind of need they'll never get anything beyond their little paycheck and their little pleasures.

"A few men are different. They know what they want. Want it enough to fight for it. To kill or even die for it if they have to! Every mountain looks unclimbable. To a man who doesn't know the word defeat, though, even the highest mountain has to yield."

"You really believe that, Dick? That stuff about the power of will?"

"Yes. Because that's the kind of man I am—and the kind of man I think you are."

Galloway glanced up at him. The blue eyes were welded to his. After a moment he had to look away. "Well, I guess we'll see, won't we? . . . Okay, let's talk salvage."

"Good enough," said Keyes softly.

Smoothing a napkin on the table, Tiller sketched a rough outline of a sub on it. "Do you have any idea where the stuff is?"

"Not precisely. But I've thought about it and done some research. Actually a lot of research. You have to realize, I've been thinking about this for years."

"I can believe it."

"Well. This model of U-boat, the Type Twenty-one, was called the *Elektro-boot* because of the oversize battery, for more endurance and speed. Now, all submarines are sensitive to fore-and-aft balance. According to my dad's sea stories, transferring torpedoes, pumping fuel, even crew walking forward or aft, and they had to retrim the boat." Keyes placed his finger aft of and below the conning tower on Galloway's diagram. "Given that, the best place to put a one-ton weight not originally in the design would have been somewhere here, near the center of buoyancy—as low as possible. Perhaps they dismantled one of the battery cells and stacked the gold there in ingots." He removed his finger and looked at Galloway. "Make sense?"

"Sure does." Galloway finished his beer and signaled for another. When it came he said, "When I was with SEALS we inserted from an old diesel sub a couple of times in Nam. U.S., but they can't be that different. As I recall, you got to the battery by pulling up the deckplates in the main corridor. If it's really there I expect the plates are either locked or welded down on it. So, we'll need the underwater cutting torch, and/or explosives." He jotted the two items down on the napkin. "Next: entry. The hatches were open, as I recall. So we can get in through there."

"There's a hole blown in the port side, low in the hull. That's what I was looking at when you found me."

He stared at Keyes for a moment. "In the port side? A hole?"

"I saw it. Fairly large, too."

"Good—that may be more convenient than the hatches. We'll see. Lights—we'll need hand-held lights. Airbags, big ones. Line, plenty of it. New regulators, new O-rings for the compressor. . . ." He looked up from the paper, the questioning look back. "I just thought of something else."

"What?"

"Booby traps. I remember my—my father telling me the Krauts would set demolition charges as they abandoned ship. To go off if someone entered, so she couldn't be salvaged from shallow water by the enemy. Did your dad mention anything like that?"

"I don't think so. But I've never been aboard a submarine. A lot of what he told me I didn't understand. Or didn't think at the time was important to remember."

"We'll have to be careful, then." Galloway bit down on the pencil. "And we won't have much bottom time to play with, either. Maybe a diving vehicle would be the answer—to carry more tanks, let us stay down into decompression times. I know a guy in Beaufort's got one."

"Can he keep his mouth shut?"

"What'll he know? I'll just tell him I want it for salvage work."

"Whatever you need, get it. I'll pay for it. The question is, can you do it?"

Galloway finished off the beer. He rubbed his chin, then suddenly grinned up at the blond man. "Yeah," he said. "That's the question, isn't it? You want more water, or a Coke or something?"

"No." Keyes unfolded himself. "You going back to the boat?"

Galloway got up too. "Yeah, let's get some sleep."

As they stood at the desk Galloway slipped a local paper from the rack. He was folding it over, intending to read it back aboard, when he saw the headline halfway down the front page: "Men Sought in Death of Hatteras Resident."

"Hold it," he said. Keyes, who was paying the bill, raised his eyebrows. Galloway read the article rapidly. Halfway through, the other man came around him and began reading over his shoulder.

Clifton Aydlett had died in a fire at his home two days before. Lyle Galloway of Kinnekeet, N.C. and another, unidentified white male were wanted for questioning.

"Oh no," said Keyes.

"Christ. Christ! Old Cliff dead."

"And they think we did it."

"This is rough," Galloway muttered. "It's rough enough on me. It's going to be hell on Shad."

Keyes looked at him sideways. "Are you going to tell him?"

"We can't let him find out from anyone else. That'd be the last straw. No, we've got to tell him."

"Would you rather I did it?"

"I'm not sure. Let me think about it."

"Thanks, keep the change," Keyes said to the waitress. "Coming?"

"I think I need another beer now."

He felt the other's hand on his shoulder, just for a moment, and then he was gone. When the door closed on Keyes and the night, Tiller Galloway stood by the desk for a moment. Then he went to the bar. He ordered another draft and stood with his foot on the rail and drank this one slowly.

He considered what he had just learned, and what he had just been told. It was quite a story. It might all be true. It might be partially true. Or Keyes could be lying through his teeth for a reason he, Galloway, would understand only when it was too late.

His client couldn't have been involved in old Aydlett's death though. Or could he? No, Galloway had been with him every moment. But he could have hired someone else. It could even have been an accident: a blind man bumbling around in there with all that paint and varnish, a kerosene flame—it was only too possible.

What should he believe?

He could think of only one way to find out.

twelve

Hirsch slammed the restaurant door behind her. She was so angry she stumbled down an unremembered step. To be shut out of his business, after she had counseled him. Stood up for him at parole review. Even served as his unpaid crew—not without endangering her career. If Mr. Moulton found out how she was spending her vacation time he'd have her off Galloway's case fast as a parole hearing for Sirhan Sirhan.

What a fool she'd been! But there was a limit to how far she'd go for him. And she'd just reached it. Rubbing the bruises on her arms she walked rapidly and blindly past gift shops, fish markets, tackle shops, hardware stores and chandleries, small motels set back from the waterfront street.

But as she walked her anger cooled into a kind of rejected melancholy. She stopped to gaze at the fluted leaves of a fig tree. She looked in the window of the City News bookstore for a while and then went on, strolling now and looking about her. A tint of red, a fragment of day still lingered in the west, reflected in the still waters of a marina basin. Against that tint of rose a lacework of masts and drying nets edged the darkening sky.

Gradually she realized she was not alone. She glanced around. A few were trawlermen, in bib overalls or green work trousers, clean white T-shirts, and billed hats. Tourists, wearing jackets against the sea wind, carried tote bags and guidebooks. Pleasure boat owners swung along in summer dresses or blazers. But most looked to be local teenagers. They were all walking in the same direction. She moved around a car parked awkwardly across the sidewalk, and stopped to listen.

Music lifted for a moment ahead of her.

She came out a few blocks later at a small park. Cars and vans were jammed along its edges. Kids were lying on the hoods, on the grass, the older teens and a few self-conscious younger marrieds dancing to amplified rock played by a local group from an old-fashioned bandstand. She only half took it in. She was becoming angry again. She found a bus bench down a side street and sat down, throwing her legs out. Not stopping to think, she lit a cigarette.

Yeah, he had potential, she thought, blowing a stream of smoke into the sea wind. But he had problems too. Big ones. Galloway was ill at ease in freedom. He thought he was finished as an honest man. That was natural. Everyone felt that way. She'd told him that often enough! But for some reason he didn't believe, somewhere deep, that he could do it. Or else—and she'd considered this too—he didn't want to, was just biding his time till the restrictions of parole were over.

She wondered if he'd grown in four years in prison. If he hadn't, then sooner or later he would be tempted again, and there would be nothing, nothing at all, anyone could do to help him then.

The group shifted to old Creedence Clearwater, and she leaned back against the wood and closed her eyes. When the solid mass of the street, the town, the earth began to roll under her she put out her arms, bracing herself. It was like that whenever she came back after time at sea with Galloway. She thought about him at the wheel during the storm. Her anger ebbed as she remembered how strong he'd been, and at the same time, when the cleat tore out and she thought they were lost, how gentle. When the hair on his arms was wet it curled into tight curls, like the curve of foam behind the boat when she put it into a tight turn. . . .

She recalled herself sternly. She had to set her feelings for him aside. She knew she had a weakness for older men. She'd even felt it, briefly, for Keyes.

This deal he was sucking Galloway into . . . at first she'd thought it a positive step, a good job for Tiller, more challenging than blowing the occasional wreck or recovering lost outboard motors. She didn't know what he wanted, only that it involved salvage. That was legal. If Keyes knew of something out on the sea bottom, it was his to recover, as long as he declared it and paid taxes afterward. Naturally he wanted to do it without publicity; anyone else had as much right to bring it up and sell it as he did. So at first she'd had no reason to assume there was anything untoward going on.

But then someone had tried to kill them. And the longer she spent around Keyes the less she trusted him and the more she feared. She remembered that awful scene over her bikini. It made her wonder if he was even sane . . .

"Mind if I sit here?"

"Go ahead," she said. Then something in the voice jogged her memory, and she opened her eyes and looked up.

The old man was smiling at her in the starlight, the cold eyes and time-ravaged face distinct even in shadow. "I've been waiting for you for some time," he said.

If her throat had not closed with terror she would have screamed. She threw up her arm, gathered her legs under her, her eyes blown wide.

"No, don't run," he said softly but urgently into the sudden silence of a break between songs. Scattered clapping came from the audience, hidden by night. "Don't cry out. I'm sorry to startle you, but you and I must talk."

The next chord rolled over the scattered audience, cut into the susurration of her breath. She stood watching him, ready to run, but he did not move.

"Who are you?" she said, her throat unlocking at last. The fact that he was so old calmed her a bit.

He had taken something from inside his suit coat and was holding it up. She bent closer cautiously. Some kind of folder, leather, with a card inside.

"Perhaps you can't read it in this light. My name is Yitzhak Ruderman, Miss Hirsch. I am of the Mossad. You may recognize us as the major Israeli intelligence agency."

This time the shock was less. She still stared, but now she could speak. "Intelligence? I don't understand. Why did you try to—"

"Kill you?" Ruderman chuckled apologetically, though the shadowed eyes did not change. "A mistake. A flawed interpretation of orders based on an incomplete understanding of the situation. We seldom operate that way, I assure you. And really, we didn't know you'd be aboard."

"I see," she said, though she didn't. "What do you want?"

"Can we find a less public place to talk?"

She hesitated as he pointed back down the street. Should she? She wished she had more street experience, knew her job better. Would it be dumb to go with him? She wished for Galloway, even Keyes, but there was no one near, not even strangers. Finally she decided that she would. He was so old and frail she felt she could handle him, as long as he was alone. She put her hand in her purse, as if there was a gun in it. "All right. Just for a moment. I warn you—I'm a law officer."

"I understand."

The car was different. Instead of the Mercedes this was a Buick, new, shining some undefinable but bright color under the starlight. It was the one she'd walked around a hundred feet up the road. This made her wonder how long he'd been watching her. She slid into the passenger side, keeping the door open and her eyes on him. He closed his door, took out a pack of cigarettes, and offered her one silently. "No, thank you," she said. "I quit."

"A moment ago—"

"I mean, I'm trying to."

"Ah," he said. He lit his with a small gold lighter. As it illuminated his face she saw sad eyes, graying hair. He puffed for several seconds, as if organizing his thoughts.

"Bernice Hirsch. Twenty-three years old. Born in New York, Orthodox family. Honor student in high school. Two years at Cornell, two more at Columbia. Political involvement, demonstrations against nuclear arms and against repression of Soviet Jews. Religious involvement since high school, none. Graduated with a degree in psychology. Came to North Carolina after her parents ended her affair with a married doctor. Now a parole officer with Dare County, living alone in a rented cottage in Kitty Hawk." He glanced at her.

The only thing she could say was, "So you're a good boy, you do your homework."

"Tell me, Miss Hirsch. How did a nice Jewish girl from New York end up in North Carolina?"

"That's my business. Maybe I wanted to get away from all that nice Jewishness. Why?"

"Because we want you to do something for us, Miss Hirsch. Something important to our country."

"You mean Israel, don't you?"

"That is our country. Yours and mine. The country is the people and the people are Israel."

"Wait a minute, Mr.—Mr. Ruderman. You're assuming way too much. I left that behind when I left Cornell. That doctor you mentioned was Pakistani. I'm not . . . I'm just not into being a Jewish princess anymore."

He settled deeper into his seat, half-turned toward her. In the darkness she could see his silhouette and the dying star of the cigarette. "Oh? But being what you are is not something you can run away from. It's not a matter of choice. You are what you are from the moment you are conceived. The world did not begin with us. To deny our blood changes nothing; its laws operate whether we acknowledge them or not. We merely deny our deepest selves."

"Nice try, but tough luck. My guilt gland doesn't work anymore. Let me tell you something you missed, Mr. Ruderman."

"I want to hear it."

"My father lost his first family. They left Germany before the war and went to Paris. The Nazis caught them there. I don't know what he had to do to survive. He never talked about it. To the end of his life he never bought anything made in Germany."

She had a sudden image of her father while she spoke, of his wary, shielded eyes, mouth always closed. And then, immediately, of his face above her all the Fridays of her childhood, candlelight in his beard, his heavy hand on her head. Looking full at the light he would mumble, his mouth still nearly closed, asking God to make her like Sarah, Rebecca, Rachel, Leah; his eyes defenseless then, but still inaccessible, distant and hurt, unreachable now by anything in this world. "He was a good man."

"And?"

"He died of cancer. Terribly. All his piety and mitzvahs, good works, they were useless. So maybe it's naive. But I just can't believe in a god who does that. It's easier not to be a Jew."

"You're a bitter young woman. But forgive me, this is not a new story. I—"

She was suddenly violently angry. Why was she telling him all this? "Forget it. I don't want to discuss it, damn you! Why don't you just tell me what you want?"

"All right. I will try to make it simple for you. We want the man who hired your boat."

"Keyes?"

"What he calls himself doesn't matter. His real name is Erich Straeter. He was *Schutzstaffel.* SS."

"Him? No way! He's way too young."

"They took them very young during the last year of the war. And a little dye, a little exercise—he does not look his age, that's true. But it is Straeter."

She was still suspicious, but she thought it over. If it was true . . . perhaps that was why she felt so strange around him. Why he'd made that scene, why he looked at her and brushed against her in the close quarters of the boat. She'd thought it was sexual, but . . .

Ruderman seemed to guess what she was thinking. "Many of them took a special interest in young Polish and Jewish girls. They liked to cause them pain. In ways, my dear, that I would not like to have to describe."

"If he is SS," she said slowly, "or was—why are you telling me? What do you want me to do about it? Help you capture him, put him on trial, like Eichmann?"

Ruderman finished the cigarette. He chain-lit another, and the spent butt made a fiery arc into darkness. "No. Capturing him is secondary. We'll get him. But first we want what he came here for."

"He came to the Banks for some kind of salvage. That's all I know."

"We know that, of course. He is looking for a wreck on the sea bottom off the cape."

"If you know everything, why bother to talk to me?"

"You'll see. He has found what he wanted?"

"Well—yes, I think he has."

The red glow twitched. "And what was it, Miss Hirsch? If you don't mind telling me."

"I don't see why not. I heard Tiller say, after they came up, that it was some kind of submarine."

"Ah," said the old man softly. "Ah. Very good."

"Now you can tell me something. What's this—Schroeder—"

"Straeter."

"What is he after? What's down there? A weapon, or something?"

"A weapon?" the shadowed man repeated. "No. More dangerous. Any weapon of those days could kill only a few."

"I don't understand you."

"It's gold. A lot of it. From all over Eastern Europe. From the Holocaust, Miss Hirsch. Pried from Jewish pockets by terror and from our mouths by murder. For that gold, rivers of blood."

She was silent. He went on, his voice intimate in the closed car. "Enough, girl, to pay thousands of troops, buy thousands of guns. Straeter, and the other leaders, are ready. They have preserved their ideology for decades, waiting like a seed. They think now it is spring. In South America they will present themselves as a bulwark against communism from Cuba and Nicaragua. They will speak a different language this time. Wear different uniforms. But they have the same goals. All they need is what is out there."

A shadowy hand waved toward the waterfront, and by extension, she supposed, toward the dark sea beyond. The cold voice seemed to turn toward her. "There are over a million Jews in South America, Miss Hirsch. Perhaps your father never told you what the Holocaust was like. But you must have imagined it, you must have heard. Will you let that begin again?"

"Why don't you just go to the FBI, or something, and have him arrested?"

"Think, Miss Hirsch. Any such funds are ours by right, and we intend to have them, but how could we prove that? We are better off without official attention. In that respect this man's penchant for secrecy, his arrangements with your friend, are admirable. We will let them recover it for us. We are, after all, operating in a foreign country. Publicity could embarrass us—and could lose us what is rightfully ours."

A clock ticked on the dashboard. That was the only sound. After a moment she said, "You must have some reason for telling me all this."

When the old man opened the glove compartment a courtesy light came on.

"This is a shortwave radio, Miss Hirsch."

"I think—can I borrow your lighter?"

He held the flame for her while she lit one of her own. She tossed her hair back and glanced at the thing. It looked like the beeper Dr. Jamail used to carry when he came to her apartment in Prospect Park.

"So? What about it?"

"We will monitor this frequency day and night. All you need do is signal us when the gold is aboard *Victory*."

"If I did . . . what would happen then?"

"We would handle everything after that."

She paused, then shook her head. "No, Mr. Ruderman. Sorry to disappoint you, but I'm not getting involved in this mess any deeper. I'd planned to go home tomorrow, before Tiller sails again. I think I'll stick with that."

"You won't help us?"

"I really don't see any reason to. You sound perfectly capable of handling the situation."

Ruderman smiled. "Well—I won't argue that. But we do need you, Bernice. I won't offer you money. That would be an insult. But I have to point out one other thing."

"What?"

"Galloway."

"What about him?"

"He's in this too."

"Sure he is. I mean, it looks like it. But I'm sure he doesn't know anything about this, this Straeter—about his past. It's just a paycheck to Tiller. You won't implicate him, will you? I have to have your promise."

"You have it." Ruderman smiled. "In fact, he deserves to be paid well for what will be hard and dangerous work. We would be generous to Mr. Galloway. Considerably more so than his current employer."

"What do you mean?"

"A man like Straeter would never leave him alive with such a secret. He will kill Galloway, and of course the black man as well, as soon as he can dispense with them. He has already killed Mr. Aydlett's father."

"What!"

"Burned his house," said Ruderman calmly. "With him in it. He was an old man. Blind."

Hirsch shivered. She looked at the radio, then picked it up. It was surprisingly light.

"We need no promises from you, Miss Hirsch. Simply take it back aboard with you. If you don't become convinced that I am telling the truth about Straeter, throw it overboard. But if you are, if you see that you and the others are in danger, use it."

She slipped it into her shoulder bag.

"Remember," he said softly, as she opened the door, "you must call us at once when it is aboard. Don't delay a moment; that is the point when he will become truly dangerous."

Outside, on the road, she looked back to see him leaning out of the driver's side, watching her. She turned back, suddenly, on impulse. "One more question."

"Yes, Miss Hirsch."

"The note. The message you gave me, when we first met . . . what did that mean? Who is Tarnhelm?"

The old man chuckled softly. "It's not a person. The Nazis were in love with Nordic mythology, the idea of the Götterdämmerung, the fall of the gods. The Tarnhelm was a kind of magic that could prevent it, or some say rebuild Valhalla after its destruction. It's meaningless, it was just their code name for the gold . . . but Straeter, you see, recognized it immediately. Didn't he?"

She remembered his expression, that moment of surprise before he'd feigned puzzlement. "You're right, he did."

He said nothing more. Yet she lingered, looking back at him. In the faint wash of starlight he still looked sinister, but she saw now that he was not. In a way he was heroic. An unobtrusive old man . . . "Thank you," she whispered. "For the warning. For the help."

He made a weary gesture. "Shalom, child. Go in peace."

• • •

Galloway sat on the pier and watched the sky.

One of the finest things about the Banks, he was thinking, was the stars. No city skyglow to wipe them out. No concrete and steel to bar you from them. If you were free enough, if you could reach high enough . . . they hung just out of his grasp overhead, glowing and shimmering in thousands. Burning like the napalm rush of coke against a night black as the inside of your skull when night bell rang and the block lights went out and you slid under the blanket and crossed off another day of your sentence, another day of the one life you had been given and had thoroughly soiled, ruined, and destroyed.

His life . . .

A shift of wind brought music to him for a moment. Someone's radio, he thought. He was considering another beer when he heard the distant thunder of tuned pipes. A few minutes later tires grated on gravel behind him in the lot. He got up. A long black hulk crouched there, rumbling, its Cyclopean eye glowing and vibrating. He lifted his hand, staring into the glare. After a moment a thin silhouette detached itself, hesitated for a moment, then swung to earth. The eye went out. The figure limped toward him in the darkness.

"Jack?"

"Tiller, that you? Hey, good to see you." They shook hands.

"Feeling all right? Sure you're up to going to sea?"

"Sure, man. Makin' money, aren't we?" The boy laughed. "Ribs are sore, but doc said guys my age either die or recover fast. I figured if I could make it here on this hog I could handle some time at sea."

"Well, that's great. Say, whose cycle is that?"

"Sharon's brother's."

"How are you and Sharon getting along?"

"Okay." Caffey shrugged. "She got to play nurse a little. I think she liked it."

"Did you?"

"I guess so."

Galloway grinned in the dark and cuffed him. "Look, I got some things to do. Why don't you go aboard and bunk down forward."

"Sure. Just let me grab my bedroll."

"And let me have your keys, would you. I got an errand—"

"No problem," said Caffey agreeably. "But be careful. He said he'd kill me if he found a scratch."

The Harley was enormous, the kind of cycle Galloway had dreamed about when he was Caffey's age. Its engine sounded like the Reos on the boat—when they ran, he thought. With luck it might get him back by dawn. He wheeled it carefully out of the lot, trying to remember who Sharon was. Then he had it, a slight pale girl. She reminded him of . . .

Christ, he thought then, I screwed her mother in high school. The realization left him feeling incredibly old.

He had not driven much in the months since leaving Raleigh, and of course not at all for four years before that. He put the machine on the twin lanes of 70 east, toward the Outer Banks, and kept it in third for a mile or two to get used to it. As he increased speed the marshland and then a low forest began to flash past, the stars keeping him company above the strip of road, and he settled himself in the deep saddle to think.

It took almost four hours to get to Hatteras Island, though it was less than fifty miles from him in a straight line. He had to wait twice for ferries, once from the mainland to Ocracoke, then again to Hatteras itself. At last the familiar beam flicked overhead, wiping out the stars, and he slowed. He gassed at the Red Drum in Buxton and headed north on an all but deserted road. Behind him Hatteras Light dropped away. Empty marsh and dune, Park Service land, opened darkly before his humming tires.

The lonely roar of surf followed him for miles north along the shore. From the speeding machine he looked out on the sound, shimmering silver beneath a newly risen moon. To his right, between occasional gaps in the dunes, came the answering glimmer of the breaking sea. Past tiny villages, a few score scattered homes, lifted on pilings to let hurricane surf roll beneath. Past the rising bones of the new condominiums, with his brother's name on the signs. Past the shuttered windows and flaking shingles of the old lifesaving station. He thought for a moment of his ancestor, pulling a boat out and back through January surf thirty feet high, a sea not a man in the crew expected to live through. When he was a child he'd thought him a hero. Now, he was not sure. He might have been a fool.

The wind tore at his ears. It was all in the way you looked at things . . . and the way the world looked at you. The island of his childhood had still been the Hatteras of legend: a sparsely peopled community knit close by isolation, kinship, and a fierce yet silent pride. His shame and regret made sense to him because he had been one of them. But was it reasonable, was it fitting anymore? So much had changed. When he was hand-holding high his stepmother had told him the names of everyone they met. Now barren dune and heron-haunted marsh had become sudden towns, thousands of anonymous and interchangeable people with anonymous and interchangeable accents; they knew no one and no one of them knew another. Why should he care or grieve over his private guilt? The name Galloway meant nothing now. The old ways of trawlers and surfmen were gone. Real estate, building, peeling dollars from tourists like leaves from artichokes—that was the future. Those who realize that, like my brother, he thought, will survive. And those who don't will be destroyed, or destroy themselves. Like my father.

Like Lyle III? No way, he answered himself over the roar of the machine. This boy's going for the score.

But he was still thinking of the old days when he turned off the main highway. He cut the ignition and rolled onward, downward, in silence and darkness. The track was so narrow brush hissed against his legs. The old man had liked it out here, despite the mosquitoes. Refused to leave the placid sound, the sandy hopeless garden, the rickety pier his grandfather had built. . . .

Galloway pulled the cycle over when the marl ended. When he kicked down the stand he paused for a long time. The smells of the night pulled him backward through three decades. It had been years since he had stood on this silent sandy path, with the yaupon pressing close and fragrant under the moonlight. But he had been here many times since. In dream, immured by stone and steel, surrounded by the sleep-stink of hived males.

Back then he had been a different man.

The house was just as he remembered it. Big, and old, and dark. The turn-of-the-century ornamentation at its eaves fretted the sky. He could just make out the carved dolphins. He hesitated for a long moment at the edge of the lawn. But no light showed. He glanced at his watch. It was well after midnight.

At last he moved forward. The wooden steps creaked as they always had, familiar as childhood, yet strange as dreams. The screen door opened silently to his touch, unlocked, unlatched as of old. On the porch a rusting refrigerator glowed faintly. The house smelled familiar and yet different. Was Anna still here? He didn't even know if she was still alive. Hell, this house could belong to someone else by now. She'd never written him in prison, never answered the letter he wrote her when his lawyer, dropping by for the last time to tell him his appeal had been rejected, had told him that his father was dead.

He moved into the entrance hallway, into darkness like the bottom of the sea. Felt his way around a corner and eased open a door.

The old man's office was just as he remembered it. Dustier, perhaps, but the big chart of the Atlantic still hung on the wall and the brass chronometer, tarnished now, beside the plaques from ships Lyle Galloway II had served on and commanded. Its unhurried hollow tick made him shiver. He pulled the flashlight from his pocket and crossed to the filing cabinet. A forty-year career, seaman to solid-stripe admiral, in four dusty drawers . . . he found the proper folder a third of the way down. He flipped it open and shuffled rapidly through yellowing papers. Then stopped.

CONFIDENTIAL At Sea, 11 May 1945

From: Commanding Officer, USCGS Hiram G. RUSSELL
To: Commander, U.S. Atlantic Fleet and Chief of Naval Operations
Subject: Destruction of German Submarine—Report of.

The following is a report of particulars of action undertaken on 9 May 1945 between USCGS RUSSELL and USS ARNOLD and a German submarine. The action resulted in the loss of ARNOLD and the destruction of one German U-boat, type and manning unknown. . . .

Galloway read it quickly but with care, then stopped. He reread the last page. He flipped it closed.

Keyes had lied.

There was no mention in the report of a German chief machinist. There had been no survivors at all. His father had depth-charged them all in the water. Galloway saw now why the report had never been released. And understood, now, a little of his father's grimness, the iron rigidity with which he had met any deviation by his younger son from what he saw as the right.

And that was not the only puzzling thing . . .

He was just beginning to think about it when the lights came on in the room. He turned, dazzled, still holding the report.

"Lyle?" said the woman with the gun.

"Hello, mom," he said slowly.

"No. Not that. Not anymore."

She was old now, he saw. Five years had done that to her. Once she'd had broad shoulders, she could lift him when he was nearly full grown. Now she had shrunken, gone gray.

"Anna," he said.

"What are you doing here? Have you broken in?" Her eyes went to the desk. "What are you here for?"

"Dad's old action report. On that submarine he sank."

"Why do you want that?"

"I'm curious."

"You're mixed up in something criminal again. They told me you were paroled. They should have kept you in Raleigh."

"Now, Anna, hold it. We haven't seen each other since dad died."

"Your father didn't die, Lyle. He loved life—as long as he could live it with honor. You killed him."

The lack of sleep, or the long ride on the Harley, made him feel suddenly weak. He gripped the edge of the desk. His stepmother had changed. Once they had been close. Now she was an old, bitter woman. With his father's carbine in her hands.

He took a deep breath. "I didn't come back to take anything. I've never asked for anything of his. It's all yours. I'm sorry it happened the way it did, all of it."

"Liar," she said. Her lips were inflexible. "Criminal. Drug dealer. Murderer." The little rifle trembled in her hand. "I should shoot you now for being in here."

He made a careful judgment, very careful, and moved toward her. She stepped back. "Stop," she said. "Stop right there!"

"Mom—"

She pulled the trigger. As he had hoped, but not known, she had not understood how to load a cartridge from the magazine. He took it away from her gently, smelling her familiar scent, and went down the hallway to the front room. It was the same. She had kept it all the same, even to his own mother's picture over the old DuMont television that had not worked since the day Kennedy went to Dallas.

"We forgot you, Lyle," she was saying behind him. "And Otie and I, we don't need you. Or want you. Get out, Tiller. There are other places to live. You can only hurt us. Get out of here and never come back."

He looked back as he opened the door. The light was behind her now. He could see her hands doubled into fists; could see withered breasts under the cotton nightgown, could see how old she had grown. But he could not see her face, her expression, alone in the house, alone with the dead. He closed the door gently, hearing the same rattle it had always made as it set, and went toward the machine.

He did not quite make it. In the moonlight, in the bushes, he came across the old rowboat, his grandfather's, in which he and Otie and Mezey Aydlett had played surfman long ago. Galloway fell to his knees beside it, burying his face in the loblolly needles, sobbing helplessly into the night-cold sand of Hatteras.

thirteen

It was just after dawn on Wednesday when Galloway, squinting into the new sun, steadied *Victory*'s wheel in mid-channel and advanced the throttle.

It had taken a full day of dawn-to-midnight work to locate and load the gear they needed and to jury-repair for sea. Now, shading his eyes against the glare, he examined the strange short chop of the outgoing tide as it met the Atlantic outside the low whalebacks of Shackleford Banks. Underway at last, he thought. His feelings about it were mixed. He kept wanting to look over his shoulder. At last he did, looking not directly at the others but at the torpedo shape the old PT towed a hundred feet astern.

"It's holding, Tiller," said Jack Caffey. The boy motioned to the bridle-rigged line that led from *Victory*'s stern to the bright orange thing she towed. "Those aft cleats are solid. I don't know what went wrong with that forward one. The deck must have gone dry rot."

"Keep an eye on it. I'm going to crank her up."

The diesels hammered louder, and smoke swirled away in the fresh wind. Keyes came up from below. "The tune-up helped," he said, stepping up beside Galloway. "Though you really need to pull them, get 'em rebuilt."

"I can do that when we get back."

"Hell, you can buy yourself a new boat then."

Galloway ignored that. Instead he said, "Those exhausts sound better too."

"I patched them with Mar-Tex. Clamped sheet metal on the worst places. They'll stand up, I think."

"Thanks."

"Nice weather today. This is a funny sea here. One day storm, the next mild and bright as the Caribbean."

"It's had that rep for right many years." Galloway looked out over the sunny blue expanse, dimpled with whitecaps, then upward to a cloudless sky before he lowered his eyes to the chart. He walked his fingers from tan to deep blue. "We can cut the cape close in weather like this. At fifteen knots—no, won't be able to do that with this thing astern. Say ten. That'll be nine, ten hours back out to the wreck."

"That'll put us there around three or four. We can dive then—maybe twice before we lose the light."

"Yeah," Galloway agreed absently. He turned again to look back at the vehicle.

Twenty feet long, the little submersible had cockpits for two divers and a trunk aft for extra tanks and equipment. Batteries powered a single centerline screw; planes and rudder controlled attitude and direction. The stick was in the forward cockpit. Half-submerged for towing, it slipped through the water on the end of its line like an orange porpoise.

His eyes followed the line to the afterdeck. The boat was crowded with crates, diving gear, tanks of gas for the torch. A small wooden box nestled beneath a seat, lashed carefully with shock cords. In case the torch was not enough.

Caffey said, "What's the matter, Bern?"

Galloway saw that she was sitting quietly on the transom, rubbing sunscreen into her arms and glancing from time to time at Keyes.

"Oh, nothing. Tiller, you want me to do anything?"

"I guess you could start on the flying bridge. I didn't get to that yesterday. Too busy buying out Morehead City. Saw's in the tool locker. And we need to hook up the new sounder."

"Right." She tucked the sunscreen into her shoulder bag and picked her way forward over the cluttered deck to the ladder. Her new red cotton slacks flapped in the wind like signal flags. Galloway looked after her, unsure what to make of her mood. The morning before she'd surprised him by apologizing for her temper. She no longer wanted to leave. In fact, she insisted on coming with them. But that didn't mean things were the same. Something had changed about her—something he couldn't quite place. She spoke less, for one thing, and he had not seen her smile once yesterday, though she'd worked hard at restowing the gear that had come adrift in the storm.

She puzzled him, but she didn't worry him. What worried him was the fourth member of his crew. Shadrach Aydlett sat impassively on one of the aluminum lockers, his elbows on his knees, his scarred hands dangling. He said nothing and did not look at the low land passing down their port side, or at the sun, which was laying a flashing path as if gilding the road to their common goal. He stared at his hands.

Galloway and Keyes had woken him the morning before. Galloway, staring down at the compass, remembered how, sitting on the bunk opposite, he'd shaken the big man gently, then extended a cup of coffee. Aydlett had sat up, blinking, then turned his eyes to it.

"That mine?"

"Yep."

"Thanks."

"How you feeling this morning, Shad? Your eyes better?"

"Yeah, that burnin' all gone. Feel like a million now." He sipped at the coffee, then looked up in surprise. "Irish?"

"We got something to tell you," said Tiller. "Something bad, Shad."

"What it is?"

He held out the newspaper.

The big man had sat motionless, staring at the print. His lips moved. Then they stopped.

He looked at Keyes. Then he looked at Galloway.

At last he said, "Which one of you lit the fire?"

"Look, Shad, you were there. You saw us leave. Neither of us did it."

"You could have come back later—Jesus! Why'm I talkin' to you?" He jumped to his feet. The cup rolled to the deck, shattering and spilling. "I'm going to—"

"Sit down!" roared Galloway. "Listen to me, Shad! Cliff had that old kerosene lamp lit. He lit it for us when we came. After we left he must have gone to put it out and knocked it over by accident."

The waterman rocked forward, his fists doubled. His face was a foot from Galloway's. "Bull crap! How I know that?"

"Because I said so!"

Keyes stood up. "Knock it off, you two. Shad, I'm sorry about this too. I only met your dad once, but he impressed me. Now here's what I think. I think you ought to go on home and help your brother—"

"Like hell! You want me to leave? Now you know where your wreck is? No way, my man. Shad Aydlett is going to do what his daddy set him to: stay right here. And get our cut at the end, me and my brother's."

"Don't you even want to call?" said Galloway.

"Abe knows where I am. With you."

"Damn it, Shad, you can go to Frisco. We're going to spend all day here repairing. We'll wait for you. Only thing we ask is, don't let the cops know where we are."

"Why not?"

The blond man said, "Because they'd take us into custody, and question us, and that would waste weeks. Everything we're doing out here would be in the papers. I have a feeling that if we're going to do this job, we've got to do it right now."

"You must think I'm one stupid nigger. I'm supposed to bite on this? Grin, and leave, then soon as Shad gets around the corner you cast off. Horse shit! My daddy told me before I left, 'You watch your ass close now, Shadrach. Don't trust them two at all,' he said. 'Neither of 'em; that Galloway boy's gone to the bad, anymore he's crooked as they come. They'll as soon kill you as look at you.' Only it was him that got killed."

"I told you I didn't kill Cliff. Hell, I loved him, Shad. He was to me more like my dad than—"

"Shut up. Listen to me now, I'm givin' you fair warning. You is safe till I got our share of whatever you is after, Tiller. Then I am going to hunt you down and kill you."

The three men stood in the narrow, close-smelling cabin, wordless at last; it had all been said.

So that was where they'd left it. Yesterday Aydlett too had worked hard, but with a brooding introspection that Tiller had never seen before in him. And their progress had been limited by the fact that they had to shop in pairs; neither Keyes nor Aydlett would go out of sight of the boat without Galloway along. Even in the crowded harbor, even as they worked together, Galloway had felt the distrust grow ever more pervasive, till now it seemed to fill the boat.

The bow passed the Beaufort Inlet sea buoy. They were in the open Atlantic. Galloway glanced at the chart and fed spokes to the wheel till 160 met the lubber's line on the compass. Out to Cape Lookout, then a left around it for the long run out to sea.

Now he began to think about Keyes.

What was he to think about a man who lied, it seemed, about everything? First there'd been the historian story. That hadn't lasted long. Then this routine about his father escaping a sinking U-boat. Believable, beautifully embroidered with detail, but again, totally untrue. Galloway had proved that to his own satisfaction.

Should he even believe that Keyes was after gold? Or was that just another of the man's disposable truths, nestled one within the other like the successive skins of an onion?

Was there any gold off Hatteras at all?

And if there wasn't, what was Keyes really after?

And what about the thing that had started this entire imbroglio? The three skeletons in the raft?

He stood with his legs braced against the rise and fall of the boat, watching the compass and the sea ahead. Occasionally he lent the wheel a spoke, or borrowed one back. Behind and above him he heard the others, Caffey coiling line, Aydlett clearing his throat hoarsely, Hirsch's saw blade snoring as she hacked at the stumps of the tuna tower. But only part of his mind steered and listened. The rest was engaged in a desperate search for insight. He was trying to imagine what landing in the raft in wartime must have been like; trying to reconcile old Cliff Aydlett's account, incomplete though it obviously was, with what was possible; and from this, like a chess player deducing his opponent's game, trying to decide what lay behind it.

They had come ashore from the central dark, through night and fog. Born from the sea foam, but of Mars rather than Aphrodite. Torn from it like a fragment of night the raft had come ashore, to ground on the Banks, that fragile yet resilient barrier between sea and land. Had they thought that beach the mainland, where they might disappear in a heterogeneous, mobile population? Instead they'd landed on Hatteras. On the barren dunes that had fought back the sea for twenty thousand years, and amid an armed, untrusting people.

But why had they come ashore? Keyes's explanation had been that they were survivors. But there hadn't been any. Therefore the U-boat must have landed them earlier, just before its encounter with Lyle Galloway II and the *Russell.* Had the three on the raft come with hostile intent? He couldn't imagine that, not in 1945. Were they spies? Again, it was the end of the war.

The blond man had mentioned a mutiny in his last fiction. Perhaps he was weaving his fabrications of partial fact. Could they have been mutineers, put off in a raft near shore instead of being shot?

No, because why then would they have a chart, and moreover, one showing the intended track of the craft they were leaving? And pistols? And cash, and even ration coupons?

Each conjecture arrived at a contradiction. Something mysterious had happened that night almost half a century ago. Clifton Aydlett might have known. The old man might have had the bit of data that would make sense of the whole shadowy picture. But he'd never told anyone. And now he never would.

Galloway felt the last grain of fact slip through his fingers, leaving him with an empty fist. All right, he thought, narrowing his eyes to the sun. The only thing he could do was what he did when he entered a strange inlet and could not quite see the conformation of the channel ahead. He'd wait. Deliberately postpone his decision till he was closer, till he could see more clearly. If you waited and watched long enough there always came a moment when the heat haze and the motion of the boat ceased, or neutralized each other, allowing you for a fleeting instant a flicker-glimpse of the truth.

When it came, he would have to be ready.

"Buoy ahead to port, Tiller."

"Thanks, Jack. That should be R eight. We'll keep this course for a while. Okay, who's ready for the first trick on the helm?"

• • •

After leaving Cape Lookout behind they ran east through the morning and afternoon, taking fixes with the old loran hourly, then more often. At last Galloway sent Caffey to the roof of the wheelhouse with binoculars.

That was when things went sour. Hour on hour passed, the boy searching restlessly, four more pairs of eyes reading the sea from the cockpit as *Victory* idled around in vast circles. At six Galloway began to wonder if the storm had taken their mark. He turned on the new sounder and began mapping bottom again. But nothing showed. Another hour passed. Keyes hung near the chart table, becoming increasingly unpleasant. At one point he all but accused Galloway of stalling on him. "I thought you had it pinpointed," he began.

"Are you crazy? Have you ever tried to find something on the bottom of the ocean before? I have. It ain't easy."

"We found it before. And you wrote down the coordinates. All we have to do is go there. I think—"

"We were lucky as hell that first time. That's all. Damn it, what do you want, man? If this thing was easy to find everybody and his brother would be out here tearing it apart for scrap."

"He's right," said Aydlett from behind the two men.

That silenced Keyes for a time, but tempers were ugly all around. At last, when it was too dark to continue, Galloway sent Keyes and Hirsch forward to drop the anchor. The new line was still on wooden drums, and they snarled it. Their argument was audible all the way back to the cockpit. Caffey went forward to help. When the danforth was down he came back along the gunwale, favoring his side just a little. "Set like concrete," he said.

"Can't do any better than that." Galloway grinned at him. As the others came aft he raised his voice. "I know the weather's good, but we'd better keep a watch. Since I don't intend to burn an anchor light."

"Good idea," said Keyes.

"We'll grab some dinner, then I'll take it till midnight. Jack till two, Dick till four, Shad till dawn."

"What about me?" said Hirsch.

"You can have ten to midnight if you really want it."

"You want us all up at dawn?" Caffey asked then.

Galloway nodded. The boy rolled his eyes and groaned. "I should have stayed in my sickbed."

"Get my violin. Go on, lay below and see what you can find us to eat."

When the meal was over and the rest had turned in he perched himself on a cylinder of oxygen and looked out across the dark. It had fallen clear and cool, and above him the faded band of the Milky Way glowed dully behind the stars. Two low lights glittered on the horizon, masthead and range of a passing ship. Bound north, he thought. She's giving Diamond Shoals a wide berth. As well she might. He reached for one of the boxes. We'll have some moon around eleven, he thought. It'll be pretty out here then for Bernie.

Uncapping the bottle, he raised it in a toast to Polaris before he took a long swallow.

"Till?"

The shadow was slim and moved with a certain caution. "Hey," said Galloway. "Siddown, Jack. Glad you came back up. Want a drink?"

"No thanks. You shouldn't drink when you might be diving."

"I know . . . say, I'm really glad you're aboard. I didn't get a chance to say that yesterday."

"I'm not so sure I ought to."

"What's that mean?"

Caffey hesitated. They had both been speaking in murmurs; his next words fell to a whisper. "I mean—well, seems like a lot of stuff is going on I don't understand. Everybody's so tense. What's with you and Shad, anyway? I've never seen him like this."

Galloway explained briefly about Cliff Aydlett.

"Wow. I didn't hear about that. You think Keyes—?"

"No, I was with him the whole time. I think it really was an accident."

"Keyes scares me too. Till, what are we out here after, anyway?"

"He says there's gold in the wreck."

"Gold . . . *gold?* You *saw* it?"

"Not yet. Just the exterior. It's an old submarine."

"Sounds deep, too."

"It is."

"Tiller—look—"

"What?"

"Are you sure this is a good idea? Being out here with these two guys. I wouldn't trust either of them behind me with a knife. And such a deep dive. I mean, gold or not, do we need this job that much?"

"This could leave us both sittin' pretty, Jack. We're talking millions. Enough to get you through school and set up in business and still rich."

"We don't need that much money," said Caffey, his young voice troubled. Galloway saw his profile turn up to the stars. "I'm not even sure I *want* that much money."

Galloway watched him for a long moment. At last he reached out and clapped him on the back. His double cousin was the only one aboard he didn't have to worry about, whom he could trust without reserve. Just then, under the stars, he loved Jack very much. "Don't give me that bullshit, boy. Want it or not you might get it."

"I guess it would be nice to have."

"It sure would. Oh, I almost forgot. Come over here." Caffey came over. Galloway tilted his ear closer and whispered, "I brought a gun aboard. It's under the mattress in my bunk. If things get out-and-out savage, I want you to use it."

"Jesus," said Caffey, straightening. "I hope you know what you're doing, Till."

"This isn't the first shady deal for me, Jack."

"And you paid for it."

"Go to bed, kid. Go to bed."

When his cousin had gone below Galloway looked at the sky for a time. He reached for the bottle again, weighed it in his hand, then put it away. He'd have to be sharp tomorrow. He had a feeling it might be a very long day.

fourteen

Galloway woke half an hour before the sun. He stared at the overhead, wondering where his usual hangover was, feeling the rock and sway of the boat. At sea? Then he remembered. Moving quietly, he took the sextant out of its box and went topside. Aydlett was on deck, sitting on the locker. The two men exchanged looks before Tiller turned away. He checked his watch and lifted the instrument to his eye.

Breakfast was a short affair, and silent. Instant coffee from the alcohol stove in the galley, bread and raspberry jam, a box of granola bars passed around while Galloway computed and then plotted the star fix.

The celestial reduced their whereabouts to a polygon half a mile across. Tiller drew it in on the chart.

"We're somewhere in there?" said Keyes, bending over it as he ran a cordless shaver over his jaw.

"Right. Depth sounding puts us on the seaward edge. We'll run a little way back west, say quarter of a mile, and we should be over the wreck."

"What about the buoy we dropped before?"

"Keep an eye out, but it looks to me like the storm carried it away. We'll have to do an expanding square search till we catch the wreck on the pinger again."

It took three hours before the sounder's trace jagged upward. At the same moment Caffey's voice rang out. His seventeen-year-old eyes had picked up the little red and white marker, dragged below the passing crests by hundreds of feet of water-soaked line. Galloway sent Aydlett forward to give him a hand with the boathook. The waterman went reluctantly, his face like a storm front. When he held up a fist Tiller shut down the engines. "Okay, we're here," he announced. "Let's get *Charlene* ready to go. I want to get in some bottom time today."

"Charlene?" said Keyes.

Galloway hauled on the bridle and the little vehicle came obediently alongside. Its name was stenciled on its nose. He swung himself over the side. Jack followed, bare feet landing lightly. Air hissed as the buoyancy chambers blew clear and the orange hull rose higher in the water.

"Okay. Start handing down that pile."

Filled air tanks, twin units, with regulators attached. Galloway and Caffey stowed them in the trunk aft. When six were aboard Galloway climbed back on the boat. "Enough for now. Let's see those decompression tables."

"I worked it out already," Keyes said. "It's—"

"Don't tell me." Galloway frowned at the tables, did a calculation with a grease pencil, and tilted it toward him.

"Same as I came up with."

"Yeah, but it's better to work the deep ones out twice. Twenty minutes bottom time, then three decompression stops, total decomp time thirty minutes." He looked at Caffey, who had been pretending indifference. "Feel up to diving, partner?"

"You bet!"

"Today's your day. Wet suits—we'll be losing a lot of body heat over that long a dive."

"Wait a moment. I'm going down too."

"And me," said Aydlett.

"Keep your shirts on, both of you. There'll be plenty of work to do down there."

Keyes glanced up, eyes surprised and then angry. Tiller looked at him, waiting. Bernie watched them both, half bent to the gear. At last the blond man smiled, a movement of the lips that added no hint of warmth to his eyes. "Sure," he said. "Okay. You're the boss."

"He ain't mine. I'm goin' in safety, like last time."

"You don't learn easy, do you, Shad?"

"Kiss my black ass, Galloway."

He sighed. He didn't feel like having it out with Aydlett again. "Whatever makes you happy, Shad. But you better hold on to the line this time."

"You goddamn right I will. I don't expect you to come after me no more."

Tiller sighed again and reached for a wet suit top.

He reviewed the procedure briefly with Jack as they dressed out. Each diver would be wearing a "double," two of the large tanks, as he climbed into *Charlene*. He would breathe from them during the descent and exchange them for fresh ones from the trunk as they ran low.

There was plenty of air. That was not the problem. The problem was nitrogen. They'd have to ration air used versus bottom time so there would be enough left for decompression—stopping on the way up to wait for the gas to leave their bodies. A direct ascent from 180 feet to the surface would mean the bends—painful, crippling, quite possibly fatal.

"Ready, Till?" Caffey's voice was nasal beneath his mask.

Galloway nodded and slid down his own. Atlantic and sky contracted to flat glass surrounded by rubber. He felt Hirsch behind him, tugging down his tanks, tightening straps. At last she slapped him lightly on the shoulder. When Caffey disappeared he lurched heavily to the transom and toppled over it into the water.

He spent a few seconds submerged, adjusting his buoyancy and letting the current drift him aft. When he came abreast of the vehicle he hauled himself up into its forward cockpit, cursing as the doubles dug into his back, and flooded the buoyancy tank. His last look up at *Victory* showed him Keyes, eyes steady and cold, squatting on the bow; Hirsch, leaning on the transom, looking down at them anxiously; Aydlett, behind her, fitting a fin to his foot with a determined expression.

His faceplate slipped beneath the surface then, and they shimmered and were gone. Just in time, he remembered to cast off the tow line. He pushed the stick forward, and twisted round to check his partner as they began to glide downward. Behind him, in the rear seat, Caffey was looking up. He too turned his face mask to the roof of the sea.

Their sky now was a moving mirror, like liquid mercury. Through it golden light shuddered diagonally down into the blue. Their bubbles streamed behind them, silvery jellyfish rocking toward the surface. The black hull of the boat was the only shadow.

Better visibility today, Galloway thought. A lot more light was pouring into the ocean. They'd be able to conduct a thorough reconnaissance of the wreck. He wanted to decide on a plan of entry today, maybe even get inside for a quick look. If he kept his head and moved briskly they could get a lot done in twenty minutes.

He shoved the stick left. The vehicle began a circle as it glided downward. The sporadic rumbles of their exhalation punctuated an eerie silence. Every few seconds he had to clear his ears, an indication of how rapidly they were descending. Desert-dry air hissed past his tongue, tasting of rubber and metal. The restless mirror receded, became a uniform turquoise haze above them as they passed fifty feet. As they sank the sea deepened through azure to cyan, still shot through with moving light, though the gold had deepened into the emerald green of old bottles.

He removed his attention from the sea and concentrated on flying *Charlene,* watching his depth gauge. At 140 he pulled back on the stick, leveling them fore and aft, and pulled up a toggle switch in front of him.

The whine of an electric motor filled his ears. Galloway banked, and they circled cautiously lower.

The sea floor gradually came into view below. It was flat, white, a sandy desert littered with small tan rocks. Nothing grew on the bottom, nor had he seen any fish yet. They continued the circle till a gray shadow loomed ahead. He steered for it, then suddenly cut the motor. They sank slowly to the bottom and grounded, rocking gently in the current.

It was the wrong wreck.

He sat motionless, the stick loose in his hand, and looked up at the bow of a destroyer. The stem rose proud and straight, as if she were steaming over the ocean floor, and the superstructure was erect and almost undamaged—till it ended, chopped clean a few yards aft of the stack. A few bluefish, hard little mouths pursed, milled in and out of the shattered windows of the bridge.

Caffey reached forward to tap his shoulder. He signaled, palm up—What's happening?

—Nothing. Forget it. We'll make a circle, keep looking.

The motor purred a high note and they lifted lightly from the sand, bumping twice over rocks before they became waterborne.

Tiller completed three circles around the destroyer, each wider than the last, before they found the U-boat. It lay, he estimated to himself, between two and four hundred yards northeast of the remains of the *Arnold.*

He examined his mental state as they purred toward it. So far, at least, he was not much affected by the depth. He was conscious of a mild elation, a slight high; but he could cope with that, even welcome it to counter the blue gloom and claustrophobia that haunt every diver who ventures beyond the brilliant colors of the near-surface.

The sea was much brighter this time than on the first dive. With clearer water he could make out, in less detail as it stretched away from him, the general outline of the sunken submarine. He turned the vehicle to run along the starboard side, in the direction of the bow, repeating his observations to himself to fix them in his memory.

It was big. Even allowing for the magnifying effect of water, it seemed enormous. The gray-black hull, covered here and there with patches of pale growth, was heeled to the right at about a forty-degree angle. He repeated that to himself. Bow slightly lower than stern. Right plane badly crumpled, apparently by contact with the bottom, as was the blunt bow, the thin plating of which had been peeled away on the underside to reveal a long tube. Slowing, he pulled a hand light from under his seat. Focused on the dark mouth of the tube, the spot of yellow illuminated a smoothly curving dome within.

The head of a torpedo. Tiller clicked the light off thoughtfully. He circled to the left and slid along the other flank of the wreck.

From this side, the high side, the hull seemed pregnant in its silent convexity. The starboard list exposed its belly to them. Save for the fairing of the ballast tank and the flat upper deck its underside was smooth, the steel covered with a coat of mud and coral which, as he touched the button of the lamp again, glowed briefly with flame red, saffron, the rich brown of long-fallen maple leaves. The port plane was tilted high off the sea floor and seemed undamaged. A slow stir beneath it proved to be the same grouper he'd seen before. It was, he thought to himself, just as ugly.

Halfway down the port side he saw the first evidence of attack. A foot-wide hole had been punched through the flat deck downward toward the pressure hull, part of which was visible through upward-twisted gratings. He remembered the emotionless prose of his father's action report. One of the hedgehogs. But this had not been the fatal stroke. Beneath the mangled deck the pressure hull was dented but still sound. Below and astern of the hole it flowed smoothly aft undamaged to the conning tower. He studied it as they crept nearer, slowing the electric motor to the whish-whish of a barely moving ptop.

He'd seen sunken U-boats before. There were two others off the cape, in shallower water, sunk in the early days of the war. He'd taken sport divers out to them a few times. This boat was different. It was bigger than the old Type Sevens. The conning tower was streamlined, built for speed beneath a storm- and war-lashed surface. There were no handrails or antennas to create turbulence. His eyes fastened for a moment on the rusting snout of an antiaircraft gun protruding from a low turret, then slid down and aft as the vehicle crept on.

The hole Keyes had told him about came into view aft of the conning tower. He thought: This is what sank her. It was low in the hull, a gape of blown-out steel plate, jagged and shadowy. A mass of pipes and cables, the boat's entrails, writhed from it. Wires moved gently in the current, tangled like a scuppernong thicket, coated with weed. It wasn't the easy entrance he'd hoped for. In fact, Galloway thought, it might be as dangerous to enter there as to risk set charges on the hatches.

The tapered stern, tilted up from the sea floor, displayed a complex arrangement of skegs and screws to view. The aft torpedo doors yawned open, blackness within. He wondered which of them had murdered the men on the *Arnold.*

Charlene banked, dropped, and scraped to a halt on the afterdeck of the wreck. The two divers moved awkwardly to extricate themselves from the cockpits. When he was free Caffey swam to the deck, trailing the vehicle's safety line behind him. He half-hitched it to a rusty grating. Galloway finned after him. When he reached the sub he paused to unwrap a flat package. The end of a line drifted up. He seized this and tied it off before pulling the toggle.

They watched the buoy soar upward, trailing line, until it was out of sight. Caffey looked at him.

—Let's go forward, Tiller waved. His partner nodded, switched on his hand light, and moved slowly after him toward the conning tower.

Their first stop was some thirty feet aft of it. Galloway sank flat on muddy steel and aimed his light at the underside of the engine room hatch. The handwheel looked clean. No wires, nothing that looked suspicious. He shifted his position and examined the hinge, then aimed the torch straight down. He grinned suddenly, wondering if the ghosts of the crew were watching, and if so thinking how funny the two of them looked. The Kraut ghosts had gone a long time between laughs.

He shook his head in annoyance. The nitrogen was getting to him. He half-rolled to one side and pulled his tank gauge up. Another 1100 pounds. He motioned Caffey closer and checked his. My God, he thought, the kid breathes air like it was free. He was almost at reserve pressure. He pointed back at the vehicle, rapped his tanks, held up two fingers, pointed to himself.

—Change your tanks. Bring me a fresh pair too.

The boy mimed a salute and Galloway returned his attention to the hatchway. He had worked his head and shoulders a couple of feet down into the trunk when a loop of wire froze him. Probably a switch, he thought, something to indicate to the diving officer whether the hatch was closed. But would permanent wiring hang loose like that? Confused, he backed out clumsily.

Aluminum bonged against rusty steel. It was Caffey, struggling with the new tanks. Galloway bit into a fresh regulator, cleared it with a puff and tentatively asked for air. It came, dry as a fine wine. He struggled out of the old pair and strapped on the new. He glared at Jack, who stared back, eyes puzzled.

At last he fished the grease pencil out of his vest and wrote laboriously on the deck: BREATH SLOW CONSRV AR. He pointed it out to his cousin. Caffey examined it like an archaeologist reading Cretan, then motioned for the pencil. He painstakingly added two Es and an I.

Galloway made a rude gesture. Caffey returned it. They swam upward together.

The conning tower hatch was flanked by the bases of the periscopes so closely he had to wriggle between them. It was halfway open. Jammed? He put his gloves on it, set his fins on either side, and yanked.

He almost blacked out with the sudden storm of pain in his back. An involuntary scream lost him his regulator and got him a mouthful of cold salt water. He grabbed for it, releasing a storm of bubbles, and got it back in and cleared. The pain receded and, single-minded as a drunk, he looked back down at the hatch. It hadn't moved.

He shook his head at Caffey and pointed forward. The forward torpedo-loading hatch was next. His cousin, in the lead, hardly bothered to look before pulling himself inside. Galloway had the presence of mind to grab his ankle before he disappeared. When he backed out Galloway shook his finger at him, thinking The kid's blotto. He doesn't care about the risks anymore. Got to keep a cool head down here. He examined the inside of the trunk very carefully. To hell with this, he thought then. If we go in here we'll have to crawl all the way aft to get where we want to be. He motioned to Jack to follow and swam over the deck edge and around the curved expanse of the hull.

Waving the boy clear, he approached the blown-out hole. He played the light around and inside the edges, noting the positions of the wires and pipes as carefully as his numbed mind would allow. At last he shoved off from the hull, sank to the level of the hole, and cautiously approached it.

The first barrier was a tangle of brownish, smooth-looking cable. When he shoved it aside the motion detached the brown coating; it slid off in curved fragments and then dissolved into roiling silt, further obscuring the interior. Following his light he moved forward cautiously, right hand advanced. It found the rusty edge of what seemed to be a second, interior hull. More wire, muddy skeins, barred his path and he wriggled under them, reaching back to keep them from fouling on his tanks.

On past a jagged pipe, under a twisted beam. The water cleared a little and he found himself with slightly more room. The pale yellow cone of his light rested for a moment on dials, handwheels. He was inside. The double hull, he thought, must have been either ballast or fuel tanks.

Pausing to breathe, he held the lamp to his air gauge and then his watch. Only five minutes' bottom time left, another ten on this set of tanks. We're both using air too fast, he thought. It must be the cold; his lips and cheeks were numb with it; even his fingers, in heavy cotton gloves, were growing stiff. He took a consciously slower breath and drifted upward, pointing his light down a kind of corridor. The patch of brightness wavered over crowded, angular, confusing shapes, then steadied on a black oval: an open door, beyond which lay nothing that gave back light.

Something tickled his neck, and he spun slowly to look. It felt sticky. It followed his head. As he turned it slid downward, clinging viscously to his ears, his hood. He drifted a last inch upward. The back of his head bumped gently into the overhead.

He reached up, into something soft. It clung to his arm. When he tried to shake it off he drew it down across his cheeks and his lips, clenched tight on the mouthpiece. It burned, and a sticky dense taste filled his mouth.

He recognized it then. Fuel oil seeping from ruptured tanks and floating here, trapped within the top of the pressure hull. He tried to scrape it from his face, but succeeded only in spreading the jellylike mass. The interior seemed to have grown darker; he looked around, waving the light in his free hand. Nothing, only night. Either his light had failed or the mess had covered his mask. Ah, hell, he thought drunkenly. What a nuisance.

He was thinking about how he'd have to clean it off his wet suit now when his regulator made a peculiar sucking noise, and jammed.

fifteen

Bernie lingered by the gunwale after Galloway and Caffey submerged, watching their breath foam and break on the slick surface of the sea. The old torpedo boat stirred beneath her, a slow roll like a rocking cradle. Aydlett gruffly asked her to check him out. She did and a moment later he went in too, holding a length of rope. When she lost sight of him she straightened, stretching sensuously in the growing heat of cloudless morning.

Only then did she realize that she was alone with Keyes, and would be for at least an hour while Tiller and Jack were below.

She shivered and dropped her arms, looking round the deck. The blond man, in shorts and sandals and with his chest bare, was replacing the unused gear in the lockers. When he caught her glance she dropped her eyes.

"Looks like we have some time on our hands."

"I guess so."

"Getting warm up here. Want something cold to drink?"

"No, thank you. I'm going to—" she had been about to say sunbathe, but changed that to "—work on the deckhouse. Some fresh paint."

He nodded, though his glance was sharp, then bent to his own chore. She walked by quickly, trying to keep her body from betraying her. He did not look up as she passed and she exhaled in relief and hurried down the companionway.

In the chain locker she selected sandpaper, brush, and a half-full can of Cawlux yacht white. She was about to leave when her eye fell on a paint chipper. A foot long, steel, with a sharp edge. She hesitated, then took that too. She hauled the can up after her by a line on the handle, to avoid going aft again, and carried it to the top of the pilothouse.

From twenty feet up she could see for miles. A white speck danced on the waves a few hundred yards away. She watched it for a moment, shielding her eyes, then concluded that the men below had sent up a buoy. At last she bent to work with sandpaper and then brush. She did a square meter and then another. The day grew hot. Patches of sweat appeared at her back and arms and crotch, but she kept her shirt and jeans on.

Despite the discomfort, work gradually ceased to occupy her mind. She still sanded and painted, but her mind went on to other concerns. Such as a cigarette. Since her conversation with Ruderman she'd gone back up to a pack a day. Luckily she'd bought a carton in Morehead City. But they were belowdecks, and *he* was there. She decided to think about something else. About Galloway, for example.

Yes, about Tiller. If there's really gold down there, she thought, he's the one to get it up. Despite his drinking, which she had counseled him about, she knew he was an excellent diver. He could do anything underwater.

But prison, or his guilt about his father, had robbed him of something central. He had the ability and skills to make an honest living; no, he was capable of far more; he could start a company, for example, as her father had. But he didn't want to. The easy dollar was all he cared to take, enough to buy fuel for the boat, liquor for him, and drinks ashore for the women he brought aboard from time to time.

That made her angry, even thinking about it. Of course there was no requirement for parolees to be celibate. And Nags Head in summer was one vast singles bar. But it irritated her.

She knew why. She had accepted at last that she was attracted to him. Her decision to come back aboard, after what Ruderman had told her, meant nothing else.

She smiled to herself. He was so transparent. He acted so masculine, rude and callous and competent. But that was only a defense mechanism. His loneliness and torment were obvious to anyone who took the time to get to know him.

But he didn't respond. And that was frustrating. Galloway seemed not to care about love or involvement, just as he was indifferent to success.

If only he *wanted* something, she thought, battering fiercely with the tool at a patch of blistered paint. But he didn't. He seemed content to drift through life alongside a stinking wharf in a half-rotten boat and run fishermen and divers out a few times a month. Enough money for food and whiskey and transient women. That was all Tiller Galloway seemed to want.

But in the last few days—she twirled the brush slowly in the can as the idea struck her—he *had* been different. More involved with people. And he was drinking less. Straeter had brought him a challenge. Something out of the ordinary. Certainly it had the lure of easy money. But that, she hoped, wasn't all Tiller saw in it.

It was hard, inexperienced as she was, to know what to do. There were written guidelines you could follow; Moulton had given them to her. But Tiller was not an average client. Perhaps she should have advised him against further work for Keyes as soon as she suspected the man. Or at least gone ashore herself.

But it was too late for her to back out now.

Look on the bright side, Bern, she thought, watching sweat drip from her forehead onto fresh white paint. Between you and Ruderman maybe this will turn out all right. You can't foresee everything.

But it was dangerous. Not only to her but to all of them. When the gold was aboard . . . she pictured the transmitter in her mind, now hidden in a roll of clothes at the foot of her bunk.

She hoped the old man came quickly when she made her call.

Something cold touched her foot, and she jumped. It was a bottle of apple juice from the ice chest. She took it silently from Keyes's extended hand. He stood on the ladder, looking around.

"You going to paint the whole thing today?"

"Thanks. Well—as much of it as I can."

"There's no hurry."

"I want to get it done."

"All right," he said equably. "I'll give you a hand." He came the rest of the way up the ladder, chest gleaming with sweat and pale hair, and stepped onto the unpainted section of deck.

She moved back against the freshly painted rail, trying to mask fear with a smile. "Sure. I mean, if you want, that's fine."

He took the brush from her and their hands touched. She turned away from him after a frozen second and knelt to her work again. She felt his eyes on her back as she began sanding around the new antenna mount. Sound casual, she thought. Keep it light. But all she could think of to say was, "How long have they been down, Dick?"

"About thirty minutes." His voice was friendly. "Say. Tell me something. Bernie."

"What?"

"Do you find me attractive?"

The rasp, rasp of sandpaper stopped, then resumed. The noise seemed loud to her in the silence that had come over the sea. "That's . . . an odd question for you to ask."

"It has to do with your behavior, which is also odd. At first you seemed to be attracted to me. But since we went into Morehead you take every chance to avoid me. Is that two sides of the same coin, I ask myself. Yes, it could be. But there could also be some other reason. So I'm asking you now: Which is it?"

"Well." Time, she thought. Play for that. Flirt with him a little. "You're definitely a good-looking guy."

"For an old man, you mean."

"For an *older* man. You're . . . handsome, sure."

She heard him set the can down. She tried to continue sanding, but stopped, trembling, as he brushed the damp hair away from her neck.

She remembered Ruderman's words. *He liked to cause them pain.* Was this how it began? With caresses and love words? When does he change—when I acquiesce? When I resist? What happens—does he hit me, use a rope, a knife? She started to shake. Her hands closed around the paint chipper and she stood up. His hands stayed on her. He was much taller and she had to lift her head to see his eyes.

And then she froze. Her terror and strength alike seemed to drain out of her. For a moment, looking in sudden peace up into their pale stare, she wanted to give him all he wanted. Only let him tell her what it was, and she would—

She snapped her gaze away, and tried to push by him, to get away. Instead he gripped her wrists, bent her backward against the rail, and kissed her savagely.

"Please—"

"Afraid?"

"I don't mean to . . . tease you. The way you said I did."

She felt him go rigid against her. What now? He let go of her wrists and stepped back, frowning. Behind her back she gripped the sharp tool so hard her fingers hurt. She was turning it point outward, steeling herself for what she would have to do, when a choked cry came from below them, alongside the boat.

"Dick! Bernie! Help. Tiller's been hurt!"

• • •

Galloway came to with someone's fingers in his mouth. Before thought came he bit down on them and on the sick taste of oil. Someone cursed. The fingers retreated and he turned his head to one side and coughed and retched uncontrollably.

He lay motionless after the spasm had passed, trying to get enough air. Only gradually did he understand the rough warmth of wood against his cheek and realize that he was lying on *Victory*'s deck in a flood of sunlight, yellow and red through his closed lids. He tried to rub at his eyes, but someone stopped him. He allowed his face to be cleaned with a wet towel.

"Can you hear me, Tiller?"

"Yeah," he grunted. The effort set off a fresh fit of coughing. He wondered if he had swallowed any of the stuff. His stomach heaved again at the thought.

Bernie had his hands; he felt her stroking them. "Don't touch your eyes. They're okay, but you've got oil all over your arms."

"Paint thinner," he gasped.

"To clean it off with," Keyes interpreted.

"I'll get some. We'll need rags too." She ran forward.

Galloway pried open an eye. The sun made him blink. It was beautiful. Above him Keyes was looking at Caffey, who was sitting in full gear in the sternsheets, panting after climbing aboard without help. As he watched, a dark bullet head appeared behind the boy: Aydlett. The black man threw his mask up into the boat and hoisted his dripping bulk after it, his eyes fixed on Galloway with undisguised hostility.

"Jack, did you get any of it? Swallow any?"

"Some on my suit. None on me."

Hirsch returned with a kerosene-soaked rag, but Galloway shoved her away, struggling to get up. "You came straight up?" he said thickly.

"Oh, calm down." Caffey pulled off his mask and scaled it across the deck. "I got up to thirty feet before I remembered, but I did. I checked you and you were breathing so I went back down and did the decomp stops by the clock." He smiled. "Well? How'd I do in the pinch?"

"You did damned fine," said Galloway, managing a weak grin. He reached for the rag and scrubbed at a hand. The brownish mass came off reluctantly and his nose wrinkled. Four decades in salt water did not improve German ersatz diesel fuel. It stank.

"What's goin' on here?" said Aydlett.

"We ran into some oil on the wreck, Shad. Got in Tiller's regulator and stopped it."

Hirsch said, "Hadn't we better get him ashore?"

Keyes looked at her angrily, but Galloway forestalled him. "Hell, no. I'm breathing and I haven't got the bends; we'll keep at it. Thanks to my brave young dive buddy. How'd you get there so fast, Jack?"

"Pure dumb luck—if my head had been straight I'd never have gone in after you. But I didn't seem to care." He shrugged. "I waited outside for all of about two seconds after you disappeared. Then I got bored. Why let you take all the chances? We're partners, right?"

"Yeah, I remember how you charged into that forward hatch."

"Same feeling. Crazy kind of high. So I went in after you. I saw your light fall and when I clicked mine on you were fighting with something on the ceiling. I had no idea what it was, so I stayed low and grabbed your legs. I stuck my regulator down your throat and got you back to *Charlene* as fast as I could."

"Well, I'm proud of you." Bernie kissed him on the cheek, then crossed to Galloway and bent down. "And very happy that you made it back."

This kiss was longer, and full on his mouth. Galloway tensed, surprised. When she stood up he saw her look directly at Keyes, smiling coolly.

Keyes turned away. Galloway sat up, just managing to stop a groan. As he began to undress, Hirsch smiled at him. He stared back, wondering what was going on. Turning her eyes away, but still with that slight smile on her lips, she dipped up a bucket of seawater and began sluicing away the vomit and oil.

• • •

Half an hour later Galloway came back on deck in clean work trousers and a blue dungaree shirt. His hair was still gummed in tufts and his eyes and lips were raw, but he looked vital again. He also carried a strong smell of liquor. He squinted up at the sun. "Dick, we might as well get in another dive today."

"You ready for another, after that?"

"You're the one who told me how little time we've got to do this. Now listen. I'll brief you on what it's like down there, and what to do." He pointed. "The wreck's over there—"

"Tiller, can I talk to you?"

"Of course, Counselor Hirsch. What do you need?"

"In the cabin. In private."

When the companionway hatch banged closed she turned to him, hands on her hips. "Listen, Tiller. I don't think you should go down alone with him."

"With Keyes? Why not? He can dive."

"Don't treat me like a fool! I shouldn't have to give you explanations. I'm not working for you. But he as much as attacked me when you were down! I don't like him, Tiller, and I don't trust him alone with me or anyone else—especially on the bottom with you."

"Okay, okay," he said, putting his hands on her shoulders; he was surprised to feel that she was trembling. "Say, you're really upset. He *attacked* you? I'll have a talk with him, tell him hands off Dare County's bureaucracy. But look, he wouldn't try anything underwater."

"Tiller, he already tried to kill you once underwater!"

"That was narcosis. He didn't know what he was doing."

"Are you sure?"

"Reasonably."

She turned away from him and he let his hands drop. Her eyes darted to the hatch, then came back up to meet his. She moved closer. "I have to tell you something. I don't think Keyes is who he pretends to be."

"Who is he, then?"

"I don't—know, exactly. But I think he's more dangerous than you think. Maybe he was in the SS. Weren't they taking them in young at the end of the war?"

"I don't think he's old enough. He sure didn't grow up in Germany, you can tell that from the way he talks. But did it really take you till now to figure out he was some kind of Nazi?"

She was speechless. The words seemed to melt their way down into her. Galloway watched her for a moment, then grinned and reached behind the chart table. He took a long swig, wincing as the whiskey burned his lips, then offered it to her. She shook her head angrily; he capped the bottle and replaced it.

"You're not the only one who gets suspicious. Remember when I threw you out of the restaurant? I had a talk with him then. He gave me a long story about how his father was on that U-boat and survived the sinking, then later how he was in South America and happened to hear something about some gold being aboard it. That's what he's after, gold.

"Well, I didn't like the sound of it then. So I checked it out. And you know what? My old man didn't recover any survivors. All he picked up were bodies, and not in very good shape, either. So his father wasn't on the boat. Lie number one.

"Lie number two. That crap about 'overhearing conversations'—just that, crap. The big boys don't air things like that at cocktail parties. I don't care if they're in harvesting machines or drugs or politics. They don't talk business, they talk about their golf scores and next year's tax structure. No, I figure this guy's in with the head honchos down there in

New Berlin. He may be working for them, or maybe he's trying for a fast score on his own. Either way it's a dangerous hand. I don't blame him for playing it as close as he can."

"You don't?"

"Not a bit."

"And knowing who he is, are you still going to help him get it?"

He looked at her for several seconds and then sat down on the starboard bunk. He reached for the bottle again. "Obviously I am. I'm out here."

"I mean once he's got it. What are you going to do then?"

He took a slow sip, considering her question. "Well—if I was going to play it absolutely by the book, I guess I'd watch my chance and call the Coast Guard at Ocracoke or Hatteras Village. The government'll show up and take custody. There'll be a hell of a row over who owns it, but I should get ten percent salvage whatever they decide."

She puffed her cheeks in relief and sat down beside him. His bare arm was warm against hers. "Good. Good. It'll be dangerous, but . . . I'm so relieved, Tiller. I thought I was the only one who suspected him. And if they got that money—"

"I suppose that would worry you more than it would me. Yeah. But look, having it wouldn't change much for them."

"With a lot of money they could buy things. Weapons."

"Nothing that matters." He leaned his head back against the bookshelves. His face had gone distant. "What does a Fascist group need most to succeed? Answer: a leader with a capital L; a self-willed, ruthless man with a psychopathic sense of mission. Without one, no matter how much money or arms they got their hands on, the real key to success wouldn't be there. And fortunately they're rare.

"So I think that, even if they got their hands on this, it wouldn't have such terrible results. A few rich old men in South America would get richer. That's all."

"But they won't."

He sighed and looked at her. "But they won't."

"We'll have to keep a real close eye on him, Tiller."

"Yeah. Real close."

She smiled at him; they were agreed; it was all right now. She debated for a moment saying it, telling him she cared about him. But then she decided that it could wait. With a little time, maybe, he'd say it first himself. Yes, that would be better.

"Let's get back on deck," he said, getting up. "We've got a lot to do."

Caffey had hauled *Charlene* alongside and was unloading the used tanks. He looked up as they came out on deck. "We divin' again, Till?"

"Let me look at the tables." He made some calculations, examined his watch again. He waved Keyes down from the flying bridge, where he was watching the horizon.

"We've got a problem."

"What is it?"

"Stay time. At the depth the wreck lies we don't have but a few minutes bottom time each dive. And this looks like a long, rough job."

"So, we do a little each time till we're finished," said Keyes. "Right? I thought you were all ready to go, a minute ago?"

"I changed my mind. Okay? Now listen. The point is, we're building up nitrogen each time. You don't purge it all when you decompress. We've got to rest between dives; otherwise we run risks—big risks. I don't feel up to it yet; Jack and I could both use a few hours topside. And we need to run the compressor, recharge these tanks. So here's what I suggest: We'll all three of us go down together after supper."

"That'll put us into darkness below."

"Yeah, but we've got a buoy on the wreck now; we don't have to do any looking around. And it'll be dark inside the hull no matter when we dive. You done much night diving?"

"No."

"It'll be okay. There's a headlight on the vehicle and we have plenty of batteries for the hand lights. I'll start the compressor going and we'll have full tanks at eight. Sound good?"

"I want to get this done quickly, Tiller."

"I know, Dick. Believe me, I don't want to hang around anchored off Hatteras an hour longer than I have to. We'll work as fast as we can."

Keyes nodded, eyes back on the horizon.

"Now—how about something to eat?"

"Sounds good to me," said Caffey. "Whose turn is it? Let's see—Shad, you haven't done any cooking yet."

"And I ain't goin' to."

They all looked at him. The big waterman was squatting on one of the lockers. His arms bulged out of his cutoff T-shirt and his thighs bulged out of the cheap nylon swimming trunks. His eyes were red-rimmed from salt. Altogether he looked extremely truculent.

"Shad, you got to do something aboard here. You want a cut, you got to share the work."

"You got my contribution, Galloway. The map was it."

"Shad," said Keyes then. Aydlett looked up at him. Without a word the blond man jerked his head toward the companionway.

Aydlett sat there motionless for a moment, blinking. Then he got up and went below. A moment later they heard a match scrape and then the rattle of pans.

Galloway looked after him, his face thoughtful. "Okay," he said at last. "The rest of us, let's get these tanks charged."

• • •

The long afternoon ended with a spectacular Atlantic sunset, etching high streaks of cirrus fiery against cobalt even after the sun vanished. Now only a pale glow lit the western horizon, and as night gained confidence stars snapped on one by one to the east.

Galloway flipped a switch and the anchor light joined them. He looked aft on the shadowed deck and touched another. A floodlight went on, illuminating three wet suits and heaps of gear laid out for donning. He closed the pilothouse door and went out.

"Nine double tanks aboard, all filled and checked," said Caffey in a conspiratorial whisper.

"Torch?"

"Right here. Plus gas. I tell you, this truck's full, Till, won't another ounce go in her."

"Where's Dick?"

"Taking a leak. He'll be right up."

He picked up one of the waterproof flashlights and leaned over the gunwale. The sea's quiet tonight, he thought. No wind. The deck hardly moved. The beam of his light, refracting downward into dark water, showed the anchor line sagging in a lazy arc. He ran the pale circle aft over the vehicle, which bumped gently against the side, then clicked it off and looked up at the Pleiades.

Keyes came up. He glanced around. "You boys ready?"

"Yeah. Let's get dressed."

Galloway took his time. A night dive was different from day work. He gripped each piece of equipment several times, memorizing its geometry and heft. They would be diving by feel, not by sight. He hooked tools into a multipocketed belt, snapping pockets closed over smaller items. Those that were left over he put in a net bag and handed to Jack.

Keyes was ready first. He clambered down, fins in hand, putting them on just before he lowered himself into *Charlene.* Galloway followed him. Caffey, last down, hesitated—there were only two seats. "Hold onto the tail fin," Galloway said in a low voice.

The boy nodded, and made a feet-first entry astern of them. They waited for several seconds after his splash subsided.

"Where did he go?"

Caffey surfaced. "I'm too heavy," he said, spitting out the regulator, which bubbled briefly before cutting off. "Wait a sec." He fumbled with his belt, treading water in the darkness, and then tossed a weight over the gunwale. It thudded onto the deck, just missing Aydlett.

"All ready, then?" said Galloway, and received two brief nods in reply. "Be careful back there, Jack. Stay clear of the prop."

The motor hummed, loud in the calm, and the vehicle moved slowly out of the circle of the floodlight. Hirsch, watching it go, raised a hand and waved.

Galloway ran northwest by the compass for several minutes on the surface, then slowed. He pulled out his light and searched the rippled sea around them. "Anyone see the marker?"

Two other lamps flashed on. "There it is," said Keyes, holding his light on the sphere.

Galloway placed *Charlene*'s nose against it and cut the motor. He leaned out to capture the buoy with a loop of line, then he made both ends fast to the towing padeye and tugged on the knot. It held. He looked over his shoulder at the other two. They were shadows against the stars.

"Regulators," he said.

He tucked his own in his mouth, took a breath, and pulled the plug. Cold mounted from his feet to his waist, his chest. The ocean closed in silence over their heads; the stars wavered, and were gone.

Entering the sea by night, Galloway thought each time he did it, was like dying. They sank through absolute blackness, made deeper by the dim luminescence of his instruments. The bubble and squeak of their breathing filled the sea. He watched the depth gauge edge downward, too slowly, and valved air from the buoyancy tank. The needle moved more rapidly. Twenty-five. Thirty. As they passed forty feet he reached out and flipped on the headlight.

A brilliant beam lanced into darkness from the vehicle's nose. It created an eerie effect. Despite its power it illuminated nothing, revealed only itself. Tiny living things in the water scintillated, reflecting and dispersing the ray till it became a feeble wash, a ghost, then nothing. The light poured into the utter night into which they sank, but nothing returned.

Fifty. He leaned forward and checked the padeye by feel. The loop still circled the buoy line, dragging along it as they dropped. They were sinking straight and true.

Seventy feet. In the wet suit he felt the thermocline as a sudden cold bathing his face. Eighty. Something silver flashed in front of the beam, gone too quickly to identify, like a bomber through the searchlight of a defended city. He checked the gauge. They were dropping faster now. The air in the buoyancy tanks, in their suits, was compressing, making them heavier as they bored into the sea.

A hand light swept across him from behind. Caffey or Keyes. Galloway looked off into the blackness, seeing nothing, then again ahead. He was looking directly in front of the vehicle when the thing swam through the beam again. He stared after it, his lips set around the mouthpiece. It had been swimming slowly, in its searching pattern.

A hammerhead.

Galloway had a sudden memory of his childhood. Cape Point, when he was small. It was a sudden and complete memory, like a snapshot. In the background, the lighthouse and his father, both looming, both old and enduring; in the foreground himself, small and new, sand crunching under his sneakers. When the tide drew back her lips the sea left many things for boys, as if to tempt them to her. Splintered baulks of iron-bolted wood, once the ribs of ships. Sea glass, frosted like opals. Salt pools, limpid and calm.

He had found hammerheads in one of them. Tiny things, just born, but even six inches long they were perfect. They were fighting among themselves in the puddle, but when he thrust a stick among them they attacked it instead. He flipped one out and clubbed it, as boys will, to see how it took death. He still remembered the semicircular slash of jaw under the impossible head, set with row on row of teeth, tiny and as perfectly cut as the edge of a hacksaw. In the dimensionless light of the beam he couldn't even estimate how large this one was. Four feet? Six? Possibly more—they reached fifteen feet off Hatteras, and he himself had seen several twelve-footers.

He hoped there were no more of them about.

The luminescent needle swept past 120. He twisted a valve for a moment; air scraped, and the descent slowed to a drift, a gentle settling. The sea grew suddenly icy cold. We aren't a vehicle, he thought, watching plankton glitter upward through the beam. We are a dead creature, falling from the blue realm of the sun toward the endless night of the abyss.

At 160 the periscope shears glowed pink-yellow in the headlight. He oriented himself by them. They had come down pointing roughly parallel to the wreck. He reached forward to tug on the loop. The knot came free. *Charlene* continued to settle. He steered forward and left. The wreck loomed up at the edge of the beam, drifting upward as they drifted down.

At 180 they hit, harder than he'd intended. Sand grated on the rounded bottom. The vehicle tipped slightly and stopped. The beam steadied, lighting a bare strip of bottom ahead of them. Galloway unfolded himself and swam free, holding the flash. He shoved the grounded vehicle around till the U-boat loomed up ahead of its light. Caffey rocked it, wedging stones under the keel till the beam centered itself on the blown-out entrance to the hull.

Galloway moved steadily, not exerting himself, breathing like a mechanism. Occasionally he squeezed all the breath from his lungs, to avoid carbon dioxide buildup. He pulled out tanks, passing a set to each of the others. They weighed little underwater; each diver could tote his own spare. He checked his watch. Good time so far.

He glanced around. Brilliant shafts of light burst from each diver's hand. They probed the darkness, flashing over sand and metal, but the man behind each remained invisible. He kicked off the bottom and headed for the brightly outlined darkness ahead.

First order of business: Clear the entrance. He brought the cutters into position and set to work, shoving the severed wire back into the dark. A steady *snap . . . snap* told him Caffey was following suit to his right. When the last cable fell away he replaced the tool in his belt and swam forward. He wriggled under the bent pipes, as before, and waited inside the hull for the others.

Keyes came through, pushing his air ahead of him. Galloway waved to catch his eye, and motioned him downward. The other glanced up, at the inverted pool of oil, and bubbles burst from his regulator. He sank. Caffey came through next, yanking at his tanks as they caught on an edge; his curses were almost audible. Galloway grinned, then caught himself and steadied down.

He bubbled air, waiting to sink to silty steel before he took another breath. Around the mouthpiece his lips were already wooden. The water was like black ice.

Turning slowly, he directed his light into the dark tunnel that lay ahead.

sixteen

Shadows loomed at the edges of his beam. As he propelled himself forward, staying close to the floor, they became massive machines. Motor-generators, he thought. They were in some kind of electrical room.

The door to the next compartment was half open, an elongated crescent of darkness beyond. Galloway reached out, then paused. With light and tools and extra tanks he was just too burdened. He checked the gauge of the set on his back: 800. He began to change off, though it was early. The first, he reasoned, could remain here as a backup. There were clanks and bubbling behind him as Keyes and Caffey followed suit.

When his regulator thudded with new air he thrust his hand through the gap and flicked light into the next compartment. A narrow corridor, dim at the far end. More machinery. He swam through, banging the housing of the light on the coaming. The sound tolled through the long-dead hull like a distant, muffled bell.

He swept the beam from side to side, then upward into a vaulted maze of pipes and valves. The overhead here was free of oil. The silt was thinner too. It lay lightly on the upper rims of valve wheels, on connection boxes. The machinery was outwardly whole. A ball peen hammer lay rusted to the deck. He swam slowly down the passage, noting where a food locker had burst, spilling its contents across the canted deckplates into a pile of unidentifiable debris on the starboard side.

Another watertight hatch, this one closed. Galloway paused, shivering a little as the cold explored down the back of his wet suit, studying the complex dogging mechanism.

A hand came over his shoulder. Keyes's. It flipped a toggle down, then jerked the wheel counterclockwise. It resisted at first, then gave way with a grinding noise. Fine rust reddened the water. It spun easily for two or three revolutions, then seized again so solidly both men had to crank it through the final turn.

They were both straining against it when it yielded. The hatch groaned and began swinging to starboard, squealing and rasping on its flaking hinges. The list accelerated it and then it clanged to a halt, dimming the water around it with fine silt.

The first thing Galloway noticed about the compartment beyond was the floor. The deck was divided into meter-wide squares of embossed metal. Each square had semicircular cuts in the outer edge. Evidently they could be lifted to inspect or repair the cells of the heavy battery immediately beneath.

A slow wave of giddiness hit him and he almost giggled. The high, right on time. He pulled himself through the hatch, noting that it had locked itself open. That was good. It couldn't swing closed behind them. He swam rapidly down the center of the compartment, focusing his light briefly around the outline of each plate as he passed over it. They all seemed normal, not even bolted down. Here, beyond the sealed door, there was no silt at all. Save for the rust that glowed russet under his light, all was unmarred by the decades, preserved by the sea.

A vertical tube loomed, like a column supporting the curved overhead. Galloway followed it up with his light to where it penetrated the hull. It was the lower periscope housing. Control room directly overhead, then; they were under the conning tower.

So far, at least, he felt all right. Lighthearted, but within reasonable bounds. Yet he knew he was thinking and acting far more slowly than on the surface. He was in control, but it was the kind of control a man exerts after three martinis at a party. He can, with concentration, still respond to a pass or an insult, but the finer judgments are beyond him. His anxieties drop away, he unstops his ears to the siren songs his conscious denies. Galloway admonished himself sternly to bear down. He swam slowly around the shaft, and stopped.

A litter of bones lay on the deck, one arm curled round the housing. A few pieces of metal lay around it. Buttons. One gleaming coin.

He could see it as if it had just happened. The attack. Men rolling from bunks that had suddenly become death traps. The scramble to leave the sinking boat, where every man on the hatchway ladders fought to displace every other. The explosion aft, and then the plunge. This sailor had managed to dog both hatches before his compartment flooded. But to no avail. His ship was in her last dive.

Galloway's hand tightened on the periscope. He must have heard the keel of the U-boat dig its grave and his in the sandy bottom. Must have waited in the dark, hopeful at first, then slowly despairing. Till sometime later—hours? days?—he had breathed enough carbon dioxide into his steel coffin to slide him into the last black sleep. And then the sea had come creeping in, drop by drop.

He stared for a moment longer, then swam on. A scrap of decayed cloth crumbled away in the backwash from his fins.

The next hatch was dogged as well. Galloway examined its edges inch by inch, then opened it gingerly. This has to be it, he thought. Placing a heavy cargo any farther forward would tip a submarine hopelessly out of trim. If it wasn't in this compartment there was no gold on this boat. The door was recalcitrant and he had to shove. At last it too shuddered open. He thrust his light in before him. A moment later he bubbled noisily in relief, and waved the others forward.

Three squares beyond, a steel plate had been laid across the battery covers. Reaching from bulkhead to bulkhead, it was secured to the deck by heavy bolts. He swam inside, exulting, and then halted. The job would not be as easy as he'd hoped. A thin, almost invisible wire was looped from bolt to bolt.

He checked his watch as the other two swam inside. They'd been down for fifteen minutes. It seemed like an hour. Not much time left. Caffey headed directly toward the plate. Galloway pulled him back and shook his finger at him like a nurse admonishing naughtiness. He aimed his light at the wire and mimed an explosion with one hand.

—Careful. She's ready to blow.

—Right. The boy nodded slowly. —Sorry.

Keyes swam over the two of them and continued on over the steel plate, keeping the tips of his fins well clear of it, and sank to the deck on its opposite side.

Galloway moved closer. His flashlight traced the filament as it curled into a hole drilled through the head of each of the massive bolts. Clever, he thought. You can't unbolt it without snapping the wire. He looked more closely at where the bolt joined the plate and saw the cavity of a weld spot; then another. Three all told. Each bolt was tack-welded to the plate.

He lay on his stomach and tried to persuade his increasingly stupid mind to reason.

Safeguards like this operated by holding a relay open until the wire was severed. Then the relay closed, either ringing an alarm or detonating a charge. The wire was grayish. In spite of its thinness it would have to be insulated if it led through steel. Could there still be a current flowing in it? He couldn't think of any power source available in 1945 that would supply electricity after over forty years' immersion in salt water.

On the other hand, if breaking the wire would have set off a charge, why hadn't it gone off when the power source had been shorted out by the sea?

One answer, he thought fuzzily, might be that the battery was sealed, but the relay wasn't. The battery, with the small load imposed by the loop, might have lasted long enough for the relay to corrode fast in the open position. That, in its turn, meant that he'd have to be careful not to jar it. Any residual voltage at all, even the contact of dissimilar metals in seawater, could set off a sufficiently sensitive detonator. And explosive—that lasted forever.

If, of course, there was a relay at all. He was thinking more and more slowly. It was hard to keep his mind on the job. He wanted to turn graceful somersaults. He reached a hand up to rub his face, found his mask in his way, and was starting to remove it when he caught himself.

Keyes was watching him from the other side of the compartment. His slightly protuberant eyes, flat and cold, seemed to flicker in the light of the flashlights. Galloway brought his hand down from his face and motioned Caffey over. He fished the grease pencil from his vest and wrote in sprawling letters on the deck: GET TOCH.

His cousin frowned behind his mask for a moment, then his face cleared. He flipped him a thumb and left.

Keyes was still watching. Galloway waited until Caffey had had time to reach the outside of the hull, then reached for his belt. Drugged as he was, he felt his pulse accelerate as he poised the cutter and looked up.

The blond man nodded, and Galloway nipped the wire. The jaws slipped through easily and the two cut ends curled apart, waving in the water. He looked at them stupidly for a moment, forgetting what he'd planned to do next.

Something rattled behind him. It was Caffey, trailing two rubber hoses; the heavy tanks of compressed gas were still aboard *Charlene.* He handed the torch to Galloway.

He blinked hard and waggled his head. He cracked the valves, liberating a spurt of bubbles. A lighter was built into the cutting head. As he squeezed it the flame burst into life, flooding the compartment with brilliance, casting their shadows knife-edged and enormous on the bulkheads. The water boiled furiously around the cutting tip, absorbing the heat, and he was able to get quite close to the work, squinting against the glare. (He remembered only now that he should have brought the filter insert for his mask.) Holding it with both hands, he drew the flame slowly in a four-inch circle centered on each bolt head.

He completed the last circle, turned down the flame, and propped the torch near the door. It rumbled and popped, illuminating the compartment. He waved to the two others, and pointed down.

—Take hold at each end and lift.

He looked at his watch again as they swam to their places. He had to stare at it for several seconds before he could calculate the time from the position of the hands. Bad shape, he thought. Only minutes left. He and Jack would have to go up then. There was still gas in their tissues from the earlier dive. Keyes would have a few safe minutes longer.

He made a lifting motion with his thumb. The kneeling divers vented clouds of used air as they strained. The plate screeched sideways perhaps an inch, then Keyes's end came up enough to clear the bolt heads. Galloway tried to favor his sore back as he helped the two of them pull the sheet steel out of the way.

A meter-square pit was revealed by the removal of the decking. He probed it with his flashlight. Some six inches below the deck level was a surface of green metal. He did not touch that. He worked around it with the light, peering up under the deckplates. At last he saw what he wanted. A relay box. It was attached to the side of the green thing. An armored cable led from it to somewhere he could not see.

He presumed it led to the explosives.

Galloway studied this for several seconds, feeling fatigued and bored. He could think of no way to disconnect the relay without risking initiation of the charge. Any jar or vibration might close the contacts that led to the detonator. He could cut the cable, but as he did so the jaws of the cutters would short the wires inside. He chewed his mouthpiece for a moment, then decided, Well, if I can't make it safe, maybe I can work around it. He picked up the torch again and turned up the cutting flame.

Working as carefully as he could, Galloway burned a sloppy rectangle out of the steel deck. When he set the torch aside his teeth eased off the rubber. He now had three inches of clearance around the relay.

He stared down into the hole for a while then, his mind vacant, and at last recollected what he was about. He thrust his arm into the hole, down the side of the green box, and felt around. It was about two feet on a side. His fingers explored what felt like a handle. This seemed promising. He pulled on the handle experimentally.

It rocked.

Galloway stopped. He hadn't expected that. If it moved that easily it was light. Therefore, he reasoned painfully, it might not be full of gold. He glanced across the compartment. The mind behind Keyes's narrowed eyes had obviously come to the same conclusion.

They would have to lift it out, and see what else was in the cell.

He communicated this to the others. The three of them pulled the box upward, very carefully, scraping it against the deck edge away from the relay. It was even lighter than he'd thought. That could be misleading, he reminded himself. It might be buoyant here, yet heavy in air. But it wasn't gold. When it was free they laid it on the deck.

Galloway examined it closely in the flickering glare. Distantly, through the intoxicant haze of nitrogen, he felt excitement. Bronze, yes, he'd guessed that from the verdigris tinge. Stained green by decades in the sea. The lid was hinged and hasped, held down by a corroded brass lock. Stamped into it was—he peered close—yes, an eagle and swastika, and above that the double-lightning runes of the SS.

He glanced at the others. Keyes, across from him, made an impatient gesture. Galloway nodded. He was impatient too. He lifted the torch.

The flame sliced through the hasp like a sharp knife through modeling clay. The lock clanged off the deck and disappeared into the open void below them. Galloway braced his knees and battered the lid up with the heel of his hand.

The box was packed to the top with currency, neatly stacked, neatly banded with white paper. Blue hundred-pound notes with portraits of King George VI. Fat sheafs of red notes, Cyrillic-lettered, with pictures of workers with raised hammers. Ornate notes that said 1000 Cruziero. Others he didn't recognize. And fully half of the top layer was a familiar green.

He looked across the lid at Caffey. The boy's eyes were wide.

Galloway's hand hovered over the rows. The part of his mind that never ceased watching noted dispassionately that it was trembling. At last he picked up one of the stacks of hundred-dollar bills. It was a full inch thick and lifting it revealed more beneath. He steadied this in front of his mask. The picture was of Benjamin Franklin; series of 1934; Secretary of the Treasury, Henry Morgenthau, Jr.

On the other side of the stack was a beautiful engraving of Independence Hall.

Keyes motioned impatiently. Galloway was holding it out to him when one edge of the topmost note flaked into green silt. They stared at it. When Galloway rubbed his fingers slightly the rest of it evaporated, disintegrated, became a falling murk of water-rotted green paper.

A hand came past him and plunged into the box. Around it hundred-pound notes crumbled into powder. Keyes grabbed the box, overturned it. The red, brown, green, blue bundles slid out onto the deck, melting as they tumbled like sugar cubes in hot tea. The particolored murk swirled up around their lights, eddying to and fro as the three men groped through the quickly darkening water.

A heap of frayed powder stirred uneasily on the deckplates.

Galloway, his throat closed in horror, thought: the gold. It had to be here. Where was it? He leaned over the hole where the box had been, moving the torch to send its guttering glare into every corner of the battery cell.

It was empty.

He stared for a moment, unbelieving, then thrust the torch at Caffey. He pulled off his fins and slid through the opening, careless of the jagged weld edges, pushing himself toward the bottom through the swirling paper snow.

The space was about four feet wide. The hull side of it was curved. Hastily welded steel walled it off forward and aft from the rest of the battery bank. The remaining side was taken up by four huge cable penetrations and a run of dozens of smaller wires. There was no way to get into the adjoining cells. Under his feet was a metal grating covering the ballast; under that was the outer hull.

The compartment was empty. The money was gone, disintegrated. And there was no gold. Galloway slammed a fist into unyielding steel, hardly feeling the skin peel off his knuckles. He looked at his watch, then at the two masks above him, and pointed upward. Their stay time was over. They had to surface immediately.

• • •

Galloway coiled the torch hose on one arm as they swam back through the hull. At last the probing beam of Caffey's light showed mangled piping. The three men paused at the hole that led to open sea.

Charlene's headlight, still burning brightly, shone into the wreck. As Galloway peered out the sea around and behind it seemed darker, more impenetrable and menacing, than it had when they entered the hull. Our flashlights are getting weak, he thought dimly. They've been on since we dove. That's why the dark is so close. But the headlight made a bright path across the rock-strewn bottom.

He was exiting the wreck, his eyes on the light, when very slowly, very distinctly, a silhouette passed between it and him. Radiance spilled around the heavy body, the raked dorsals and trailing jet-plane caudals. The scissor tail sculled gently to and fro as it slid out of the beam, back into darkness.

He stopped just outside the hull and sank to the bottom. He swept his waning light after it, but it bored into blackness and vanished without trace.

Sharks generally circled for a time before they came in close. He motioned to Caffey and Keyes to come out. Keeping his light trained to the right, he launched himself toward the headlight.

This time the fish came in from above. He did not see its approach until a flick of its tail sent it curving along the bottom away from them. His light traced a dim spot along brownish-gray flank. A moment later it had nosed up and vanished into the blackness to their left, giving all three of them time to contemplate the grotesque shape that led that tapered, gracile whip of body.

A hammerhead. Probably, he thought, the one we saw on the way down. But this was no four-footer, as he'd guessed from that swift glimpse. This was mature, not far from fifteen feet long. And if this was the same shark, that meant trouble. That meant it had stayed around, feeling the strange bubbling throb the torch must have sent through the water. It had waited for its slow-swimming prey to reappear.

Because it was hungry.

Galloway turned to explain to the others, but their eyes told him they understood. He pushed past them and wriggled into the hull again. The shark was dangerous. But it was a possible danger. Whereas, he thought, the bends are certain. If he and Jack didn't get topside fast, they could be dead in a few hours.

He handed the first set of used tanks out, following it with the second. When he squirmed out with his own he gestured, drawing their eyes. He made a circle with his hands, then held the spent doubles out defensively.

—Form a circle. Fend it off with your tanks.

They nodded. Caffey bent to pick up his tanks from the bottom.

That bend saved his life. The hammerhead came from the right again, so swiftly they had neither warning nor time to move. Its fin flicked and the rush of water bowled the boy along the bottom. He recovered himself at the edge of the lit path, groping at a flooded mask. He set it, tilted his head back, and cleared it. Then he looked slowly about for his light. It lay glowing feebly in the dark, several feet away.

Come back, Jack, Galloway thought. But Caffey didn't look at him. Don't go for it, he prayed. Come back with us. Quick! He began to move toward him.

Caffey swam back toward them, abandoning his light. Galloway hauled him back under the overhang of the hull, gripping his shoulder.

The three of them picked up the tanks, holding them waist-high like shields.

Back to back, phalanxed like Greek warriors, they swam slowly out into the open. Caffey led, facing the beam. The two older men guarded the flanks and rear, hand lights stabbing at the darkness around and above them.

It'll come now, Galloway was thinking dully. It's through circling and waiting. It'll come in fast and come in for blood.

He remembered his hand then. The knuckles scraped raw on rusty steel, the black curl like smoke . . .

It came from Keyes's side, a sudden flat hatchet of head with a two-foot-wide gape beneath it, and crashed against his tanks, throwing him against Galloway. Tiller's light caught the tip of its tail for an instant before losing it again. It seemed to be turning. He braced himself. Thank God it can't stop, he thought. A shark, with its primitive gills, had to keep swimming. If it didn't, it could come in from above and take our heads off like plucking grapes.

The shark came unseen and hit Caffey again, striking so hard his tanks spun away into the dark. He gripped his wrist, groaning into his regulator. Galloway pushed ahead, sandwiching him behind himself and Keyes.

If only we could see it coming, he thought angrily. It can hear us in the dark, but we're blind. Waiting. Staring into the night, like prehistoric men watching for tigers before fire was—

Fire.

He pulled the torch from his belt, gripped it between his legs, and twisted the valves open. A storm of bubbles attacked his face, but he held on until he had set it by feel. He lifted it above his head and squeezed the lighter.

He had opened the oxygen to maximum and the flame leapt out blue-white, like an electric arc, but in a tongue of fire six inches long. It made not a roar but a continuous explosion. The light reached out sixty feet to catch the shark at the aphelion of its deadly orbit, flank to them, already turning inward.

He took advantage of the moment to look around him. Caffey had drawn his diving knife. The sliver of steel glittered in the unearthly radiance, but it was about as dangerous to a big hammerhead as a toothpick. Keyes had not yet seen the shark. He was looking backward, and Galloway followed his glance.

The U-boat, lit from stem to stern against the black, lay frozen like the Flying Dutchman in a hard roll to starboard that would last until its atoms melted into the all-dissolving sea.

He jerked his head back to the hammerhead. It had neither wavered nor slowed at the sudden flood of light. Seen head-on the shark formed a brightly lit star. It grew rapidly larger, and Galloway realized it was headed for him this time. He brought his tanks up with his left arm to cover himself, and thrust the torch out as well in an unconscious fending motion.

The shark flicked its tail and hit him. He was smashed backward and spun facedown to the bottom, hands empty. The sea flickered and went out. He flattened himself against hard sand, breathless, defenseless, waiting for the end.

Something gripped his arm. It hauled him upward and toward the still-visible headlight. He began swimming again, recovering his breath. Ten more yards. Five. Then he was climbing into the forward cockpit. He groped for a spare flashlight and looked back.

Keyes was in the rear seat, pulling off his tanks. Caffey hovered over the stern, passing the last set of fresh doubles forward. Galloway swept his light around them. No sign of the shark. Keyes tapped him on the shoulder then and when he looked up held something for him to see. The ends of the torch hoses, bitten off clean. There was no sign of the torch itself. Galloway nodded. Despite the sick silly grin sticking itself to his face, he felt suddenly immensely tired. He reached back and began the switch to the fresh tanks.

The motor hummed. They headed upward, preparing themselves for the long boredom of decompression.

• • •

"Are you sure the shark got the worst of it?"

None of them answered Hirsch. Keyes slumped in a corner, his face slack with exhaustion. Caffey, biting pale lips, was winding layer on layer of adhesive tape around his wrist. Galloway flinched as he dabbed his favorite antiseptic into the multiple cuts on his face and hands. He held the bottle up and finished with a long pull. It went to Caffey; when he put it down, choking a little, Galloway offered it to Keyes, who hesitated for a long moment before giving a tired shake of his head.

"Jack—*what happened?*"

Caffey looked up, forgetting his hand as the light of battle recalled filled his eyes. "Wow. You should have been there, Bern. Pass after pass! He was sure we were supper. I figured he might be right until Tiller lit the torch. Soon as he did, it made for him, and got it on the next strike."

"Got the torch?"

"Tiller was holding it in front of him when the shark hit him. The flame went out and the hose went whipping off after it in the dark. When we pulled it in from the tank end the cutting head was gone. Bit off clean."

"It swallowed it?"

"No, he stuck it in his pocket," said Caffey, in mock disgust. "Jeez, think about how that felt. A hot torch in its gut. No wonder it cleared out."

They noticed then that Keyes was not joining in the laughter. "Hey, there, my man. You all right?" said Aydlett.

He looked up. He looked older. Drained. "I suppose so—physically."

"You look wiped out—all of you," said Hirsch. "What's wrong?"

"I was so sure it was there . . . so sure," Keyes said in a low voice. "But it wasn't."

"What do you mean?" said Aydlett, standing up abruptly. "Not there?"

Caffey said, "Cool off, Shad. It's the truth. Zip. Zero. Nothin'."

The big man stared around. He seemed at a loss. Keyes went on, talking now to Galloway in an exhausted monotone. "I'm sorry, Tiller. Still, you're out nothing. I can cover your expenses and damages. Thanks for your help."

Galloway reached over and slapped his back. "Chin up. Think of it as an adventure. Right? Something out of the run of—what was it—marketing insurance. Whatever that is."

The tall man smiled sourly.

Hirsch said, "Wait a minute. You mean—what are you saying, Tiller? That there wasn't anything there?"

"Not an ounce. The cell was bolted shut, all right. Booby-trapped, too. But there wasn't a thing in it but a tin box."

"The gold wasn't in that?"

Galloway felt too depressed and exhausted to explain about the cash. He could still see the blocks of currency turning dreamlike into silt. "Nope. Bum steer. Goose chase. That's all."

"And the cell was empty aside from that."

"I went down into it. Not a thing. Two steel walls, obviously jury-rigged, connecting cables, and then the grid keeping some ballast from shifting."

"Then that's it," she said.

"What's it?"

"The ballast. Ballast is supposed to be heavy, right? What did they use in those submarines?"

Galloway and Keyes stared at each other. "Mercury," whispered the tall man at last. "The U-boats used mercury. Since it was liquid it could be pumped fore and aft, for trim adjustment. She's right. It's got to be what we thought was ballast."

And Bernice Hirsch put her hand to her mouth. Too late, she realized she'd just spoken a warrant for her own execution.

seventeen

It was half past two and the stars were glittering madly midway through their wheel when the companionway hatch slid back. Keyes was wearing his Birkenstocks and Galloway, nodding on a locker near the stern, did not hear him until he sat down beside him.

"Christ! You startled me."

The tall man murmured, "Didn't want to wake you if you'd dropped off. You've earned your sleep today. How's the back?"

"Not so bad. Jack gave me a couple of his pain pills. And a few stiff ones helped." He nodded at the nearly dry bottle. "I can still feel it, though. Torn muscle, most likely."

"You should have it looked at when we get back in."

"Maybe I will."

"Look, why don't you just go on below, Tiller? I'll take your watch."

"Thanks for offering. But I'm wide awake again now."

"Sorry."

"No problem. I can sleep late in the morning. Weather looks like it'll hold for a couple more days."

"Don't turn complacent on me, Tiller. We're still not sure it's there."

"I have a hunch Bernie's right. It's in the ballast."

"If it isn't?"

"Then getting up early won't change anything."

"You're a philosopher," said Keyes, from the dark side of the deck.

"No. Just cranky and half drunk."

Except for the lapping of the waves against the hull the night was quiet for a time. Galloway thought: He's making an effort to be agreeable. And it was working. At least through the haze of Percodan and alcohol. He thought of having another, and decided against it.

"Why so pensive?"

"Just thinking . . . tell me something. If it's there, and we get the stuff up, what do you plan to do with it?"

"Head for shore fast. Rent a closed truck from U-Haul or Ryder and check it into one of those rental-storage places. Then New York first, I think, on the way to Switzerland."

"I mean, what will you do with that kind of money? You don't give me the impression of needing it to eat, like some of us."

"I don't, no. But I don't imagine spending it will be too hard. It'll cost money just to keep possession. Even with bodyguards and constant travel I can't keep it hidden forever."

"I see what you mean. Sooner or later your . . . friends will put two and two together and get three. They'll come after you for the missing number."

"They understand greed, but not when they're the ones being cut out. The U.S. government might be interested as well. But I'm primarily afraid of the old men in Argentina."

Galloway waited, then asked the question. "You're a Nazi too, aren't you?"

"My father fought in the *Unterseebooten.* I told you that."

"That's right, you did, didn't you?" He leaned forward. "And I checked my father's records. He didn't pick up any survivors. His last depth charge attack killed all the men in the water. So that was a lie."

"Your ad," said Keyes, after a pause. He laughed then, startling Galloway a little. It was the first time he'd heard the blond man laugh and it was surprisingly attractive. "I guess I've got a confession to make, Tiller. I'm not exactly what I represented myself as. Hell, I've never even been to South America."

"What number story is this?"

"Three or four, I guess. Anyway it's the bottom line."

"Is there a reason I should believe this one?"

The other man shifted in the darkness. Galloway found himself holding a billfold. "Go ahead, take a look. You'll find the driver's license on top. And my personal card."

Galloway examined them. They both said Richard R. Keyes. The photo on the license was undeniably the man beside him. The card said Consulting Architect, Futron Enterprises, Houston, Texas.

"Interesting."

"Think so? You want the real story of my life? All right. Say, do you mind if I finish this up?"

"Thought you didn't indulge."

"Just a swallow. To be companionable."

"Help yourself. More down below."

Bourbon rattled into a mug. After a few moments Keyes resumed. "Yeah, it's been interesting so far. For a long time I drifted, though. Couldn't seem to get anything going.

"See, I grew up out in southern Cal. Spent a lot of time on the beach. Surfing. Not doing much. I used to want to make films. My foster parents threw me out of the house finally. I went to L.A. for a while, trying to break in, but my name wasn't Levine or Gold—you know what I mean, don't you?—so they froze me out.

"So I hit the road. Bummed my way down to Mexico City, Guadalajara, Acapulco. Worked here and there—sold hot dogs, guided tourists, danced with old ladies, did some blue movies. Got sick as a dog in Yucatan, hepatitis, and the U.S. Consul had to ship me back. Worked on the docks for a while in Galveston—"

"I could see you knew boats."

"Forklifts too. The draft picked me up there."

"That's right, you said you'd been in Vietnam."

"First Cav, Binh Dinh Province. I was wounded in White Wing, one of the early search and destroys. Stepped on a pressure-detonated one-oh-five—"

"I know those," said Galloway.

"Then you know how lucky I am to be walking around. It was as if God spared my life for some reason. Anyway that was the end of my service. They shipped me back to the States and I spent the next six months in a hospital in SanFran. It was there I realized that we were going to lose that war. Not in Vietnam, not at the front. At home.

"After I got my medical discharge I went back to school. I decided to be an architect. For a few years I tried to get grants, to design ideal communities. Arcosanti was my dream, I wanted to be another Paolo Soleri. I didn't do very well. Then I met some men in Texas who were involved in metal futures, oil, commercial land development—shopping centers and expensive, exclusive residential communities. They were movers and shakers, high rollers, the real thing. They needed talent. I stayed with them for ten years. They opened my eyes to what the real issue of our time is."

"What's that?"

"The war with communism's been lost, Tiller. We just won't admit it yet. America has power, but it can't act. The Jews and the fellow-travelers are in the driver's seat. That's why this mess keeps getting worse in Central America. We could bomb the Commies out of Nicaragua in a month. But Congress is too rotten soft.

"No, the old free-enterprise America's down the tubes. These men in Texas—they're planning now for what comes after."

Galloway said, "So you *are* a Nazi."

"No, but in some ways they weren't too far off the mark. Sure, I believe there's a race of men destined to rule others. But they're not necessarily Nordics. They may not even be white, all of them. That was the Germans' mistake, they had the right idea, they were just too exclusive about it."

"That's broad-minded of you."

"Thanks. I try to think for myself, develop new solutions. A political hobbyist, you might call me. You'll smile at this, but I was with the Weathermen for a while, in the sixties. Made speeches and organized. I was a good speaker. Even headed up a chapter in Los Angeles. Till I realized they had no real chance of achieving power. Then I lost interest and went to Mexico."

"I see," said Galloway. "Southern California, L.A., Mexico, Galveston, Vietnam, Texas. Confused kid, filmmaker, bum, architect, political hobbyist. Have I got it right?"

"Exactly."

"But if I believe that story, how do you explain knowing about the raft, the U-boat, and the gold?"

Keyes grinned. "Sharp. But obviously I did know about it. Because we found it. But everything I just told you is true too."

"I don't see how—"

"Then obviously I haven't told you everything. And I'm not going to. Not yet." There was a trickle and a thud as he finished the bottle and set it down. "You won't share the gold with me, Tiller? Since you don't understand how I knew about it, and you don't like my politics?"

"I didn't say that."

"I didn't think you would. What will you do with your share?"

"Pay off my many creditors. This tub is the only thing I own. And it's not even in my name."

"You owe a lot?"

"Maybe not that much to you. A lot to people on the island. Legal fees, things like that."

"I see. Well, you won't have that problem after this."

"I hope not."

"Tell me something," said Keyes, his voice remote and hollow from the dark. "You left the military under a cloud. I know that. But you had family. You were still respected on Hatteras. What made you dabble in the drug trade? That's a dangerous way to make a buck, isn't it?"

"None of your damned business."

"I see. Tell me, Tiller, are you a Nazi?"

Galloway said nothing for a moment, then chuckled. "Okay. Your point. I had family here, yeah. But the admiral was Coast Guard all the way through. Honor. Family name. When the service booted me so did he."

"That must have been hard to take."

"It turns you off on staying clean anymore. After that there was only one thing I could figure was worth the effort."

"Cash?"

"Cash."

"And you know," said Keyes slowly, "You were right. When I was a kid I spent a lot of time thinking about things like that. At first I thought I had a mission, that there was some destiny for me to follow. I tried politics, then I tried art. Then I grew up."

"Defined how?"

"I realized that money and power are the only things worth the attention of a man."

A full five minutes went by and neither of them spoke again. At last Galloway sighed and got up, cursing under his breath as the movement reactivated the pain. "Well . . . if you're going to stay up, check the engine room before you turn in."

"Something wrong?"

"This is an old boat. The rot's gone pretty far. Wake me or Jack if the ooze gets above the floorboards and we'll run the pump. It used to go on automatically, but . . ." his voice trailed off.

"Interesting," said Keyes, staring at him. "About the hull, that is. Okay, I'll check it before I turn in."

Galloway went slowly down the companionway to his bunk. He lay staring at the overhead for a long time before his eyes finally slid closed.

• • •

Tiller woke suddenly, in the dark, to a woman's scream.

He rolled out instantly, reaching under the thin mattress. He gasped as his feet slammed into the deck. Then drugs and booze fought back pain and he ran, free hand extended to ward off unseen obstacles. The door to the engine compartment was ajar and he pushed it open and went in.

The first thing he saw was Hirsch. She lay curled small in the filthy water of the bilge, hands raised to protect her face. Keyes towered above her, aiming another kick. When the door slammed open he turned, a snarl twisting his mouth.

The snarl froze as he saw what Galloway held in his hands.

Galloway took two steps, shifted the carbine to his left hand, and carried the swing up from his waist. The punch snapped Keyes's head into the cover of a circuit breaker. He shook himself, then raised his fists. But Galloway had turned his back on him and was helping Hirsch to her feet.

"You hurt, Bernie?"

"I think I'm okay," she said shakily. She took her hands from her face warily, looking toward Keyes, and he saw the bruises beginning to darken on her cheek and around her eyes.

"What's goin' on?" said Aydlett, coming in in his trunks. Caffey was behind him in stars-and-stripes jockey shorts. The boy saw the gun and his eyes widened.

Galloway ignored them and swung toward Keyes. "Explain," he said, his voice deadly. "Right now."

Keyes bent to the deck. He fumbled for a moment, then came up with something small. He held it out. Galloway took it, glancing at Bernie. She stood hugging herself, head down, oil-matted hair over her eyes. When he held it up to the swaying bulb his eyes widened.

"A radio transmitter."

"Jeez! Tiller, who was she—"

"Shut up, Jack. Who were you calling with this, Hirsch?"

She tossed her hair back then and raised her eyes. Despite the swift darkening of bruise they were determined, defiant, harder than he'd ever seen them.

"Friends."

"Who?" said Keyes.

She neither answered nor even looked at him. "Answer me, you little bitch," he began, "Or we'll—"

"Tiller. You told me you were going to turn this over to the Coast Guard. This is better. It's time to let somebody know."

Galloway didn't answer. He examined the tiny set once more, carefully. He and Keyes looked at each other.

He turned, and swung it against the water jacket of the port engine. The plastic cracked at the first blow. He swung it twice more before throwing what remained into the bilge.

He did not look back at her.

"Coast Guard," Keyes was repeating. "You told her—what? That you were going to call them, when we found the gold?"

"That's what my parole officer advised me to do. I don't know if I would have. But she seems to have forced my hand."

"I see. Yeah, I see it. Blow the whistle, claim your salvor's cut, and to hell with me, eh?"

"It would've been legal, anyway. We'd have gotten title to it eventually—if your story held up."

"You weren't going to do it," said Hirsch suddenly.

"Bernie—"

"No. Don't bother. I understand now." She shuddered. "You weren't going to call at all. You want that gold as much as he does. *You're just like him.*"

"I don't know about that. But you're damned right I want my share, yeah."

"You can't do this, Galloway. You can't do it to yourself. Not again."

"Go to hell," he said then. "You're not my conscience."

Still staring at him, she put her hand to her mouth.

Her scream broke Keyes's control. One stride and his hands were around her neck, forcing her down. Caffey yelled and dove at him, but the older man shrugged him off; the boy staggered into a bulkhead. "You little bitch," Keyes said, in a detached, unemotional tone. "Dirty little Jewish whore—"

The butt of the carbine made a hollow sound against his skull. Galloway, holding the rifle reversed like a bat, looked down at the crumpled figure.

"Look out!" screamed Caffey, behind him.

Galloway turned in time to duck the fire axe. The blade whacked deep into a beam and stuck. Aydlett let go of the handle. He came for Galloway, his big scarred hands held wide. Then one of them moved, to his belt. When it came back up it held a fid.

"Shad—goddamnit, what are you doin'!"

"Killin' you, Tiller. Just like I promised I would."

The six-inch taper of steel feinted toward his eyes. Galloway got the carbine up just as the point dropped and lunged toward his stomach, too fast and close to avoid. He was anticipating it in the pit of his gut when Caffey grabbed the waterman's arm from behind.

Aydlett jammed his elbow back without looking. It caught the boy in the bandaged ribs. His mouth opened soundlessly; he let go and reeled back. But by then Galloway had the barrel up, a round in the breech, and the muzzle firmly centered on Aydlett's massive chest.

"Siddown, Shad," he said.

The man glared down at him, then glanced at the barrel. For a moment Galloway thought he might try to brush it aside. His finger tightened.

Aydlett squatted slowly on the deck.

Galloway breathed out. He looked down at Hirsch. "Help her up, Jack," he said tightly.

"Right." Caffey, pale and scared, jumped to obey. He tried to lift her in his arms and failed. At last she moaned and sat up. He helped her to her feet and they moved together, stumbling on the coaming, out of the engine room.

Keeping a weather eye on the glowering waterman, Galloway moved to Keyes and patted him down. That done, he looked around the compartment, satisfying himself that there was nothing serviceable as a weapon in reach of either man. He sat down on the bilge pump and put the carbine across his lap and waited. After several minutes he saw Keyes's fingers curl toward a fist.

"You're covered, both of you. Don't bother."

Keyes propped himself up. He rubbed his head, wincing. At last his eyes steadied on Galloway and the gun.

"Is that what you hit me with?"

"Uh-huh."

"Where did you hide it? I searched this boat the night I came aboard."

"I brought it on after that."

"You can put it away now. I'm okay."

"That's what I intend to discuss."

"We're on the same side, Tiller. We are the hard ones. We both want what we can take. And neither of us cares about anything else."

"I can't trust you anymore, Dick. Especially with Shad on your side. As he obviously is."

Aydlett grunted something. Galloway ignored it, still speaking to Keyes. "Anyway, it's obvious you can't control yourself. I'm no angel. But I'm not going to let you murder people on my boat."

"You know she's ruined our chances."

"Not necessarily. Not if we move fast. You caught her transmitting. Do you think she got through?"

"I don't know."

"Assume she did. The closest base to us is Ocracoke. That's four, five hours for a cutter, even if they start right away. It'll be light soon. Maybe we can finish this up before the Coast Guard arrives."

Keyes rubbed his head again and looked at his hand. "Nice job. No blood. You really think we can get it up that fast?"

"Maybe not all of it. A good part, maybe. What have we got to lose? Jack and I will work as fast as we can."

Keyes stood up. "Jack and you and I."

"No. I'm going to lock you and Shad in here, Dick."

"No, you're not. Listen, Galloway. You don't know who you're dealing with. I advise you, don't do this to me." He moved forward, his hand open.

The safety of his father's gun made a loud click as it released. Keyes stiffened as the muzzle moved to point at him. The two men were close enough to touch.

He sat slowly back down on the deck beside Aydlett.

Galloway got up and went to the hatch. He paused there, turning to meet the others' eyes. "Listen. Both of you. Bernie may have done the best thing for all of us. She called before any of it came up. There's no way the Guard can prove we didn't intend to call them once we were sure it was there. If they'd caught us with it underway it would have been a prison term. A long one.

"But now, whatever we have on deck when they arrive, that's legal salvage. I propose we split the salvor's fee three ways. If Jack and I hump hard, Dick, when the legalities are over you'll have expenses and a substantial profit; Shad, you'll have a clear third. What do you say?"

The two men sat on the deck, one blond and blue-eyed, the other black. But the hatred glittering in their eyes was just the same.

"All right, have it your way," said Galloway finally. "Stew away down here and be damned. But don't try to wreck the engines, or open a sea cock. You'll drown, as they say, like rats."

Keyes nodded then. He cleared his throat, and with immense effort seemed to tamp down what was raging within him. "Can I say something?"

"Fire away."

"You're not thinking very well, Tiller. She didn't call the Coast Guard, as you seem to think."

Galloway lowered the rifle fractionally. He waited.

"I think she's working for someone else."

"Who?"

"Most likely, those South Americans I told you about. The Nazis."

"*What?* You're paranoid as hell, Keyes, you know that? She's Jewish! She's also a first-term parole officer fresh out of college. Working for *them?* That's not even worth a laugh."

"Then where did the transmitter come from?"

Galloway stopped. He remembered it in his hands.

"That's not Coast Guard style, is it? Okay, maybe it isn't *Die Spinne,* but it's somebody shady. Whoever they are, if they get here and we're still around, we get nothing, Tiller. We don't get a cut. We don't get a salvor's fee. In fact—"

"Yeah," said Galloway slowly, looking at him. Much as he hated to admit it, the man had hold of something. "The bomb at Harry's. I don't think she'd work for Nazis. At least knowingly. But she—well—damn it, who *would* she do something like that for?"

"I don't know, but you see what it means. Whoever they are they wouldn't want press attention, official attention any more than we do. Instead there'll be an accident. *Victory,* motor vessel, missing off Cape Hatteras, no survivors."

Galloway stared at the oiled darkness of the carbine barrel. "You're starting to make sense."

"Good."

"Except for the fact that I need this to keep you from killing someone. Maybe me."

Keyes stood up. He stretched casually and looked up at the bulb. Its stark radiance left pools of shadow under his eyes. "You forget that I need you, Tiller. I can't run *Charlene.* And you need me, to expedite and convert what we recover ashore. A parolee can't travel. Nor can he walk into a bank and ask for change for a bar of bullion. Can he?"

"No." Galloway stared at him. "Maybe you're right."

"Try me."

"What about Shad? Since he seems to be working for you now? Why, I don't know."

"We understand each other," said Keyes. "He's a good man. But maybe he'll give us his word as well."

"My word for what?"

"Not to attack Tiller again."

"If I said that I'd be lyin'," said Aydlett.

"Shad, Shad." Keyes smiled sadly at Galloway. "He's too honest for his own good."

Caffey came back and stood just inside the door. He had pulled his cutoffs on, but still looked scared. "How is she?" Galloway asked him.

"Getting cleaned up."

"Good." Galloway nodded at Aydlett, who had squatted motionless through the conversation, his eyes shuttling between Keyes and Galloway. "Shad here's decided he wants to be tied up belowdecks. There's some seizing wire in the tool cabinet there."

When the waterman's wrists were satisfactorily bound to the engine block Galloway relaxed slightly. "Let's get one more thing into the deal, Keyes. Hirsch. You don't touch her. If you so much as talk to her, that's it. The partnership's dead."

"She betrayed us, Tiller. Don't you think you're being too concerned about her?"

"You heard me. Bother her again and whoever gets here after we leave finds you face-down in the water."

"That's blunt enough," said Keyes. "That's the way men should talk. All right, I agree." He held out his hand.

Galloway didn't take it; but he did, after a long moment, drop the muzzle. Turning away, he led them up the companionway to the deck. The other man's footsteps were close behind.

I knew this moment was coming, he thought, feeling the hair prickle on his back. I always felt it when I was with him. It was like looking across the bars of a zoo into the yellow eyes of a wolf. It was caged for a time; but someday it would not be. There was always that feeling that someday the bars would be down between him and me.

But he'd made his decision. He was through hedging his bets. He'd have to let this one ride, and right or not, live—or die—with the roll.

Topside a new day was beginning. The eastern sky was opalescent and a low haze lay between the sea and the last dying star.

"Jack?"

"Here." Caffey came back from the bow.

"Here's the plan. We're going to get as much up as we can in one dive, then move out quick. We'll figure out what to do after that."

Caffey looked worried, but he nodded. "I'm with you, Tiller."

"Thanks, partner. We'll hit the water soon as we can dress out. Get *Charlene* ready." He looked at his watch. It was a little after five. "Where's Bernie?"

"Up there." He pointed toward the flying bridge. As far away from us, Galloway thought, as she can get. He climbed the ladder carefully. Raising his arms sent pain shooting upward into his neck and shoulders.

She came into his view, silhouetted against the opal sky in cotton drawstring shorts and one of Caffey's cropped Nags Head Divers sweatshirts. She was smoking a cigarette, sitting stiffly upright on the fresh paint of the flying bridge.

"Bernie?"

She didn't move. He said to her back, "I don't know what's going on in your head. I don't know why you did what you did. But I figure you did it for one reason: You thought it was the right thing. Am I right?"

She looked away from him, off to where the horizon was lighting with rose and orange.

Galloway gritted his teeth and pulled himself over the edge. When he stood above her she looked up. He could see the tracks of tears on her cheeks, but her eyes were dry and hard now.

"So. You saw what he did to me, and then you had your talk. What did you decide?"

"I'm going down."

"With him?"

"Yes."

She lowered her eyes from his face. There was no more liking, no more respect in her look. In the space of a few seconds she had become a different person, one who would spend her life hating him.

He hunkered down and unslung the carbine and laid it beside her. "Here. I'm leaving this with you."

She glanced down, then up. "I don't like guns."

"You don't have to. Listen. It's already loaded. To use it push in this button here and then pull the trigger. It's full auto, it'll keep firing till you let go."

She glanced at it again, as she would at a snake, but put her hand on it. "Why are you giving it to me?"

"To protect you."

"Who from? Him—or you?"

"I guess I deserve that, in a way. Okay." He stood up, his voice final. "If you want to use it on me feel free."

"Tiller. Wait."

"I've got to dress out."

"This won't take long. What are you trying to do? Get it up before they arrive, then run?"

"Something like that."

"It isn't right, Tiller. What's down there isn't yours."

"Whose is it?"

"The people it was taken from."

"What? They're dead, Bernie. They've been dead for a long time."

"To their heirs, then."

"Look." He glanced around the horizon, then squatted again. "Look, damn it! Who the hell are 'their heirs?' That gold came from all over Europe. Who knows who it belongs to? As far as I'm concerned, if it's in U.S. waters, it's free salvage. It belongs to whoever brings it up."

"Don't you think Israel has the most right to it?"

"Israel." He stared at her for a long moment. "Jesus, I never thought of them. . . . So Keyes was right. Okay, Hirsch, let's have it. The full story."

She looked away. "They contacted me in Morehead City. A man named Ruderman. I wasn't sure I agreed with him at first. Now, seeing what it's doing to you, I think he's right. But you didn't answer me, Tiller. Don't they have more right to it than you and Straeter?"

Galloway frowned. "Who?"

"Your new partner. He's a Nazi, an SS killer. I tried to tell you."

"He's pretty far gone, but Keyes is no German—he's one of our own far-right nuts. I think—"

"Galloway!" The voice came from below, unmasked and hard-edged now. "Tiller! You up there?"

"What do you want?"

"Jack and I are dressed out. We're waiting."

"Be right down." He put his hand on her shoulder; he felt her stiffen under the thin cloth. "We'll talk about it later, all right? Maybe we can work something out with part of the money. To square things a little. But I can't do things the way you want and wait here for them. Frankly I don't trust them any more than I do him. And one more thing."

"I thought you were a decent man," she whispered.

"Listen, damn it! If anybody—*anybody*—shows up while we're down there, don't let 'em aboard. Make them wait until we surface."

He waited for acquiescence, even a nod, but she did nothing. She was looking out to sea, and the hating look had come back. He squeezed her shoulder again and went to the ladder.

"And I thought I loved you."

It wasn't loud, but Galloway heard it. He stood by the ladder for a moment, looking back at her bowed neck. Then he turned and went below.

• • •

The water seemed colder than it had before. Galloway shivered as it flooded between his suit and his skin. The dawn light turned to ice as

Charlene dipped her nose into aquamarine. He switched the motor on to increase their downward speed. The propeller began to thrum and water tugged at his mask. He wriggled lower in the seat and brought them around, spiraling round the line as they descended.

He shivered again. He could still feel Keyes behind him. He knew now he'd seriously underestimated the man. He was far more dangerous than he'd thought. Cleverer. And more persuasive. Now that the spell of his personality was wearing off, Galloway regretted he hadn't kept him locked up aboard. He'd acted stupidly. The man behind him couldn't be trusted as a diving partner, couldn't be trusted at all. Those pale, slightly bulging eyes induced a kind of narcosis, like breathing nitrogen at seven atmospheres.

Somehow he'd won Aydlett over too. No—Galloway understood suddenly; that had taken no hypnotic spell. The man sitting behind him had simply told Shad point-blank that the fire in the little house had been no accident, that Galloway had killed his father as well as his brother Meshach.

Galloway wished then he'd had time to find out exactly what game Hirsch was playing. She was young, but she had a kind of toughness. She hadn't meant harm. Like most people her age she thought that what was right ought to be done because it was right, because that was how life ought to be lived.

He smiled tightly against his mask, remembering a time when he'd been like that. Believing that all you had to do was what was right and that life would reward you for it.

Only the world didn't play by those rules. And it seemed you only found out what the rules were when the game was almost over. Certainly he was in deep now, for stakes far higher than a ton of gold.

He was playing with the man behind him for all their lives.

He checked his gauge. They were descending, but too slowly. He pushed the nose farther down. The rush of water increased and he put a hand to his mask to keep it on.

But now, he thought, I'm old enough to know. I've got one last chance at the jackpot and this time I know how the wheel is rigged. You've got to follow the reward and not the right because the right always lies with someone else, the one with the best lawyer. The smart man always goes for the cash.

The gold below them, like everything else under heaven, belonged to whoever was smart enough, fast enough, and strong enough to take it and hold it against the rest.

The U-boat loomed up below. He kept *Charlene*'s nose down, aiming just aft of the conning tower. It grew swiftly. At the last moment he pulled the stick back and they skimmed over the deck, missing it by inches, and then dove again the last twenty feet to the bottom. The vehicle slammed into the sand. It plowed along the bottom for several yards before it stopped, nose up. He forgot to turn the motor off and the prop made a frantic chuk-chuk-chuk against the seabed before he cut it with a chop, already levering himself out of the cockpit.

Caffey was off-loading the extra tanks when he got to the stern compartment. Keyes joined them in pulling out canvas lift bags and cargo nets. Heavily loaded, the three divers made for the U-boat's side, swimming as fast as their gear permitted.

The blown-open hole yawned ahead. A school of spadefish milled aside as they approached, flashing silver and black. Galloway looked after them. Today the water was clearer than before. The sea was lit through, even this deep, with the wavering blue of the rising sun. The two other divers swam gracefully, steadily, trailing him in the gloom. Streams of silver-blue bubbles burst at short intervals from their regulators, soaring upward, expanding to great shimmering umbrellas as they rose.

He cached the lift bags just outside the pressure hull, and motioned to Keyes and Caffey to do the same with everything but one set of spare tanks apiece.

Galloway paused when he reached the interior. It was dark after the bright sea, black as the pit of a mine. He clicked on his light. Its dimness surprised him. He'd forgotten to change batteries. But it would do, now that he knew the layout of the wreck.

When the others joined him he pushed onward. Through the engine room, the generator room. He barely gave the remains by the periscope a second glance.

The compartment was just as they'd left it. He peered into the empty battery cell, sweeping his faint beam from side to side. Behind him he heard Keyes's spare tanks hit metal. Something felt odd to him. Perhaps it was the sameness. So much had happened topside in the few hours just past that he found it hard to accept that nothing had happened here. The metal box lay as he'd left it, tilted on its side, the heap of powdery rubbish silted beside it.

Except for that, nothing had changed here, 180 feet beneath the surface of the sea, since 1945.

He grimaced, angry at his wandering mind. They had to work, and work fast. He swung his legs around to slide down.

It felt like a lightning strike at the base of his back. The sudden, unanticipated agony knifed through the beginning glow of nitrogen rapture like a bayonet through a soap bubble. Red patterns kaleidoscoped behind his retinas. He slowly straightened his body till the pain backed off, then dug his fingernails out of his gloves and his teeth out of his mouthpiece. At least this time he hadn't spat it out.

He pointed to Keyes and then to the open hole.

The light blue eyes narrowed behind the mask. They flicked from Galloway to Caffey.

Keyes slid feet first into the cell, still watching them as he dropped down. Galloway leaned over the access. He sent the yellow spot of his light over the other's back, steadying it on the metal grid that formed a floor.

Keyes was bent double in the low compartment, digging at a section of grating. He lifted first with his fingers, then braced his knees against the curved portion of the hull and strained. The grid remained in place. He crawled to another and pulled at it. It too refused to move. Fastened, Galloway thought, holding the beam steady. Or more likely corroded, welded tightly over the ballast channel by rust.

—Wait, signaled Caffey suddenly. He drove himself out of the compartment with powerful strokes of his fins, sending water roiling back into Galloway's face. He was back in seconds with the hammer they'd passed on the way in.

Keyes flinched when it clanked down beside him. He hefted it, then lifted it high and drove it down. No good. Water blunted the stroke to that of a healthy infant; it bounced off the grating with a hollow clink.

Keyes reversed the hammer head, leading with the ball. Two shorter blows made the central grating shudder. Particles of rust floated free. He dropped the tool and tugged. It came up with a screech and he heaved it aside and reached down.

His hand reappeared, dragging out a pig of metal.

It was flat gray-black in their focused lights, unmarked and uncorroded. All three of them looked down at it in Keyes's gloves.

Keyes let it sag to the deck. His right hand moved to his leg, came back with an unsheathed knife. He scraped at the bar like a whittler at a stick. Thick strips of what looked like hardened tar corkscrewed down through the water. At last he stopped and lifted it to their lights. One entire face of the pig was scraped clean.

It was the color of the sun.

Keyes turned it to and fro before his mask. At last he boosted it the final foot to Caffey's eager hands. Its weight pulled Jack off balance and he scrabbled at the deck to keep from falling in. Behind his mask, as he fondled the thing, were the eyes of a boy loved for the first time. They were tranced, dazed with the presence of something so long dreamed of he'd despaired of attaining it. Galloway smiled just to see him.

Another bar came up, and a third. Looking down, he saw that Keyes was hefting each before heaving it upward. The stack grew rapidly to three and then four high around the perimeter of the hole.

Galloway reached out for one then. Joy ran through him like the lightning jolt of coke. It was here, gold, the stuff of tales and dreams, of his fortune and his future. He stripped off a glove and sank his thumbnail through tar into the hardness beneath. He tried not to think of those who had trusted last in the heavy metal that lay in growing stacks around them. Who had tried to buy off their murderers with cash. Who had laid their rings and baubles aside to step into the showers.

He looked at his pressure gauge. Time for a tank change. He signaled to Jack. They changed out and lowered a set to Keyes. He was handing up bars more slowly now, feeling far back under the gratings before dragging them out into the light.

Galloway tried to think as he cinched the new tanks. Now they had to get the stuff out. He hadn't planned on doing it all in one dive. They'd just have to lug the bars out one or two at a time.

Keyes handed up a brick and made a circle with his fingers. The last one. He pulled himself out of the well and motioned impatiently to the stack, then to the hatch leading aft.

Tiller picked up a bar and felt himself grow heavy. Each brick, barely a foot long, weighed over twenty pounds. Just outside the hull, he thought, would be the best place to spread out the nets. They could lay the bars directly on them, attach the air bags, inflate them, and go back for more. He picked up another, clutched them both to his chest, and started aft, kicking hard to keep from sinking to the floor.

The three men settled to work. They moved fast, driven by the sweep hands of watches and the luminescent faces of gauges. They passed and repassed one another in the silent, silted corridors. Their lights played over mechanisms and bulkheads. Occasionally they picked out for an instant a heap of whitened bone, hand pointing now to an empty trove.

Galloway counted ten trips for himself and stopped, sucking hard at his regulator, near the periscope well. He sank to the deck beside it. His breath creaked and roared in his ears. The depth narcosis was growing stronger. It disorganized his thoughts, filled him with a mindless gay carelessness. He fumbled for his air gauge and flogged his mind into motion. Not much bottom time left. He forced himself into movement again, biting into rubber at a renewed torment in his back.

This was no torn muscle. The boom that had slammed into his back when he was pulling Caffey free had broken something. And the ceaseless activity since then had made it worse.

But you can't stop now, Tiller-me-boy, he told himself. Every bar you tote is one-third yours. Ten trips so far, two bars each, three divers working. What was that—sixty? He'd give one each to Jack and Bern. So eighteen, he thought, are mine! He tried to work out the value of 400-odd pounds of pure gold, but narcosis was making reading an air gauge impossible, not to mention arithmetic.

He was pretty sure it would make him rich.

He lunged gasping through a fuzzy cloud shot with pain. Night and fog darkened his brain. Lift . . . haul . . . wrestle clumsily between jagged plates of steel . . . drop a weight onto the straps of the lift net . . . and go back. He came clearly to himself once out on the sand, lashing up a netful of yellow metal. Neither Caffey nor Keyes was in sight. Two of the lift bags lay scattered where he had dropped them. So three were filled and gone. He smiled at his mental ability and aimed the bubbles from his regulator into the mouth of the gaily colored bag. A few breaths sufficed to balloon it out. He let it go and watched it for a moment, his mind vague, as it rose majestically toward the brightness far above. Then he dropped from consciousness again into a region of drunken greedy instinct.

• • •

Some time later he came to himself again in the battery compartment, alone. He peered stupidly into the hole. It was empty. Won, he thought, exultation a bursting sun in his chest, a crazy grin wrapped around his mouthpiece. Safe home with the big prize, the golden reward, the payoff. Dick or Jack must have gotten the last bar. Strange, he thought drunkenly, they didn't let me know. They must have their heads in the bag too.

Something grated behind him, but he ignored it. He was rubbing his cheeks. They felt like wood. His mind meandered. His hand floated up to his eyes. He stared dully at the round black thing on his wrist. It was important, but he couldn't remember what it did.

Maybe, he thought vaguely, you've been down too long.

The idea didn't particularly worry him. Now that he had the gold it seemed an absurd fancy that he could get the bends. No. That couldn't happen to Lyle Galloway III.

Just then he noticed that he was getting very little to breathe. He dragged harder at the regulator, but got less air with each try. Reserve, his brain supplied at last. He reached back and rotated the valve. Air flowed over his tongue again and he sucked it in greedily. That meant only a few hundred pounds remained, though, and that would go fast at this depth. In fact it would be barely enough to get him out to *Charlene.* Urgency penetrated his fogged mind. He spun clumsily, then paused. His hand light was too dim now to see much, but something was different at the far end of the compartment. One of the bags, or something else they'd discarded, lay in a heap near the hatch. He swam up to it.

It was Jack Caffey. His eyes stared up through a flooded mask. He was motionless except for the gentle sway of one arm. From the side of his wet suit a curl of blood twisted like dark filigree around the hilt of Keyes's knife.

Galloway raised his light slowly to the hatch. He tugged gingerly at the dogging wheel, then braced his arm and pulled hard, ignoring the pain. But he knew already that it didn't matter. Keyes had locked it from the other side.

eighteen

When the orange fin had disappeared, the last ripple of wake merged with the sea, she pushed herself slowly to her feet. Feeling more alone than she ever had felt before, Hirsch stared around the horizon. She prayed for a mast, a plane. For any sign of help or intervention . . .

Nothing broke the empty circle of sea. Nothing met her eyes beneath the blue bowl of sky except a few high clouds and the new-minted penny of the sun, hanging just above the distant sawblade of the horizon.

She was alone. She sat down again and rubbed a hand across the fresh yacht white. The smoothness of the new paint was reassuring.

On it lay the gun. She looked down at it, exploring her bruised cheek with her fingertips. She'd fired one just once in her life. In the crime lab, her last semester at school. She hated guns. She was afraid of them. But she was more afraid of Straeter.

Not as much as she had been, though. Something new was growing in her. Something grim and determined. Yes. If she had to, she could use it.

And Tiller?

We won't think about Tiller, she told herself. He's sold out. We just won't think about him anymore, ever.

At last she picked up the gun. She poised it at her shoulder and tried to aim. It was awkward and heavy and she lowered it to her lap. She turned it over and found the safety. She pushed it in and then out again, then laid the gun aside gingerly on the deck.

That left only one thing to do. She slid down the ladder and went below to the galley. In its lockers she found kippered snacks, granola bars, canned creamed corn, Keyes's tofu, canned ham, a dried-up onion, two full bottles of bourbon, and half a loaf of nearly stale pumpernickel. She picked up the Hormel, then paused. At last she put it back. Instead she made a kipper sandwich and ate it slowly, wiping the oil from her chin.

Now what. She went into the head and washed her face. She changed the sweatshirt, which was growing hot, for a blue halter, then went up on deck again. She closed her eyes for a moment before she looked out at the sea, hoping for a gunboat. Or perhaps a rusty freighter would be more realistic. But when she opened them there was no ship in sight at all. Except for a pod of porpoises far away, sending up white splashes as their backs arched from wave to wave, the sea was completely empty.

For the first time she wondered if they were going to come at all.

Their contact had been so brief. The engine room had been hot and close. The smell of rot and gasoline had made her feel sick. She'd turned the thing on, she remembered, and called three times, at one-minute intervals, as the old man had instructed. She'd had to keep her voice low—*he* was fifteen feet away, behind one thin bulkhead—but on the third call someone had replied. The voice was so distorted with static or distance that she could not tell if it was Ruderman or someone else.

"Can you hear me?" she muttered.

"Yes. Go ahead." The voice was tiny and remote.

"I'm here. We found it, I think."

"Is it aboard yet?"

"No. They're going to try to bring it up tomorrow, at dawn."

"Good. Very good! We will be there soon," Ruderman, or someone, had said, satisfaction evident even in the distant whisper.

And then Keyes had stepped through the hatch, and she'd frozen, unable to move or speak as he sauntered toward her, till he saw what was in her hands and his eyes widened and his fist split her lips into a scream that still echoed in her mind.

She leaned over the rail. The teak was still night-cool against her arms. She looked down, into deep blue water. Ten feet of it was crystal. Thirty was smoky. A hundred and eighty was opaque as concrete. She wanted to dive in, feel the sea flow and part before her eyes. What was happening down there?

She raised her head suddenly. Off to the right—had there been a ripple at the corner of her vision? She stared till her eyes burned, but whatever it was did not repeat itself. The dolphins, she thought. For a moment she'd hoped it was *Charlene* breaking the surface.

She clicked her fingernails on the rail, then turned abruptly and went into the pilothouse to look at the clock. Only seven-ten. But it seemed as if they'd been down all morning. She looked at the starter switch. She thought of turning it and taking *Victory* miles away. Galloway's key dangled, the chain swaying with the roll of the boat. At last she shook her head. She couldn't leave the two of them out here. The third one, yes. She would leave him to the sharks with pleasure.

She remembered then what Caffey had told her about Aydlett.

The waterman looked up when she appeared at the engine room door. They stared at each other for a moment. Hirsch thought: He's so huge. She felt afraid of him too, now. But he should be safe as long as she didn't get too close. She took another step inside.

"Are you all right, Shad?"

"Not too bad."

"I thought I'd check and see if you wanted some breakfast. We have instant coffee, and I could make you a sandwich."

"Be hard for me to eat it," said Aydlett. He shifted a bit on the floorboards and she saw that his wrists, behind him, were tied to part of the engine. "Think you could loosen up one of these?"

"I don't think I'd better. I like you personally. But if you're on Keyes's side, forget it."

"Well then—"

"But I'll bring it. I guess I could feed it to you."

He looked at her steadily, then shrugged.

When she came back from the galley he ate from her hands, his breath warm on her fingers, the dark eyes flashing up at her but neither in hatred nor gratitude as far as she could tell. When he'd finished the coffee she asked him if he needed anything else.

"Kind of like to take a leak."

"You'll have to handle that yourself."

"Just joking you, Miz Hirsch. I do thank you for breakfast."

"Fine," she said coolly, and left.

• • •

On deck again she sat on one of the lockers, banging her bare heel against it, and looked at the sky. A few low clouds, wispy, more a prediction of good weather than a threat of bad, shone orange above the lifting sun. The wind was slight. Even the waves seemed lazy, as if on a day like this they felt it too much work to rock the boat. It was good weather, especially considering where they were.

She climbed the ladder again and searched the horizon. Still nothing. Ants crawled down her legs; when she slapped at them they turned to sweat. She rubbed her face and sighed, thinking vaguely about a cover cream for the bruises.

A splash came from behind her and she whirled. It was the little vehicle, orange nose pushing the sea aside as it headed toward its mother boat.

For a moment she was relieved. Anything was better than this waiting. But then she saw that only one hooded head showed above the low hull. She ran to the edge of the flying bridge and leaned, staring down.

"Tiller?"

He didn't look up. Didn't hear me, she thought. *Charlene* turned to come alongside and she heard the whir of the motor only when it stopped. Sun flashed from the man's mask as he glanced up at her. She still could not see who it was. She looked from his face to the water beyond. The top of a lift bag broke the surface a few dozen yards off, but there was nothing else. No other divers. No bubbles. He was alone.

When he pushed up his mask she saw that it was Keyes.

He dropped the mask over the side, then shrugged his tanks into the water. They sank, the regulator storming bubbles for a second before water pressure closed it. He looked up then, and saw her.

"Throw me a line."

She didn't move. The voice was low, precise, without inflection or color. She had heard it before. In the engine room. It was the voice of the other. The voice of the thing that had hidden for so long beneath the smooth, agreeable, at times even attractive man who called himself Richard Keyes.

"No."

He looked from her to the boat's side, and kicked his fins off into the water. His weight belt fell free. They too slipped from sight. He eyed the distance, swung his arms back, and vaulted aboard over the gunwale. The little vehicle drifted slowly away.

Keyes watched it for a moment and then looked out toward the bag. It had moved a few feet past the boat, carried by the current. He stripped off hood and vest and threw them too over the side.

He came to the foot of the ladder and stood looking up. At last he smiled and said, "Come down here."

She shook her head.

"All right. Then I'll come up."

He started up the ladder. She backed away. Her hands shook as she picked up the carbine and steadied it at waist level.

"Don't come any closer," she said then.

"What?"

"I said I've got a gun. Stay down there! Where are Tiller and Jack?"

His head came above the level of the deck. He was grinning.

"Oh, they're dead," he said.

She pulled the trigger. His grin flickered as he saw what she held. But he kept climbing. Then, as she struggled with the weapon, the smile came back. It was wider now, but even less human. He stepped off the ladder. As his hand closed on her wrist he began to laugh.

At the same instant her finger remembered the safety.

• • •

Smiling stupidly, Galloway followed his bubbles upward.

Silver mushrooms, he thought, bright dancing bubbles, mercury jellyfish. A passing yellowtail swerved and he saluted it gaily with his free hand.

His other was knotted in the inflated vest around a thin body. Galloway giggled into his slackening hiss of air as they lifted gracefully toward the light.

He could not remember much about the past few minutes. Another part of his mind had taken over. A part that operated without consciousness, that functioned as faultlessly, automatically, and mindlessly as an electronic circuit. Only flashes came through from time to time to his waking self. And most of them were not thoughts but simply images, so that he saw what went on without acting or willing; the tiny ever-observing point that each man considers most truly himself was only a dazed passenger.

This was how he remembered opening the hatch at the far end of the compartment, leading forward, deeper into the wreck. He remembered vaguely a cave-dim charnel house of silt-strewn bones and skulls, and here and there among them the scattered lethal ogives of 88-mm shells. A huge moray eel slid uneasily behind racked cylinders. Torpedoes. One lay half-inserted into a tube, its rails still in place. A bare ulna glimmered ghost-pale where the massive weapon had rolled sideways to crush a man. He'd looked up at the trunk to the forward hatch, seeing the loose-hanging wire now from below. You can take this route now, that part of his mind that now had control had told him quietly. It does not matter now if it explodes.

And he remembered dragging Caffey behind him all this time.

The intoxication dropped away suddenly fifty feet from the surface, leaving him with the worst headache he'd ever had. He sucked a shallow breath from the boy's tank, blinking warily around. He'd been sober enough to leave the knife in, but a thin scarlet smoke still marked their path upward. Blood in the sea . . . if a shark hit that scent trail he might have to abandon his cousin as toll for his own escape.

But not until. He wound his hand into the harness till it hurt and reached up to valve air, stopping their ascent. He was already on reserve;

he breathed as slowly as he could as the minutes of decompression ticked by. They would be dangerously abbreviated. But still he had plenty of time to remember that it was Tiller Galloway who had thought, not that he could trust Keyes, but that he would cooperate, because cooperation would help them all.

Now Keyes had the gold. And Jack had death. He stared upward, searching for the dark vee of the hull against the sky.

He wondered what he would do when he saw it.

His air gave out then. Galloway lifted his watch. It hadn't been long enough. His blood was still full of nitrogen. But there was no choice.

He went up.

He broke the surface gasping, lifting his head for real air. He sucked it in greedily. It was rich with water vapor, incredibly delicious. Panting, he glanced around as a crest lofted him.

There. At sea level his horizon was minimal, but he caught *Victory*'s truncated upperworks half a mile distant. He turned on his back and began to swim. He felt naked, like a trout fly being slowly played across the water. Like shark bait, waiting for teeth to close on his pumping legs . . .

It was a long time before he saw progress. Swimming in full gear was work, especially towing a body. But gradually the boat's cabin and then her hull rose slowly above the choppy sea. She seemed to be stern to him. Simultaneously he heard the rumble of her engines.

"Come on, kid," he said to Jack. "Come on, son. Only a couple hundred yards more. You can make it. You're a surfer, aren't you?"

But his partner didn't answer.

At last he could see the waterline. He was beginning to think he might make it when something smacked the water and went buzzing away over the sea.

I must really be tired, he thought a second later. She's shooting at me and I'm still up here waiting for it.

He dived, dragging Caffey down with him. He found the boy's dangling mouthpiece. There'd been no more air on the bottom, but up here, against the reduced pressure, he might be able to coax a few more breaths out of it.

The sea heaved above their heads. He swam in as straight a line as he could judge for fifty kicks, then stuck his head up for a fix. The pilothouse showed white to their right and he corrected course. Two more bullets whacked near his head as he surface-dived. A spent slug spiraled past, glinting copper. Jesus, he thought, that's good shooting.

Why the hell was Bernie firing at them? For a gun-shy woman she was shooting too goddamned close for his liking. The little carbine was a short-ranged weapon. Its sights were only graduated to 300 yards, and the cartridge had just enough poop to get there before it lay down.

But it was deadly at close range. And he was getting closer by the minute.

He broke water again, hardly letting the sea roll off his mask before he was back under. But this time the sea erupted around him, boiling with streaks of lead. The water turned into bubbly trails, each tipped with ten grams of heavy metal. He finned downward in near panic.

That wasn't Bernie. Whoever fired that burst had handled a full-automatic weapon before.

And that meant Keyes.

He stopped swimming. It would be suicide to close the boat now. He checked Caffey. His side was still bleeding, a thin mist of scarlet fogging the water around them.

But there was nowhere else to go. Galloway hung motionless. They were at least forty miles from the nearest land, and the Gulf Stream would carry him away from it. Not to mention sharks . . .

He turned toward the boat again.

What, he imagined desperately, was Keyes seeing? He was seeing bubbles. This shallow they'd come streaming up just behind him, a white froth in salty sea. Keyes's sights would be steadied just ahead of the trail, waiting for the black dot of Galloway's head to show.

In fact, it was the way his father had hunted U-boats. Keep them down until they had to come up for air or die. And then kill them, quickly, because there was no way to tell surrender from attack before it was too late to matter. So they came up and died . . . and young Coast Guard lieutenant commanders became admirals and heroes.

He made out a silhouette in the fuzzy green ahead. He burrowed downward as he neared it, leveling off at ten feet. When he was under the hull he reached up for a rudder skeg and held on, sucking what he knew were his last ounces of tanked air. He looked at the motionless props.

Again he tried to put himself in his enemy's mind. Why was he still here? Keyes should have simply abandoned him to the sharks and the sea. That he hadn't probably meant he hadn't got the gold aboard yet. Could he do that alone? Certainly; he could haul it aboard with the anchor winch. Then Galloway remembered Aydlett; he'd have plenty of help.

But he hadn't. He was waiting; had waited to be sure Galloway was not coming up. Waited, ready to kill.

Was it a precaution against whoever Hirsch had called—who might, if they arrived later, fish any survivors out of the sea and get the full story?

Or was it less logical than that? Was it simply that like a shark, once seeing blood curl darkly in the sea, the man called Keyes had to kill and kill again until no one around him was left alive?

Galloway wondered: What would such a man do to a woman?

• • •

The muzzle, spitting flame and sound, jolted upward in her hands.

Hirsch dropped it. It fired once more as it hit the deck, tearing a furrow through the fresh paint. Splinters stung her legs.

Keyes had stopped in mid-stride, his mouth opening. His hand moved to his body, and she saw the little tear in the black rubber of the wet suit.

He swayed for a moment, staring down at her, then went down on one knee.

He felt for the gun, his eyes still on her.

When his bloody hand found it he rose again. She watched, not believing what she saw. Gradually, even as his free hand found the hole and probed it, the smile was returning.

"Get down there," he said, pointing down to the stern with the barrel of the rifle.

She slid around the edge of the bridge, staying as far from him as the rail allowed. "What are you going to do?"

"Shut up. Get down that ladder."

"Where?" She heard her voice shaking as if from somewhere far away. She could not believe this was going to happen to her.

"Not that way. Not the bunkroom. Into the engine room."

As they came single file through the hatch Aydlett struggled to his feet. "My man. You made it back!"

"Hello, Shad."

"Where's Galloway?"

"Dead."

"Goddamn, I wanted him."

"Well, you had your chance. I just made better use of mine." Keyes turned to her. "Untie him."

She tore at the wire. Too fast; her nail broke short and she moaned a little, not remembering how this set him off till he hit her from behind with the gun barrel.

"There. It's off."

Aydlett grunted in relief. He brought his hands around and stood up, massaging his wrists. "So. Now what?"

"Well, we got some gold to get aboard. But first I wondered if you wanted some of that." He motioned to Hirsch.

Bernie was leaning against one of the engines, feeling dizzy; her legs were trembling, she couldn't stop them. Distantly she heard the waterman say, "Some of what?"

"This little tramp's on her way over the side. Just thought you might want to enjoy yourself first."

Aydlett looked at her. Bernie caught his eye, just for a moment. Then she lowered her head. He looked back at Keyes.

"You want to watch, that it?"

"That's right."

"Think I'll pass, this time."

"Too bad," said Keyes. Hirsch felt her arm seized. He thrust her through the hatch and pushed her up the stairs.

"Go back aft," he said.

Her whole body numb, she turned to obey him. It felt as if she floated rather than walked; the stern seemed a thousand yards away. Behind her she heard the waterman say, "Hey—where's Caffey?"

"He's dead too."

"And you're plannin' on killing her?"

"I will if you'll get out of my line of fire, damn you!"

"Just listen here a minute, friend. I wanted to gut Galloway 'cause of my dad. But I don't like the way the rest of this is goin'. You seem to be set on killing everybody aboard here."

Still walking, Hirsch looked from side to side, not knowing what she sought. Tiller, Jack—anyone or anything. But there was no one. The sky and sea were empty.

"Well, Shad, you got a point there."

"Good. Thinkin' we should let her go myself."

"That's not exactly what I had in mind. I was figuring on having you help me get that gold aboard. But I guess I can manage that myself."

"What's that mean?"

"It means you can join her."

She turned to look back; to see Aydlett, turning suddenly, finding himself on the wrong end of the gun. The blond man was motioning him back. Toward the stern. Toward her.

"No, go on," Keyes was saying. "We'll just clear out all the deadwood around here. It's not like I enjoy your company. Move, boy!"

"You're crazy, Keyes!"

"Get back there, Aydlett."

"We agree to split it. Okay, look, I can do without my share—"

"Too late," said Keyes. His mouth moved below the pale blue eyes. "You poor fool. Did you really think I was going to share a ton of gold with a simple nigger like you?"

Her legs began to shake. She turned when there was no more deck and hugged herself. When she raised her eyes the big waterman stood halfway between them, rigid, facing Keyes. She could see that he'd made up his mind to jump.

"You bastard," she heard him mutter.

She closed her eyes then, intending to pray. But instead, without volition or intent, she had a kind of vision. It was of Shabbat again, but this time it was no memory, she was there; she could smell it. The *schalet* in the oven, perfuming the house with simmering barley and meat and beans; the bite of phosphorous and then burning wax as her mother, throwing the shawl over her long dark hair, waved her hands before the candles and then covered her eyes for a moment before gazing with the surprised joy of a gentle child at the light. And then all the eyes, her father's and brothers' and mother's turning to her; herself moving forward, believing then, one with them, lifting her trembling match to the fresh white wick. *Blessed art thou O Lord our God, King of the Universe, who has sanctified us and commanded us to light the Sabbath light.*

The carbine cracked, a single shot, and she started. She peeped between her eyelids.

Aydlett lay like a fallen tree across the deck.

She could pray now. And she did, murmuring it half-aloud, the ancient Hebrew of the Viddui. Not for rescue, or mercy. Only the same stark words every Jew had said at death since Abraham.

The Lord is God.

The sound hit her like a thunderclap. She flinched all over. Then stiffened.

Hardly believing that she was still alive, she opened her eyes. Keyes was leaning against the rail, rifle raised, sighting on something out on the sea.

She was not alone. And not alone, she might still have a chance.

She jumped into a desperate sprint. Her feet slapped on the deck. She had to leap over Aydlett's sprawl, but Keyes never turned. As she crouched by the wheel two more shots cracked out. She could see the splashes through the window, but couldn't see what he was aiming at. It looked like empty sea.

Hirsch bit her lip and hammered her fist on the wheel. It *had* to be Tiller and Jack. He'd lied, they weren't dead. But they could never get aboard as long as Keyes had the gun.

Something dark bobbed on a crest, then vanished. A burst of fire whipped the water where it had been like a thrown handful of rocks.

What could she do? Attack him with bare hands? He'd shoot her down in an instant, and her sacrifice would not buy the others another minute of life.

She had to have a weapon. She scrambled down the companionway, into the galley. A bread knife gleamed up at her when she slammed open the drawer. A good, stout, sharp blade. She turned it in her hand. It would kill. But could she? Did she have the courage to face death in the hope of saving the others?

That was easy. If they didn't live, neither would she. If Keyes killed them she would be next.

As her hand tightened around the handle the last of her fear fell away, and something quite different took its place.

• • •

Below her, at that same moment, Galloway felt his tanks go finally and completely dry.

There was no more time. He had to put his plan, not half thought through, into effect at once. Shooting or drowning, Tiller, he thought. That's what your greed bought you. That's the prize your golden ticket drew.

You fool.

He hauled dead weight upward. Pinning it under the arms, holding it against the keel, Galloway tripped his harness. His tanks dropped away. He kicked his fins free and let them go.

He began to need air. He pulled furiously at the unwieldy parcel in his arms, grinding his teeth. At last it was positioned to his satisfaction and his clawed fingers found the buckle beneath the boy's vest.

Ten pounds of lead dropped away, and the body grew light.

He shoved it upward, and pushed himself in the same motion to the left, forward and up along the opposite side of the hull. He counted to five while the ache in his throat grew. Air bubbled from his lips. Each time he swallowed the madness went a step away. But when it came back it was worse. At "four" he tripped his own belt, watching it fall away into the deep blue abyss.

At "five" he launched himself upward, arms outstretched.

He snatched for air and for the handhold he knew should be there. Instead he got a wave in his open mouth and gripped only the smooth side of the hull. He slid backward, his fingernails chipping paint. The water closed green over his staring eyes and water filled his throat.

His body revolted, screaming red pain. It coiled and leapt upward again, legs thrashing at the sea.

Air at last—and—his arm scrabbled along the side—a handhold. His fingers locked. He hauled himself up and got his other arm over the gunwale. The first thing he saw was Aydlett, face down and unmoving. So Keyes had disposed of him, too, when he'd got what he wanted from him. Galloway threw a leg up, twisting his torso, and was reaching for his knife when a nova exploded in his back.

His mouth opened in a soundless cry, his eyes rolling upward. His legs jerked and his hands drummed against the inside of the gunwale. The knife thudded to the deck on the far side.

The sound was obliterated by three shots close above.

He came back from the nonself of unendurable pain to find his body slipping toward the waves. He tried to pull it back. Caffey's floating corpse wouldn't fool Keyes for long. But his arms were quivering taut on the gunwale just keeping him where he was. He tried to get a foothold, but nothing happened.

He realized that he could not move his legs.

Galloway slipped farther. He hung face-down over the water, staring down into it.

This, he thought, in the blinding clarity of the final moment, is where you brought yourself at last. Your grandfathers risked their lives for strangers, for ten dollars a month. Your father fought at sea, defended his home, for a hundred. It was not the money that made them heroes. It was because it was their duty.

He had sold their honor and destroyed his own, for cash. And now he'd sold his life, and the lives of others, for a golden ticket that led only down forever into the glittering sea.

The waterline sucked at the waves, dripping barnacles, and a stink of rot came up from it. Only one arm held him. He closed his eyes as weakness and nausea swept over him. He wanted to let go. To drop back into the cool green and never leave it again, to drift downward into the dark sleep . . .

The sirens were singing. But something deep, something he'd never called on before, had not yet given up. It held yet, though it could not prevail. He felt his fingernails tear off as they slid slowly up the inside of the gunwale. Then he heard steps. He closed his eyes again, and waited for the merciful shock of a bullet.

A hand grabbed his hair. Another took his shoulder. Galloway groaned once as he was hauled bodily back over the gunwale. The rest he bit back. He half-fell, was half-dragged to the deck and across it into shadow. He waited till the pain had lessened a little and opened his eyes.

The pilothouse roof was over him and Hirsch's face was close above his. She was whispering. But more shots from above drowned her words. Faintly, after the firing stopped, he could hear the tinkle of empty cartridge cases dancing on plywood above them.

"What?" he muttered.

"Where's Jack, Tiller?"

"That's what he's shooting at. He's already dead. Keyes killed him on the bottom."

"He shot Shad a moment ago."

"I saw."

"He was going to kill me next." She lifted her head and looked swiftly back to the deck. She put something in his hand: his diving knife. "We've got to try, Tiller. If we both go up at the same time, on opposite sides—"

"Whoa. Don't think I can do that."

"Are you hurt?"

He tried hard, looking at his legs. Sweat dripped from his forehead. "No gŏ. I can't move them."

Her eyes were fierce. "All right. Good-bye, Tiller."

"Wait. Goddamn, Bernie, don't!"

She paused, halfway to the ladder. "You know he'll kill us anyway."

"I know. But don't go up after him. Wait at the bottom of the ladder. Let him start down. He'll only have one hand free then. It's not much, but . . ."

She nodded.

Silence had succeeded the last burst. Galloway dragged sweat off his face. He visualized the other man peering down, trying to make out the features of the floating corpse. Or would he be satisfied that now both of them were dead?

Footsteps sounded on the deck above, heavy, dragging. They neared the ladder. Hirsch slid catlike to it, gripping a gleam in a pale hand. She crouched, and her lips drew back.

And Galloway, watching her, suddenly saw something else new in the new clarity. It was about her. She hated violence. She tried to stop it, not by punishing, but by healing those who dealt in it. She was an intellectual. By his standards she was naive. She would not fight until she had no other choice. But then she turned savage.

He knew then that Keyes, despite the gun, had no more than an even chance of living through the next ten seconds.

"Galloway!" The voice above them was harsh and strangely high-pitched.

"Here."

"Somehow, it doesn't surprise me. But how did you do it?"

"Just luck," said Galloway.

"You know I've got to kill you both now," said the voice above them, still high, but strangely reasonable.

"Why's that?"

"Because if I don't you'll kill me."

"Whoa now." He glanced at Hirsch; she was holding her crouch by the ladder. "I've got no such intention."

"You're a dangerous man, Galloway. You killed Aydlett's brother. And his father. You'll kill me if you have half a chance. This is self-defense."

Galloway raised his voice. "What about Jack, Keyes? Did I knife him too?"

"He surprised me. I thought he was going to attack me. But I didn't kill the old man."

"Who did?"

"Don't play coy with me, Galloway! You're just like me. Out for yourself. Well, now it's you or me. I'm sorry—I respect you—but you've got to die."

A diving boot appeared on the topmost rung. Blood dripped from it.

Below the ladder, Hirsch brought the knife up, staring at the blade.

A voice rolled over them, slow, guttural, and enormous. The boots paused. Hirsch jerked her head around, and her eyes seemed to congeal.

Galloway, seeing her look, dragged himself up with his arms, careless of the pain, till he could see through the bottom of the windshield. "Damn," he muttered. "What—"

"It's him," Bernie said. Her hands leapt to her face.

"Who?"

"Ruderman. The man I called!"

Not a hundred feet away, a short old man looked down on them from a glistening black tower. He lowered the megaphone and gestured to someone below. As Galloway stared, beyond thought or understanding, two other men appeared beside him. They carried submachine guns, which they immediately pulled to their shoulders to aim down at *Victory*'s deck.

nineteen

"I repeat: Put down your weapons now or I will open fire."

The three of them were motionless for a long moment, staring up at him.

Keyes was the first to move. He came slowly down the last steps of the ladder. He did not look at Hirsch, nor she at him.

"This is your last warning!"

He bent then, and placed the carbine on the deck. When he straightened he lifted his head for a long moment, looking across the water, then reached out to support himself on the rail. Blood seeped from the anklets of his wet suit.

Galloway, too, was staring up at the submarine.

The old man was leaning over the coaming of the conning tower. His gray hair ruffled gently in the breeze as he looked silently down at them. The two gunmen stood motionless on either side. A moment later two sailors appeared behind them, cradling heavy machine weapons, which they set up in mounts and swung to cover the boat. The old man glanced at them and said something that did not make it across the water.

Bernie raised a hand, hesitantly, and waved. Looking down, Ruderman lifted his palm slightly in return.

Galloway, once the astonishment passed, pulled himself up into the chair at the wheel for a better view. Generally submarines looked much alike, but this one struck his eye oddly. The tower was grayish-black, faired smoothly into the hull, which was slowly coming into view above the surface amid a rumble of bubbles. Still ballasting up, he thought. In contrast to the smoothness of its topside lines the underwater hull was foul with sea grass. It rolled ponderously, even in the light swell. The whole ship looked out of proportion. It took him several seconds of observation and progressively greater puzzlement before he realized why. It was smaller than any sub he had seen before, not much longer than *Victory*, though the deep hull would displace several times the tonnage of the old PT.

When three feet of freeboard showed, a steel shoal heaving slowly in the blue sea, a hatch hinged open in the deck aft of the tower. Two men climbed out. They were dressed entirely in white. A shapeless bundle came up after them, pushed from below. It was unrolled and half inflated before Galloway recognized it as a rubber dinghy. Moving quickly, they launched it from the side of the sub, then looked up expectantly to the man atop the conning tower.

Ruderman raised the megaphone again. "On the *Victory*. There are five of you. I want everyone out in plain sight."

Bernie stepped to the side, moving past the motionless Keyes without looking at him. She cupped her hands to her mouth. "Jack Caffey . . . he's in the water . . . dead. Straeter killed him. He shot Shad Aydlett too."

Galloway, watching Keyes, saw the blond man sag suddenly into the wood. Yet he said nothing.

Ruderman nodded. He lowered the megaphone and called something down to the two in the dinghy. They started a motor and cast off. As they came closer Galloway saw the weapons in their hands.

The raft circled at a safe distance, inspecting them, then returned to the submarine. It nuzzled the ballast tank, bobbing uneasily as Ruderman and another white-suited man clambered down into it from the deck. When they sat down the buzz of the outboard rose to a whine. The little craft backed off, spun in a tight circle, and headed straight for *Victory*'s stern, bounding over the swells like a porpoise.

A man of about twenty, with close-cut blond hair, was the first on the diving platform. He looked them over carefully, blue eyes cool over the short barrel of a submachine gun. He flicked them away only to take a turn on a cleat with a line that sailed up from the raft.

One by one the others climbed over the transom and fanned out on deck. A chunky man with spiky brown hair and a readied automatic bent to Aydlett. When his fingers came away bloody he rolled the waterman's limp bulk into the scuppers. A slim swarthy man followed him up into the cockpit. He was armed too. He kicked the carbine down the companionway steps. They spread out, weapons ready, and stood waiting in silence.

Ruderman, his hands empty, climbed cautiously over the transom. The blond boy gave him a hand up. Like the others he was dressed in white, a loose coverall with the sheen of nylon. The first thing he did was unzip a pocket and pull out a pack and a lighter. When he had a cigarette lit he propped his hands on his hips and looked them over. Gradually a smile deepened the furrows around his mouth.

Bernie began to laugh. "You came just in time. He was about to kill us." She started toward him, arms outstretched.

"Stop there," said Ruderman. "Karl, if she comes another step, cut her down."

"Jawohl," said the swarthy man, studying her.

Galloway struggled to sit upright.

Hirsch stopped, her hands still out. The old man regarded her with a half-smile of amusement or irony. "Thank you, Miss Hirsch. For your help. But now it is time to shatter your little dream."

"What do you mean?"

"Get back by the cabin. We'll discuss you two in a moment."

She heard the iron in the tone. She paused for a long moment, her face blank, then moved back to stand beside Galloway. Putting one hand on his shoulder, she faced the men with the guns.

Keyes was alone now, facing them. He slumped against the gunwale, holding himself up with one arm. The pool around his boots was growing.

"It's you I'm interested in first, Mr. Keyes. Did you really expect to succeed in this? Barefaced theft of our property?"

"I thought so," muttered the tall man, in tones the two in the cabin could barely make out.

The short man laughed. "You underestimated us. That is a mistake Americans often make. Why, I really think you are surprised to see us."

"No. But I didn't expect you to show up like this. Nor so soon."

Ruderman nodded. He looked down at the deck. "I see that you have been hurt."

"It's not too bad. She missed the lung."

"Lucky for you. Do you want a doctor? I have one aboard."

"A doctor," repeated Keyes. Surprise was mixed with wariness in his voice. "Are you serious? I mean . . . sure, I could use some help."

"Perhaps in a few minutes, Mr. Keyes—if I get the right answers, and quickly."

The old man turned, to address all three of them, and suddenly there was no more humor in his face. "Now. I want to know a few things. No evasions, no lies. I don't have time for them. First. Where is the gold?"

"Under the lift bags," said Galloway. He glanced at the compass, then pointed. "The Gulf Stream's going north—you'll find them off in that direction, not very far."

Ruderman snapped orders in rapid German. Two of the three bodyguards went back over the transom. The youngest and blondest remained, gun level, finger on the trigger. As the dinghy whined away the old man walked slowly toward the cabin. Bernie's hand tightened on Galloway's shoulder as he stopped two feet away.

"Hello again, Bernice. And this must be Captain Galloway. I'm pleased to meet you at last."

"You know my name. Is Ruderman really yours?"

"As good as any, and better in most circumstances than some." Faded hazel irises surrounded by nets of sun wrinkles studied him. "You seem relaxed, Captain. That impresses me."

"Thanks, but it's because I can't get up. Something's wrong with my legs."

"How did that happen? Was it—" he glanced at Keyes—"his doing?"

"Mine as much as his, I guess, when you add it all up."

"Would you like my doctor to help you?"

"Your Nazi doctors don't have a real good reputation. I'd rather just have you let us go."

Ruderman laughed. "Warrior stock! And you were one yourself once. It shows. . . . As you wish. But we could give you something to ease your pain."

Galloway shook his head quickly, before he could think too much about it.

The old man shrugged, and turned to watch the submarine. An opening yawned in the afterdeck now, some sort of repair access, and a collapsible davit had been rigged over it. A swimmer was already attaching a line to one of the lift bags; the dinghy was towing another toward the ship. An electric motor hummed. The boom groaned but held as the bag collapsed and the net beneath came up dripping from the sea.

"Yes, excellent," breathed the old man. He crossed the deck and stood, once again, in front of Keyes. "Now. There was something else. A bronze box. Perhaps you recall it?"

"We found it. But it was ruined—"

He screamed as the old man's fist came into his chest.

"It's true," said Galloway, from behind them. "We found the currency. It must've been millions. But it was in the water too long, and the acid in the batteries . . . anyway, it came to pieces in our hands."

"Captain, I hope that is the truth. There are good ways to die. And there are bad."

"No, it's true. I pulled it out myself." He hesitated, then decided he might as well ask, might as well know what they'd all died for, now that it was all over. "Where did it come from? The money, and the gold?"

Ruderman raised his eyebrows. "You haven't understood?"

"Not entirely."

Through the window Galloway saw the davit dip again, saw the U-boat list as a second netful surged upward into the light, hung, spewing water, then was swayed aft and lowered into the hull.

The old man stared at him for a moment longer, then lifted his eyes. He examined the high clouds, the horizon, then shouted harsh Spanish over the sea. On the conning tower a man came to attention, then raised binoculars, began to search the sky. Ruderman turned his attention back to Galloway. "It is strange, Captain, that after your father almost wrecked our plans, you should have set them right again. Strange, how you and the Tarnhelm have become intertwined."

"Oh—your message. Some kind of magic helmet that makes you invisible, wasn't it?"

"Invisible, yes; but more than that; its wearer could change into any form he desired." The old man reflected; at last he went on, a little reluctantly. "In the old myths it was the key to recovering the Ring of the Nibelungen, you see. That gave power over gods and men; it alone could rebuild shattered Asgard, after the destruction of the old gods . . . I suppose that is what it meant, to the man who chose it." Ruderman stared at Keyes, who was breathing shallowly. Flecks of blood stained his lips where he had bitten them. "Heinrich was fond of the old myths, maybe too fond. . . . Mr. Keyes did not tell you what it really meant?"

"The gold, I guess."

"Nothing more?"

"I don't think he knew anything else."

"Perhaps our deepest secrets are still secrets, then. And that is good. But you, Captain Galloway—I want you to know them. For a reason, as you'll soon find out. As for you two—" he smiled tightly at Hirsch and Keyes—"I see no reason for you not to hear this. You may be interested. And I don't think we'll have to worry about undue publicity."

He chuckled and eased himself down on one of the lockers, not far from Keyes. The wounded man stared at him, his face pale as piano keys; Galloway wondered how far he was from shock. Behind Ruderman the young blond stood alert, his eyes dangerous as the muzzle of his gun.

"Operation Tarnhelm—it is of course the same word in German—was one of three that the SS planned in early 1945 for execution after the defeat. It was the last one, and the most important."

A siren wailed across the water. Ruderman stood up and shaded his eyes. When he sat down again he was smiling. "It was an ambitious plan, but perhaps too romantic. Like many plans our . . . former leadership made. But we've finished loading. One phase of it, at least, is finally complete."

Galloway nodded, glancing at Bernie. She was staring at the old man, her face dead. "Go on," he said, switching his attention back. "What else was it about? If it wasn't just the gold."

"First things first. In May of 1945 I was a young officer in the SS. Junior, but with an excellent record in the East. I was called to Berlin to receive my orders from Himmler in person. I was to go to the naval base at Kiel-Wik and take charge of two cargoes. One had come by train from Silesia in East Prussia. The other I brought from Berlin myself."

"He's not Straeter," said Hirsch suddenly, "*You're* Straeter. All those things you told me about Keyes—that was *you.*"

The old man bowed slightly toward her from his seat, but his eyes stayed on Galloway. Tiller nodded. "The train—that would be the gold."

"Exactly. In Kiel I found that the Germania Werft shipyard had readied two U-boats for the mission. Both were of the newest types—"

"*Two* U-boats?"

"Yes. One was the new diesel model. Larger and faster than the older diesels—there would have been no Western Front had we had it in 1943. The other was something entirely new. A smaller craft, but with unlimited diving time. Thirty knots speed underwater. Totally self-contained propulsion." He nodded into the sun, toward the sleek gray-black shape. "The Walter boat."

Galloway ran his eyes over it again. "I've read about 'em. Wasn't there some problem with the fuel?"

"There was. Concentrated hydrogen peroxide is deadly stuff. Corrosive, sensitive, and terribly explosive." His withered hands plucked at the coveralls. "One of the many precautions we have to observe. I can't smoke aboard, for example. But as you see, we coped."

"You've kept her in good shape."

"Four decades is not long for well-maintained machinery. There are older ships in your Coast Guard. This boat was lying on the bottom of a river for most of that time. Fresh water—and an excellent hiding place.

"But to return to my story . . . we left Kiel for Argentina. Both U-boats, in company. But off Hatteras we met a certain young destroyer captain, who crept up so quietly and skilfully on a snorkel wake that we were taken by surprise."

Galloway strained to remember the action report, read by a flashlight in a room where he was no longer welcome. "That explains something that puzzled me. It was the second U-boat—yours—that torpedoed the *Arnold.*"

"Who? Oh, the other destroyer. Yes."

In his effort to remember, Galloway saw a light flicker on in his mind. He imagined men running across the decks of a stricken submarine, falling under a hail of fire. Men plunging into the dark sea for refuge. And then, suddenly, the whole scene obliterated by an inexplicable detonation.

"You torpedoed the other U-boat, too," he said slowly. "With your own men aboard."

"Kapitan Dietz did that, yes. He is dead now. But I ordered it."

"Why?"

"It was necessary. If your father had not killed them all for me, I would have had to." His eyes crinkled at Galloway's naiveté. "If they were captured they might have been forced to talk. What they knew was that important. Believe me, they would have understood, even agreed. They were the cream of the Party."

"I see."

The old man looked again at the waiting submarine, then at the sky; finally, glancing at Galloway from his seat on the locker, lit another cigarette. "Your father's unexpected attack, the sinking, checkmated me for a long time. Frankly, we didn't know where we were that night. It had been a long run from Germany, and the Allied raids had made it impossible to get ball bearings for our gyrocompasses. We knew we were off North Carolina, but the exact location of the sinking was a mystery.

"But now, at the end, I win. All worked for the best; all mouths were stopped; the gold was preserved for us, till now, till we are ready to make use of it.

"You know, as I grow older I find that destiny, or the historical process, has a certain symmetry. Those who study it learn much. Those with both knowledge and a steel will, they are the ones who eventually rule. No matter how numerous the littler men who oppose them."

"What's that supposed to mean?"

"We are wiser now than we were in 1945. Far wiser than in 1939. We will not aim for world domination this time. At least, not right away. We will not make the same mistakes again."

"New ones, eh?"

"Perhaps. But the combination of this gold—and this U-boat—"

"Will do what?"

Straeter laughed then. "You aren't thinking, Captain! Please exercise your imagination. We made a five-day passage here from South America, undetected by Coast Guard planes or boats. We have been off Hatteras for a week, yet the Drug Enforcement Administration has no idea we are here. There is a certain export commodity in great demand in the United States. The market requires approximately a hundred metric tons of it a year. Our cargo capacity is five tons—ten if we carry no torpedoes. Do you perceive a business opportunity?"

"You could wrap up the cocaine market," said Galloway. "You're right, it's sweet. Who thought of that?"

"I did. All we needed, really, was operating capital—and now we have that too. So you see that things have not worked out too badly. At least for that part of the operation."

"That's right, you said there were two parts to it. Two shipments."

"Yes. Only the second was not an it."

"The second was a person?"

"Exactly. Actually, he was originally the most important element of Tarhelm."

"Who was it? One of the big boys?"

Ruderman, or Straeter, laughed. "A 'big boy.' Not at all. No, not at all."

A shout came across the water to them; the old man acknowledged it with an impatient wave of the hand. He glanced at the silent Keyes. "We will be submerging soon. Let me make this brief. The time, 1940. The scene, the Universum-Film Aktiengesellschaft cinema colony in Berlin. A popular actress disappears from view for a time. There is speculation, but nothing appears in the Party-controlled press. Actually she is in Northern Italy, where in December she is delivered of an infant. All in the greatest secrecy, because this news would have been a political disaster for Germany.

"As the boy grew older, and the early victories turned to ashes, it became even less possible for the father to acknowledge him. Later there was defeat and occupation to be considered. Early in 1945 it was decided to send him out of the country. A haven would be found, somewhere he could safely pass the years to manhood. When Himmler briefed me about it I thought it was a good plan. More, I thought I knew the perfect place for him to live. Unfortunately, though we got away from Germany in time, something went wrong. We off-loaded him in time, before your father attacked us, but the child was lost."

"Whose was it?"

"Her name is unimportant now. As I told you, she was an actress in Goebbels's UFA studios. Very beautiful, a tall, natural blond; a striking woman. She was often seen at high diplomatic functions before the war began."

"And the father?"

Straeter shrugged impatiently. "It's all so long ago, so futile—it depresses me to think about those times. Enough talk! A patrol could fly over at any time." He gestured to the guard; the man raised his gun. Galloway felt for Bernie's hand, felt her stiffen beside him.

"Just a minute," said Keyes suddenly. "Just a minute. I need to tell you something."

"I have no more time for you."

"You'll want to hear this. It's about the raft."

The old man paused, his hand still lifted. After a moment he sighed. "The raft? Very well, go on."

"Yes. You haven't mentioned it."

"No, I have not. What about it?"

"This person—this child—was on it."

"Yes, of course. That was how we planned to hide him. Here, in America, with English-speaking SS men as his 'uncles.' Where better? They would land on a deserted coast, bury the raft, and disappear in the population. They had money, documents, ration cards, everything I could think of. But something went wrong."

"Real wrong," said Keyes. "Especially for the four people in it."

"Three," said Galloway, without thinking.

"Be quiet, Captain. Mr. Keyes has something he wants to tell us." The old man's eyes glittered cynically.

Keyes braced himself. His face was drawn, his voice little more than a murmur; he was holding himself erect with will, not strength. "There were four people in it that night. Weren't there?"

"Yes. Yes, There were."

"No, I remember when my brother's 'dozer uncovered them," said Galloway. "The paper next day said *three*—"

"Shut up, Galloway! Let's finish this. Go on, Mr. Keyes. How do you know there were four?"

"It's the first thing I can remember," said Keyes, whispering now.

The hypnotic, slightly protruding blue eyes slid closed, then opened. "I was real small. Four? Five? But I remember that night."

Straeter sat down on the locker, passed the gold-housed flame over another cigarette. Without looking behind him he gestured; the bodyguard, still holding the submachine gun, moved back to the stern, out of earshot. "Go on," the old man murmured.

"I remember leaving somewhere safe, where I'd been happy . . . then fear, a long time in a cramped small bed. I ate from a bowl with an anchor on the bottom. Then I remember night. The smell of rubber. The softness of the bottom of a raft. And the way it swayed to the waves. The dark.

"Then we went ashore. The people with me spoke in low voices. I was lifted out of the raft and set gently on sand. Wet, hard sand. I was cold. Then I remember being frightened, terribly frightened. There was someone else, out there in the dark. They shouted at us in a strange language. Then the flashes began. The shooting. I don't know how it started. I was pushed down, someone pushed me into the sand, to protect me I suppose."

"What happened then?" said Galloway.

"One of the others, the men from the dark, found me there, took me away . . . I woke up later in a house with a strange woman. She seemed old to me; she might have been middle-aged. She fed me. That's all I remember for a while. Then later there were my stepparents, and a new language to learn. And after that, my childhood. What went before it was like a dream, or something that happened in a nightmare. But I remembered it. I knew I had to, if I was ever to find out who I really was.

"So I have to ask you. Tell me, if you know—who am I?"

Galloway looked at Straeter. The old man looked unsurprised; almost bored. But he said, "The three in the boat. Describe them."

"Two of them I don't think I knew. They were men. Dark clothes. I was afraid of them. The third I remember better. She carried me sometimes, sometimes I held to her hand. She had long blond hair. She called me . . . *Puppchen.* I never saw her again after that night."

Straeter stood up slowly. At last he said, "Well, there it is."

"Don't apologize. There wasn't any way you could have known. I didn't know myself."

"You remembered that night. And you read about the raft being found—"

"And I came back."

"For the gold?"

"That attracted me. Sure. But I hoped there might be something else too. Maybe I could find out who I really was."

"I suppose, you know, I should beg your pardon."

"For striking me? Forget it. You thought I was a thief. Now things are getting clearer." Keyes glanced at Galloway. "As long as we're straightening things out—you did kill him, didn't you? Old Aydlett?"

"I thought you did," said Galloway.

They looked at Straeter; he nodded casually. "Yes. And the old woman."

"You killed Mrs. Baum too?"

"We were closing off all leads."

"That's inhuman," said Galloway. "She couldn't hurt you. She was ninety years old! What was the sense in that?"

"Tiller. Cool it." Keyes flicked his fingers. "I understand him. They were old, useless; she probably welcomed it. And I planned to hit Aydlett later myself, after all this was over—for killing my mother."

Bernie whispered, "Who *is* he? Keyes?"

"Watch." Galloway looked at the two men.

Straeter bent forward, peering up into the face of the man before him. Then he straightened, seemed to reflect for a moment. Suddenly his right arm shot out.

"Yes, I see him there," he said softly. His chin lifted; for a moment his age-worn face looked seventeen again. "It is truly Siegfried, son of Odin. The anointed.

"We saved the ideals, the money, the Party, for him. For years we worked in the darkness. Anonymous. Silent. For forty years we accepted the judgment of our enemies' lying 'history.' We gloried in it!"

His head lifted. He spoke to the sky.

"Tarnhelm has succeeded! In disguise he grew to manhood. Now he returns, just as we planned so long ago. Our leader. Our Führer!"

His voice had a queer, bitter sound. Yet his eyes lit with an old fire as his arm shot out, held high, palm outward and fingers together.

"*Heil Hitler!*"

Galloway's spine prickled. It was the same declaration of faith and hatred that had sounded over these waters on a dark night forty years before. That had been unheard for so long the world had forgotten there were still men who believed in everything it meant.

"Do you know now?" he muttered to Hirsch.

She nodded, trembling.

Keyes's blond hair rippled in the sea wind, gleamed in the rays of the morning sun. Casually, almost negligently, he raised his arm to return the salute. Galloway followed his glance toward the black ship that rolled a hundred yards distant. Keyes—he supposed he ought to think of him by a different name now—was smiling. It was the smile of a man who knows at last who he is, and what he is; who accepts it, who glories in it. Not for what was past. But for what lies ahead.

The old man lowered his arm slowly. The light ebbed from his eyes. He looked down, then around the boat, as if trying to remember where he was.

"For his sake, I suppose—for the sake of all I was then, all we were and dared together—you deserved that salute, Mr. Keyes. I was wrong to think I could deny it to you."

"Thanks," said Keyes. "You did well. And I'll reward you. Let's get over to the sub, shall we?"

Straeter didn't seem to hear him. He went on, looking out over the Atlantic. "Yes, we put you ashore. But then, unfortunately, we lost track of you. But I knew someday you would return here. I was content to wait."

"Sure," said Keyes. "Let's get moving, okay? I've got a lot of questions to ask. And we've got a lot to do."

The old man turned, and called roughly in Spanish to the boy with the gun, who had stood at the stern through the conversation. He moved up beside them now.

"What's going on?" said Keyes.

Straeter said slowly, "I spent forty years in exile because of your father's mad ambition. He destroyed Germany. He nearly destroyed the Party. You helped us find the gold. For that, thank you. But for the rest, Mr. Keyes, for what we plan now, you would be merely an inconvenience."

"What? What are you talking about, Straeter? If you're threatening me—"

The old man nodded to the boy with the gun. "This is Ramon, one of our newer members. He only understands a few words of English; simple commands, that sort of thing."

"Hello, Ramon," said Keyes.

"Shoot him," said Straeter.

A single shot cracked out, and Keyes, his face unbelieving, sagged slowly to the deck.

Straeter looked down at him for a moment longer. The blond man lay motionless, eyes closed, in a pool of blood. Finally the old man turned his back on him, and cleared his throat. "Well. I believe this is all the business we have for the present, Captain Galloway. So now I will say good-bye. Will you do me the honor of accepting a gift?"

Galloway felt Bernie's look. Her eyes were burnt holes in a white face. He looked back at the old man. "You mean you're letting us go?"

"Letting *you* go, Captain Galloway. Oh, don't think it is an old man's emotionalism. We have nothing to gain from killing you. The nature of the gift will guarantee your silence.

"But, more than that, I would like you to work with us. When we begin our deliveries, I don't want to risk coming close inshore. We could use someone with a boat, and with your background and contacts, to offload and distribute our cargo—to administer, shall we say, the North American end of our new business." He shifted his smile to Hirsch. "The *Judin,* naturally, will be coming with us. My men will be glad to entertain her for a time. But yes, we will let *you* go."

"You're filth," Bernie said. "You'll fail, you'll all be killed this time. The world is different now."

"That's right, my dear," said the old man, as if to a child. "The world is different now. Far different! Terror no longer shocks. Mass killing is no longer even news. The West is dead from within, riddled with Jews and Communists, rotten with drugs and luxury. Yet there is no hurry. We will take our time, build up our position in Central America. In a few years its people will turn to us as the only alternative to communism. Now the future belongs to us—once more."

A bar of metal came up over the transom. The bodyguard staggered at its weight. When it thudded into the deck he turned again, reached down, and brought something else up too. Lighter than the metal. But this time his fingers lingered on it as he laid it beside the ingot. Visible through the thick plastic, double-wrapped, was a white, powdery substance.

"Two kilos," said the old man. "Pure, uncut Bolivian. Street value, let us say, a quarter million. I hope this repays you for your trouble."

Bernie turned to him then. Galloway saw that her cheeks gleamed with tears. "Tiller—you can't take it. You can't go along with this—"

"He can and he will. He is *ein besonnener sachlicher Mann.* A realistic man. Aren't you, Captain?"

But Galloway did not reply. He was staring down at the two objects, lying side by side on the bloody deck. Gold. And cocaine. Wealth beyond the dreams of the people he had grown up among. Pleasure to escape the hell of being what he'd become. Together they were all he had ever wanted. But that was not all he saw. For at the edge of his vision, he was also watching a hand.

The hand was pale and streaked with blood. Behind the two men who watched Galloway, waiting for his answer, it groped slowly over the smooth wood of the deck. It moved closer, centimeter by centimeter, to a piece of serrated steel and black plastic that lay forgotten between a locker and the gunwale.

It was Galloway's knife.

It was Keyes's hand.

twenty

Galloway sucked in a breath, fighting to keep his eyes steady on the bronze glints of the old man's.

As he shifted in his chair the pain seemed to move. It trickled down his spine and fell, drop by drop, into a sensationless void. That's where the trouble is, he thought. Something pinching or cutting the spinal cord. Aggravated by too-hasty decompression; nitrogen tended to accumulate at a site of previous injury.

He dropped his gaze from Straeter to the ingot. It lay canted on the deck. Silver drops spotted its black surface. It was one of the first that Keyes had passed up to them, for the coating was peeled back from one edge and the metal shone underneath as warm and yellow as sunset across Pamlico Sound.

"Well, Herr Kapitan?"

But Galloway was studying the plastic-wrapped bundle now. Uncut, he was thinking. He'd never sold, but he knew there were two ways he could go. Step on it hard with lactose or borax, then ounce it through some men he'd met in Raleigh. Or sell it as it was, in grams, a little at a time. Either way the old man's snap estimate wouldn't be far off.

And either way he wouldn't sell all of it. It had been years. But his brain had never forgotten its white-lit energy, a lightning rod through the nose. He felt sweat prickle his back, seeing it five feet away . . .

"Galloway!"

He raised his eyes slowly. Put his hand on the wheel to steady himself—and to keep their attention with motion.

"You'll let me go, you say?"

"Yes, yes. On your word to be silent, which is in your interest too. We will be in touch with you later about arrangements. Do you have some objection to that?"

"No-oo," said Galloway, drawing it out. He felt Hirsch, beside him, turn her head to stare.

"Good. We are agreed. I ask once more—would you like my doctor to see you before we leave?"

There might be many doctors now, Galloway was thinking. The spinal cord was delicate. If it was cut he had no hope of walking again. If it was just a pinch, and he kept still, got to a hospital, someday he might. And then again it might be transient, he might be able to recompress in Norfolk, be good as new day after tomorrow. There was just no way to tell.

"The doctor," he repeated, as if considering it. At the fringe of his vision he saw the pale fingers slowly engulfing the hilt, like a starfish closing around an oyster. He glanced at Hirsch. Her pupils widened suddenly and jerked back to his; she'd seen it too. "Well . . . is he a good man?"

Behind the two Germans, his upper body braced on the corner of the locker, Keyes was raising himself slowly on one arm. His face came into view, bloody from lying on the deck. His eyes were deadly, protuberant, blue, fixed with hate and insane determination.

"Yes, very good. Paraguayan, educated in Europe . . . listen, you must choose now, Galloway. I can stay here no longer." Straeter glanced toward the submarine. Sailors were moving around the davit, dismantling it, manhandling the boom down into the large hatch aft. He swung back. "For the last time, do you want assistance? Answer now! And you, woman—"

The blade caught the old man low in the back. He twisted, screaming, and toppled forward, his hands behind him.

At the same instant Galloway flung Hirsch forward with all the power he could put into his arm.

The blond bodyguard swung on Keyes, who was slumped back with a slight smile on his lips, and stitched a short, professional burst across his chest. He was half turned back to Galloway when Bernie slammed into him. He staggered backward toward the stern, dropping the weapon. For a second he contemplated the handle of the bread knife that she had till now concealed in the back of her shorts. Then he hit the transom, sat down on it, eyes still astonished, and toppled backward into the sea.

Galloway surveyed the carnage on his deck. The old man lay face down, the black grip of the knife growing out of a kidney. Keyes lay near him, shuddering out a breath; as he watched, the blond man's open eyes froze, and the red froth at his mouth went still. But at the same time, a faint groan reached Galloway from farther aft.

"Shad," he called. "Shadrach, you hardheaded bastard, is that you?"

"My head, my head." Aydlett's hand groped along the bloody bullet scar that furrowed the side of his skull. Below it one eye pried itself open; the other was swollen shut. "Oh, Jesus, I feel sick."

"How long you been awake?"

"A while . . . didn't seem like the right time to say so, though. I heard him say, about my pop. The son of a bitch. Let's kill 'em all, Tiller."

"No other way to get out of here alive. Get me the carbine, Bernie."

She ran for the companionway; a moment later she handed it to him, and picked up the Schmeisser herself. She pointed it in the direction of the U-boat, half-closed her eyes, and triggered a burst, pulling the muzzle back down as it jumped into the sky.

Galloway had meanwhile trained the carbine out of the side window of the pilothouse. He set the peep sight for wind and distance and the selector for single shots. He aimed carefully, slumping forward into the butt, and fired. The man who held binoculars on them from the U-boat's bridge threw his hands skyward and disappeared.

He shifted the front sight farther aft and squeezed three slow rounds into the mass of men who were struggling to get below. Behind him Hirsch fired another burst, this one better aimed. Bullets clanged off steel. The men around the hatch redoubled their struggles for cover.

A sound like tearing canvas came across the water, and a hailstorm struck the old PT. The heavy machinegun slugs smashed through wood and aluminum and plexiglas. They picked Straeter up and threw him across the deck to sprawl grotesquely against Keyes.

"Down!" shouted Galloway, but Bernie had already dropped and was wriggling forward. "Shad, get up here, damn it!"

"Comin'. Comin'." Looking punch-drunk, Aydlett scrambled toward them on all fours. As he reached the deckhouse the gun clattered again from the conning tower, winking like a welding arc, and the second joined it. Galloway covered his head with his arms as all the windows burst in at once. Chunks of the fragile foredeck and bulwarks flew apart, ragged fragments wheeling into the sea, splinters showering across the open deck.

"Get down. Low. I left some of the frag armor in the sides when I rebuilt this bitch."

"Tiller, what we going to do?"

"Fight." The firing slackened; he bobbed up, squeezed, but the striker clicked hollowly. He pulled out the magazine, stared at it for a moment, then let it and the empty weapon thud to the deck. "I guess we can't even do that."

"Here. Use this." She thrust the Schmeisser into his hands.

They were waiting for him when his head showed again. The machine-gun flashes came through a wall of spray as the sea erupted a few feet short of the old boat. He narrowed his eyes, as a man does against rain, and held the chattering weapon's sights a few feet above the black hull. When it went dry he ducked down again.

"Why'd you stop?" said Aydlett.

"Out of beans . . . Bernie. Look, I'm sorry I got you into this. I thought we could force 'em to submerge."

"Don't apologize!" Her eyes burned up at him, and then he felt her lips soft and hot on his. Just for a moment. "At least *he's* dead. Tiller . . . will the engines start?"

He peered aft. The gunwales were ragged, but most of the fire had come in high. "They might. Why?"

"Couldn't we run into them?"

"Ram," he corrected automatically, even as his mind explored it. The old patrol boat had stout bows, but nothing made of wood was equal to the pressure hull of a sub. It would be suicidal.

"Only thing left to do," said Aydlett. "At least get us alongside, let me loose on deck—"

"Shape you're in, Shad, that might laugh them to death," said Galloway, grinning despite himself. "But you're right. It's all we got left."

He turned the key, mashed the starter button, and heard the whine above the guns. The pistons thudded lifelessly. He held the switch down, bending its mount into the instrument panel.

The old Reos choked and then fired. One caught and then the other, though with an eccentric vibration that ran up through the chair to chatter his teeth. Damage below, he thought. Bound to be leaking too. But *Victory* was gathering way through the water.

And fortunately too, he thought, they were already well inside torpedo range.

"First good luck today," he shouted down. Shad and Bernie looked up at him. Her face was a mix of exhilaration and terror. His was a battered mask of rage.

Galloway shoved the throttle all the way forward and left it there.

The firing had slackened as they began to move. Changing magazines, he figured, or letting the barrels cool for a moment. But as *Victory*'s bow began to swing both gunners saw his intention simultaneously and opened up again, hammering at them now without pause.

"Tiller, get down!"

"Can't." But he bent as low as he could and still see through the shattered windshield.

The inside of the cabin exploded as the guns found the range. The heavy slugs went through plywood with little damage, blowing out jagged holes where they exited, but where metal edging or bolts or instruments lay in their path they too became deadly missiles. The depth sounder burst into cogwheeled shrapnel. The binnacle blew apart in a stinging cloud of glass and alcohol. The top rim of the wheel exploded into splinters as Galloway ducked to escape the blizzard of lead. Bernie lay digging her nails into the deck, wincing as bullets clunked into the plating by her head. With a dull thud the fire extinguisher disappeared in a cloud of choking blue powder. The lockers aft rattled as slugs caromed around inside them.

Galloway raised his head again after a moment. White water seethed at the U-boat's stern. Something tore through the roof, whined past his ear. He ignored it and swung the broken wheel left, aiming the bow aft of the conning tower. They were still gathering speed, but without much farther to go. Fifty feet away—thirty—

"Hold on!" he shouted.

With a ripping sound *Victory* struck, throwing him to the floor as the bow tilted toward sky. Aydlett crawled to him and grabbed his arm. "You okay?"

"Not exactly. But still breathing."

"We hit 'em?"

"Felt like it, didn't it?"

Hirsch stood up for a quick look, dropping instantly as another burst came through the naked windowframes. "Tiller. We're up on its back. Right beside the conning tower."

"Good."

"Can we get off here? Can we get away?"

Galloway lay motionless for a moment, eyes closed. The pain was incredible. "Don't think so, Bern. Felt like we tore her bottom out. She's finished."

A long groan and scrape came from beneath them. The boat shuddered and lay slowly over to port.

They waited for the first white-suited man to come over the side, gun in hand.

A slow vibration came through the keel. The old boat slid farther over, then partially righted. Galloway felt her give a slight jog to the side, almost as if she were partially afloat again.

"Help me up, Bern."

She put an arm under his and hauled him up. When he could get his arms on the wheel he pulled himself the rest of the way onto the seat. He looked out to starboard. They were almost free of the black hull. And he saw why.

The U-boat was sinking.

When he'd run *Victory* up on its afterdeck the additional weight had forced the stern under. Now the sea was cascading into the big afterhatch, still propped wide for back-loading the davit. Tons of seawater were destroying the delicate trim, lifting the submarine's bow as her stern settled into the hungry sea.

Not to mention pouring onto electrical switchboards, generators, engines, the volatile fuel this experimental ship ran on . . .

A puff of smoke, or steam, blew green water out of the open hatch, but it swirled back in.

Victory slid free as the *Unterseeboot* settled beneath her. Her screws bit water again and she described a slow, wallowing curve away. A last rattle of fire came from the tower. The rounds arched high, raising spurts of foam far beyond the circling PT.

Galloway and Hirsch watched, their hands locked. Beside them Aydlett braced himself on powerful arms, staring at the sea.

The U-boat's stern disappeared, leaving a swirl of bubbles and smoke. The bow tilted high, showing its graceful deadly curves, the oval outlines of torpedo tube doors.

The first detonation threw a spumy foam a few feet above the frothing surface aft of the tower. Its concussion rattled *Victory*'s loose fittings even before the sound reached them through the air. The bow rose higher from the water, as if struggling to remain afloat.

The second explosion tore the ocean apart. A cloud of steam and smoke and spray rolled out from the stricken ship, lit from within by flashes of blue fire. Above the cloud part of the bow leapt from the water and crashed ponderously back into the sea.

But the Atlantic, though split asunder, swept back in. From behind the gray shroud of steam and vapor came low rumbles, smaller explosions for several minutes. They gradually grew fainter, subsiding into the depths.

Victory staggered at a wave, heeled slowly, and dipped her bow. Galloway looked away from the rolling cloud.

"She's taking a lot of water," he said.

"Can't we do something?"

"I'll go below, get the pump workin'—"

Galloway leaned forward, caught a liquid glimmer at the foot of the companionway. "Forget it. Her guts are torn out. She'll be going soon."

"What can we do?"

"Find something that'll float. That's my advice."

The old boat had her head down, like a tired hound. Her rolls were heavier, and she came back more slowly from each one. Galloway nursed her around and pointed her into the mist-shrouded patch of sea. A chemical smell bit at their nostrils. Small items littered the jostling waves: a length of board, an oil can, unidentifiable flotsam. They came out on the other side seeing nothing more. Galloway pulled the throttle back to idle as the propellers, lifting out of the water, began to shake the stern.

"What's that?"

He looked after her finger. It was an orange object, rolling slightly a few hundred yards away. Galloway reached for the binoculars. A bullet had mangled one lens. The other side was whole. He raised it and peered.

"It's *Charlene.*"

"Will that do?"

"Might could."

"Hold three of us?" said Aydlett.

"It might," said Galloway. "If we don't take a lot of luggage."

He sent Aydlett and Hirsch aft, to lower the stern a bit, and edged the sluggishly moving boat toward it. Halfway there the engines died. "Water's got to them," he said. "Bernie, think you can swim it from here?"

When he turned to see why she hadn't answered she was already in the water, doing a graceful crawl.

The sea was halfway up the companionway steps when she brought the little vehicle alongside, threw a bow line up to Aydlett, and swung herself up after it. "You ready?" she said briskly to Galloway.

"I guess so."

"Shad, give me a hand with him."

He tried to help with his arms, but even so they almost dropped him over the side. The transfer was made easier by the fact that *Victory*'s was now only a little above the water. He settled himself in the seat. Aydlett, above him, said "What else we goin' to need, Tiller?"

Galloway checked the gauges in front of him. "Well, we've got a compass here. Get yourself a life preserver, and some line, we'll have to make you fast somehow. Grab the chart. And a tarp from the aft locker, and the boat hook. You'll have to rig us a sail."

"Water? Food?"

"Water if you can get to it. Don't stay below too long."

"Right." He reappeared in seconds and started handing things down. Beer. Flashlight. Chart. Flares. Galloway had turned on the ballast pump and the little craft began to bob jauntily in the lee.

"Hurry up, both of you, damn it," he called. The multicolored sea was lapping at the freeing ports. His nose wrinkled; the spreading film was diesel fuel. The old PT was near her end.

"Tiller."

He looked up. Hirsch was holding up the plastic sack. It was torn; whiteness ran down her arms in a slow heavy stream.

"Jesus, Hirsch—"

"Look out below!"

She had reversed it, got both thumbs in the tear. Now she pulled, showing her teeth, and it opened suddenly end to end. She tossed the torn sack over the side between Galloway and the hull. The wind caught a streamer of it and it blew out over him, powdering *Charlene* like a frosted doughnut, whitening the waves. But only for a moment before it dissolved, whirled downward.

"Pure, all right," said Galloway, looking at the innocent sea.

"And then there's this." She bent, disappearing from his view for a moment, then straightened. She held up the oblong of tarry metal, grimacing at its weight. A bullet had hit it and the scar gleamed in the sunlight.

He stared up at it. The golden ticket home. All that was left. All that he needed.

Their eyes met. "It's not ours, Tiller," she said, half lowering it.

"That's not what I'm thinking about."

"Are you sure?"

"Hold it!" said Aydlett, coming up behind her. "What you at, girl? We put sail on this thing, we'll need ballast. Good gust, it'll spill us in a second. Don't even think about gettin' rid of that!"

Galloway grinned. "Nice try, Shad. But horseshit. We're overloaded as it is. Give it here."

She slid it toward him over the rail. He held it there, balanced on the teak, for just a moment. Then he took his hand away.

The sea took it back. Leaning, he watched it drop away, glittering and winking. The golden sparkle grew faint, grew green, drifting downward through slanting rainbowed light.

It was gone. "Hell," said Aydlett.

"We're better off without it, Shad. Come on, she's starting to go."

Hirsch, after a last look around, stepped over the splintered teak and settled in her seat. Aydlett swung himself down after her, a coil of line round his elbow and hand.

"Ready, there, Bernie? Ready, Shad?"

"Ready, Tiller."

"Let's cruise."

Aydlett popped tabs on three Millers and passed them out. Galloway pulled a few yards away, the motor humming. They watched as the sea lifted, sniffing at the deck.

It ran its tongue across the canted forecastle and nipped at the cabin windows.

It swallowed the anchor for the last time.

With a bubbling sigh *Victory* lifted her skirts. Swaying rows of seagrass, a pale line of barnacles like a chorus of tiny startled mouths. Her rudder swung to one side, tapped to the other, as she rolled for the last time, showing them for a moment the two bodies lying side by side on deck, intertwined like sleeping lovers.

Together, silently, they toasted her.

When she was gone Galloway put his hand over his eyes for a moment. Then he straightened in his seat, looked at the compass, and turned his head from side to side for the wind.

"Shad, see if you can get that tarp up. With luck and this breeze behind us, we should pick up Hatteras Light sometime tomorrow."

"Yo." The waterman crawled forward, spun a swift fisherman's bend into the bullnose.

"Tiller."

"Yeah, Bern?"

"I'm—I'm sorry I screwed up. Trusting Ruderman. Straeter, I mean."

"We both made mistakes, Bernie. Mine cost Jack's life this time. And Clifton's, and Mercy's—"

"No! Bad reasoning! *They* killed your cousin and the others, Tiller. Not you."

"I guess you're right."

"I'm glad you turned it down," she said, from close behind him. Her hand came over his shoulder. "I'm glad you turned it all down. I know how much the old Galloway wanted it. But I knew you'd win."

He considered for a little while, then reached up. He held her hand for a long time, feeling the warm pressure of her fingers. "I'm glad too."

After a moment he added, "Bernie?"

"What?"

"I don't know if this is the right time to say this. I don't know how bad hurt I am, for one thing."

"Is it about you and me?"

"Yeah. Come on, help me out."

"No."

"No?"

"No. I mean, the answer may be yes, but you've got to ask the question yourself."

"Uh-huh. Well, do you think you'd like to—when we get back—do something together?"

"That's not the right question. Try again."

"Shit! Goddamn it!" He banged his fist on the hollow fiberglass. "Okay. It's like this. We argue. We fight. But when things get rough, like in the storm, like today, suddenly I realize I need you. When it gets hairy, there isn't anybody else I'd rather have beside me." He glared at her. "I think that means something important. It means, I want you in my life. Maybe it won't work, maybe we're too different—but I want to try. You want that?"

She looked at the sea for a long time. The sea that had swallowed so much. Had it swallowed the old Galloway too? Then she remembered his face, when he'd let the gold go.

Yes. That was down there too. She tightened her hand on his. "Tiller."

"What?"

"That was the right question. At last. And I have the right answer, too."

"Get your lips off her, Galloway, you old goat," called Aydlett from the bow a moment later. "We're rigged! You people ready to sail?"

Together, they set their backs to the wind.

DATE DUE

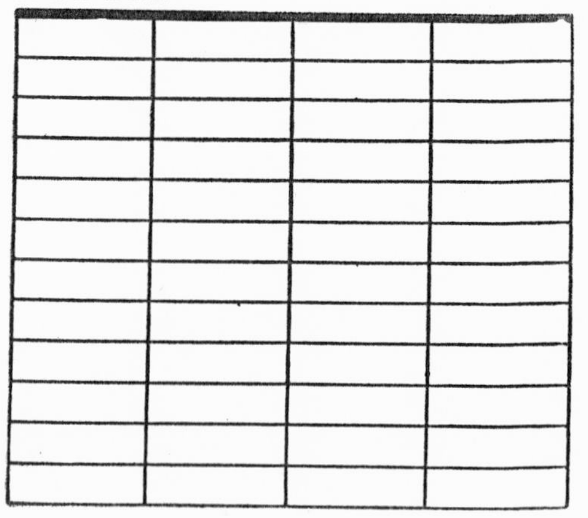